W9-AHR-512

MAGGIE BRIGHT

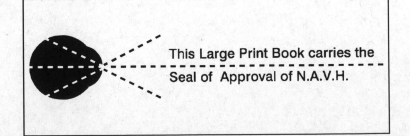

MAGGIE BRIGHT

A NOVEL OF DUNKIRK

TRACY GROOT

THORNDIKE PRESS
A part of Gale, Cengage Learning

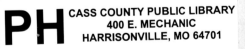

GALE
CENGAGE Learning·

Farmington Hills, Mich • San Francisco • New York • Waterville, Maine
Meriden, Conn • Mason, Ohio • Chicago

GALE
CENGAGE Learning®

LIBRARY OF CONGRESS CATALOGING-IN-PUBLICATION DATA

Groot, Tracy, 1964–
    Maggie bright : a novel of Dunkirk / by Tracy Groot. — Large print edition.
        pages cm. — (Thorndike Press large print Christian historical fiction)
    ISBN 978-1-4104-8142-9 (hardcover) — ISBN 1-4104-8142-5 (hardcover)
    1. World War, 1939–1945—Naval operations, British—Fiction. 2. World War, 1939–1945—France—Fiction. 3. Yachts—Great Britain—Fiction. 4. Large type books. I. Title.
PS3557.R5655M34 2015b
813'.54—dc23   2015013842

Published in 2015 by arrangement with Tyndale House Publishers, Inc.

Printed inMexico
1 2 3 4 5 6 7 19 18 17 16 15

For Alison, Annie, Cynthia, Lorilee,
Sharron, and Shelly,
Fellowship of the Gimlet Eye

Those who go down to the sea in ships,
Who do business on great waters;
They have seen the works of the Lord,
And His wonders in the deep.

— PSALM 107:23-24

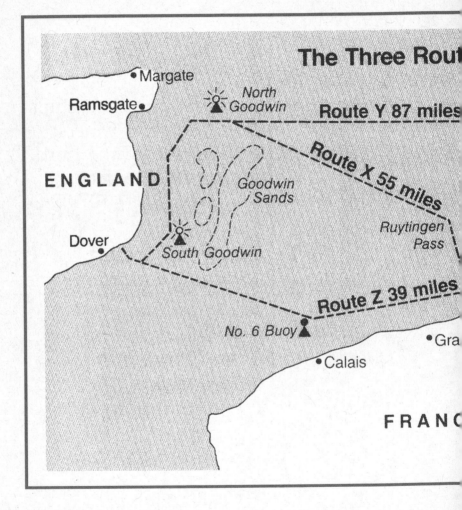

The Three Rout

Route Y 87 miles

Route X 55 miles

Route Z 39 miles

Margate

Ramsgate

North
Goodwin

ENGLAND

Goodwin
Sands

Dover

South Goodwin

Ruytingen
Pass

No. 6 Buoy

Calais

Gra

FRANC

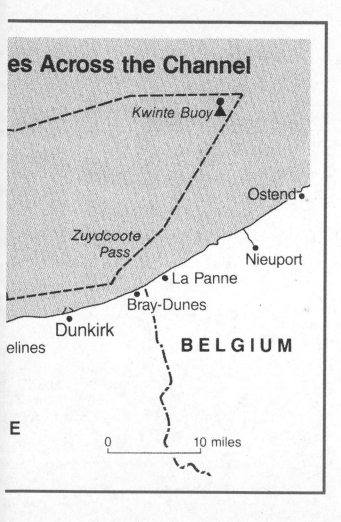

es Across the Channel

Kwinte Buoy

Ostend

Zuydcoote
Pass

Nieuport

La Panne

Bray-Dunes

Dunkirk

elines

BELGIUM

E

0   10 miles

1

Somewhere in Belgium
May 1940

There is nothing more disturbing than the sound of an animal in pain. Animals can be put out of their misery, but men, men cannot.

"What in me is dark, illumine! What is low, raise and support!"

"Will someone *please* shut him up?" shouted the British officer.

Artillery shook the hut. Bits of dried earth rained down on the officer's map. He flicked away a single lump. The British Army was in *retreat.* Had England ever met such a rout as this? How would they face those at home — if they made it home?

The man in the corner howled. When he didn't shout strange things, he howled, and not just any old howl; it came up in an eerie building groan and let loose at a peak, put the hair straight up one's neck.

At the peak of the latest unholy howl, a figure appeared in the doorway, hesitant, uncertain — just the person.

"You there!" said the officer. "Yes, you. See the man over there? He's yours."

The private looked at the bandaged man. "What do you mean, sir?"

"Get him to Dunkirk. He's done something heroic."

"I only came to tell you —"

"Yes, yes, we're overrun!" A boom shook the hut. "Bronson!" he shouted over the private's head. "Get *over* that canal and tell McIntire's unit to *pull out. God,* have mercy!" He stared at the private. "Still here?"

"But, sir —"

"Let me be clear: You are no longer part of any unit. You've been plucked from your lovely little fraternity, you now have an independent commission, and *he* is *yours.* Move!" Then, bellowing, "Bronson!"

Private Jamie Elliott went to the bandaged man making the horrible sound. A medic finished the last of his dressing, and looked at Elliott with some sympathy.

"All yours, mate. At least he can walk."

"What's wrong with him?" said Elliott.

"Shell went off, right by his head. When he's not howling, he quotes Shakespeare."

12

"Milton, actually," said another medic, bandaging another man.

"Who cares? It's poetry, and it's awful."

"I think it's rather interesting. I like to listen to him."

"That's because you're a pansy, aren't you?" said the first medic. He looked at Jamie and shook his head. Then he looked at his charge, who had quieted at last, and said, gentler, "He's a captain. Lost all his men, poor sod. Risked his life to bring a message to another unit, saved *their* lives, came back to his own and they were blown to bits. Last one died ten minutes ago. A brigadier put him in for the Victoria Cross."

A boom, and earth rained down.

"Their fatal hands no second stroke intend!" shouted the bandaged captain.

"Well, that was relevant." The medic grabbed the captain's rucksack and stuffed in rolled bandages. "Change it as often as you can; keep it clean as you can. It's a great rotten hole, but I have no time to stitch it. Keep the bandage *tight*. He's lost a lot of blood. He'll need water as often as you can scrounge it." He thrust the rucksack at Elliott. "Go."

The ground shuddered, earth rained, and Elliott grabbed the captain's arm.

"Which way to Dunkirk?"

"That way, mate, twenty miles or so. You can't miss it — it's burning."

2

Elliott's Boatyard
Bexley-on-the-Thames
London

No topic has more lurid appeal than when one is nearly murdered in one's bed by a member of the clergy.

Clare Childs did not begrudge Mrs. Shrewsbury the right to pick the incident down to atomic particles. It was the most exciting thing to happen in the old tweedy's life, and Clare was convinced the Shrew was grateful it had; but it had occurred *weeks* ago.

"More tea?" Clare offered.

"In a blink, your life changes. You are sixty-seven. Retired. Prepared to serve out the rest of your days in good deeds and usefulness. Yes, dear. Thank you." She paused before taking a sip. "I can still see his eyes. They glowed red."

They were brown. And frightened.

15

"Going to the Home Front meeting this afternoon?" Clare said brightly, though she knew it was fruitless to try and change the subject until Mrs. Shrew played it out to the bitter end.

"We'll see him at Madame Tussauds one day," she said with grim relish, eyes glowing a bit disturbingly themselves over her teacup. "Right next to Jack the Ripper. His clerical collar will be a chilling counterpoint. I wonder what name they'll give him."

"As he hasn't committed any murder —"

"That we *know* of . . ."

"I don't know that he'll grace an exhibit anytime soon."

"What *would* they call him?" Mrs. Shrew mused. "He's an American. He's a vicar."

"I don't think they call them vicars in America. Not from the novels I've read. He is an Episcopal priest. Perhaps it's Father something or other."

"Father . . . Slasher. Father Maim. The papers called him the Thieving Priest — such an insipid moniker for such gruesome potential. They got it all wrong."

"The papers also said he had made off with 'a mysterious package.' Where did they get that? Nothing whatsoever is missing." Clare scowled.

" 'The tearful owner of the *Maggie*

Bright . . .' "

Tearful! Oh, why did the Shrew have to remind her?

"I've got it! The Reverend Yankee Maimer."

"Really, Mrs. Shrew . . . sbury." Clare had to stop calling her Shrew in her head. "You must put the matter out of your mind. It isn't healthy."

"What *I* wonder is why there hasn't been an inquest. I have longed to give testimony. At the very least we should have been thoroughly questioned."

Here was the one point upon which they agreed. Why hadn't someone come? The night the incident took place didn't count, as there had been no one from Scotland Yard to question them, only the arresting constable. No one from the *Daily Mirror* had questioned them, either; no wonder they got their facts wrong. "Well, things *are* a bit busy just now. War and all. Perhaps —"

"Yes, but do you see, that is *exactly* my point. He could be a German spy! I didn't buy that trite New York American accent for one moment. Neither should you. A girl of your sensibilities. Offering *tea* while we waited for the police. If it hadn't been for that man to subdue him, I don't know what we should have done."

"You did all right with the kettle . . ." It was a wonder the poor man's skull wasn't fractured. "And the shrieking."

"It was a distractionary move," Mrs. Shrew said modestly. "I occasionally employed the tactic on my students. Did you notice the staccato cadence of the shrieks?"

"I did."

"Puts the perpetrator off center."

"It did that." Poor fellow probably thought he *was* in a Tussauds exhibit — as a victim.

"Hail the ship!" came a call from outdoors. "I have news!"

"It's that man," said Mrs. Shrew disapprovingly, because it was proper to disapprove of men, though she smoothed her hair and brushed toast crumbs from her bosom.

Clare slid from the tiny dinette and ran up the ladder.

"Good morning, Captain John!" She smiled at the man on the dock. "Any news from your son?" She dared to ask because he appeared quite chipper this morning.

But the question did dampen him for just a moment. "No. Nothing. Bit odd — I've gotten a letter twice a week." Then he smiled. "I'm sure all is well. Stopped the Jerries in their tracks, no doubt, and Jamie

18

leads the pack. Too busy to tell me about it!" He waved a piece of paper. "I have the information you were after!"

The timing couldn't be worse. And yes — there was Mrs. Shrew, right behind her.

"Information?" she called as she appeared at the hatch. Her voice always took on a slightly musical note when the captain was about. "What information?"

There was no signaling Captain John to be discreet. He'd already torn off his hat, eyes only for Mrs. Shrew. "Well, good mornin', Mrs. Shrewsbury!" he said, as if heartily surprised.

"Good morning," she sang. "What news, Captain? Has the barbarian invaded our shores? Ha-ha-ha!"

"Hasn't come to that yet. We'll be ready if they do. Only, I've found where they've stowed the Burglar Vicar. He's in a jail in Westminster. Awfully far from Bexley, don't you think? Don't know why our own jail didn't suit." He nimbly stepped over the narrow plank from the dock to the *Maggie Bright.* "Here you are, love."

Clare meekly took the paper.

"*What* is that?" said Mrs. Shrew.

"Only it's a paper with an address on it," said Captain John. "Where they've locked up the BV."

Clare winced at the shrieking staccato silence.

Mrs. Shrew slid to her side. "It is worse than I have feared," she said, voice breathy and low, no music in it. "You have developed: a *fixation.*"

"What's this?" said Captain John, looking with concern at Clare. "You do look a bit peaky . . ."

"Your tea. Your concern. Your *kindness.*" Mrs. Shrew turned upon the captain. "And *you* have thrown petrol on it!"

"Hang on," the captain said defensively. "I've done what?"

" 'Put the matter out of your mind,' hmm?" said Mrs. Shrew. "While you go about developing a sick, sordid, *victim* crush!" Her eyes glowed, and fell upon the paper in Clare's hand. "I cannot let you have that." She reached for it, but Clare held it high.

"Mrs. Shrew — sbury, *honestly.* There is no fixation. There is only deep curiosity about why this man was on my boat. He had no intention to harm us in any way. I am quite sure of it. He was *looking* for something. I want to know what he was looking for — why it was worth risking jail."

"You don't believe that rubbish about his wife due for their first child — asking us to *let him go* for their sakes before the police came?"

"I don't know what to believe. I do know he was after something. And there was something about him — something innocent. And worried. And . . . well, rather pathetic."

She became aware of her grasp on the mast stay. She followed the stay up to the mainmast.

The *Maggie Bright* was the most beautiful thing she'd ever seen, a gallant, lovely, hearty girl, and entirely in Clare's hands: her two noble masts, the fifty-two feet of her length and the sixteen feet of her width — *beam,* Captain John implored her to say. But it wasn't until Clare had signed the papers of ownership transference that she knew something sacred had been turned into her keeping — as if a spray of oath-taking fairy dust had erupted at the last scratch of the pen.

Clare felt as if the previous owner, of whom she knew next to nothing, trusted her. Trusted her to keep the fittings polished, the decks scrubbed, the bottom clean, to keep her free of leaks — to keep her ready for any adventure, surely crouching at the very next corner. Perhaps all new boat owners felt this glowing responsibility.

But Clare had believed from the start that *Maggie Bright* was something special.

"I have a right to know anything that concerns my vessel." A gust of wind came singing through her lines. Fittings rattled a counter-point. "If that is a fixation," Clare murmured, eyes moving along the foremast line to the bowsprit, "oh, I am fixated."

"Oh, go on — she's right, you know," said Captain John indulgently, nudging Mrs. Shrew with his elbow. "Knew she was a sailor the minute she saw old Mags."

"Sailor, perhaps," Mrs. Shrew said. "Detective inspector, certainly not. *I* was the one to catch him in a lie. 'Why are you here?' I asked of the Thieving Priest, after the captain had restrained him —"

"*Restrained* is a stretch," said Clare. He sat meek as a lamb, sipping tea while waiting for the police.

"— and do you recall what he said? 'I am in England for the Lambeth Conference,' and he said it *quite carefully* as if it had been *long rehearsed.* 'Lambeth Conference!' said I. 'Well, that *is* a surprise . . . as there hasn't been a *Lambeth* Conference since 1930, and there isn't one now! Besides all that — what would the *Lambeth* Conference have to do with your presence on this boat? Who are you *really — Father* Fitzpatrick?' Oh, what a

22

trump! Do you recall his face? Like catching a student in a lie!"

"Yes — and he wouldn't say a word after that, would he? Not a single word about what he was looking for." Clare just *knew* he was on the very brink of confession when Mrs. Shrew had gone all Lambeth on everyone.

"He was *looking* to kill us. Do you not know feral nature when you see it? Try teaching school in Liverpool. West Kirby."

"I intend to find out what he was after." Clare studied the paper thoughtfully.

It hadn't been just worry in those eyes. It was desperation. And in the end, as he was led away, it was defeat.

Yet there was something else. She folded the paper. Something she had not felt in over ten years. Just a flicker. She had to find him again to see if it were true, to see if she had only imagined it.

"Hang on," the Shrew suddenly said. "Who's that?"

They turned to the direction of her gaze — the boathouse at the end of the dock.

"Who's what?" asked Captain John.

"I could *swear* someone was watching us. And when I noticed, he ducked away. Around the corner of the boathouse. By the shrubbery."

"You want I should check it out?" said Captain John, looking very capable.

Mrs. Shrew studied the area for a long moment and then said doubtfully, "No. No, it's quite all right. Must be I've got the Burglar Vicar on my mind." She turned a severe look upon Clare's piece of paper. "Someone else certainly does."

"Really, it's nothing." She slipped the paper into her pocket. "Join us for tea, Captain John?"

"Had mine, could use more, thanks," he said. He followed Mrs. Shrew below.

Clare hesitated before descending.

She'd raise the sails today and give them a good scrub down, less to check for mildew than to see Maggie's glory unveiled, if only at her moorings and not filled with sea wind. She'd check the mail and see if she had any new applicants for renters, *not* invaders of her sanctuary, as her lesser part mourned. Bright vision saw renters like Mrs. Shrew as a means to an end, and that end was to raise funds not only for the adventure of her lifetime, but quite likely the lifetime of *Maggie Bright*.

Vision! Courage! Singularity of purpose! That would conquer all.

Still . . .

"I thought you might have a secret, old

girl," Clare said softly, caressing the wooden grain of the hatch cover. She glanced at the shrubbery by the boathouse, then curled her hands around the hatch cover and swung below.

3

Bartlett, New York

Murray Vance threw down the chalk and
messed up his hair. He shook his fists at the
door, then stood deflated until the knock
came again. Smoothing his hair, tucking in
his shirt, he went to the door.

How did they find him? He'd ask
someday, sure there was a leak at the *Times.*
Likely Eddie the elevator boy, that two-
faced river rat. Said he wanted to draw
someday and Murray believed him. You
know what? That's what comes outta being
nice to people. They use you. That's what
he was learnin'.

"I ain't so green anymore," he muttered.

Murray put his hand on the doorknob,
and some of the mad went out. Aw, kids
after autographs, not a big deal. He was a
kid not so long ago. For them, a tiny
salamander sittin' on the *M,* and he'd make
the tail curl into the *V.* But he always felt

stupid with adults. Had nothin' to say to them. No salamander for them.

Murray opened the door to a pleasant surprise.

"Say! Mrs. Father Fitz! I thought you was an intruder! What's cookin'? Where's the padre?" His eyes dropped to her very large stomach. "Holy smokes — you got a whole nursery in there?" He bent to the stomach and called between cupped hands, "Hey, kid! You a girl, you come out lookin' like your mother, boy oh boy, are you gonna stop traffic!"

Confident he had paid her enough compliments, he straightened to smile at her — and his smile quit. She'd been cryin'.

It was then he realized that *A,* Father Fitz wasn't with her, and *B,* she'd never stand in his doorway without the Fitz.

"I've received a telegram, Murray. David's been arrested." She talked some more. She'd tried to contact the American embassy in London, couldn't get through. Tried to contact Congressman Wilson — they said he'd acted outside of American interests, nothing they could do.

She talked some more. He didn't hear it.
This is some good cement, isn't it?
Best stuff ever.
Murray was eleven, and the Bartlett Road

Commission was fixing the downtown sidewalk. They mixed cement in a great cement mixer. It tumbled down into a wheelbarrow. They pushed the wheelbarrow to a square hole framed by wooden forms, and down the cement poured, pushed along the chute by men with long-handled scrapers. A crowd had gathered to watch.

Murray stared at the miraculous gray substance pouring into the hole. Infinite possibilities crashed down on him at once, and he suddenly knew what cement was capable of, and wondered why they all didn't go a little crazy. But the crowd seemed to think they saw an ordinary thing, and no one shouted, "Cement! Cement!"

No one except Murray. But that wasn't the worst of it. For at some point — Murray didn't know when, maybe when they finished smoothing it flat with the wide scrapers — he launched out and belly flopped into the middle of the cement-filled pool.

He rose, and watched the cement ripple down his body. He made his bare feet go up and down. Infinite possibilities became infinite inventions, and he wished with all his heart he could draw. He saw cement held in the air. He saw cement in oceans. He saw it mixed with other things, like coffee grounds, Buck Creek silt, talcum powder; he saw it tumbled with ground seashells, he saw . . .

. . . an angry crowd, and furious cement workers, and his screaming mother.

Sound came back and shame rushed in — he saw his teacher who told other kids to steer clear of him, and his mother's boss from Florsheim's Cuff Link Factory, and a startled young priest. His mother's boss shouted at him, wagging his finger, and Mother switched from shouting at Murray to shouting at her boss, and Murray cried out for her to stop, for she could lose her job. The cement workers shouted too, cigarettes bouncing at the corners of their mouths. A policeman came running to find out the fuss. People shouted and people laughed and people pointed.

Murray wanted to die.

Then suddenly, no one laughed. No one shouted. They stared.

"I wonder what it's capable of . . ." said a calm voice beside him.

It was the young priest. He was ankle deep in cement next to Murray, but he wasn't looking at Murray. He was examining a handful of dripping cement.

It was all over his trousers. It smeared his black coat.

He sifted it between his fingers. He lifted it to the light.

Then he noticed Murray. "This is some good cement, isn't it?"

And Murray cried out, "Best stuff ever."

Never even took off his shoes.

Murray rubbed his fingers together, surprised he didn't feel cement.

"We know where this is goin', don't we," he said to Helen. He shoved his hands in his pockets. He walked the room. "I ain't goin' to England. Hemingway said never again should this country be pulled into a European war through mistaken idealism. I put that in my speech. You know I got elected to the committee? Keep America Out of War? Me and the padre, that's where we part ways."

He picked up an ashtray, looked at the bottom, put it down. Fiddled with chalk in his pockets. Walked the room.

Helen said nothing. She just stood there, crying, wearing the same perfume.

"That's what he gets for stealin' my girl. He got himself into this, he can get himself out. Goes off when his wife is pregnant. I wouldn't've left."

He picked up a paperweight, tossed it hand to hand, put it down.

She just stood there. Crying.

"It'll look bad, me goin', just on the committee. Papers'll find out and they'll get it wrong. Well, I ain't settin' foot on foreign soil. We can't solve our own problems, how can we solve theirs? The American Institution of Public Opinion said 95 percent of Americans don't want another war. And 92 percent say —"

She brushed hair behind her ear. It was the signal she and the Fitz worked out long ago to help him stay on track.

"You know why he went," she said softly. "*A, B,* and *C, Murray.*"

"I've outgrown *A, B,* and *C!*"

"I know — I'm sorry. I'm just upset."

He messed up his hair.

Aw — truth was, it still worked.

He found the chalk in his pockets and crushed it to crumbs.

"*A,* if he went because of the malarkey my old man told him, he's as crackpot as my old man was. *B,* you know how hard it is to get to England? Place is surrounded with German mines. Not to mention German submarines in the Atlantic and —"

"Murray, I haven't told you all of it." She looked down, trifled with a button on her coat. "David found the *Maggie Bright.*"

A.

A.

A.

He couldn't think of a *B* yet because he didn't have an *A.*

"That why he's in jail?"

She nodded miserably.

"Tried to break in?"

She nodded. "I'm sorry to tell you this way."

He wished he could put that sun back on her face. He used to make her laugh.

He sifted chalk crumbs in his pocket.

There was only one person on earth he'd let use him, and one person he'd be used for. He pulled his hand out of his pocket and studied the powdered chalk on his fingers. Rubbed his fingers together.

"*A*, I'll go get him. *B*, don't worry."

"Oh, Murray." More tears came, and Murray took up walking and reaching for things.

"*A*, I am worried," she said. "I can't help it. And now I'm worried for you." She dragged the heel of her hand against the tears, and her voice went quavery. "But *B* . . ." She laid a hand on her stomach.

He flicked a dangly bead thing on a lamp shade, watched it swing.

" 'Member the last journey? Six years ago?" He flicked it again. "That was steppin' outta Bartlett. I don't count trips to

New York City as journeys. Those are work related. Forty-three minutes from Bartlett to New York City by train hardly constitutes a journey. That's what it says on the schedule, forty-three minutes — yeah, 57 percent of the time! That's false advertising. If it was 97 percent —"

She brushed hair behind her ear, and he stopped talking.

She suddenly smiled through her misery. "Do they know who Murray Vance is, in England? I wish they knew him like I do."

He rubbed the drawing callus on the side of his middle finger. "I get mail from England."

"I hope you get back to it one day. You made me laugh."

He caught her perfume, and turned away, and reached for things.

The Fitz was like the basement of his house, a place you don't go much but what you gonna do without it? He was the rock bottom of Murray's life. He anchored it.

The only mistake Murray's mother ever made was introducing her boss's daughter to the Fitz.

"Look in on my ma, will ya? And get my mail? Holy smokes, the logistics!" He clapped a hand to his head. "A ship to Lisbon, a train through the continent, a boat across the English Channel — it's mined; hope I don't get blown up. There goes the kid's godfather. Hang on, hang on. Let's write down the details. When's the next ship out?"

Off he went for pencil and paper.

What you gonna do without a basement?

Hang on, Padre. Ol' Murray is coming.

4

Somewhere in France

"What in me is dark, illumine. What is low, raise and support."

No chance for good-bye, no chance to explain. With those guys a whole year, sharing care packages from home and trade secrets on girls, and suddenly this, hustling a broken half-wit to a place on fire.

Private Jamie Elliott bent to yank the tongue of his boot back in place. It kept sliding down the side of his foot.

"Trial will come unsought. God towards thee hath done his part — do thine."

"Shut *up!*"

Little rest or food for two solid days, always on their feet, always moving, sometimes ditch-diving to avoid bullets from a low-strafing airplane, sometimes hiding in terror from German patrols which usually turned out to be civilians running scared; and always, always with a constant

35

backdrop of this eerie howling and quoting.

The thought summoned direct response from the offender, Captain Milton, who now stopped in his tracks, put his arms wide, and with loud lament aimed right at God, shouted: "Hast thou made me here thy substitute?"

"Shut it!" Jamie pushed the man. He stumbled forward and regained his shambling gait.

Did his men find out what happened to him? Kearnsey will worry. Drake will say it's war, and act like he doesn't care. Lieutenant Dunn likely sent someone out, and hopefully that someone had discovered Jamie's fate. But he did not know theirs.

"Too well I see and rue the dire event, that with sad overthrow and foul defeat hath lost us heaven."

Jamie shoved the captain harder than necessary, and he stumbled and fell. Discovering himself upon the ground, he wrapped his arms about his head and rested in the dirt, his backside hiked in the air. Looked like Lawrence of Arabia doing some worshippy Arab thing. Jamie waited. He shifted his weight. He wondered how to secure the boot tongue.

"All right, all right. Get up. You're not that bad off. I've seen a man carry his hand in a helmet."

Not a lick of action until two weeks ago, and nothing but action since. Whole German Army crashed on them like a thousand thunderstorms, and now chased them like monsters from a thousand nightmares.

"Come on. Get up. Let's find some water."

Why was it burning? Dunkirk wasn't an ammo dump, it was a seaside tourist town. No way could the Germans have made that much ground that fast. Was it being bombed? If so, why Dunkirk? Calais was closest to Dover, wasn't it?

But here was the real question: When will the army stand and fight?

"What's the matter with him?" A steel-helmeted soldier stood beside him. No stripes, no need to salute.

"Got hit in the head. Knocked a bunch of sense out of it." Jamie looked at the soldier. Dusty, unshaven, wary, haunted, and hunted — looked like Jamie felt. "Who are you with? Any news?"

"Queen's Fusiliers, the 2nd — what's left of 'em. We're scattered to the four winds. I only know two direct orders: it's every man for himself, and head for Dunkirk."

"Every man for himself?" Jamie repeated, hardly believing such words came out of his mouth.

"Aye." Watching the captain, the soldier unscrewed his canteen and handed it to Elliott. "What'd he say?"

"Oh, he goes off like that. If it's not poetry, he howls like a shot dog." Jamie took a swallow and handed back the canteen. "Thanks."

"Something yet of doubt remains," the captain groaned, "which only thy solution can resolve!"

"When do you think we'll stand and fight?" said Jamie.

"Dunno. But you better get him off the road. There's a whole village coming. Half of Belgium, looks like."

Jamie had seen hundreds of people on the road over the past two days, mostly terrified civilians carrying or pushing whatever they could. All hurrying, hurrying. A few hurried past now, staring at the man with his face in the dust. They looked like the soldier — haunted, hunted.

"Where are they going?" Jamie said. "Dunkirk, like us?"

"I don't think *they* know."

"We'll make our stand at Dunkirk, then?"

"Not a clue. Well, good luck, mate." The soldier walked off a few steps, then turned. "You know the new directive about the injured, don't you?"

38

"What directive?"

"Leave any wounded behind."

Jamie stared.

"Heard it from a major. He got it straight from the top."

Jamie felt a strange, hot flush. "Never heard of such a thing." He looked at the captain.

The soldier shrugged. "Makes sense. Why chance losing two fighting men for one who may die anyway? Leave 'em for the Germans to sort out. Maybe they'll swap for 'em later." He gave a little salute. "See you in Dunkirk." Off he went.

Jamie kicked the ground. "Curse my sodding, rotten luck!"

If someone else had got to that hut before him, *that* man would've got stuck with this job. But no — Jamie had pushed past other would-be chumps to end up king chump of them all.

"Come on, move! We don't have time for this!" Jamie booted the captain's hip, and he fell sideways.

Where were Kearnsey and Drake, his two best mates? Blown to bits in some trench?

"Did you hear what he said?" Jamie shouted at his ear. "I could leave you for the Germans! Perfectly in my rights!"

He could not shake the belief that if he

was with his unit, they would be all right. They would make it if they were together. A year with those men. He cared more about them than he did his own brother.

He opened his mouth for another go at the captain, but squinted at a bright new spot on the captain's bandage, and went to a knee for a better look.

"Oh, what have you gone and done?"

"Dazzled and spent," the captain whispered hoarsely. His lips looked like corrugated tin, creased with dust. Jamie hadn't thought of the captain when the soldier had given him a drink. "Sunk down, and sought repair of sleep . . ."

"Yes, well, we're all tired." A bleary mind played tricks. A few miles back, what Jamie thought was a corpse in the road was only an artillery-blown tree limb; half a mile later, what he thought was a limb was a corpse. "Look, you can sleep later — do you understand? We've got to get someone to stitch this or you'll bleed to death, won't you? No bloody Victoria Cross for you, then."

He looked back to where they'd come from. If refugees would soon flood the road, surely one of them had to be a doctor. He looked around for a place to stash the captain. No houses about. A long fenced meadow on one side of the road, and on the other, a dead horse in the ditch, killed a day or so ago by strafing aircraft. It was still harnessed to a crashed cart.

"Come on, mate. Upsadaisy." He hooked his hands under the captain's armpits and pulled him up. "We'll get you sorted, and I'll go find someone to fix your head. Here you are. A nice horsie to keep you company. Doesn't even smell much. See? He's looking right at you, you can tell him all your Milton. Now don't move. Stay. Understand?" He held his hands up. "Stay *right there.*"

He walked away from the captain with the terrible knowledge that he could keep on walking, and all would be in his rights.

5

Clare Childs scanned the stops listed on the side of the double-decker bus. She leaned in to ask the driver, "Excuse me, does this change for —" she glanced at the paper — "someplace close to 12 Brookby Road, Westminster?"

The driver nodded and rattled off the changes. She listened carefully, boarded the bus, dropped in some coins, and took a seat.

What secret did *Maggie Bright* keep? Clare had gone over every inch of the boat after she'd signed the papers with Mr. Hillary, her family's solicitor. She'd had Captain John go over every inch, too; he had assured her that not only was *Maggie Bright* seaworthy, and that the stout old girl had seen many sea journeys — not a river cruiser, was she — but that ownership of Maggie for the price of the back taxes was certainly fair; *too* fair, he worried. Mr. Hillary, however, a large man with an improbably shrill voice, had assured them the boat would have been Clare's scot-free, were the bequest not used as collateral against a loan. The former owner of the boat, an Arthur Vance, was a boyhood chum of her father's with apparently no heir of his own.

For days after the encounter with the Burglar Vicar (as Captain John called the man), Clare prowled about Maggie, pulling out sticky drawers and peering into tight damp places. She took a torch and examined every inch of the deck lockers above, the cupboards below. She emptied out the larder, and found only a packet of ancient mildewed crackers that had fallen into a chink.

All she had was a boxful of old newspapers that the previous owner had collected — American newspapers, curiously enough — with a few oddments in it: a brittle old sea sponge, a cheap figurine of a dancing native girl, and a few mildewed sailing books and navigation charts. But the Burglar Vicar hadn't taken this box. He had gone through it, plainly enough, as it certainly appeared ransacked, but nothing was missing from it.

He had, in fact, taken nothing at all — and easily could have. Clare's purse was right on the chart table. A new portable wireless, a valuable first edition from her uncle's bookstore — things of some value, and quite in the open, untouched. Mrs. Shrew's money was also untouched, though she likely slept with it strapped to her stomach; there could be no safer place.

"What were you after, Burglar Vicar?" Clare mused. She looked at the paper. He went by the name of Father David Fitzpatrick, so Captain John's friend discovered.

She hated this unfair dread that the *Maggie Bright* was somehow under siege. It was her home. She had one again, and nothing would take it from her. So she faced this fear much like she once faced a bully of a dog, who growled and barked at her every time she came home from school; she was so tired of being afraid of the thing, and angry at being afraid, that one day *she* attacked *it,* and punched it right on the muzzle.

Poor thing.

She would not punch a priest. But she would not leave that police station until she had answers.

She noticed the headline of the abandoned newspaper in the seat next, and took the paper to her lap. *BEF in Holland; German Offensive Checked.*

Where was Captain John's son, "over there"? Perhaps when he came home, he might find himself a new stepmother — what a ghastly thought. The woman had answered the advertisement for Bed and Breakfast on the Thames, and really meant to have breakfast *every morning* — and Clare had to fix it!

Clare smiled ruefully. The bed and breakfast scheme turned out to be far more work than she had planned. Still, her jar labeled *Operation: Circumnavigate the Globe* now had enough money in it to rattle when she shook it.

She laughed out loud. She'd need more than rattling coins to make a go of it.

Vision! Courage! Singularity of —

She yelped when she saw the name of the current stop and jumped from her seat.

In the little jail cell he shared with no one, Father David Fitzpatrick selected another memory with which to entertain himself. The entertaining ones usually involved Murray.

"What's glory, Father Fitz?" he had asked one day, while they fixed slatted bushel baskets for the basketball courts at the YMCA.

"Drat you, Murray," David had said, and

45

laid down his hammer.

Murray would expect nothing less than a real answer, not the off-the-cuff ecclesiastical reply that would satisfy, if not truly inform, the average parishioner who often cared less about an answer than asking an impressive question — though David enjoyed impressive questions.

"How are your classes coming?" he asked. Murray would know it for his way to work out the answer.

"Swell. There's a broad who — there's a *young lady* — who sits beside me, and if she don't have the most gorgeous set of legs God put on the planet . . . I drew them instead of the bowl of monochrome fruit. It wasn't doing anything. The legs did somethin'. They hollered to be drawn."

"That's glory. It hollers to be drawn."

"I knew it! Them legs were glorious."

"*Those* legs were glorious. Did you get in trouble?"

"Not 'til after the professor saw my drawing and asked if he could keep it. I said nothin' doin', *then* I got in trouble. Speaking of legs, how is Helen? I mean — Mrs. Father Fitz?"

"Aw, she's wonderful. Loves to go for walks. There's a trail in the woods at Shea Park. My favorite place is that dark and

46

close area down by the creek, where I look up and see a great canopy of layered leaves. So many different shades of green, and if the sun is out, I see golden pinpoints of light come through. It feels secure and close, everything around me and everything above me; it's beautiful, and still, and fragrant, and I get such a sense of well-being there's often an ache in my heart. Not sure what that ache is. But I think it's glory." He picked up his hammer.

A week later, he and Helen found a wrapped present on their doorstep. It was a framed watercolor of a vaulted canopy layered in green, golden pinpoints of light, the closeness discerned, the fragrance caught, the stillness felt. It was so stirring that David could never say what he thought of it, anything at all would never come close; he could only murmur agreement with whatever everyone else said.

At first they hung it in their dining room, but knew it must be shared. It now hung in the foyer of St. Dominic's in Bartlett. He lost track of how many times art collectors came to ask if it was for sale. David stood before it when he needed to, and never failed to come away with an ache of well-being.

Murray easily understood glory. It came

to him in a rectangle gleam on a fixture of chrome, in the smell of a box of new crayons, in the feel of a teapot's curve. Murray seemed to encounter it daily, ever since he sought to know what it was, and seemed to encounter it far more than David did. The cares of the world, and of his parishioners, often stopped glory from getting through.

How endearing seemed those cares, now that he could not get to them. How he ached to see his people and hear their troubles, to see what he could do to bring guidance and hope.

He could think about them, and he could think about Murray. Helen and the baby, he kept far from mind and heart.

He mined another memory, and found the day he picked up Murray from his trip abroad. He came hooting and trampling down the white-railed, zigzagged gangway, announced that he had disowned his father, and said he was dying for New York food. All hope for the long-plotted father-son reconciliation had vanished before David could even say welcome home.

"You got a visitor, mate."

David looked up. He could scarcely make sense of the words, they were so very unexpected.

"Well, let's not dillydally. Haven't got all day." The policeman held the cell door wide and swept his arm to where David should go.

David walked the corridor in a daze. He'd seen no one but guards and inmates for three long weeks. As he knew no one in England, who would visit now? Two men from Scotland Yard came once, but never came back. Not that he said much to gain their attention — he'd said nothing. He couldn't. There was too much at stake.

"Have it your way, then," the older of the two had told him and could not have been more affably indifferent — but not his partner.

"If you fancy a chat, ring me up," said the younger man with a smile not meant to be warm, and bestowed his card between two fingers like a hot tip to the races. The clear implication was that this younger man, William Percy, could make things go well for David if he did.

Something about William Percy stayed with David. As a parish priest at St. Dominic's for twelve years, he knew personalities. Percy had a chilly manner ill-fitting for one so young — he couldn't be past his early thirties, yet seemed to have the hardness of a man who had seen the worst human nature had to offer and had given up hope or desire for human nature's redemption. His eyes were so pale they were nearly the color of wheat, and this stark color he put to good use with his cold manner — while his partner did the talking he did the watching, with a probing, unsettling force David could call leashed menace. Percy seemed to know what David was looking for on the *Maggie Bright.* It made David his enemy.

David couldn't even tell Percy they were on the same side. Couldn't tell him that he'd had an important mission, and that mission had failed.

He had not yet been assigned counsel of any kind, and when he'd asked a guard about it, the man said there was a *war* on, and who gives a (colorful phrase) about a foreigner priest who was likely a Fifth Columnist anyway? Perhaps it was irrational of David, but he had a hard time thinking of himself as foreign since they both spoke English.

He did wonder how he could trust even a lawyer; Arthur Vance had told him to trust no one, and Arthur had had his reasons. So he dared not speak a word even to Scotland Yard, and when they allowed him to send a telegram to Helen, he was quite careful: he said nothing past the fact that he had been arrested, that she should contact Congressman Wilson's office to contact the American embassy, and that he had found the *Maggie Bright.*

For three long weeks, nothing had happened. Who could be waiting for him? Someone from the embassy? Had Arthur Vance's lawyer heard of his arrest? Hope rose, and he followed the policeman into a large room.

There were chairs at long tables, and down the center of each table was a partition. At intervals along the partitions were posted notices: *Do Not Reach Over Partition.* Many people sat across from each other at these tables. The room was filled with layered cigarette smoke, softly squabbling visitors and inmates, a crying baby and a few busy children, and armed policemen at intervals all along the wall.

"Right. Thirty-minute visit. No reaching over the partition. No reaching under the table. You will be watched at all times. Your time starts now. Your visitor is there. Well? Go on, then. Off you go."

But David couldn't move. The policeman gave him a little shove. In a dream, he went to the table. His visitor had been too interested in the coping along the ceiling edge to notice.

"Murray," David breathed.

Murray Vance rose from the other side of the table, stuck out his hand, yanked it back at the sharp command from the nearest policeman, shook it theatrically as if burned, and settled for the biggest, most beautiful, most welcoming grin David had ever seen.

"Whaddya say, Padre? What's cookin', eh? You look terrible." He took off his hat with a flourish, set it on the table and smoothed his hair. "Don't they feed you jailbirds, Father Fitz?" He said it in the comical Brooklyn accent David loved, the one Murray put on just for him: 'fadda,' and 'jailboids.' It was heaven on his ears. "Maybe I can get you a sandwich." Murray looked around the room. "Hey! Anyone got a sandwich for this man? I can pay." He looked at a cop. "Say, are sandwiches allowed? I can toss one over the wooden thingy. Says don't reach; doesn't say don't toss. Well. He ain't havin' any. No one's got a sense of humor around here."

"Murray, tell me I'm not dreaming."

Murray grinned. They sat down. "I'm here to haul your fanny back to the States. Say, I got some black licorice in my suitcase from Helen — I mean, Mrs. Fitz — but they won't let me bring it in. Bobbies, they call 'em. Sometimes constables. I like the way

52

they talk, but can't understand 'em half the time. Gee, it's good to see you! This is the best I felt in two weeks. That's how long it took to get here. Well?" Murray looked around, tapping his fingertips on the table. "Where do I sign you out? How does it work? They take American cash? I brought a lot. Just in case. Emptied out my bank account. Left some for my mother in case I explode from a mine."

Pleasantries over, he finally eyed David. "Frankly, Father, I'm glad you ain't dead. You was reckless to come, but we'll put it behind us and chalk it up to live and learn." He adjusted his shoulders. "It's dangerous here. This country's at war. Don't look like it, but it is. Over *there,* they say, south of here, on the continent. Not even their land. *That* shoulda been a big fat clue against goin' to war."

That old glorious rapid-fire speech, that American accent. David closed his eyes. "Just keep talking, Murray."

"*Keep* talking? That's the first time you said *that.* Where do I post bail? They know about bail, right? Things are different here. We speak the same language, but things ain't the same." He grinned. "Remember when you posted bail for me? Eh? Never thought I'd return *that* favor. Say, you'll never guess — met someone at the train station who knew me. Ain't it a kick? All the way to England? He's fifteen. Him and his friends thought I kicked the bucket. They had a wake. Lit candles. Cried. Real somber affair. Says he wants to grow up and draw too. I only half believed him 'til he said he has every *Rocket Kid and Salamander* ever published. Can you beat it? Even when it was just *Rocket Kid*! His dad got him the last two he was lookin' for for Christmas. Not even my ma has every one. She's missing volume 2, number 11. Yeah, yeah, I know, *A, B,* and *C,* but guess what? I offer the kid fifty bucks for it. Fifty bucks! Guess what he said? 'Nothin' doin'.' Offered a hundred. No dice. Glad he didn't take me up on it. Kid's the real deal, you know? They ain't all rat finks."

And as Murray babbled, hope bloomed.

One more chance.

Of all people, that chance had to be Murray.

"I told the fella at the desk you ain't a bad man. You're just misguided."

David couldn't help a chuckle. For years, that's what he'd told others about Murray. He clasped his hands together. "Listen, Murray . . ."

"Let's get outta here, eh? I'm starvin' and

54

I ain't slept. Too much changin' ships and trains and cabs. Where do I ante up?" He looked around, tapping his fingertips. "I left a lotta dough with that bobby. I don't like it outta my sight."

"Murray . . . a man from Scotland Yard said the courts won't allow for bail until I tell them why I was on the *Maggie Bright*. She's beautiful, by the way."

"Well, *tell* them why, and we're on our way."

Absolutes never went well with Murray. David folded his hands. Whatever happened, he determined to remain calm.

"I can't."

"Sure, you can."

"I can't, and you know why."

Murray's cheerfulness dissolved. He stared at his tapping fingers, which had picked up pace.

"So nothing's changed," he said, face coloring.

"*A, B,* and *C,* Murray," David said, hoping his calm tone would help to avert a scene.

"Everybody keeps telling me *A, B,* and *C.* You don't think I've outgrown that?" Murray raised his eyes. "Why didn't you listen to me? What's the *matter* with you to come?" His voice rose. "Scaring her to death?

55

Leavin' her in that state? You know you made her cry?" He raised a fist. "If I had half a brain I'd stick this right down your throat! For makin' her cry, and for believin' filthy lies!"

"Your father didn't lie. There is proof. I came to get it."

"I'm tired of you defending him!"

"Keep it down over there," a policeman warned.

"And I am tired," said David. "I am so very tired of always trying so hard to get through to you."

Surprise, like water, dashed over the glowering face.

"Why is it always a fight, Murray? You're the most stubborn, pigheaded, obstinate fellow I know. If you don't want to believe it, out the window it goes. If it's not funny, or pleasant, or happy, or fascinating — it has no part of your world. You're just as blind as the people you draw those posters for."

"It ain't our war!"

"Dead children are my war."

"Charles Lindbergh said —"

"I don't care what Charles Lindbergh said! I cared what your father said!"

Murray snarled, and clamped his fists over his ears. David wanted to throttle him.

But . . .

But relentless compassion struck David's heart. Why, God, did you create some people thus? Murray was ten times more aware than the average person of *everything,* and his imagination was the keenest receptor of all; David had come to understand that if someone said *ocean* to Murray, he tasted salt and rode the swells — he encountered the enormity. Murray's keen reception faculties meant that he had encountered what Arthur Vance had brought to them. He took it in, he knew it, he felt it more than David ever would. It meant he knew evil like David did not, like he never would.

"Murray," he said heavily, knowing he was about to murder the final scrap of innocence in him, "your father's friend, the American journalist in Berlin — he confirmed that it's true. He confirmed every word. God help us."

Murray's face broke, and his chest heaved. He shoved himself arm's length from the table, gripping the table's edge. He put his head down. "There ain't nothin' for Rocket Kid in this. Ain't nothing he can do."

"Murray, there's a packet. A parcel of some sort. We have to —"

"No one could let that happen." Murray was shaking his head. "No one could go

57

along with it. I won't believe it!"

People in the room stopped talking and stared.

Why had it fallen to David Fitzpatrick to do, and to say, such terribly hard things?

"You're not a child anymore, Murray. Act like a man."

Murray went very still.

David sent a swift glance about to make sure no one was listening, and leaned in. "The packet has photographs. The photographs are evidence. They're pictures of documents, of ledgers, of . . . children. Evidence of everything your father told us. Someone risked his life to get it to the journalist. We have a moral duty to find it. We must bring it home, and get it into the right hands." He hesitated over the next part. It would be hard for Murray.

"The *Maggie Bright* is docked at Elliott's Boatyard on the Thames in a small village called Bexley. It's just west of a town called Teddington — not far from London. Just get to the Thames and follow it west. Your father hid the packet aboard the *Maggie Bright*. Find that packet, Murray. You'll believe me."

Murray raised his face, white from encounter.

David's resolve nearly faltered. "Oh —

son." He resisted the urge to caress that head. "Maybe I don't know what I'm asking of you. But the packet is so important that I am alone. I trust no one but you. We must find it and get it home. The world needs to know, so that we can do something about it. Your father was to bring the packet to the States. I had arranged for a meeting between him and Congressman Wilson, when we got word of . . . his death. The journalist told me that your father —" No. Not that, not yet. Maybe not ever. "That . . . he told an English bishop about the packet. This bishop has the ear of Anthony Eden, and Eden has Churchill. Churchill, God willing, will one day have Roosevelt."

Murray was very still, his face impassive, and white, and hard.

"Look around you. Would I have risked this if it were not true? Would I have come all this way, would I have left Helen —"

Murray snatched his hat and stood abruptly.

"Murray — no! Wait!"

He was nearly to the exit when he stopped, turned, and came back. His face was as cold as his voice. "Two days out on the Atlantic, I get a call to the captain's room. Helen sent a cable. Baby was born May 7. It's a boy. You're a father, Father. Congratulations and

I got you a cigar. And now it's two you left. Just like my old man." He shook his head. "I came to fetch you home, knowin' all the while you don't deserve them, not when you pull a stunt like this, but I'll tell you what — that kid ain't growin' up without a father. Not her kid. You think I care about some packet? I'll get you out if I gotta bust you out 'cause you ain't some savior, not anymore — you got a family. *You* made that choice, and if you won't take care of them —" he shook his head, lip curled in disgust — "savin' the world don't matter. It's lost already if a man can't take care of his own." His tone lowered. "You listen to me: Something happens to you 'cause of this, then *I'm* moving in, *I'm* taking over, *I'm* Helen's man. I'll raise that kid as mine, and I ain't ever gonna tell him about you. Ever. You just think about that, Padre."

He went to the door, slammed it on the way out. A notice of rules fell from the back of the door.

So much to sort through, so much all at once, but one thing shone clear — for the first time since David had known him, Murray hadn't thrown a fit when very angry. He stayed calm. He kept it under control. He acted like a man.

He leapt to his feet, shouting, "Well done,

60

Murray! Well done!"

"What difference does it make if he has more than one visitor in a day?" Clare Childs demanded of the man behind the desk. "You're saying I have to pay *another* fare to come all the way from Teddington — with a miserable amount of changes, not to mention the *time* it took . . ."

"I don't make the rules."

She pressed her fingers against a headache. "Well, if I can't get in to see him today, I'd like to be reimbursed for my fare, thank you very much."

"I'm sorry. That's not possible."

"But this is unreasonable! How am I supposed to know if I'm getting here before anyone else?" Tears stung Clare's eyes, and she hated that they did, but they were tears of frustration for wasted money. "One visitor per day — ridiculous! Who makes these rules? This is outrageous!"

The middle-aged woman behind her patted her shoulder. "You poor dear — is it your husband? Your fiancé?"

A slammed door took the attention of all.

A harassed-looking young man with dark hair stood glaring at no one in particular. Then he came up to the desk next to Clare.

"I'll have my bag now."

The accent caught her ear.

"Excuse me — there is a queue," said the lady behind Clare with some indignation. He looked at her, then at the sergeant behind the desk.

"Say, how does bail work here?" he asked the sergeant.

The sergeant pointed to the end of the queue. "There's a *queue,* the lady said."

"What's a queue?"

"Yanks," the man muttered. "A *line.* You must wait in line. Wait your turn. They take turns in America, don't they?" He looked at Clare, shaking his head in disbelief. "You want your fare reimbursed?" He jerked a thumb at the young man. "Talk to the Yank. Next, please."

Clare stepped aside, staring at the American. He put his fists in his pockets, and went to the end of the queue. He looked rumpled and tired and very out of sorts.

He was the one who visited the Burglar Vicar? *He* usurped her visit?

Were they friends? Were they in cahoots? Some sort of criminal ring?

Were they related? They didn't look alike. The dear BV, of whom she suddenly felt unaccountably protective, had light-brown eyes, thin brown hair, and was of average height. This American had nearly black eyes, black hair, and was taller. If anyone was a burglar, it was this fellow, not the other. Had a rather dark, intense look . . .

How could she possibly leave without saying something?

What could she possibly say?

He certainly had the attention of everyone in the room — his accent, his apparent agitation; Americans were very demonstrative, it was true, but . . . and yes, oh dear, he was *muttering* to himself. . . .

She walked past very slowly and stopped to slowly button her jacket. He was not only talking to himself, he was fidgety. Hands in his pockets, hands out. Back in, back out. Off went his hat, tossed from hand to hand, back it went on. And all the while he chattered to himself in a low murmur, as if he were in the room all by himself.

"Treat me like that. Think I haven't outgrown *A, B,* and *C*? Here's an *A* for you: I shoulda married your wife. Eh? Whaddya think of that? Here's your *B*: That kid should be mine. That ain't enough? How 'bout a *C*? That kid should be mine. How 'bout a *D*? That kid should be mine. *E:* that kid should be mine. *F:* that kid —"

"Should be yours?"

Startled, he looked down at Clare. It

seemed to take a moment for him to register that she had said anything at all. In fact, it took a very long moment, and oh dear, what was meant to be a cute little sympathetic yet introductory quip threatened to prove an insult. Then he noticed all eyes on him. A flush came, and he looked away.

"You're from America, the sergeant said?" Clare said brightly. "Oh, I've always wanted to visit." She wanted nothing of the sort. Couldn't stand America because of its isolationist policies. "Heard so much about the Grand Canyon. Have you been?"

He shook his head, not meeting her eyes, though his discomfort seemed eased. At least it seemed he'd come away from a very intense place. "Too far away," he murmured. "I'd like to go. Ain't been outside New York much. This is only my second time. Don't know how I'd get there, ain't learned to drive yet, probably never will — probably go by rail, then." He shrugged, and brightened a bit. "Might be fun. Ma's wanted to go. We could pick up my uncle Bill and aunt Fran in Philly. That's the kind of —"

"You're from New York, did you say? Oh — I've *always* wanted to visit New York City!" She hated big cities. "What's it like?"

"It's swell." Then he shook his head, as if

catching up with his words. "No, no, it's not swell. Not all of it. I can only take so much, then I want to get back to Bartlett. I only work there, see, I don't live there. When you say you're from New York they all think you mean the City. New York's a big state. From Bartlett it's forty-three minutes by train, 57 percent of . . ." He shook his head again, as if to clear it, and didn't speak for a moment. When he did, he spoke with more reserve. "No offense, miss, I got a lot on my mind. I don't feel like talkin', unless you can talk bail."

"Bail?"

"I gotta post bail for my friend. You got bail bondsmen here, right? They do that in England?"

"Your . . . friend?" she dared to ask.

"Father Fitz. Came all the way here to get him, and now . . . Well, it's not lookin' too good. They won't let him out 'cause he won't talk. Maybe *I* can talk for him. *I* can straighten it out, like he always done for me. Who do I gotta talk to? The bobby behind the desk?" He looked around the room. "Someone else high up?"

"Talk about what?" she asked innocently, hoping to catch him off balance for a few more details. Oh, she was shameless!

"Well, see —" But he closed his mouth.

"Well done, the padre said. He saves it for when he's *really* impressed, and he'd be impressed to know that for once, I shut my mouth." He grasped his lapels, now looking very pleased with himself. "I don't gotta lay *all* my cards on the table. It's been a pleasure, miss. You're a real inspiration. I hope you get to the Grand Canyon someday. If you do, give it my regards." He lifted and replaced his fedora, and turned his attention to the front.

She couldn't contrive a single reason to keep standing there, so she murmured, "Likewise," and walked out the door.

"Daft?" she asked herself outside the police station, thinking furiously, pacing three steps to, three steps back. "Don't think so. There is something odd and peculiar about him, but not in a *criminal* way. He's certainly gabby. Reminds me of Giles Wentworth."

I hope you get to the Grand Canyon someday? Give it my regards?

"Well, that was certainly sweet. And he meant it." Something about him was very much like the dear BV.

What did G. K. Chesterton say about the talkative man? He doesn't have anything to hide. Or maybe it was that the talkative man has no pride. He is not so *careful,* he doesn't *watch* himself, not like someone with pride. Or someone with a guilty conscience. Something like that.

The chatty American was *not* a criminal. She had a feeling for criminals. Well — she had a feeling for malice, and neither of these men had malice within.

Not like her uncle, the Privately Amused. They were quite different from him.

Clare stopped pacing. The dark American reminded her of the BV in the same way that *he* reminded her of — but, really — two, at the same time?

"Oh, you are being foolish," she told herself fiercely, and wondered if she had indeed developed a dreaded *fixation*.

She realized her hand was pressed upon her heart. She felt for the locket.

"I miss you," she whispered, tears suddenly stinging. "More than ever. I haven't had anyone to remind me of you. And now there are two."

The American emerged from the police station, carrying a suitcase. He looked very unhappy. The *intense* look had come back, very dark and inward.

He stood quite still for a rather awkward amount of time while people passed. He simply stared at the street, didn't move an inch. Then he looked left and right, as if trying to decide which way to go.

"Oh dear," she said.

Cards, said he?

Put them all on the table, she told herself.

She walked up the steps, murmuring, "Courage. Vision. Singularity of purpose." She produced a cheerful smile. "Hello again. I'm — waiting for my bus."

He nodded. "Hello."

"Listen — wherever you're staying in London, I've got a better place. It's quiet, and it's just outside this poisonous city."

"Poisonous?"

"I can only take so much of it. Then I want to get back to . . ."

She went all electric, felt lifted to her toes.

"Look," she said quickly, "I own a boat on the Thames, and I'm raising money to be the first woman to singlehandedly circumnavigate the globe in a ketch-rigged yacht. It's currently a bed and breakfast. Your friend paid a visit a few weeks ago in the form of a foiled burglary. I came today to find out what he was looking for. I have one cabin available, and you can stay in it if you like. The price is seven pounds a week, and that *includes* breakfast. It isn't cheap, but it's . . . unique and idyllic. Who *wouldn't* want to stay there?"

She was trembling and hoped it didn't show.

"Captain John Elliott owns the boatyard. He keeps an eye on my boat, and on me. He is very fond of me because of my sailing dream, and has become my . . . sworn protector. If you try anything he will kill you. Mrs. Iris Shrewsbury is a current paying tenant, and is skilled at swinging kettles and shrieking. There. That is all of it."

"What's her name?"

She knew instantly what he meant, wondered at it.

"Maggie Bright."

He gave a very strange smile, one of bitter amusement and something else. She couldn't tell what, and didn't know if she couldn't read him because he was an American or because he was a stranger. He certainly looked very uncomfortable.

In fact, he looked miserable.

Just as she was ready to turn and run as fast as she could, he said, "I ain't stayin' nowhere."

"Well — well, what a providential co-incidence," Clare said idiotically, because she could think of nothing else. "You *do* look awfully tired." He looked very sad, too, as woefully wretched as had the BV. "Some tea would be just the thing. Shall we find a place to grab a pot, and you can think it over?"

He nodded, and she led him away.

Inside the police station, the sergeant behind the desk suddenly remembered. He held up a hand to the next in the queue, and picked up the telephone. He sorted through the clutter on his desk, and found the card. William Percy. Youngish to be a Scotland Yard detective.

"Yes, this is Blake. Westminster Station. William Percy, please. Thank you. Yes, Blake here — you wanted me to ring up if anyone visited the American priest? Yes, he just left. His name is Murray Vance. Yes, I'm quite sure. Yes, Vance, that's the name. Well, I'm looking right at his signature. No, I haven't a clue. Hang on — there's no call for that! Well, it wasn't a *long* visit, you wouldn't have had time to *get* here, would you? No, I don't have that kind of manpower, that's *your* job, as you frequently tell us. Good *day.*" He replaced the receiver, muttering, "Snotty . . . bloody . . ." Then he said brightly, "Next?"

6

The topic, and he started it, was why on earth did England go to war — Clare nearly spat tea. Oh, I don't know — has to do with a fellow named Hitler and his roving gang of thugs who thought Europe belonged to them and they blew things up and killed people to get it. Nothing much.

Honestly!

Murray Vance was his name. After the waiter had taken their order for corned beef stew, bread, and tea, Clare had exclaimed in a nervous rush, "Well, isn't it interesting! The man who owned my boat was a Vance. But he was British, you see. Died in January. Heart attack I'm told. Terrible shame for him. Terrible inadvertent good fortune for me. Wait until you see her. She will absolutely break your heart."

The subject meandered from Britain's declaration of war in September of '39, to the long "phony" war as the papers called it, to the fall of Denmark just a month ago, and all the devastation since — Norway fell, and Holland only last week, and now Belgium and France were under siege. Not so phony after all.

Cursed decorum! She wanted to push past all this opening nonsense and get to the Burglar Vicar and whatever business brought him to England.

Clare sipped her tea and tried to think of things to say while he ate. She did harbor a particular fury over what happened to Norway.

"I saw a picture, once. A collection of peaceful Norwegian sheep farmers in a lovely mountains-and-lakes setting. It's absolutely awful, what's happened. The Norwegians were neutral. It somehow made them more *innocent* than the Poles. It was the suddenness, I suppose, this ransacking ambush of Hitler's. The suddenness seemed particularly evil. So pouncing. On peaceful people."

She tried not to notice as Murray ate stew with disturbing precision. Clearly he was famished. The bites were huge and rather off-putting. He swallowed, and said, "You sayin' it was less evil of Hitler to wipe out Poland than it was to take over Norway? Ain't buyin'. Where does that make sense,

Clare? Twelve thousand innocent civilians died in Poland. Ain't that evil?"

How easily he called her Clare, as if they'd known each other all their lives. Though it would be strange, she supposed, if he called her Miss Childs. Still, he was so informal. The familiarity was both refreshing and faintly uncouth.

"Of course it was evil. Maybe I really liked that picture. It was particularly innocent."

The spoon paused, midair. "Pictures got power, I'll say that. Guy I know changed his politics 'cause of one." The spoon resumed.

"Changed his politics? Because of a picture?"

"Yep."

Goodness, she hoped he didn't eat like this *all* the time, especially for breakfast. She saw her profits eaten up right before her.

"I *should* mention," she said delicately, "in case I didn't make it clear earlier, that only breakfast is included in room and board."

"Say, can we get more of this bread? Hey — mister! You there, mister . . . waiter guy." He stifled a belch, and said to Clare, "What do you call 'em here?"

"I'm sorry, but that was a bit rude," Clare said, eyes slightly wide to make her point.

"You *are* an American, but still — you must learn the rules of the road." She turned to the waiter and said smoothly, "Yes, *very* sorry, but could we trouble you for another plate of bread, please? Thank you *very* much. *Very* sorry." Behind her hand she whispered apologetically, "He's American," and gave a wink. Hoping the exchange educated, she turned to Murray. "Did the photograph change his politics for the good?"

"Nope. The good senator shoulda stayed an isolationist."

She couldn't help a smile. "You are talking to a Brit."

The young man grinned. He was a few years younger than she, and when he smiled, he seemed positively boyish. *"A,* you can't help that. *B —"*

"B, did the Burglar Vicar tell you anything interesting?" Clare said in a rush. "Sorry, but I'm quite mad to know his business with the *Maggie Bright,* and can you possibly blame me? It's my boat. It's my home. What could he have been looking for? I have no money. Spent my entire estate acquiring the boat. It was bequeathed to me, you see, but I had to pay a dreadful amount of back taxes before I could get it. Spent all I had. My point is, I have nothing of *real* value,

except for a necklace which has sentimental value only. So *why* was he there? Why the *Maggie Bright*? I have a right to know. I don't believe for a moment it was a random burglary. And why am I sure he is a good man, not a bad one?"

Murray's face hardened, and oh dear, that place of dark intensity returned. "He is a good man. He's here because of a bad one. He's here because of lies the bad one told." Then he shook his head, as if catching himself. He looked at his spoon, dropped it in the bowl and pushed it away. "All that business is his, not mine. I'll say it straight — I'm outta this with a ten-foot pole. You wanna know, you heard what the bobby said — be first in line tomorrow. He got himself into this fix, he'll do the talkin'. Not me. So don't ask me again." He adjusted himself, and then muttered with less heat, "Please."

Clare slipped her hands into her lap so that he wouldn't see white fists.

All was amiable up until now. Now, Murray Vance sat in a closed, moody silence, and Clare could think of nothing to say.

The American paid the check, leaving a ridiculously huge tip — which Clare did *not* correct — and they hailed a taxi, not a bus. Clare felt somewhat recompensed that someone else wasted money today.

75

■ ■ ■ ■

"No references?!" the Shrew staccato-shrieked in Clare's head. "You — didn't — get — *references* — on — this — man?! Where is that teakettle?"

"Do you mind if we make a stop at my uncle's bookshop?" Clare asked Murray over Mrs. Shrew.

They shouldn't. He looked very tired. She was being a very bad hostess.

Murray surfaced from his dull gaze out the cab window to say, "Yeah. Sure." Even tired, he was an amiable sort. He also seemed to have completely forgotten his rude forthrightness at the café. She wasn't sure she liked it that he had forgiven himself so entirely.

She gave directions to the cab driver, and settled back, brooding.

Why should she care what Mrs. Shrewsbury or the captain thought?

Clare pondered:

She did indeed care about Mrs. Shrew's approval. (This surprised her.)

She cared about Captain John's approval. (This did not surprise her; he was a dear.)

Murray was a complete stranger with no references. They would never approve his presence on the *Maggie Bright.*

But Murray was the key to Father Fitz-patrick. They must approve!

They would make her life miserable if they didn't.

She did not care what her uncle, the Privately Amused, thought.

He made her life miserable regardless.

Not anymore! Ha-ha! Remember that, Clare.

Why did she want to parade Murray to him?

The last thought startled her.

The glorious freedom since she'd quit working at the bookshop and started the B and B took on ever-new psychological significances: What was her *motive* to go to the shop right now? Was it to flaunt her independence in a shallow, childish way? Certainly. But she frowned. It wouldn't change her uncle. That superior, condescending, manipulative, privately amused, and quietly vicious man would still find reason to apply that superior, condescending, manipulative, privately amused, and quietly vicious *smirk.*

No, now that she truly thought on it, her uncle did not factor in. Clare's heart rose. She wanted less to display her freedom to come and go as she pleased than to buy time to get to know this Murray Vance. Then she could pour heaps of details upon Mrs. Shrew, and so soften the calamity of a reference-less tenant. For surely, Mrs. Shrew would be convinced that yet another American sought to murder her in her sleep (or do far worse) if Clare could not immediately convince her otherwise.

Clare's motives were correct. She cared what the *right* people thought. It meant Uncle's hold on her was lessening, soon to have the strength of a cobweb before a crashing bayonet. Her heart rose to a smile.

"Right," she said crisply. "I need to know more about you. Lots more."

He roused with a snort, and wiped his mouth. "Was I droolin'?"

"To be frank, Mrs. Shrew—sbury will want to know that you are not a potential exhibit for Madame Tussauds. I must convince her of your conventionality."

"My what?"

"Your normalness."

He gave a short chuckle. "Never accused of bein' normal."

"Nor I. Nevertheless . . . do you have a girlfriend?"

"She left me for an older man."

"What do you do for a living?"

"I design posters for the Keep America

Out of War committee and other isolationist and noninterventionist groups."

"Oh dear."

"It's great work. They're well funded. I make as much as I used to. Well — almost."

To the cab driver she called, "No, no — the next left. After Brumby Court."

"Is that a problem?"

Clare bit her lip. "How do you feel about lying? We could say you design posters for the opera. Or the movies! I have a splendid *Wizard of Oz* paste-up that a friend gave me. Seen it three times. You see, Mrs. Shrewsbury is an ardent politician. Keeps me apprised. And unfortunately, is not a fan of current American foreign policies — she is especially not fond of your ambassador, Mr. Kennedy. Calls him *very* rude things. No offense."

When he didn't answer, Clare ventured, "Are you offended?"

"I'm too tired to be offended. In fact, I can't remember what you just said." He rubbed his eyes. "Remind me in the morning. Won't speak to you for a week. See, I ain't slept in . . ." His hands dropped from his eyes. "Huh. Must be a long time. The only time I don't talk a lot is when I'm tired."

"You must not be *very* tired, then," she

suggested. She added soothingly, "We'll get you sorted soon. Your cabin is the best. It's my favorite, but *I* need to be in the captain's cabin. *I* need to be in the heart of everything. Listening. Aware. Alert to the slightest change, and you will not know what that change is until it comes. Once you know your vessel, the *slightest* alteration to its daily rhythms, anything out of the ordinary, will get your attention. Dreadfully important on a boat — it's your life, you know." She added, "Captain John is a dear. Teaches me a great deal about the *feeling* things of being a sailor. It's how I discovered the Burglar Vicar: *keen alertness.* Right. Your parents. Your siblings. What can I tell the Shrew about them?"

Murray smacked each side of his face, and gave himself a shake. "Ah, let's see: Tell her my old man was a philanderin' yutz who left when I was four. Later he died. My ma's a retired secretary, lives in a cute little bungalow in Bartlett. You kinda remind me of her. She's chatty, see. And strict. You make me wanna watch my grammar. I got the bungalow for a song. You should see the place. Proudest day of my life, drivin' her up. Got a nice carport, garden. She always wanted a garden. No siblings."

His voice had grown hoarse with fatigue.

80

She cracked on mercilessly.

"How were your grades in school? Were you an exemplary student? Did you do anything noteworthy or hopefully heroic in your community? Where did you go to college to design posters, or does it come naturally? And how are you connected to Father David Fitzpatrick?"

"Terrible grades. Nothing heroic. Noteworthy . . ." He chuckled, his expression rather sly in fond remembrance. "Yeah. Lots of noteworthies. Not the kind you want, I think. What were the others?"

"Schooling," Clare prompted. "And Father Fitzpatrick."

He smacked his face. "National Academy of Design, New York City. The Fitz put me through. I dropped out my last year 'cause I got famous and boy, the padre blew his stack on that, tried to get me to — no, no, no, that's all I'm gonna say about him."

He sat up. "You ain't gonna trick me. I ain't *that* tired."

"You mean . . . he paid for your schooling?" Clare asked, very interested.

"Mostly. I worked odd jobs. I think some of the dough came from my old man, though I ain't supposed to know. Could never figure out where the Fitz got it. He's poor. Always givin' stuff away. Kind of irresponsible. Most irresponsible thing he ever did, outside of comin' here, was make me his kid's godfather. I wanted to crack his head."

"He sort of . . . directed your schooling? In the absence of your father? Well, that's very decent of him. Would you say he is sort of a father figure for you?"

Another expression of remembrance came, this one soft.

"He stepped in cement for me."

"Is that an American metaphor?"

He came to himself. "No, no, no — I ain't gonna fall for it."

"Oh, bravo! I *knew* he was decent. Now. I must learn very important facts about *yourself,* and quickly. Tell me something comfortable and inspiring. Do you read books? Smoke a pipe? Oh dear. I wish we'd known each other all our lives. I wish you were an American cousin. I don't suppose we could say you are. You see, I need to tell them something that says, This man is *not* a burglar or a killer."

He shrugged. "Tell 'em whatever makes *you* know I ain't."

"A million things. They won't appreciate the subtleties."

"Like what?"

"A bad man doesn't talk as much as you."

"Holy smokes, sister — you must be a saint."

"A bad man does not come all the way to England to retrieve an errant priest."

Amusement left. He looked out the window.

"What was he here for, Murray?" said Clare.

"A package, Clare." His voice had gone hoarse.

"What's in it?"

"It's supposed to prove something that cannot be true."

"About what?"

His face was pale, whether from fatigue or something else, Clare didn't know. But now something else descended on it, a darkness, a down-pulled shade.

She shouldn't intrude, not on this. Something felt very wrong. Here, that boyish innocence left and something alarming took its place.

Rubbish. "What is it supposed to prove?"

He shook his head. "It will change you. It will change everything."

"I'm a big girl. What's it supposed to prove?"

"It's supposed to prove something about humanity. If it's true, we're finished. It'll mean somethin' got inside us. If it's true —

I quit. I'll find a place where none of this can find me. I'll find a place where things are how they're supposed to be. I won't tell you 'cause you're nice, Clare. It'll change you. It'll change everything."

"I notice your grammar improves when you are upset," Clare said a bit breathlessly, fascinated by that dark intensity.

He turned a hostile look upon her. "Why did he give you the *Maggie Bright*?"

It shocked her speechless.

"Why you?" The next words came slow and deliberate: "Why did it go to you?"

How slowly the world turned at moments like these.

"How could you possibly . . . ?" Clare looked out her window. "I don't know. I've wondered ever since."

"I don't believe you."

"Whatever I say will sound silly."

After a moment, he said, "Try me."

Oh dear.

"The owner was an old friend of my father's. My parents died when I was eleven. Ever since, I've been looking for a place to call my own." She felt for the locket. "I didn't know that a place looks, too. You see, I believe she was meant to be mine. *She* wanted me. It was less that I had come to her by some whim of a man's allegiance to a boyhood friend, than that she had come to me, as if she were sent to me, as if —" she waited through the ache in her throat — "as if my parents had sent her from heaven. I know how silly that sounds. But I like to believe they are still trying to take care of me, that they sent me another home because the one with my uncle was unbearable.

"I know with all my heart *Maggie Bright* was meant for me, because she changed my life. She was glad the day I owned her. She trusts me, and because of that, I trust her. And she tells me that this Father Fitz had very good reason to be where he was, as if *they* are coconspirators, more than Maggie and I, and she tells me I should —" To the cab driver, she suddenly called, "I've changed my mind. We'll go directly to Bexley-on-the-Thames, not the bookshop." Gazing out the window, she said, "I don't belong there anymore. Freedom doesn't look back."

The only place she wanted to be was on her boat, and with the thought came the glorious joy that it was hers to go home to all of her days.

After what must have been a very long while, she came to herself, and looked to see what the American thought. He was fast asleep. His arms were crossed. His face was utterly free of care, and rather bunched up and puckered with his head sunk on his shoulder. She didn't know him well enough to think he looked rather adorable, but if she did, she would.

She also felt quite sure that a potential exhibit for Madame Tussauds would not feel free to snore in the presence of a stranger.

"Blake again. William Percy, please. Yes, I thought you might be interested to know that your suddenly popular prisoner had *two* other guests today, besides the Murray Vance I called about. Well, I don't know — one was female, lovely, and British — I didn't count her at first, because she didn't actually *see* him, she couldn't get in because of the one-visit rule, but she certainly *came* to see him. It just now struck me that you might want to know. And now the latest visitor just left — another American, male, much older. Rather ratlike. A bit shady. The word *furtive* comes to mind — you could cast him in a Hitchcock film. Yes, he was American. No, he *wasn't* German, didn't I just — No, no — I said I didn't *get* their names, as — Hang on! There's no cause for that. I can't very well ask them to *sign* their names if there's no *visit,* now, can I? Is that sensible? This is a *courtesy* call, sir, I thought it might *interest* you." He replaced the receiver *without* saying good day. "Sodding . . . rude . . . relics of . . ." He mustered a smile. "Next, please?"

7

"What in me is dark . . ."

"Yes, yes, illumine," Jamie finished for him. "Drink up, mate. Thatsa boy. Probably filled with sheep bits. Captain Milton, meet Mr. Belgium Doctor. He's going to fix you up."

The angry little doctor stood in the middle of the small, dark hay shed, one hand on a hip. His neat white shirt stood out in the gloom. He turned in place, shaking his head.

"C'est impossible," he finally declared, flinging out a hand. "Zee light — terrible. My, my, my tools — no *antiseptique.* And zee Germans. Zey come! *C'est impossible!"*

"Mr. Belgium Doctor, meet Mr. Bren." Elliott raised his rifle. "Fix him, or you'll need fixing."

Disgusted, the doctor went to a stack of musty hay bales and set down a small brown leather case the size of a large wallet. He began to roll up his sleeves.

It had taken two hours to find him. Another half hour to get him to come, and that, only when Jamie had unshouldered his rifle. Another half hour to scout out the nearest shelter and drag the semiconscious captain to it, another half hour to find water in a sheep trough.

"British *thug.*"

"A thug, eh? I've been eight months in your country. Eight months on a line erased in a day, like it never existed. Eight months, for your protection! This is how you repay us?"

The Belgian's dark eyes pierced. He rolled a sleeve with precise movements. "You are not here for me. You are here for your safe island. Get me bandages."

Jamie took the captain's rucksack and rummaged. He found a battered book — *Paradise Lost* by John Milton. He tossed it back, rummaged, found several rolled bandages. He took one and regarded it with a twinge of guilt; two days, and he hadn't yet changed the bandage. He was too afraid the wound would come apart if he did. He handed it to the doctor. "There's more if you need them."

The doctor set it aside. He unwound the ties on his case, and unfolded it.

Now that he had his way after pulling a

rifle on a civilian, Jamie cast about for something conversational. "You've got the, you know — thread stuff for the job? Catgut? Isn't that what they call it?"

The doctor sent him a swift, seething glare.

"Right. Just do a good job." He looked down at the captain. "All right, Milty?"

Captain Milton lay on the ground. He held both sides of his head, groaning softly, breathing faster as if caught in a nightmare, as if sunk to a private place of wrestled hell. Jamie had seen him like this before. Was it pain, or was it something else? Did thoughts of his men bring on that agony? When it was over, he'd always resurface to a wary, bewildered reality. Jamie had the urge to pat him on the head and speak kindly to him, then, like his old dog Toby.

He knelt beside him.

"Doc's gonna fix you up. But there's nothing to numb it. Here's a harness strap, see? Cut from your friend the horse." He worked the man's mouth open, and slipped the leather piece between his teeth. "There's a British soldier's whiskey, eh?"

And something strange happened: the brown eyes looked *right* at him, first time in two solid days, and it looked as if he had something to say. Something real.

Something not from a book. Jamie hesitated, then dislodged the strap, fearing if anything came out it would only come out Milton.

"Solitude sometimes is best society," the captain whispered apologetically.

He felt a little jump — that *was* direct to him. Even if it came from the book, it was like real conversation, and he understood it. Maybe the man had been trying to communicate in Milton words all along. His own wits blasted out, the wits of Milton blasted in.

"It's all right, mate. Sometimes . . . we can't talk about things." He couldn't imagine losing his whole squad. Couldn't imagine finding them blown to bloody ribbons. He'd go loony as the captain.

Brown eyes still with him, the captain whispered, "The mind is its own place, and in itself can make a heaven of hell, a hell of heaven."

"That it can." He patted Milton's arm.

The doctor drew near with a water-soaked rag and needle and thread. He laid these on the captain's stomach, and knelt, with clear distaste, in the dirt. He removed the dirty bandages. He wiped the wound with the cleanest parts of the old dressing, tossed it aside, took the water-soaked rag and dabbed very gently at the gash. Even gentle movements released fresh blood. Jamie's stomach roiled, and he wondered how the doctor would stitch up that dark mishmash. The doctor gestured to the captain's rucksack, and Jamie retrieved another bandage roll.

Jamie thought he'd start right in with the needle and thread, but instead, Jamie watched as he used his fingertips to apply delicate pressure on the skull near the wound, and then fan out incrementally all around the captain's head; as he did so, he gazed off, and let his careful fingers do the seeing. He frowned, and didn't say what the frown meant. Was the captain's skull fractured? Like an egg, broken in place? The doctor finished the probing, wiped fresh blood, and reached for the needle and thread.

"Brace yourself, Cap'n."

"Trial will come unsought," the captain said, and took the strap between his teeth.

"That it will." Boy, they were on a roll.

The doctor went to work.

Jamie very nearly did not come back.

He'd seen it all quite clearly. He'd just take off, track down his squad, and they'd make for Dunkirk together. He saw the reunion in his head. I was hoping we were shut of you! Look what Hitler threw back, lads! He'd tell his tale, they'd tell theirs, and they'd be on their way.

But could he tell them he'd left a wounded man?

It made cold sense to leave the wounded. Jamie could fight, Milton could not, and by the look of things, England would need every man she could get once they rallied from this first blood.

He didn't know why he came back. Only, he couldn't imagine what an enemy would do with a babbling man like this, a man just now starting to communicate, a man stuck inside a rotten, battered cage. Jamie was just now starting to crack the Milton code.

What in me is dark, illumine: Why did I survive, and not my men?

What is low, raise and support: Someone out there . . . help.

He sat beside the captain, his back to the doctor's work, and waited.

8

What Murray liked best about the movie *Beau Geste* was the way the sand blew over the dune in the opening scene, revealing the film's title. Thrilled him every time. Now that's art, he'd say to whoever sat next to him at the Palladium.

When Murray first saw *Maggie Bright* at her berth on the Thames dock, it was as if sand blew over the dune.

Good to see you, Mags, he called out in his heart.

Little Miss Chatty Clare was all fluttery and proud and saying something, but Murray set down his bags on the dock and went to work 'cause oh, she hollered to be drawn.

He pulled out a pad of sketch paper from the side pocket of his briefcase. He took out his pencil box and sorted through it until he found a Kimberly 4B with a reasonably sharp point.

He hadn't seen her in six years, not since

he was seventeen. His father or Clare had changed the sails — they used to be white — and now the mainmast sail, currently furled, was an ugly salmon color, as was the foremast sail. Unless, pray his heart out, they were sail covers. Couldn't tell from here.

The rest of her was the same. Oh, there were some pots of flowers and herbs on the deck, which his old man never had, some painted paper Chinese lanterns strung out in a cheery red and yellow dotted line, some colorful rag rugs thrown about, and — well, there it was, a painted sign with curlicue letters that said *Bed and Breakfast.* A short garland of red flowers dangled from a corner of the sign.

Sixteen feet at her beam, fifty-two feet on her length, and add another three feet if you count the retractable swimming platform off the port stern his old man put in the summer Murray was seventeen. Same beautifully paneled woodwork and shiny brass fittings that made other yachties pause for a look when she came into a marina. Same lettering on the transom, which Murray could not have done better, his mother's name when his old man met her one summer at the resort on Long Island: *Maggie Bright.*

Clare watched Maggie come to hollerin'
life beneath his pencil.

When he finished, he withdrew as he
always did from a drawing, backing out
from one reality into another, and cocked
his head.

Clare studied the drawing, and then
looked up at him. She looked at the boat,
back to the drawing.

He felt a pleased flush.

"Like it?" he said like a little kid.

"Don't be ridiculous. It's marvelous. I feel
foolish."

"Why?"

"I just do."

The drawing time gave him a chance to
get used to seeing her again. Things might
go easier when he went aboard. The cabin
Clare had described was his. And Clare's
was his old man's. It raised a sweat in his
scalp.

"It's perfectly foolish," Clare said with
unexpected fierceness. "You're wasting your
talents on propaganda posters. Father Fitzpatrick surely knows this."

Murray put his pencil and drawing pad
away.

"Wait — give me the drawing. I have an
idea."

He retrieved it from his briefcase, and

gave it to her.

She studied him for a moment, and then sighed. "Well, come on then — let's meet our fate. Please try not to look like a burglar. Or a murderer. Don't even frown. You look very intense when you do. Be on your *best* behavior, for Mrs. Shrew is going to kill me but we may as well present a good show. And remember — you know *nothing* about the dear BV. We must *not* let on that you are connected."

"Why?"

"She'll think another American has come to kill her. Oh dear, there she is. Courage, now." She swallowed. "Courage. Vision. Singularity of purpose. That will conquer all."

She didn't look like she believed a word.

Clare needn't have worried.

She used the sketch of Maggie as a peace offering for bringing a disapproved man aboard. She held it out like silver before a werewolf, and after a sharp look around Clare at Murray, whom she had instructed to stay safely behind her, Mrs. Shrew snatched and studied the drawing.

It was somewhere in the middle of Clare rushing to say, "He's another paying tenant, you see, isn't it wonderful? He is an

97

American and his name is Murray Vance. I know he is a man, but isn't that a *splendid* drawing of our Maggie? What a clever little creature there on the bowsprit. Such talent, wouldn't you say?" when Mrs. Shrew grabbed her own throat, not Clare's, and said, a bit strangled, "Good heavens — *the* Murray Vance? I thought you were dead! I wore black."

Astonished, Clare turned to Murray. He gave a charming smile, spread his arms to display himself, and said, "I ain't dead."

"Do you know," said Mrs. Shrew, her voice now musical, "that my nephew and his friends are your *biggest* fans? They have a club. Rocketkids, they call themselves. Not very original, but they are young. Oh, please tell me: When *will* you get back to the funnies? Haven't read anything new since January. Are you on hiatus?" She gasped, and a hand flew to her mouth. "Are you on sabbatical?"

"If sabbatical means I'm here to refill the ol' tank, sure am, ma'am." Murray pushed up his hat. "Things got mossy in the old magic well, see. Hopin' a change of scenery will help."

Oh, well done, Clare silently admired. He was very good at deception.

Murray looked down and patted his

stomach. "This is where I drop the bucket, see, and when I crank it up, I just look and see what I got."

"*That's* where you found Rocket Kid?"

"Doin' the backstroke."

"And Salamander?"

"Same place, one year later. Rocket Kid rescued him. Buncha punk kids were beatin' him up."

Mrs. Shrew made a very small noise. Then she covered her lips with a set of fingertips, and ventured, "Tell me — please — Salamander is *not* dead, is he? Oh, he can't be! True, such exquisite sorrow with your last comic strip — yet you left a *trace* of ambiguity as to his *actual* demise. All of your fans suspect the same. We — that is, the Rocketkids — refuse to believe he is dead. You can tell me. I promise I won't say a word."

Clare certainly hoped that Salamander, whoever he was, was very much alive as both sets of fingertips now hovered at her lips. Clare looked anxiously at Murray.

"You kiddin' me?" Murray said. "Ain't no Rocket Kid without Salamander."

"Just so!" Mrs. Shrew sang. She pressed a hand against her heart, laughing in relief. "Oh, I knew it. Bravo! Mr. Vance, I don't suppose I could keep this?" she asked very meekly and hopefully and obsequiously of the drawing — Mrs. Shrew! Meek! Hopeful! Obsequious! Clare could only stare, feeling faintly nauseous.

"All yours," Murray said.

"Oh, thank you ever so much!" She gazed at the drawing, extremely pleased. "It's so *good* to see Salamander again. Could I ask you to sign it?"

"Of course." He did so, and handed it back.

"Look — there he is again!" said a very pleased Mrs. Shrew, showing Clare. There was a tiny salamander sitting on the *M,* its tail curling into the *V.* "How clever!"

"Yes. Well. Shall we go below and get you sorted?" said Clare. "You'll want a washup before you turn in — the head is directly across from your cabin. *Head* means *loo* on a houseboat, by the way. *Bath*room, I think you say in the States. Though of course, there's no bathtub — this is a boat, you know. Can't afford that sort of water usage. Very impracticable. I do miss bathing. In a bathtub. I do *wash,* of course — I'm perfectly clean. One learns to get along without a bathtub while maintaining perfect . . . hygiene."

She colored. Had she ever said the word *hygiene* in front of a man? Mrs. Shrew had put Clare completely off center.

Who *was* this man? Suddenly he was *the* Murray Vance?

"Isn't it too early to turn in?" protested Mrs. Shrew. She laid a hand on his arm. "Love to hear how you intend to save Salamander."

"He's very tired," Clare said quickly, at the same time Murray said, "So would my editor." They glanced at each other. Clare said to Mrs. Shrew, "He hasn't slept in days."

"What?! That's no way to treat the Muse!" Mrs. Shrew declared. "Off you go!" She shooed him to the companionway. "We'll fill that well to overflowing! *Maggie Bright* is just the ticket for you!" She waved him on. "Embrace your destiny, lad!"

"I'll be along directly," Clare told him.

They watched him go below.

"I can hardly believe it," squeaked Mrs. Shrew.

"Yes. Ah. Met him by chance in London. He was looking for lodgings. What great luck, don't you think, to find someone who comes with his own references? *International* references? Good old . . . Rocket Kid." She'd never heard of Rocket Kid.

"Was 'Embrace your destiny' a bit much? I don't want to fawn. Oh! You are sixty-

101

seven. Retired. And one day . . . you meet Murray Vance, who becomes a fellow tenant. What a wonderful world. Oh, to be thirty years younger."

"Do you mean forty?" Oh, the naughty words fell out before Clare could stop them. At least she didn't say fifty.

"He's not *that* young," Mrs. Shrew said sharply.

But you are that old, Clare thought unkindly, and only because Mrs. Shrew had something to talk to him about, and Clare did not.

Not unless it involved a priest. And there, Murray wasn't talking.

"Do you know what this means? We get to help Murray Vance find his muse again! I've guided young minds all my life; it seems as though it was preparation for my biggest task of all. My nephew will go absolutely crackers."

"I'll have to tell the captain he has some competition," Clare dared to say, only because Mrs. Shrew was quite bemused.

"Hmm? What? Shall I get him some cocoa? Do Americans drink tea? Oh, we can show him the box! He'll be delighted!"

"What box?"

"The box the Burglar Vicar ransacked. With all the newspapers in it. Do you know that whoever owned this boat was a more devoted *Rocket Kid and Salamander* fan than — than my nephew?"

"How so?"

"Why, it's the *entire* collection! Even when it was just *Rocket Kid*! Every single one from the very beginning — until that first week of January, 1940. I was quite astonished. Found three I hadn't read. It's a rare find, really. That box is probably worth a mint, or will be one day, especially the ones that are just *Rocket Kid*. Isn't it interesting? How could the collector know what he was collecting? What instinct. Did he *know* it was the start of a worldwide sensation? My nephew is from Australia. They're positively mad about *Rocket Kid* down there. They have festivals. Costume parties. Frolicking picnics round the billabong, ha-ha!" She studied her drawing, and said softly, "What amazing instinct this collector had."

A very strange feeling came to Clare.

"Right. We must make a plan," the Shrew took up briskly. "A Muse Retrieval Plan. This is *quite* serious. It will affect the entire world. I shan't sleep at all tonight. He used to make me laugh. He still does, but they are *repeat* laughs — as if everyone doesn't know it's all been *filler* material since January. Stuff that doesn't advance the plot at all."

"Oh dear," Clare breathed.

Arthur Vance died in January.

Arthur Vance had collected every comic strip ever published by . . .

His son.

9

If Jamie had hoped the tide had turned for communication with Captain Milton, he was disappointed; the portal that had cracked open seemed to close as surely as the doctor had closed the wound.

The doctor had left hours earlier without a word, even after Jamie had thanked him. The captain huddled against a bale of hay in a corner of the shed. Jamie sat on a bale opposite, looking at him. First time, really.

He was of average height and build and looks, with dark hair sharp against the white of the bandage. Midthirties, maybe? He wore a wedding ring. Did he have kids? He had no identifying name on his ill-fitting jacket, no stripes to indicate rank, no ID tag, no name on his rucksack. Nothing personal in there save the book and some shaving supplies, nothing else except a packet of tea and a few tins of apricots. Maybe his belongings had blown up with his squad. It explained the loss of his jacket. It didn't explain why his shaving kit and the Milton book had survived.

He hadn't said anything Milton, direct or indirect, since the doctor left. He'd dropped down into himself again, if not to that place of wrestled hell then maybe to a place of simple survival. He looked like a child, digging in bewilderment at his ears, staring at his wedding ring for a foreign object.

That moment before the doc fixed him, was it real? Didn't the captain actually look him in the eye, didn't they share a few words of understanding, Milton or not?

"Say something, Cap. I know you're in there."

But he acted deaf, body and soul, shell-wrecked on the outside, maybe grief-wrecked on the inside.

Jamie sighed and got to his feet.

"Look, I'm afraid we've got to keep moving. We've got to get to Dunkirk. Do you understand? The Germans are coming and I won't get caught on the wrong side of the line, wherever it's finally drawn." He went to the captain. "None of this is fair. Not the shape you're in, not what's happened, and it's *bloody* unfair that I have to flog a half-dead man who hasn't a clue what's going on. Makes me feel like Genghis bloody

Khan. But there's nothing for it. Come on, then. Upsadaisy, Captain. Here we go. Steady, now. No, this way."

They emerged from the hay shed into a bright and humid afternoon, and started walking west.

Hours later, Genghis bloody Khan opened a tin of apricots and made Milton drink the juice. He tried to feed him the apricots, and it went well for a few bites, but then the captain got a queasy look and threw it back up. The force of it produced freshened bloodstains on the bandage. Jamie changed the bandage, promised Milton no more apricots, and got him moving again.

Some of the boys Jamie served with had never been to London, let alone France and Belgium. And now they'd been to Germany, too, if it counted to see the face of a German behind a gun. That was days ago, on an eight-mile stretch along the Franco-Belgian border that Jamie's division was supposed to hold. They didn't hold. They fought for a murderous two hours, and fled — rather, they were *ordered* to flee.

Yesterday he and Milton caught a ride on the back of a lorry with a group of guys and rode for hours. If the medic was right, and Dunkirk was only twenty miles off, they should have arrived yesterday. The lorry ran out of diesel, with no supply truck or fuel dump in range. To make the vehicle useless for the Germans, the men drained the oil and let it run until it seized; for good measure, they trashed the belts and yanked wires and punctured the fuel tank, then they gathered their gear and walked away. Jamie tried to stay with them, but they moved too fast for the captain.

He realized later how lucky they had been for the ride. Hours of walking now produced an arc of blisters at the top of Jamie's feet where the boots did not give. If he unlaced them and pulled back the tongue, it made them too loose and produced blisters on his soles when his feet slid around. The best he could do was pad an extra pair of socks between his skin and the boots and lace the literally bloody things up again.

He unshouldered the Bren and switched it to the other side. The heavy automatic rifle could be set to fire single shots or bursts. He missed his Lee-Enfield. A 1914 model, to be sure, but it wasn't as heavy and it was the weapon he'd trained on. He'd left it with the boys when Lieutenant Dunn sent him for orders. Pulled the Bren off a dead soldier on the road. He'd never fired a Bren.

Jamie walked behind the captain. A man with a horrible wound like that would be in the emergency ward back home. Jamie had him hoofing it like some sadistic drill sergeant. He wished he could find a motorbike.

He came to himself, and glanced about — he'd gone into that walking stupor, and just now realized that for the first time in two days, he saw no one else on the road.

They came to the outskirts of a little village. The posted sign at the side of the road, just before the canal bridge, said *Montmartre.* The other side of the bridge opened into a place with houses on either side. Maybe they could find somewhere to rest for a few hours, take up again at dusk; Milton's gait had gone a bit weavy.

"Winning cheap the high repute which he through hazard huge must earn," said the captain.

"Well — welcome back, old man. Have a nice holiday? You know, sooner or later you'll *really* regain your senses, and I'll be in serious trouble. You'll remember all sorts of things. Try and keep in mind it was in your best interests."

"To perish rather, swallowed up and lost in the wide womb of uncreated night, devoid of sense and motion. Shall we then live thus vile, the race of heaven thus trampled, thus expelled to suffer —"

"Why can't you find something cheerful to say? Isn't there something cheerful in that book?"

Captain Milton stopped walking.

Jamie had a hopeful flash that it was some sort of response. Then he saw what the captain did.

All along the road for two straight days they'd passed evidence of war: abandoned army equipment, abandoned home goods that were too heavy for civilians to push or pull or carry. But they sometimes passed dead soldiers or dead citizens, strafed by aircraft since enemy ground forces had not yet come through. In the dire haste to get to Dunkirk, Jamie could do no more than avert his eyes and wish the departed souls well. Haste was a relief, then, with no moral obligation to tend to the dead bodies.

Jamie came beside the captain.

Two small girls lay in the ditch, tumbled from a child's wagon. The wagon half covered one of them, whose face was turned away. Then Jamie realized it wasn't turned; she *had* no face, strafing bullets had made off with it, made it blend with the dark compost of the earthy ditch.

The other little girl lay staring at the sky,

face cold and sweet, eyes filmed, delicate eyebrows raised as if in surprise. Black curly hair with a purple ribbon, black-and-white checked dress, white lace at the collar, a great dark compost hole in her chest.

Jamie's head swam, and he pushed away from the captain. He stumbled about, and then stared at the sky.

Surely, even a fighter pilot could see they were kids. He took a few steps forward.

"How could you?" he shouted, shaking his fist at the sky.

Two little girls in a wagon. Maybe pulled by a big brother. Big brother gets hit, family leaves the little girls who are clearly dead, grabs him, goes to the . . .

He swiveled toward the town. No, no, something wasn't right. It was too quiet, too . . . empty. No one on the street. No dogs.

No one on the road for a while, and it usually ran with refugees. Had they taken a wrong turn? Jamie's heart began to race.

Where *were* they? How far was Montmartre from Dunkirk? He had no compass, no map. He'd always followed others. Sometimes soldiers, sometimes civilians, and they always outstripped them.

They had come to a fork a while back, and with no signposts, Jamie chose to stay on the curve bearing right. Right seemed north. Wasn't it? Or had they doubled back east?

Was this a German-hit town?

Infantry?

Milton stepped down into the ditch, slipping, sliding, righting himself. He stood over the girl in the checked dress. "For in their looks divine the image of their glorious Maker shone," he said softly. He knelt beside the body.

"Something's not right." Jamie scanned the area. "I've got a bad feeling." A wood lay on the right side of the road, just before the canal bridge, with a far more open area on the left. They should take to the woods.

He went to the ditch. "Captain —"

But tears ran down Milton's face. He touched the girl's lace collar.

"So lively shines in them divine resemblance, and such grace the hand that formed them on their shape hath poured."

"Milton. We've got to go. I think the Germans have actually *been* here."

The captain lowered his head. A tear dripped from his nose. Did he have girls this age at home?

Milton looked like Jamie felt, all undone. Maybe the same thing that broke this man and made him a Milton box had broken other things, too, maybe a wall of defense. But soldiers could not afford to come undone. No, there was no training for dead civilians along the road, for little girls murdered in a ditch, but it was a thing to be sorted later, ideally with a bottle of whiskey and a captured German in their midst.

Milton was a brave man who had saved the lives of an entire unit — they didn't hand out the Victoria Cross for being nice. And now he was broken, and now he sat crying beside a dead girl, and Jamie felt a flash of rage.

Maybe the captain felt it too — he raised a darkened face to the sky, frighteningly livid, and there came a guttural growl like a hackles-raised dog. He rose, and shouted at the sky, "Consult how we may henceforth most offend our enemy! If not victory, then revenge!"

Jamie suddenly felt better.

"Easy, easy! I'm with you on that one, mate, but I'm buggered if I'll let you wreck those stitches." Jamie slid-stepped into the ditch, and took Milton's arm, but he threw off Jamie's hand, and cried, "War hath determined us!" Then the captain gasped and clamped both sides of his head, sinking to his haunches.

"Hands up!" A steel-helmeted soldier stood at the top of the ditch, aiming a rifle.

Jamie's hands went up.

"Who are you?" the man demanded.

"Private Jamie Elliott. Queen's 9th Lancers, infantry. Who are you?"

The rifle lowered. "Private Todd Balantine, 2nd Grenadiers."

"Where are we?"

Balantine turned and pointed to the right of the bridge. "Best we can sort, looks like this canal leads that way to Bray Dunes, on the sea. West of that is Dunkirk. The word is to head for Dunkirk."

"How far is it?" Jamie realized his hands were still raised, and lowered them.

"Don't know. Twenty, maybe thirty miles due north to Bray Dunes. Truth is, we're really not sure. Not a map among us, and the town's deserted. Except for the dead. This canal will at least get us to the sea, even if it's not Bray Dunes. Maybe we can see England from there. Won't *that* be nice?"

Maybe it was just jolly good to have company again, but something about Balantine made Jamie like him instantly. He seemed friendly and capable.

Jamie looked down at the girls. "What happened?"

"Germans, mate."

114

"Aircraft?"

"Infantry."

"Infantry?" Jamie stared at him. "This far west? This far north?"

"Oh, it's worse than that. They've cut us off."

"What do you mean?"

"They've shot straight through. They've made it to the Atlantic. They've taken southern France."

Jamie couldn't speak.

"Afraid it's true," said Balantine grimly. "Last we heard, they're just south of Boulogne."

"No," he breathed in horrified awe.

"Cut through us like butter. Best we can sort, seems they met some opposition here, maybe one of Gort's divisions, then withdrew to the south to concentrate. Truth is, we don't know." He looked over the bridge to the town. "Truth is, we're lost and there's dead people everywhere. Can't've been aircraft that did this."

"But — they're civilians. They're kids."

"I know, mate," said Balantine wearily. His fair hair and blue eyes reminded Jamie of Lieutenant Dunn. "But this is war, isn't it?"

Jamie collected himself enough to say, "What's going to happen? Where will we make our stand? *When* will we make our stand?"

"Don't know if there'll *be* a stand."

"Then we're alone."

England, the last stand.

His sister and her family in Richmond. His father in the boatyard on the Thames. Now only the Channel stood between innocent people and Hitler. He could scarcely take it in.

"You've heard Chamberlain's out, Churchill's in?" Balantine asked.

"That I heard. I'm glad for it."

"We all are. He's for war, not appeasement."

" 'Bout bloody well time."

Balantine looked at the captain, who clutched the side of his head with one hand and placed leaves over the small body, one at a time, with the other. "Who's he?"

"A captain. Wounded. His head's pretty banged up. I'm to get him to Dunkirk. Those were my last orders, two days ago."

Balantine shouldered his rifle. "Well, come on, then. There's five of us. We're taking a breather for the night in a home with food and a decent wine cellar. Word is that Germans don't usually move at night. You can join us."

A weight slid from Jamie's chest. To be

with a group again was an enormous relief. "You have no idea how good it is to speak English again."

Balantine looked at the captain, puzzled. "Is he French, then?"

Jamie watched the captain lay a large leaf across the hole in the girl's chest.

"Innocence," he was whispering, lips trembling, "that as a veil had shadowed them from knowing ill, was gone."

"No. He's Milton."

10

Clare stood outside Murray's cabin, ear pressed to the door. No stirring yet, just even breathing. Must have snored himself out at last. Clare could hear the horrible racket on the other side of the boat until the small hours when either he stopped or she had fallen asleep. She'd not seen him since he turned in yesterday afternoon — he was sleeping before she went below, on his stomach in his clothing on the bottom bunk.

"Right," said the Shrew, seated at the dinette. She had a busy pencil at a notebook in one hand and a hovering triangle of toast and marmalade in the other. "I've gone to work on a Muse Retrieval Plan. Mr. Vance may wish to call it something more in keeping with *filling his pool*. By the by, I didn't have the heart to tell him that a 'magic well' is rather trite; I will guide him toward *filling his pool* whenever necessary, and perhaps that will spark a renaming of the Muse, or at least, the place where the Muse resides." She took a bite of toast.

"Right, then," she continued, after a sip of tea. "We shall divide the Muse Retrieval into two categories: Context and Content. We shall start with the art galleries, which falls under content." She made a note. "Places such as the Tate Museum. The National Gallery. We shall then visit places of architectural splendor, such as St. Paul's and Westminster Abbey and the Houses of Parliament." She thought hard. "Context *and* Content to be had in those places, I should think." She took a bite of toast. "We need more marmalade, by the by. I prefer the kind made with Seville oranges, fine cut, if you please."

Oh, do you, Clare thought sourly. Do you prefer the higher price, too? No, of course not — that must come out of my pocket.

"The box of newspapers, Mrs. Shrew — sbury; do you know where it is?" asked Clare, hoping Mrs. Shrew had it in her cabin.

"It's in Mr. Vance's quarters." She looked at Clare over her reading glasses. "The room *is* rather a collect-all." It was another you-best-learn-from-this look that Clare had come to know well. Yet what a difference between Mrs. Shrew and her uncle. Any rebukes from Mrs. Shrew were like shouts of admiration, compared. Clare learned there was nothing *in* the rebukes. It was simply normal conversation.

"Oh dear," said Clare, a hand to her cheek. "I never did have a chance to clean it out. What a frightful mess. How long has he been sleeping? At least around the clock."

"He'll have a good long wee, that's for sure."

"Goodness!" Clare turned a look on the Shrew.

"We must plan for loud conversation when the time comes. Perhaps bang a pot or two. It's awfully hard not to hear everything that goes on in a boat." She consulted her list. "Right. First, we shall do all of these things, which may take several days, and then we must embark upon a *soul* journey — which falls under content." She made a note. "*These* places can of course be considered soul journeys, but I see them useful in a *technically* constructive way — context. *Content* involves things like taking the train to Canterbury Cathedral — a very soulish place. Lovely shops, too. What other soul things can you think of? Oh! Stonehenge. Though that's a bit obvious. But then there's Cornwall — ancient and mysterious and muse-stirring. The Lake District, of course — lovely walking. Keswick. Moot Hall, endearing place, love the name. Wales! Wales." She wrote furiously. "Gracious, Tintern Abbey — couldn't be more soulish. And the sea! Oh, the sea." She gave a wistful sigh. "Though I suppose we had best confine our travel to the west; the papers say the southern and eastern coasts are being covered with barbed wire and notices of mines. Not exactly breadcrumbs for the Muse, I shouldn't think. One hates to wake up and realize war is upon us. Did you see the sandbags in London? They're going up as barricades in front of key buildings. Barricades!"

"Speaking of vicars . . . I have something to tell you."

It simply made no sense to keep it from her. Clare had woken up with the realization that she did not want to.

"Well, pull up, pull up," said Mrs. Shrew, and Clare slid into the bench across.

The *Maggie Bright* had a darling little living area that doubled for a breakfast room. A comfortable cushion-filled couch was built into the port side of the room, fitted under a long shelf of Clare's favorite books. A narrow walkway ran between the couch and the tiny dinette to Murray's and Mrs.

Shrew's forward cabins. A cold locker lay under the walkway, the pull of which fitted into a depression. There, Clare stored items which could not fit into the very small refrigerator — cheeses, bread, eggs, bacon.

Clare's cabin, the captain's cabin, was behind the companionway ladder where the living area started. It was small and smart. She had to hoist herself into the bunk every night, and it took a little while to get used to the cramped space between her bunk and the deck, but now she loved it. It was very snug and comfortable.

The captain's table was in there, too, where the wireless sat amid a clutter of wonderful sea things: battered navigation charts filled with little pinpricks from a wonderful old steel protractor; a footed, sturdy brass table compass given to her by Captain John for plotting journeys; a sailor's book of knots.

The boat's tiny galley lay on the other side of the captain's cabin, with a sink, a paraffin cooker with a clever gimballed design — allowing it to swing on two pivot points and remain level when the boat was not — and a tiny Electrolux paraffin fridge.

The stern cabin past the galley was the largest on the boat, and would have made an ideal guest room for two, but it was loaded with Clare's possessions — clothing, shoes, books, all manner of odds and ends. She'd lived aboard only a few months before taking Mrs. Shrew as a renter; she'd not gotten used to the spare lifestyle of a houseboater.

The lovely dinette table had a rich patina of use — scratches and marks in the wood, but polished, cared for. Clare ran her fingertips along the edge. Everything about the *Maggie Bright* had a rich patina of use. All was close, and snug, and comfortable. How she adored a houseboater's life.

Renters, for a time, could not dampen her happiness. Four months aboard, one of them with Mrs. Shrew, had not lost a single day of newness.

Mrs. Shrew cleared aside some breakfast things, as if what Clare had to say would certainly include usage of a cleared bit of table, and sat at the ready with her pencil and notebook.

"Well — you won't need to take notes."

"Right." Mrs. Shrew laid them aside. She folded her hands. "What's the news?"

Her severely innocent, stark-blue eyes expected nothing less than a Murray Vance sort of revelation.

Clare told about trying to visit the Burglar Vicar and meeting Murray at the police station, not at some old random place in London as Mrs. Shrew may have believed.

"Goodness! What was he there for?"

"Brace yourself: to see the Burglar Vicar."

"No!" She went positively saucer-eyed. "Whatever for?"

"It seems Murray Vance has been something of a ward to the Burglar Vicar — whose name, by the way, is Father David Fitzpatrick. Murray calls him Father Fitz, or 'the Fitz.' "

"The Fitz," Mrs. Shrew tried out. "Go on."

"Apparently, all the BV said about his wife and child was true. It seems that Father Fitz *is* here on a highly important and quite possibly diplomatic mission — a mission on the *right* side, *our* side, the side of *good* — that frankly . . . Murray will *not* talk about."

Mrs. Shrew made appropriate noises of consternation.

"Oh, he's quite close about it. Says it's none of his business and none of mine; said point blank that if I wanted to know more, I must go and speak to the Fitz himself. Oh dear." She paused, worried. "It does seem a bit irreverent to call him the Fitz. I will stick with Burglar Vicar."

"You must visit him immediately," declared the Shrew.

"Oh, I have plans to go straightaway this morning and get there before anyone else. I will *not* leave until I find out why he was aboard my boat."

"I should think not! Diplomatic mission!" She looked over the clothing Clare was wearing. "No wonder you've abandoned your shipboard trousers for that smart skirt and blouse. You look like a girl." She peered suspiciously. "Is that lipstick? Well, I must say, it *is* pleasing to see femininity replace those horrible androgynous styles of the twenties and early thirties."

"Not quite sure when visiting hours are, but I intend to get there before street shops open — that should be early enough. Now. That is that: to sum up, Murray Vance's mentor tried to burgle this boat for what appears to be a very good reason. Murray came to England to bring him home — of course, while retrieving his muse in the process," she added quickly. Then she fastened onto Mrs. Shrew's eyes. "But . . . there is more."

"Go on," said Mrs. Shrew breathlessly. She spoke into her fist. "Oh, why do I feel this is the best part?"

"It certainly is strange. Brace yourself. The former owner of this boat, the one who died in January — was Arthur Vance. I am quite

125

convinced he was Murray's *father.*"

A gasp, a lunge forward, and a hushed and saucer-eyed, "No!"

"It's true. The collection of funnies, the last name . . . and yesterday in the taxi I had detected an unusual interest in the boat, a rather belligerent interest. Before that, I noticed a very strange reaction when I told him her name." She reached for her locket. "It is quite curious that Mr. Hillary should not know about Arthur Vance's son."

And at last, the unthinkable pressed through — the only thought capable of breaking her heart: *Maggie Bright* rightfully belonged to Murray.

Why did he give you the Maggie Bright? *Why you?*

His questions now made sickening, appalling sense.

"Listen to me, my dear," the Shrew rang strong. "Maggie is yours. Arthur Vance had his reasons, and they were his own. Not his son's, not anyone else's. Do *not* let it trouble your heart."

Tears sprang to Clare's eyes.

"I'm terribly afraid I'll lose her," she confessed in a whisper.

"Don't be. That boy has soul. Anyone who knows his work knows it. He's the sort to do the right thing. I don't think it would

126

enter his mind to contest the will."

"Yesterday he asked me outright why it went to me."

"An honest question. But keep in mind he was dreadfully tired yesterday. His face was so white, such dark circles — all that charm was nothing but an exhausted put-on. Did you notice how he perked up when he drew that tiny Salamander? That's where his joy is, my dear. I wish you knew him through his work like I do. Maggie is quite safe in your hands." She handed a tissue to Clare, and said briskly, "There, there, my dear. Stiff upper lip."

Clare sniffed, and blotted, and said, "I've never read the funnies, you know."

Mrs. Shrew sat back, as if this last revelation was the one to undo her. She finally said gravely, "Well, I *am* surprised. Your love of reading. Your sensibilities. The funnies are merely another form of cultural literature, and Murray Vance is a genius. He is to *Rocket Kid* what Dickens was to *Oliver Twist.*"

"My uncle strictly forbade the funnies. When I was older, it was simply habit."

Mrs. Shrew's lips thinned. "Cruel, wretched upbringing. You must take that box from Murray's room and *lose* yourself. Oh, I just about envy you. To read them for the first time. Of course, you must be warned: *many* comic strips *are* rubbish. But there is great good to be had. You must sort out excellence."

Clare put her chin on her fist.

How did he feel, being aboard once more?

Suddenly, she wanted to be gone before Murray woke.

"I must be off. And if anyone gets there first, I *will* make someone pay for my bus fare." She slid from the bench and began to quickly clear the breakfast things. "You'll feed him when he wakes?"

"Certainly!"

"I'll stop for more provisions on the way home. Young men eat a *great* deal of food. I discovered this yesterday. I may need to triple breakfast provisions. Dear me, the new ration coupons . . . And he's American. We'll have to get that sorted."

"Where is that man?" Mrs. Shrew said, with a glance at the companion hatch. Captain John was usually along for tea at this time.

"I'll peek in. See if he needs anything."

"*Do* be careful — all sorts of characters show up at a police station. I don't care if it is Westminster. And be *sure* to ask the relevant questions first; your visit may be timed — best to cover the most important things immediately."

"I'm not a complete idiot, am I?" Clare wanted to say, but settled for, "Yes, Mrs. Shrew—sbury."

"Oh, go on then," she said cheerfully. "Call me Mrs. Shrew. All my students did. I rather liked it." She seized her notebook with delight. "Goodness! What events! I'm *mad* to know what you learn from our vicar. Quite obviously, he had some sort of relationship with Arthur Vance. And then of course perhaps *Arthur* had the diplomatic mission, and *he* had hidden something quite important that only the BV knew about."

Clare stared — no, a connection between the BV and Arthur Vance hadn't occurred to her until Mrs. Shrew said it.

"*Do* question him thoroughly about Murray — he may hold some clues to the Muse retrieval. Because isn't it interesting? His father dies in January — and that's the last we heard from *Rocket Kid and Salamander*."

"Oh dear," Clare said, dazed, laying a hand on her cheek.

"He may be here to collect his priest, but I don't doubt for one moment that this is all about collecting his muse. Gone missing since his father's death. And we —" her tone softened — "we shall help him get it back."

She fell upon her notes with hand-clasped rapture. "Isn't life just full of glorious havoc at every turn? My dear Cecil would have something to say about these extraordinary times. He's giving St. Peter an earful now, surely prodding him to join the great cloud of witnesses surrounding me; telling him to look on, just *see* what that woman is up to next. Always called me 'that woman.' Always quite proud of me. Thought of me as rather a maverick. . . ."

When Clare reached for a plate of toast crumbs, Mrs. Shrew placed her hand over Clare's and said earnestly, "We're in it together, aren't we — this glorious and dreadful time that has come upon us? Muses, and vicars, and war?" She squeezed her hand, and went back to her notes.

Clare turned the three steps into the galley. She put the plate in the sink, and meant to take down her toothbrush from the shelf above, but gripped the counter's edge and held very still. Mrs. Shrew was nothing like them.

Aunt Mary was nothing but a vacancy, ruled over by the one who had absorbed her so completely that nothing was left, her lord, her master, Uncle Sebastian — Clare made her escape just in time before she suffered the same fate, and when she did, met

Mrs. Iris Shrewsbury.

No vacancy was she; she made the air quiver for the simple fact that she was in the room. She was demanding and kind and interested and controlling, and sometimes treated Clare like a child; and in all these things she was utterly unapologetic, and in all these things there were no eggshells to tread upon, no worries that Clare was perceived as utterly incapable of correct thought or action. Such notions would never occur to the Shrew. It wasn't in her.

The Shrew, Captain John, something in the Burglar Vicar, and now Murray Vance. Clare dashed at her eyes, laughing suddenly at Mrs. Shrew's imperious claim upon Seville marmalade, glad to have found real people once more. Life seemed to have come full circle to a place long forgotten. A place she last knew as a child.

Captain John seemed pleased whenever Clare popped in to ask if he needed anything when she went out. His wife had died several years earlier, and he must miss the feminine fuss.

It was a chilly May morning on the Thames, with a brisk breeze coming down from the northwest, and she buttoned her light jacket the rest of the way as she stepped from Maggie's boarding plank to the dock. She faced east at her first footfall on the wooden dock, as was her habit; one day she would sail *Maggie Bright* east on the Thames down to the sea. She'd round at Sheerness, sail south, and follow the Channel west, then pass by the continent southward until she came to Spain and the Straits of Gibraltar; then she would enter the Mediterranean, and that would be Maggie's first full sail with Clare at the helm.

Of course — once she learned to sail.

She'd never even taken her out by motor. Maggie hadn't left this dock since she was hers. No matter! Vision, courage, and singularity of purpose would make all the way it should be.

Clare walked the dock, looking about. She didn't see the captain in the boatyard. Didn't see him aboard his fishing trawler, the *Lizzie Rose*. He must be in the boathouse at the dock's end, a little bait and supply shop for boaters. His living quarters were at the back of the shop.

She tapped on the shop's door as she entered.

"Hello? Captain John?"

No one about, and she didn't smell tea. Rather chilly in here, too — he didn't have the little space heater on. Odd. If he wasn't in the boatyard or pottering about on his fishing trawler, he was here, stocking shelves or chatting with someone or making tea behind the counter.

She turned to go, but heard a rustle. It came not from his rooms past the counter, but through the doorway to the Anderson shelter.

It wasn't any surprise for Clare to learn that before she came to Bexley-on-the-Thames from Liverpool, Mrs. Shrew was a devoted ARPer — Air Raid Precaution worker. In addition to the stack of government pamphlets on how one should conduct oneself during a war, she'd brought her own gas mask and pronounced it as the only thing up to code at Elliott's Boatyard. Upon taking a room aboard the *Maggie Bright,* she insisted that a bomb shelter go in at the boathouse. She had her own Anderson hut, a regulation-issue movable room made of corrugated iron, transferred by train from her home in Liverpool to Elliott's Boatyard, where mason workers fused it to the small supply annex built into the side of the boathouse. Clare never dreamed her name would one day label a peg upon which hung her own gas mask. A bomb shelter! Who could imagine?

The first thing Mrs. Shrew installed in a

corner of the shelter was a modesty screen, behind which sat a chamber pot. ("One must think of these things. You will thank me later.") She also made sure that the shelter remained stocked with necessities, and periodically cycled out the supply of drinking water to keep it fresh. There were sleeping cots, the personalized pegs with hanging gas masks, and a typed list of all persons in the area assigned to this particular Anderson hut.

"Captain John?"

A rustle, and a moment later, Captain John appeared in the doorway of the Anderson shelter. He was holding a framed photograph, gazing at it. "Lizzie had it done when he was sixteen. Thought it proper. Always looking after her little brother."

His lovely thick white hair was uncombed. Looked as if he'd slept in his clothing. She'd never seen him this way.

"Captain John . . . is everything all right?"

He looked up. "Hmm? Oh, yes. All is well." He looked at the picture. "Only, I thought it was nonsense, having his photograph done. Seemed vain. A waste of money. Likely said as much. Wish I hadn't — he's a good boy. He has a stout heart. He's very kind, you see. Some mistake that for . . . Well, I'm just finding a spot for it in the shelter." He gave a smile, swift to disappear. "You never know — Mrs. Shrewsbury may be right. Perhaps they all are. Old Calhoun at Evelyn's. Churchill. Eden. Only, you don't want to believe it, you can't believe it, that Herr Hitler is upon us at last. But he is."

"What's happened? Your son — is he all right?" She went to him, and discovered that he smelled as though he'd spent the night in a pub.

He polished the glass of the photograph with the cuff of his sleeve, and angled it so she could see. "That's my Jamie," he said proudly. "Handsome lad, don't you think? Took after his mum."

Jamie Elliott was handsome. Well — perhaps not *physically*. But his features were arresting. Expectant, challenging eyes, looking just off the eye of the photographer; it made you feel as though his eyes wanted to go straight to yours. A lifted chin, a confident smile. His carriage made him handsome. It was very interesting to finally have a look at this boy of whom she'd heard so much.

"Oh, I think he takes after you," Clare said warmly. "Looks to be a very clever, confident lad."

"He does, doesn't he?" Captain John said,

rousing from his reverie with a spark of enthusiasm. "That's my Jamie. Very engaging boy. Very good with people. Liked to work with customers. Never took to the water, not like Nigel, but not everyone does. I hope he knows I don't care about that. I wish I'd told him. Wish I'd said it out loud."

What wasn't he telling her?

"Mrs. Shrew wondered where you were for tea."

Any mention of the Shrew usually made him stand at attention. He couldn't take his eyes off the photograph. It was as if Clare weren't in the room.

"I should tell you we have another guest," she said brightly. "Don't know how long he'll be staying. Mrs. Shrew will have to add another name to the Anderson list. I'm sure she'll fill you in. His name is Murray Vance. An American. It appears his father owned the *Maggie Bright.* Isn't that interesting?"

But Captain John didn't answer, and Clare was suddenly quite alarmed. What had happened? Was it a letter? Did he hear some news? Was the war going badly? She'd never seen him like this. All felt as wrong and askew as the appearance of his hair.

"Well, then — I'm off to see the BV on a matter of diplomatic importance. Need anything from the grocer?"

"Quite right. All is well," he said, eyes on the photograph. "Only, I didn't want him to go. Didn't want a war to change him. But it will."

He turned into the shelter and Clare fled not for the Teddington bus stop but for Mrs. Shrew.

Mrs. Shrew pledged to get to the bottom of it. When she added a very brisk and determined, "Leave it to me," Clare felt enormous relief, and raced with a lighter heart to catch the next bus.

"Yes, this is Blake. Westminster Station. William Percy, please. Thank you very much." He hummed a few bars of Mozart. Or was it Beethoven? That popular bit sometimes played at weddings. Why he should think of a wedding march, he didn't know — should be a military march. Something was up. Something dire. All manner of grave military folk scurried about the street this morning.

"Yes, Blake here. It may interest you to know that the American priest has a visitor. Yes, *currently.* She just went in. You'll have thirty minutes to get here before she leaves. You said to call immediately — there you are. Have a good — Ah, let's see . . . a Clare Childs. Lovely girl. Very expressive. Rather captivating, actually. Yes, I'm sure it says

137

Clare Childs. Same one who was here yesterday. *Yes,* she was here yesterday, didn't I just — ? Well, she was the one who left with the American. No, no — not the ratlike bloke — the other one. Well, the *same* American I *told* you about *yesterday.* Murray Vance. Yes, they left together, didn't I — ? Well, I didn't *know* it was Clare Childs yesterday, did I, as she didn't sign the — ? Hang on! Is that any way to — ? Oh, you will, will you? Why don't you just come down here and we'll settle it — ?"

He stared at the receiver, then replaced it, grumbling, "Scotland . . . bloody old . . . Yard."

11

Well, wasn't this war just a bushel of discovery — Jamie realized how like his father he was when it suddenly occurred to him that he *liked* people, he liked to be in a group. No loner was he — not like Nigel, who took after the old man in other ways but wanted only a fishing trawler and a locker full of bait. Jamie wanted a crowded homey pub. He very much looked forward to falling in with Balantine's crew. Sure to be pure relief after two days of . . .

"A flock of ravenous fowl come flying, lured with scent of living carcasses designed for death."

"Not a very cheerful sort, is he?" said Balantine, who walked backward along the town street, rifle ready, eyes moving.

"No, he wouldn't be. But it's not always like that. Some of it's all right. What will happen when we get to Dunkirk?"

"No idea. I'm sure there's a plan."

"Like this one?" Jamie said darkly, taking in the deserted streets. "This wasn't the plan. We were supposed to stop them."

"Well, we didn't, did we? It's all we talk about." To the captain, he said, "Come along, sir. This way."

"His head is pretty bad. Look, I have to warn you, he sort of has these fits. It's getting a bit better, but he'll make a horrible groaning sound, sort of turn into himself, and sometimes it gets loud. Lasts only a few minutes, puts the hair straight up your neck, but it does go away."

"Have you heard the latest on the wounded?" The question sounded sly, like a test.

"Oh, I heard," Jamie said, his tone answering.

Balantine eyed him. "You sound like me. One of *my* men gets wounded, not gonna leave him for the bloody Germans, I'll tell you that. I'll drag him to Dunkirk if I have to."

Jamie rather liked this Balantine.

"How close do you think they are?" Jamie asked, eyeing the perimeters.

"Don't know," he answered. "But they're coming. Right now, due north is our only hope. I'll swim for England if I have to."

"Have you seen action?"

"Some. You?"

"Oh sun, to tell thee how I hate thy beams that bring to my remembrance from what state I fell —" Captain Milton stood in the middle of the street and lifted his arms to the sky — "how glorious once above thy sphere, till pride and worse ambition threw me down."

Jamie jogged back to collect him, answering Balantine over his shoulder, "Yes, if you count fleeing as action. For eight months we were on the French-Belgian line, near a decent little town we'd got to know quite well. All right, Milty? Come along." He pulled him into step behind Balantine. "Nice place. One of our guys married the daughter of the mayor. Then a week or so ago, the Jerries came down like a thousand thunderstorms. And didn't we bless Lieutenant Dunn then, for keeping on us without pity at drills. So there we were, hot at it, finally doing our job, and then suddenly we're ordered to pull out. Pull out! Couldn't believe it. What were we *there* for? It was the worst thing in the world. All that training, all the drilling, for what?" His voice dropped to a mutter. "I'll never forget the looks of the townspeople as we left. Worst day of my bloody life. Treated us like heroes when we came, when we'd not done a bloody thing to earn it, treated us like villains when we left, and we were only obeying orders. Felt rotten, leaving. Felt like we left our own grandmothers defenseless." He went quiet. "Don't know what happened to them. It's like we knew them, you know? They felt like us. Foreign, but like us."

"Your story sounds just like ours," said Balantine. "We had a woman come up to our retreating column and throw a pan of dirty dishwater at us. Here we are, mate."

They stopped in front of a large bluish-gray brick home. The bivouac was well chosen. It was the tallest building at the halfway point of the main street with clear lines of sight in either direction. It was two or three stories high — Jamie couldn't really tell, because the side they faced was flush, roof to ground, with only one window. He saw a soldier on lookout at the window.

"Look what I've found," Balantine called up.

"Well, there's a tidy catch for the day." The soldier nodded at them. "Welcome to Camp Grayling."

"Private Elliott, meet Lance Corporal Grayling," Balantine said. "He's with me, 2nd Grenadiers, artillery, and he's the senior officer of the lot. Beat out Griggs by enlisting three weeks earlier. Elliott's with . . . Who are you with again?"

"Queen's 9th Lancers. Infantry."

Grayling nodded at Jamie. "Who's your friend?" The captain had stopped walking when Jamie had put a hand on his shoulder. He stood quietly.

"Don't know his name, actually. All I know is he's a captain and he's taken a serious head wound." Jamie twirled a finger at his own head and half mouthed, half whispered, "Gone a bit daft."

"Come on in, then. Don't know when you've had tea last, but we've got lots."

"I could do for a cup," Jamie said gratefully.

It suddenly occurred to Jamie that he wanted Milton on his best behavior. When Balantine went through the door first, Jamie held Milton back.

"Look, mate, don't do anything —"

Stupid, he was going to say. Don't make me look like a fool. But Milton made eye contact. Second or third time that had happened, if it didn't last long; then his gaze drifted, and he looked down at his jacket. Bewildered, he plucked it for something he didn't recognize.

Jamie tried to smarten him up a bit, tucking in the frayed edges of a hole in his jacket, pulling down a bit of bandage to cover a protruding stitch. "Look, we're with a unit again. They're not going to understand all the —"

The captain held his hand up and turned it front and back, looking at his wedding ring.

"Just . . . keep a lid on the poetry, all right?"

"What in me is dark, illumine! What is low, raise and support!"

Jamie sat bolt upright in darkness, heart pounding. He stared about in confusion.

"Shut up, you imbecile!" came a whispered growl from the other side of the room.

"You want the Germans to hear?" hissed another.

"Milton?" The captain was not at his side, where he'd fallen asleep last night. "Where are you?"

"Thyself not free, but to thyself enthralled."

A clatter, and the sound of shattered glass.

"What's that moron gone and done?" growled the first. Griggs, Jamie thought grimly. The one he didn't like.

"He's not a moron." Jamie grabbed his boots. He pulled them on, wincing as they slid over the arc of blisters. "He's wounded, and he outranks you."

Another clatter came from outside the room.

Men came awake, reaching for their rifles.

"What's going on?" said a groggy Balantine.

"It's Professor Shakespeare," Griggs complained. "*I'll* bloody well kill him before the Germans get a crack at it. Come this far, only to have some nutter give us away. . . ."

"Oh, shut it, Griggsy," said Grayling, in a wearied tone that sounded well familiar with him. "Elliott?"

"I'll get him."

"Baylor's on watch. You best do so before he puts a hole in him."

"No luck there," said Griggs. "The little pansy's probably reading. Excellent lookout *he* makes. Never sleep a wink when he's on watch."

"Shut it, Griggs!"

They'd gone to bed some hours ago, all in various stages of inebriation except for Baylor, who had first watch, and Milton, whom Jamie would not allow to have a drink — especially when Griggs wanted to see if alcohol would make him quote something more entertaining, like Jack London or P. G. Wodehouse.

When Jamie got to the entryway of this living room turned sleeping room, glass crunched under his boots. He peered through the dimness both ways down the hall. No Milton. He turned left and followed the hall to the kitchen, where Baylor sat at the table, reading by candlelight, a rifle propped at his side.

Jamie couldn't help but agree with Griggs. Seated leisurely at a kitchen table for sentry duty, cozily reading? What a joke. Upstairs, at a window, no candlelight, and no rations if you're caught doing anything other than watching — that's what Lieutenant Dunn would have done.

Baylor looked up, adjusting his glasses. "What's all the fuss?"

"Have you seen my friend?"

"He went upstairs. Heard them creak. The stairs are down the hall and round the corner to the left. Look what I found." He closed the book and showed the cover to Jamie: *Le Paradis perdu.* Jamie shrugged. "It's *Paradise Lost,* in French. Whoever lives here has the most marvelous library. Actually found some of the lines your mate quoted last night. Quite fascinating. Have you read it?"

"Me?" Jamie almost laughed. He wouldn't be caught dead reading poetry. "No."

146

"I have. *Paradise Regained,* too, though Milton should've stopped with the first. He said it all with *Paradise Lost,* and far better. By the by, fair warning — you best keep your friend on Griggs's good side."

"He has a good side?"

"I have to admit, it's rather nice for him to pick on someone else for once. Glad your friend doesn't understand it."

"He might, and I do. That 'moron' is up for the Victoria Cross."

"Oh, I'm not sure he means anything by it — he's just angry we're not fighting. Looking for a whipping boy. Freud calls it displacement." A creak overhead, and they both looked up. "Speak of the new boy." He looked at the book. "Has he actually quoted the whole thing, front to back? In order?"

"Not a clue. Not exactly a Milton fan."

Baylor sat back in his chair. "You really need to report this to someone back home. Had me spellbound last night. Professor Cathay would go mad over him. I really should do a paper on him, for posterity at least. I should take notes. Fascinating overlap of the mental and the physical, don't you think? We must swap addresses."

"You're at university?"

"Oxford," he said with casual pride.

"What are you — what is your . . . ?" He

147

didn't run with university blokes, didn't quite know the lingo.

"My field? Psychology. I know about a dozen professors who'd love to get their hands on him."

"I better do that myself, before he breaks something else." He nodded at Baylor, and turned back down the hall.

The floor crunched at the entryway to the sleeping room. There was enough light from the kitchen to see that a framed photograph had fallen from the wall, shattering the glass. Jamie picked up the photograph, studied the French family, put it back on the wall.

He found the stairs and went up, trying to be as quiet as possible.

So much for Milton keeping a lid on it.

Yesterday when they came into the house and everyone had assembled in the kitchen to greet the new arrivals, Milton had acted the strangest yet upon meeting the men — he seemed eager, seemed drawn out of that private little box of his. He was alert and watchful, without looking anyone in the eye. At first Jamie thought it was nervous agitation in being around so many people after days with just the two of them, and hoped it would mean that lid on the poetry he had requested. It was not to be.

148

Turned out, the captain found opportunities to spout the *most* Miltonage yet, and stuff Jamie had not heard. He acted like a street-smart kid at the edge of a busy road, waiting to dart across at a break in traffic; when a pause in conversation came, off he'd launch into one line after another, just as if he were part of the banter — not that he seemed to understand what was said to him, but certainly as if he expected his comments to be perfectly clear.

As if anyone knew what to do with, "To all the fowls he seems a phoenix!"

Yet, Jamie surprised himself. He found he wasn't embarrassed at all. He found instead some sort of protection for the man, surely brought about by the duty laid upon him to get him to Dunkirk. And the man wore a wedding ring. If Jamie couldn't win this bloody war — if he couldn't even fight — he'd get this lunatic home to her, and that won something.

While two of the men — Griggs and a bloke named Curtis — acted like Christmas came early with a new toy to sport with, the other three — Balantine, Grayling, and Baylor — were the regular, decent sort who showed appropriate concern for Milton, especially when they learned he was in for the Victoria Cross. Baylor, who'd had some medical training, had unwrapped the bandage and cleaned the wound. He admired the stitch work of the Belgian doctor and pronounced it a gruesome work of art. When Jamie asked if the skull around the wound seemed dodgy, as the doctor seemed to think, Baylor gingerly applied pressure with his fingertips. He didn't seem to like the result any more than the doctor.

"Seems a bit spongy." He had looked at Milton with more concern than before. "He shouldn't be walking around, that's for sure. His skull is likely fractured, and his brain could be swelling. No idea how to set a skull. Don't let him wear his helmet anymore. It's too heavy."

At the top of the stairs was a hall. The door at the end of the hall was open. He saw moonlight.

He came into the room, pushing the door wide.

It looked like a child's bedroom. One bed against one wall, another against the opposite. In the middle of the room was a dormer window, with a small desk. From the window came a brilliant stream of silver moonlight. Milton sat on a small chair he had placed in the moonpath.

Very strange, the clumping footfalls of a heavy British Army boot in a quiet French bedroom. He could never have imagined where he'd be, one year earlier. Never imagined himself an invader of privacy, even if the residents were not home. Felt like they were.

"Captain?"

He came alongside the captain, who gazed at the moon. Dark hair tufted from the white bandage, which in the moonlight wash had a lavender tinge. The moonlight made the shadows beneath his eyes deeper, greenish; his lips, the color of pewter. He looked positively done in. He shouldn't even be upright, looking like that.

For the first time, a nudge of real worry came. How bad was that head, on the inside?

"Here's an idea: next time, just lie there quietly and say your lines to yourself. You won't break things, and people will sleep. What do you say, Cap? Speaking of, wish you'd come to your ranking-officer senses — this lot could use a captain. The bloke below us is *reading.* Can you believe it? On watch? Dunn would kill him on the spot."

The captain gazed at the moon, his fingers twisting the wedding ring in place. Then Jamie realized why he seemed to appear extra wretched — he looked as if he had come fresh from finding out about his men.

Battered sorrow lay heavy upon the moon-washed face.

Jamie sat on the bed closest, coiled springs squeaking. He watched the twisting ring.

"Tell me about her, Milton."

He didn't answer, though Jamie noticed a falter in the ring twisting.

"She'd know what to do with you, mate," Jamie said softly. "She'd know what to say if you'd lost your . . ." And though he couldn't bring himself to finish it aloud, the ring twisting stopped.

Jamie gazed at the ring. What would his father do? He'd know what to say. He was good with people.

He rested back on his elbows. He looked about the room.

"Do you know what, Milty? I'm gonna open a pub someday. I came to it on watch one night, few months back. I've got it all planned out. It'll be a nice place, a place you can get a decent meal, cheap. Comfortable, warm, great lovely fireplace, with a mantel I'll make myself. I'd like to open it on the street that ends at my dad's boat-yard, except for one problem — there's a place there already. Evelyn's. I could never give her the competition, I'd go straight to hell — she's the kindest soul you'll ever meet. And yeah, it's true — no one can beat her puddings. But mine would be a *different* sort of place. Hers is more of a café. Mine, I want more manly. Mine, I want a cup on the counter for folks to toss in change for those down on their luck, and there's sure to be those after the war. I want a place where a man can come in, order a plate of chips and fried fish like he had pockets of money, enjoy it like a king, and if he's flat broke, he can leave without paying, no questions asked. We'll just take it out of the cup."

The ring twisting started again.

"But do you know what's the centerpiece of my place? It's a very modern wireless, maybe a top-of-the-line Ekco, right at the end of the bar where folks can gather with their pipes and mugs and listen to King George tell how Lord Gort came back in mighty force and whipped Hitler and all his men. This isn't the end, you see, this running for England. I know it in my heart."

The captain's fingers stilled.

"And I want you there, with your wife and kids, when the king tells us this war is over, and your men and the little girls in that ditch have been avenged. You and I will look at each other across the room, and we'll lift our mugs." He swallowed hard. "I think you quote Milton because your heart is broken, mate, not your head."

A look of anguish passed over the moon-washed face.

"Look, I'm going on too much. Let me just say this and I'll shut up forever: You lost your squad of men. That's the worst thing in the world. But you *saved* another. And that's the best. You keep that close, captain."

The lavender lips twitched, and then a sound came from the captain, a strange, guttural clicking sound. He shifted in his chair, his fists grew white, his body seemed to stiffen, and at first Jamie feared a fit, feared the man was choking. Jamie shot up, unsure what to do, should he run for Baylor, should he — ?

"J-J-J-J —"

"Milton! You all right?"

"J-J-J-J—Jacobs," he gasped. The fists relaxed, and he sat exhausted. "Jacobs."

Jamie stood very still. After a moment, he eased back onto the bed.

"Well. Good to know you, Captain Jacobs," he said softly.

One painfully stammered word was all he could manage to deliberately speak, yet Milton's words flowed from the captain's lips easy as moonlight fell on his face.

And this time, the captain spoke with unusual grace.

"Half yet remains unsung." He lifted his face to the moon. "Good he made thee, but to persevere he left it in thy power — ordained thy will by nature free, not over-ruled by fate." He half turned to Jamie. "God towards thee hath done his part — do thine."

He seemed to expect a response.

Jamie shrugged. "Sure. Will do."

But the captain reached and clutched a handful of Jamie's jacket. He shook him. "God towards thee hath done his part — do thine."

"Okay, okay. I'll do my part."

"God towards thee hath done his part." A tighter clutch, more insistent shaking, and now a build of anxiety. "Do thine. Do thine!"

"I don't know what my part is! You've got to calm down, you'll only —"

Wait.

If *he* made it, if *Jamie* made it, then maybe to Captain Jacobs, it would be as if his men did.

Jacobs would have gotten someone home. Jamie's part was to get home.

"Someone's got to open that pub," he said quickly.

The captain closed his eyes. His hand dropped away, and he lifted his face to the moonlight.

Jamie said, "Come on, mate. Upsadaisy. Lots of walky-walky tomorrow. Let's rest that buggered head while we can. Nope, turn around, this way — two steps, right over here. Easy now. There we are. See? When's the last time you slept in a bed? Who knows, Milty — perhaps by this time tomorrow, we'll be in sight of home. I wonder where you live. Maybe that can be your next word."

Jamie went to the bed opposite and dragged a coverlet from it. By the time he draped it over the captain, he was asleep.

"Good night, Captain Jacobs."

He stood over him for a moment, then went and settled in the chair, and lifted his face to the moonlight.

As you are no doubt aware, the scene has darkened swiftly. . . . If necessary, we shall continue the war alone and we are not afraid of that. But I trust you realize, Mr. President, that the voice and force of the United States may count for nothing if they are withheld too long. You may have a completely subjugated, Nazified Europe established with astonishing swiftness, and the weight may be more than we can bear.

— NOTE FROM CHURCHILL TO ROOSEVELT,
May 15, 1940

At the moment it looks like the greatest military disaster in all history.

— DIARY ENTRY OF GENERAL
SIR EDMUND IRONSIDE, *May 17, 1940*

The unthinkable must sometimes be thought about.

— JOHN LUKACS,
Five Days in London: May 1940

12

Clare came out of the police station and hurried down the steps. She stopped at the bottom and grabbed the iron handrail. The pebbled glisten of the pavement caught her in a momentary trance.

It will change you, Murray had said of the packet. *It will change everything.*

Oh, why had she come? Why hadn't she listened to Murray?

She came to herself, clutched her jacket together, and started walking.

It's supposed to prove something that cannot be true.

"No," she whispered fiercely, panic on the rise. "It cannot."

The people on the street, the buildings and the automobiles, the very color of the air — all took on a menacing cast. All was poison and darkness and lost and hopeless if —

The walking broke to a run.

Oh, Murray! No wonder you chose isolation!

She had to get to him as fast as she could; she had to tell him she understood . . . Where was the bus stop? She stopped short — and someone from behind knocked her flat.

"Oh, gosh — awfully sorry!" he said. "Are you all right, miss? Here, let me help you up. Goodness, what a tumble. Nothing broken? Here's your purse, here's your hat — quite a smart hat it is. Good job my sister isn't about, she'd pinch it in a second. I should pinch it for her. Well, you're quite a runner, Miss Childs. Didn't expect that."

Clare paused in brushing off her pleated skirt, and looked at the man. He was dressed for the office, early thirties, rather boyish face, very light-colored hazel eyes. He touched his fedora.

"William Percy. Scotland Yard, Westminster. We followed you from the police station. This is my associate, Frederick Butterfield." His associate, a shorter and rather portly fellow in a checkered vest and a bowler hat, came chugging up.

"There's a new tack," the older gentleman gasped. "Knock 'em off their feet. Splendid, Percy, we'll put that in the manual."

"Awfully sorry about that," Percy said

159

with a wince. "Are you quite all right?"

"Perfectly," said Clare.

"And you are Clare Childs?"

She looked from one to the other. "What's this about?"

"Why did you run?" said Butterfield, breathing hard.

"Why are you following me?"

William Percy's eyes narrowed slightly. "You seem upset, Miss Childs."

"I am upset!"

"Yes, you might be," he said, "if you learned anything from the priest."

She looked again from one to the other. "I won't believe it. It's impossible." But the unchanging looks on their faces said something else. "It would mean others had gone along with it," she found herself trying to explain. "That makes it impossible. I couldn't hear another word, I had to leave. Anyone decent would."

"Have you seen this man?"

Percy reached inside his suit coat and took out a cream-colored envelope. He took a photograph from it and handed it to her. She studied the image of a man in a busy place, a train station or someplace else with a lot of people. He was looking over his shoulder. High cheekbones, thin face, thin hair. The image was a bit streaky, she couldn't tell his age. Somewhere above thirty, below sixty.

"No."

"Are you sure? You haven't seen him about Elliott's Boatyard? Or your uncle's book-shop?"

She eyed William Percy, and then studied the photograph again. "Quite sure. I've never seen him. Who is he? What's this all about?"

"He wants the same thing your vicar wants, for a very different reason," said Butterfield. "Can we go someplace to talk, Miss Childs?"

"We're doing fine right here."

"There's a café right across the street," said Percy. "Right in shouting distance of the police station."

"You can always run," said Butterfield. "You're good at that."

"I kept up," Percy said mildly.

"I don't want tea." She wanted to beg Murray's forgiveness, though at the moment she didn't know why.

"They do have nice biscuits," said Butterfield. "Fresh made, every day. Lovely cottage pie. Of course, it's not pie time . . . unless we can convince them." One eyebrow rose conspiratorially. "Shall we give it a go? It's an absolute restorative. I'm not in this part of town often enough."

"Might be a good thing," Percy commented.

She stared from one to the other. These men had no idea she was one second from a complete psychotic breakdown.

"Look — just say what you have to say quickly. I need to catch a bus."

Percy nodded at the photograph in her hand. "That man wants a parcel of papers that Arthur Vance may have hidden on his boat. He must not get them."

"It's not there. Same as I told the vicar. I've gone over every inch."

"So have we." He added, "Before the boat was yours, of course."

She studied the photograph. "What does he want it for? Father Fitzpatrick wants to bring it back to the States and give it to a congressman."

"This man wants it for Hitler."

Clare stared at William Percy.

"Arthur Vance died to keep it from him."

She looked at the picture.

"Vance was working with us. Until he was murdered."

Clare handed back the photograph. "I'll have that tea now."

Most people found it fascinating when she

162

told of her plans to be the first woman to single-handedly circumnavigate the globe in a ketch-rigged yacht. Not William Percy.

He gave no sign he was the least bit impressed, offered no polite comment or inquiry, and she found this deliberate disinterest off-putting and rude. Frederick Butterfield, on the other hand, was charmed.

"Oh, well done!" he exclaimed. "How very thrilling. You're sure to have some marvelous adventures. Always thought it would be quite exciting to round Cape Horn on some replica of a clipper ship, myself. Lashed to the foremast for fun."

The three sat at a table along the street side of the restaurant, where the police station was perfectly framed in the window.

William Percy once again took the cream-colored envelope out of his inside jacket pocket and laid it on the table. He produced a small notepad and a pencil and laid these neatly beside the envelope. His movements were just so, she noted. Surely the uptight sort.

"Such a lovely boat you have, the *Maggie Bright.*" Butterfield poured tea for Clare. "Didn't I say so, Will? Belongs in the Royal Yacht Club. You can sail, then, Miss Childs?"

"Well — not quite. I'm taking night classes in London. Navigation, twice a week." She would not tell them she'd only recently managed to pin down a barter for the lessons, promising to take the instructor's elderly parents for cruises on the Thames during the summer.

"Why, you ought to talk to William, here," said Butterfield.

"Do you sail?" Clare said, surprised.

"I should say," said Butterfield. "Won a race in some posh little yachtie affair last year. Who was it that sponsored you?"

"The Royal Yacht Club," Percy said. He laid his hand flat on the envelope. A curious little action. After a moment, he said rather peevishly, "Look, I have a difficult time with pleasantries when I am in no mood for them."

"William," said Butterfield.

Percy glanced at him, surprised, then looked at Clare and said, "Oh. Sorry." If he stopped there it would have been fine, but he had to add, "Didn't mean to say it aloud."

"Oh, I'm not fond of pleasantries either." Clare gave a frosty smile. "Especially if they're unpleasant." She looked at the envelope. "What else is in there, then?"

Later, she would remember William Percy's hand upon the envelope.

Their story came in bits and pieces, or maybe that's how Clare took it in. It's hard not to think in patches when the world goes off a cliff.

She pressed her fingertips on her forehead, averting her eyes from the three photographs that Percy had taken from the envelope and laid out in a neat line.

"Biscuits are a bit stale today," Butterfield said unhappily. "And no pie."

Percy poured tea for Clare. "Might be a good thing."

"I don't care." He lifted his chin. "I shall never have a torso like yours."

"Torso." Percy passed the sugar to Clare. "Such an odd word."

How could they speak so conversationally; how could they pour tea?

"Tell me, please," she said, trying desperately to get her bearings and starting with something more manageable, "why exactly is the Burglar Vicar locked up if you *know* he is innocent?"

"Burglar Vicar, is that what you call him?" said Butterfield, appreciatively. "I like it much better than the Thieving Priest. Oh, he's a lamb. Adore the man. Of course, we must adore him from a distance."

"We're using him as bait, you see," said Percy, rather too cheerfully. He tapped the first photograph in the line of three, the one he'd shown to her on the street. "We hope our man will show up to visit the priest."

Something finally made sense, and she looked accusingly from Butterfield to Percy. "Thieving Priest. I suppose *you* had planted in the papers that the BV had made off with 'a mysterious package.' We wondered where they'd got that."

"I have a friend at the *Daily Mirror,*" Percy said, and gave a tight little unflattering smile.

"Well, I certainly wasn't *tearful,*" she retorted. "Positively humiliating." She looked at the photograph of the man. "What's his name again?"

"Waldemar Klein," said Butterfield. His tone became less congenial. "He wants that packet quite desperately. We'd been watching your boat, hoping Klein would surface, and then along came the American priest. Didn't know what to make of him at first. Thought he might be working with Klein."

Clare steadfastly ignored the other two photographs. She wished they would put them away.

"But an English bishop, whom we'd rather not name," Butterfield continued, "another

166

lamb whom we adore —"

"Oh, honestly, Fred," Percy snapped.

"— had learned of his arrest because of the very useful Thieving Priest publicity, and came forward to tell us otherwise; unknown to us, Arthur Vance took matters into his own hands. Got hold of your Burglar Vicar to come to his aid. Didn't think the authorities were doing enough."

"We weren't doing enough," Percy said.

"We were," Butterfield said carefully, "but in a different way. In a broader sense."

"Why else would he have acted alone?"

Butterfield patted his mouth with his napkin. "Let's not argue in front of company, William."

A flush rose in Percy's face. "Arthur Vance did something real. What have we done?"

"He acted independently."

"You say that like it's a bad thing. He saved lives."

"Yes. Admirable. And it got him killed. Can we remember that part? No more saving lives for him. Might have saved many more, had we worked together."

Clare watched the exchange, fascinated and completely confused.

"He saw what's coming, Fred," said Percy in a curiously private tone. He ran his middle fingertip along the rim of the teacup, round and round. She took the chance to observe him. He reminded her of Murray Vance in the cab, when he'd stared out the window and went to a place where no one else was invited. Like Murray, he seemed to be decent enough, and like Murray, he had little peculiarities — that fiddling with the teacup, the way he'd laid out the things on the table. The way he'd laid out the photographs.

She'd certainly rather look at him than the photographs. There they sat, three motionless tarantulas.

"All Arthur Vance wanted to do was send up a warning," Percy said, cold and inward, circling the teacup rim. There was something quite arresting about that bitter tone. "And we didn't listen, and all comes to an end." He raised his eyes to Clare, and her heart picked up pace. She couldn't look away if she wanted to. Such bitterness in that flat stare. Was it that? She couldn't put a word on it. Despair? Defeat? Why did he not look away? She wanted him to look away; it wasn't professional —

"William," Butterfield said, firm and quiet. "You're frightening her."

"I'm not frightened." She blinked. "Not much. What comes to an end?"

Percy noticed his teacup. He took hold of

it, and after a moment, seemed somewhat collected.

"It seems things have gone quite wrong with the BEF," said Butterfield.

"The BEF," Clare said, mystified.

"The British Expeditionary Force."

"Yes, of course — but what on earth have they got to do with . . . ?" She helplessly gestured to the pictures.

"It may all be moot," murmured Percy, "with what is happening in France."

She looked from one to the other. "What is happening in France?"

The two men exchanged a glance.

"Look, it's all supposed to be quite hush-hush," said Butterfield, "but you'll know soon enough. Seems our boys are in trouble."

"Whatever do you mean? Which boys?"

"All of them."

"The entire British Army is in full retreat," said Percy, tightly folding his hands on the table.

Clare felt a tingling rush on her skin, sweeping to her scalp, smarting her eyes and nose.

"What do you mean?"

"They are cut off and surrounded," Percy said. "The whole bloody army. Belgium is about to fall. France will fall in a matter of days."

"What?"

France? Belgium? *Fall?*

The army in *retreat?* "Impossible," Clare breathed. She gripped the edge of the table to keep from springing up and running in circles.

"Yes, a lot of that going on these days," said Butterfield. "Lots of impossible things. But!" He thumped his fingers on the table, and said briskly, "Best we forget about the impending doom of England and all that is safe and good, and turn our attention to happier things like murdered humanitarians. Right. We've only told you about the photographs and the packet. We haven't told you about Arthur Vance. You see, we got a bit uncomfortable when we learned you'd popped in to visit the priest, fearing some sort of well-meant intrusion, and so, upon a phone call from our trusty sergeant, why, we gathered up our skirts and dashed on down."

Mr. Butterfield had transitioned to an amiable, competent professional. How could he? She took in the tightly folded hands of William Percy, and in a flash she understood — the photographs, the retreat . . .

"Oh," she said, very small. She sat back. "England is alone."

Percy looked into her, and looked away.

She stared at the photographs. "Against *that*. Against *them*."

She waited for one of them to contradict her. They did not. She felt for the locket through her blouse.

"Miss Childs, what was the nature of your visit to our vicar?" Butterfield said, as if the BEF were *not* cut off and surrounded, as if France were *not* about to fall.

"I . . ." She shook her head, blinking. "Well, I — I wanted to know why he was on my boat, of course." It came out a bit shrill. "Especially now that Murray Vance is here. He is staying in one of my guest rooms, aboard the *Maggie Bright*. The BV is something of a guardian to him. He came to fetch him home." She softened. "Does Murray know about his father? That he worked with you? That he was . . . killed?"

"We have no idea," said Percy. "Officially, Arthur Vance died of a heart attack. And he worked very *loosely* with us. He mostly worked with the English bishop on his own little scheme."

"Doing what?"

He touched one of the photographs, *the* photograph, the one that sent the world off

171

the cliff, and she gripped the locket. How could her life change forever with the simple placement of three photographs on a table? Each one confirmed the words of Father Fitzpatrick. Each one explained Murray Vance.

One was of the man Klein. One was a building called the Grafeneck Castle in Germany. And one was a child. This is the one he touched. Her stomach surged.

"I wish you'd put those away," she said quickly.

"Put them away?" He gave her a sharp look. "Yes, why don't we just put them away." His voice rose. "Why don't we put everything away, like we do." He snatched the picture of the child and held it two inches from her face. "I wish he were front-page news all over England. All over the world." She pulled away, but he kept it fast in front of her. "I hope you never forget him. I hope you can't sleep at night. I hope he haunts your dreams."

"Stop it!" she cried.

"Percy," Butterfield barked.

He threw down the photograph, and looked away, face flushed. People in the restaurant glanced over, and presently went back to their conversations.

Clare picked up the picture.

It was a child with Down syndrome. He was laughing, his head thrown back, slanted eyes crinkled in delight, palms of his hands touching. She looked at the picture of the Grafeneck Castle. It was an aerial view of a very large building shaped like a squared-off horseshoe, at least four stories tall. According to Grafeneck records, this child had been sterilized as part of Hitler's purifying eugenics program.

Sterilized.

Eight years old.

Two months later he was killed by an injection of phenol.

Tears filmed, made the photo blurry. "What was his name?"

Percy glanced at her. After a moment, he muttered, "Erich von Wechsler."

"Erich," she whispered.

The parents were told he had died of pneumonia. Four families from the same province received notices the same week — that their children, patients at Grafeneck, an institution for those with mental or physical disabilities, had died of pneumonia. An unknown staff member at Grafeneck had risked his or her life to make photographs of other photographs, and of institutional documents, and get them into the hands of an American journalist stationed in Berlin. The journalist got them to an old friend from England. The old friend was Arthur Vance.

"What was the name again, of the overall program?" Clare said, digging into her purse for a tissue. "Charity something."

"The Charitable Foundation for Curative and Institutional Care," said Percy. "A title to whitewash hell. Doctors and midwives are now required to report all births with severe disabilities or malformations of any kind." He leaned forward. "Did you catch that? *Required* to *report* them. Parents could lose custody of their children if they do not comply with sending them to these institutions."

Clare froze, digging through her purse. "Mr. Percy, I cannot take that in yet. I'm not past the eight-year-old." She glared at him. "Forgive me, but I can only absorb one monstrous thing at a time."

"Why, you haven't even heard the worst," he said acidly.

"William," Butterfield warned.

Her heart raced, her lips trembled. She seized the locket once more. "How is anything worse than a sterilized and murdered child?"

"Because some are experimented on first," he spat.

174

And that was it. He'd opened her up and all wilted. Her hand dropped from the locket. Tears spilled.

She wanted to run from William Percy as much as she wanted to reach for him as the only place of sanity in this room, for what could provoke such hatred on his face except for what she now saw so clearly within him: rage-filled helplessness.

And then . . .

There came again that capricious, reassuring wash that she had come full circle, she'd circumnavigated the world to a place where one man's rage at such evil was a good thing, a safe thing, a strong thing.

A subtle change came as he looked into her eyes, an infinitesimal easing of his pain. Had he wondered at the easing of hers?

"What is it?" she demanded. To detract from this somewhat disturbing admission of that wordless communication, she picked up the photograph and pretended to study it. "I need to know something good."

"Well, would it do you good to know that Arthur Vance was spiriting them away?" His tone had softened. "One day I will visit a tattoo parlor and have the number five burned on my arm."

The child wore a little short-sleeved shirt with whimsically striped suspenders. A woman's arm was about his shoulders. Only the lower part of her face was in the picture, a laughing smile turned toward the child. She had light shoulder-length hair, curled into fashionable rolls. Was she his mother? Someone at the institution?

Did this laughing child die trustingly, curious about the needle and syringe? Did he ask for the woman in the photograph? Did he die alone?

Was he "experimented on" first, this little boy?

She wiped her nose. "Spiriting them away . . ."

"Vance and the American journalist made arrangements," Percy said. "Someone would slip children across the waters from Emden, Germany, to Holland. There, Vance collected them and made four trips last fall, sailing five children scheduled for euthanization from Holland to Dover. Five lives, saved. The children were kept safe in a cottage not far from Dover Castle —"

"Ashton Cottage," Butterfield broke in, pleased. "Two grand old maids live there. Great fun to talk to. Though it's hard not to stare at Mrs. Barden. She has a high forehead."

"There they stayed until the bishop came to —" He broke off, and looked at Butterfield. "What's her forehead got to do with anything?"

He shrugged. "It's just very high. Goes all the way back. Thought she was bald, at first."

Percy turned to Clare and made to continue, when he looked again at Butterfield. "All I see in my mind are high foreheads. It's disturbing. Thanks for that." He looked at Clare and shook his head incredulously; but she did not miss a new expression — it wasn't a smile, but it was an easing of lines. She felt a welcomed lessening of tension, and did not miss the subtle satisfaction on Butterfield's face as he wet his finger and dabbed at crumbs on his plate. It was a look Percy did not catch, and one Butterfield did not mean him to.

Percy continued. "The bishop collected the five and got them to safe places. Meanwhile, Vance asked his journalist friend to gather as much evidence as possible from his contact at Grafeneck. Once Arthur had it all in order, your Father Fitzpatrick was to come retrieve it for the States, in hopes to alert the American press and politicians."

"Why weren't the press and politicians alerted here?" Clare asked.

"That's a little difficult to answer," Butterfield said carefully.

"It isn't difficult at all," Percy snapped. "When Vance first came to us last September, I didn't like him. He was smug, arrogant, flamboyant — the sort who flits around with movie stars on the Riviera. He gave us these pictures and told us an incredible story about Grafeneck Castle, and that a German spy was after him. Sounded like a movie script. Asked for protection, and then told us to back him in the press when he went public with his story. We refused. Told him the whole thing was ridiculous."

"That's not the word you used," Butterfield put in.

"We told him he had no *proof*. Said if we were to take him seriously, we needed names. We needed copies of documents and ledgers and institutional records. Not a movie script. He took it as a Yard-sanctioned directive. Acted as if he were part of a task force, came in week after week to boast of his progress. Said it was coming together piece by piece, and that he was collecting it into a packet. His visits were regular and annoying and the truth is, I thought he was a delusional nutter with a middle-age crisis on hand. And then —" He paused. "And then at one of his last visits —"

"I actually looked forward to those visits," Butterfield broke in, with a fond smile. "He was quite entertaining. Knew *The Rime of the Ancient Mariner* by heart. Told us lots of stories, places he'd been, famous people he'd met. Was enormously proud of his son. Told us all about the summer they sailed the Mediterranean. Arthur Vance certainly led a singular life." He squinted, and tapped his chin reflectively. "Yet for all of that . . . I think he was lonely."

"That's beautiful. Can we keep on track? At one of Vance's last visits, he . . . completely changed. It wasn't paranoia. It was something far different."

"He wasn't arrogant anymore," said Butterfield gloomily.

"He stayed for a very short time, said very little, and left. We didn't see him for nearly a month. Then one day he showed up with the packet. Showed us photographs of ledgers, patient records, had it all right on my desk. And for the first time, I truly believed him." He paused. "For the first time, he became someone I wanted to know. But suddenly he didn't trust us. Before we could ask what had happened, he repacked it all, tucked it under his arm and informed us that we were too late."

"He *what*?"

Percy gave that tight, unflattering smile. "Decided to take it to America because

England, he said, was doomed. Said he hoped Klein didn't get to him, said not to take it too badly if he did, bid us good day, and . . ."

"And Klein got to him," Butterfield finished.

The three sat in silence for a time.

"Do you know?" Butterfield said wistfully. "I miss him."

Another silence.

"Oh, Murray," Clare murmured, a hand to her cheek.

"Yes, I do hope he gets back on the bike, with *Rocket Kid.*" Butterfield smiled sadly. "World needs a good laugh."

"Because everyone can laugh in times like these," Percy said. He'd taken to his teacup, tracing his finger on the rim. He closed his hand over it.

"We *need* to laugh in times like these," said Butterfield.

"Helpless children are killed. Experimented on. I'll never laugh again. And oh, by the by, Hitler's monstrous army overtakes ours as I speak, and with the fall of France, there goes our only chance to defeat him. America won't hear from us for months, and then find us dead and colonized by Nazis. Oh, it's just a laugh riot, Fred."

The teacup burst in his hand.

He cursed, and after recovering from the brief shock, Clare seized his hand. She examined it, and began to pick out teacup pieces from his bleeding palm. He jerked at the touch of one particular piece, but she gathered his hand back and tried more gently.

The feel of his hand in hers, and now she caught his scent as she bent to her work — it was distracting. Her cheeks warmed.

"There." She placed the last bloody piece on the saucer. "You should have it checked, you may need stitches. Especially that one. Do you have a handkerchief?" she asked Butterfield.

"I don't want it," Percy said emphatically.

"Don't be ridiculous."

"I *know* this man, I've *heard* him blow his nose, I will *not* have his handkerchief on my hand. It will catch pneumonia."

"Where's yours?"

He hesitated. "I have a cold."

"Oh, *honestly.*" She wiped her fingertips on her forearm, and reached across the table to rummage about in his front coat pocket. She didn't miss the flaming color on his very cross face, and suppressed a smile. "Where do you keep it? I will *not* look for it in your trousers, you can bloody your pocket first." But she found it in the other front coat pocket. She shook out the folded square of white cloth and neatly bound his bleeding hand, tying it off tightly.

"Everything all right, guv?" said a waitress brightly.

Percy put his hand under the table, and Butterfield, collecting broken pieces from the tabletop, said, "Awfully sorry about that. Please put it on our tab."

"I saw you do it," the woman said to Percy with a sly little smile. "I've got a problem with anger, too. Try smoking Luckies. Don't know what it is, but they work wonders. Better than Player's."

"Luckies, eh?" said Percy.

"Work like a charm." She winked, and left.

He watched her go. "I better get some Luckies."

Clare picked up the photograph of Erich von Wechsler. She wanted to wake up on *Maggie Bright* in a lonely place far away where nothing like this existed. But there was no going back to the usual world, and usual included daydreams.

"It was surreal, what the vicar was saying," she said, "as if a black snake had suddenly poured from his mouth. And now to see his words in these photographs . . . I feel perfectly foolish, running out on him

182

like that. How very alone he must feel."
What a child she was. Yet how could
anything have prepared her for such a thing?
She suddenly said, "I detest this using of
him as *bait.* It's like you're lying to him."

"We *are* lying to him," said Percy.

"That seems to make you happy. It doesn't
bother you, if he's the hero you say he is?
Do you know his wife just had a baby?"

Percy took the photograph of Waldemar
Klein, studied it for a moment, then tucked
it in the envelope. He pocketed the notepad
and pencil. "That's not my concern. My job
is to get Klein. If it means lying to a priest,
if it means detaining him 'til the world's
end, which apparently is coming sooner
than we think — a song in my heart, Miss
Childs." He looked at Butterfield. "Laughter
in my soul."

"I'm not sure you have a soul, to keep him
locked up," Clare snapped. "It's monstrous.
He should be home."

"Home?" Percy said bitterly. He plucked
the picture of Erich from her hand. "Home
is invaded."

He rose from the table, and took his hat.
"I have to . . . have a talk with that desk
sergeant."

"William," said Butterfield, looking up.
"We can always hope that —"

"Fred, I don't have any hope! Not anymore, not for us. But if I can find Klein and find that packet — if I can go down like Arthur Vance, warning others — well, that's something, isn't it? We're done for. But maybe America will listen. And if they don't, I gave them a chance." He started off, looked at his bandaged hand, started to say something to Clare, then turned to Butterfield, and said in that private tone, "Don't tell her all, Fred. Not that." He put on his hat and left.

They watched him walk out of the restaurant, and then watched out the window as he crossed the street to the police station.

"Don't tell me what?"

"He's had a low time of late," Butterfield murmured unhappily.

I don't have any hope.

She picked up the photograph of Grafeneck Castle.

Hitler was no longer some caricature in political cartoons. No longer a mere bully. No longer over there.

He was here.

"May I?" said Butterfield, holding out his hand.

Clare gave him the photograph. He slipped it inside his jacket.

"I wish I was the same person as when I woke up this morning," Clare said thinly.

"We never will be again. Needless to say, my dear, keep it all quite close. And take heart — our good vicar should be on his way home soon. I think Klein is long gone, and hope Percy may soon come to that conclusion. Nevertheless, there *is* a possibility Klein may come back if he can't find the packet elsewhere. Which is, of course, a polite way of saying that your boat could be in danger, Miss Childs. Which is, of course, a polite way of saying that *you* may be in danger."

"Not with the Shrew about," Clare said vaguely. "She shrieks. Can you tell me anything about the retreat? There's a soldier, son of a friend of mine. I don't know what section he's with — division, whatever you call it. His name is Jamie Elliott. I believe he's a private."

Butterfield shook his head. "There's half a million men over there, hightailing it from a lightning rout. Your friend won't learn anything for days. Weeks, perhaps." Then the amiable face seemed to sag. "I will say this — I wouldn't hold out hope. Things have gone very badly. The unfortunate thing is that I am one of those dreadful optimists, and if I should admit there is not much hope, quite depressingly you can take that to the bank. Only a miracle will save them now, and my heart is too low to believe for one."

"What exactly is going on?"

Butterfield glanced about, and leaned in. He said very quietly, "Look, I'd be hanged for saying this, and I mean that quite literally, so you didn't hear it from me and don't ask how I know: Admiral Ramsay is working like a lunatic to pull together the entire Royal Navy and send them over to rescue the lads. Dover is in an uproar. But it's a complete logistical nightmare. Soldiers are converging from all over France upon a coastal town called Dunkirk, a little holiday place straight across the Channel from Dover; but here's the tricky part: there, the shore is very shallow, for a mile or so out. Destroyers won't be able to maneuver in for a mass embarkation. They're sure to have a deuce of a time, sending out cutters to collect our men one spoonful at a time from an enormous kettle. Promises a painfully slow evacuation." He paused, and said heavily, "Which is to say, Hitler will beat us to them. Our lads are sitting ducks."

Clare covered her mouth with both hands.

Poor Captain John! Surely the state she had left him in meant he knew what was going on with the BEF — he was an old navy veteran; he had friends in the navy.

"German panzers and artillery and infantry on their heels, to say nothing of the Luftwaffe, already mounting a bombing campaign. Our boys will arrive at Dunkirk with no idea what they're in for, surely thinking they're going to be rescued when the truth is, Dunkirk is their last stand. The situation is unbelievably grim, Miss Childs. I hesitate to say 'catastrophic,' it's like whistling for the devil, but I find no other word. Ramsay *hopes* to save forty-five thousand men . . . out of nearly half a million."

A deep shadow passed over his good-natured face, and for a moment he seemed to have forgotten Clare.

"And now we have no allies. We tried to come to the rescue of others, and find there is no one to come to ours. We stand alone, and small, before the great oppressor of our time, who brings something hideous to our island, something that will never be compatible with who we are. I have never felt such despair, never dreamed to see a day like this. The thought of losing the entire army is unbearable itself, but if our boys are not here to protect hearth and home, Britain is finished, and all that is lovely and good."

She took in the words as she looked around the café. Two women chatted at a table nearby. An elderly couple shared a dish of pudding. A young mother spooned pablum into her baby's mouth, cooing as she did.

"Look at them," Clare said, voice hollow. "They don't know everything's changed."

"Let them be innocent awhile longer."

For a time, neither spoke.

Butterfield glanced down. His stomach touched the table edge. "Gracious. I *am* getting tubby."

Clare looked out the window to the police station.

"No matter. Rationing will soon take care of that." He contemplated the last biscuit on the plate, and as if guarding against future hunger, took and bit it. "Who knows — perhaps even I, at my age, will take up arms for king and country." He chewed meditatively. "Do you know, I've never felt this before, this underlying unity — I feel connected to the man on the street like I never have. Even to thugs, for whom I now feel a great beneficence. Perhaps because at last, there are no more politics and principles. There's not rich or poor, high or low, clean or dirty. We've been beaten. We're alone. But we're together." He gave a bitter but somehow quite lovely smile. "The end of all things has a rather clarifying edge, don't you think?"

She laid her hand on his arm. "I do, actually."

"Hitler's ways are new and bold and powerful. Ours are old and traditional and plodding. And not one of us will go down without a fight for those plodding ways." He blinked quickly. "I know in my heart that is not bully-boy rhetoric. We will not have him here. Not him, or his ways." He gave a curt nod.

When the ache in Clare's throat passed, she ventured, "How did Arthur Vance die?"

Butterfield realized he held a half-eaten biscuit. He laid it down, and looked out the window longingly, as if searching for a better day, a day long gone or a day far in the future.

"I'm not sure how much you want to tell Murray. His father was tortured, you see. I'll not give those details. We made it to the hospital just before he went into surgery. He told us Klein didn't get the packet, but that's it — never said where it was, because he saved his final bit of strength to pass on last words to his son."

"What were they?"

"Do you know," Butterfield mused, as if

discovering something new, "his face was so white, he had no strength to even lift his head, but what struck me was that the man was dying, and he knew it, yet he was so calm. No panic. No desperation. There was some sort of rueful serenity about it, as if yes, the game was up, and he'd been caught as he knew he would be, but he also knew he'd done what he was supposed to do, as long as he could, best as he could, right to the end. No stout defiance about it. Just . . . rueful serenity." A faint smile, and he focused on Clare. "It was the last we saw him alive. His final words were, 'Tell Murray I'm sorry it all went to bilge.' Sailor speak, I suppose, for 'I'm sorry I left you and your mother.' "

"Bilge is awful," Clare agreed, pressing the tissue to her nose. "It's foul and nasty and part of my boat I pretend doesn't exist. Look, are you quite sure he didn't say something like 'Tell him I love him'? Can't I *please* pass along something a little more . . . ?"

"I'm sure those words were as good as, my dear," Butterfield said soothingly. "They felt so. It's how men talk, you see. We came to learn that leaving his wife and child was Vance's lifelong regret. 'I'm sorry it all went to bilge' meant 'I've been an ass and if I

190

had a chance to do it over, I'd do it differently. And PS — I love you with all my heart, and I'm ever so proud of you.' Yes, it meant all that." He let the words lie for a time, and then, mustering a transitionary show of cheerfulness, which came off as something rather brave and sad, "So what is Murray Vance like, then? Arthur *was* proud of him. Certainly a clever lad. Love to get his autograph for my son."

Clare fussed with her tissue. "I don't know, really. Only met him yesterday." She half smiled. "I feel as though I know you and your William better."

If I can go down like Arthur Vance, warning others — well, that's something, isn't it?

Such an intense man. His boyish face positively *deceived.*

She found that she had fussed the tissue to shreds.

Sounding very much like the Shrew, she collected the shreds and herself at the same time. You will take *hold* of your courage and your vision and your singularity of purpose and you will *divert* them to join ranks with men such as these and you will go down warning others. You will go down for ways that are plodding and good. That's something, isn't it?

For today, this day of days, her sailing

191

dream had ended.

She suddenly said, "Mr. Percy said, 'Don't tell her all. Not that.' What did he mean?"

"Oh . . . sometimes William is a little hard to read."

"That sounds evasive, Mr. Butterfield."

"He could have been referring to the nature of Vance's death. It was quite brutal. Affected us deeply, since we'd come to know the man. It's one thing to investigate a murder of a stranger, another when the victim is known to you . . . and known as a hero. But let's set that aside for now." He brandished a finger. "Right! You tell Murray Vance it's time to get back on the bike. We must keep on with whatever we've been given to do. We shall all of us go down in harness. I plan to go out ruefully serene, myself." He flashed a quick smile, then took his hat and secured it on his head, rose from the table, and shook her hand. "Thank you for your time, Miss Childs. Here's my card. Do ring us up if Waldemar Klein pops in for tea, though as I said, I'm sure he's thoroughly searched the boat and is long gone. Nothing to worry about. Good day, Miss Childs."

He started to go, but hesitated.

He looked through the window to the police station across the street. A softening came to his face. A troubled affection.

"My associate is the oldest of six children. His parents had their final child late in life, a sister whom he quite adores. Cecelia, six years old — little Cecy. Darling thing. Calls me Uncle Fred. Cecy has Down syndrome. And William used a word the other day, one I don't believe I've heard spoken in conversation; he said when he first saw the picture of Erich von Wechsler, and learned what had happened to him, he felt eviscerated."

Clare followed his gaze.

"He's carried a picture of her in his wallet since that day."

Home is invaded.

"You'll forgive him if catching Klein, and retrieving that packet, has become something of — as they say — a magnificent obsession." He touched the brim of his hat and left.

Percy's hand, flat upon the envelope, had contracted to a white fist.

Clare snatched her hat and coat.

13

"You're quite sure?" asked William Percy of the desk sergeant. The photograph of Waldemar Klein lay on the desk blotter in front of him.

"I don't forget faces, lad. That's him — the ratty one, not the younger bloke."

"But yesterday you said he was American."

"Half a mo." He held up his finger, and answered the telephone. "This is Sergeant Blake."

William remained composed for about five seconds, then banged the counter ledge with his fist. Klein, at last! The newspaper ruse worked! Flushed him out!

He could *feel* that neck in his fist, and it had nothing to do with justice. It was pure vengeance, and if vengeance was supposed to belong to God, then William was God's agent. He would kill Waldemar Klein for killing Arthur Vance. He would kill him for Erich von Wechsler. He would kill him for even *thinking* the barest *nuance* of thought that he could breathe in that hell-born doctrine and exhale its fumes upon his little sister.

He laughed, gave a little hop in place, smiled expansively at the woman in line behind him and even chucked her baby under its sticky chin, though he couldn't stand babies. But the surge of elation had no sooner crested than a thought came to crush it entirely.

The baby's eyes welled with tears, and it began to wail.

He strode to the bank of windows and stared across the street to the restaurant. Single-handedly circumnavigate the globe — what nonsense. And now she was in trouble before she ever left the dock.

His fingers closed over the bandage.

"What have we got?" said Butterfield, coming alongside.

"Ah! There you are! You'll never believe it. I'll lord it over you for the rest of your life." He took Butterfield's arm and hurried him to the counter.

Butterfield took in the photograph in front of the desk sergeant.

He took in William's agitated state. "Great scott," he breathed. "You don't mean . . ."

"He came to see the vicar. Just yesterday."

They stared at one another until William laughed, and thumped Butterfield's back. "Our man thought he was American."

"Well, he didn't say much, you see," said the sergeant defensively, hanging up the phone. "How could I tell? When I told him the vicar had got his quota of visits for the day, he left in a hurry. Not like *that* one, who pitched a right jolly fit." Following his nod, they turned around.

"I do like that girl," Butterfield said.

"Another *lamb* to adore?" William said dryly.

"Well, she doesn't look very lamblike now, does she?"

Clare Childs came straight for William. She took up position under his nose, and his heart gave a strange little skip at this assault of sorts.

"Look here," she said, brown eyes in a fine dangerous blaze, "if you think for one moment —"

"Funny," said William calmly. "I was just coming back for you."

Her surprise was comical. He could almost smile, but the next thought took away any desire to do so.

She noticed, and demanded, "Well? What is it?"

"Waldemar Klein has surfaced. He tried

to see the vicar."

"Oh," she said. She realized she was standing a bit close, and took a step back. Then she said, "Oh!" and clutched William's arm. "Someone was watching my boat!"

"When?" William and Butterfield said sharply.

"The other day." She squeezed her eyes shut. "Yesterday!"

"Was Clemens there yesterday?" William asked Butterfield.

"No. I pulled him off last week and put him on the Grosvenor case."

"Mrs. Shrew saw someone around the corner of the boathouse. She's not the sort to imagine things." Her gaze went blank and she started for the door, but William caught her back.

"Where are you going, Miss Childs?"

"Well, I've got to get home! It's all unraveling!" She clutched her head. "Captain John's son is in the BEF, and I've left Murray alone, and they're all quite unguarded without me. If Klein came to see the BV, then obviously his next move is —"

"He won't try anything in broad daylight," William said quickly.

"Well, he visited the BV in broad daylight," she said, rather shrill.

"William is quite right, Miss Childs," Butterfield said soothingly. "Klein won't risk it. Come, now — my associate will take you back to the boatyard, and check things out thoroughly. You will be quite reassured. We will repost a man on watch immediately." To William, he said, "Drop me at the office. I'll pull Clemens from —"

"Post me."

Butterfield studied William for a moment, then nodded. "Yes, all right. But I can't spare you too long, with the current uncertainties. No more than a few days. Any longer, and we'll put Clemens back on it." He turned to the desk sergeant. "My good fellow." He stabbed the photograph on the desk with his finger. "If this man returns, you are to —"

"Shoot him," declared Miss Childs.

They looked at her, and William said to the sergeant with a raised brow, "You heard the lady."

On the way to Elliott's Boatyard, they had stopped at Percy's flat in Merton to collect a few things. A very different William Percy got into the car. Gone was the suit, replaced with deck shoes, deck trousers, a cotton shirt, and a light jacket.

"You look as though you're ready to repel

boarders," Clare said.

"Rather yachtie of me, but it's all I could scramble for now. I'd sooner have a fisherman's look."

"Perhaps Captain John has something a bit dirtier. What do you plan to do?"

"I don't know. I'll have a talk with Elliott and we'll sort something out. I'll need a place where I can observe the boat without being observed. At least Klein doesn't know my face." He shifted gears, and turned a corner. "What were you going to say to me when you came into the station?"

Clare watched shops and neighborhoods flash past. Was Murray awake by now?

"Murray seems so alone," she murmured. "There's something very childlike about him, though he's got to be at least twenty. I feel very protective of him. He's a guest, you know."

Was the Shrew still with Captain John at the boathouse, and Murray all alone, and there comes from above a peculiar creak which he does not know is peculiar? Just how desperate was Waldemar Klein?

He murdered Arthur Vance. Tortured him to death. That's how desperate. Of course he'd try something in broad daylight. They just didn't want her to panic. She clutched the passenger-seat armrest.

"What were you going to say to me — ?"

"I've forgotten it. I'm sure it was quite a good speech."

"Looked like it promised to be." He took another corner. He adjusted the rearview mirror.

He was far too calm. As much as he wanted Klein, he wasn't even driving fast.

Maybe she *was* overreacting. She loosened her grip on the armrest.

"Perhaps I feel protective of Murray because apparently he's America's national treasure." She hesitated. "It's the Shrew, you see. And Captain John. They're all the family I have."

"What about your uncle and aunt?"

"How very strange that you should know me," she said a bit indignantly. "It feels very odd."

"That's about all I know," Percy admitted. "I'm afraid I won't be able to unnerve you any more than that."

"Well, my uncle and aunt don't count." She lifted her chin.

He looked at her sideways. "They took you in when your parents died."

She looked out the window.

"Well, I didn't like your uncle," he offered cheerfully.

She glanced at him, startled.

"We dropped by to ask him about the relationship between your father and Arthur Vance. He'd never heard of Vance. He said your father was much younger and ran with different friends."

"Why would you ask that about my father?" She frowned, concentrating. "Hang on — I do remember *someone* asking, not long after I signed the papers for Maggie . . ."

"That was our man, Clemens."

Shocked, she said, "I thought he worked for Mr. Hillary, our family's solicitor. Not Scotland Yard."

Percy shrugged. "Then he was doing his job."

"He showed up one day, said he worked for Mr. Hillary, and asked if I'd found anything on the boat. Said he was clearing up loose ends for the distribution of the will. I showed him a box full of newspapers and bric-a-brac, which he carefully examined, but left behind. He asked how well did I know Mr. Vance, and I said I didn't know him at all. Never met him. My father died when I was eleven, and I don't remember him mentioning a Vance. But then, how much do eleven-year-olds really know of their parents?" She smoothed the pleats on her skirt. "They don't observe things, then.

They would, if they knew it would all be taken."

"Arthur Vance had many friends abroad, but not in Britain. That was the curious thing. Once you had inherited the boat —"

"It was *bequeathed* to me. There's a difference," Clare said with feeling. "It should belong to Murray. I don't know how to feel about it. If I allow myself to feel anything at all, I'm quite terrified I will lose her." She felt for the locket.

"Yes, well, once you had . . . *received* . . . the boat, and when we'd spoken with your uncle, he didn't seem happy at all with your good fortune. Hinted that he had spent a great deal of money raising you, and that the boat should be his in recompense. I wouldn't have been surprised if he had produced a ledger to that effect."

"But he did keep a ledger! Every nick I made on a bit of wood, every meal I ate, every article of clothing — it all went into the ledger. He took it out of what my parents left me when I turned twenty-one. Not a penny more, not a penny less."

Percy was silent, but she noticed that his hands had tightened on the steering wheel. "I wasn't with the man five minutes and he made my skin crawl," he said. "Ten, and I wanted to kill him."

She studied him. "He usually fools people."

"Not as much as you'd think. I know his sort. I'll take an honest criminal over him any day. Most pathetic man I've ever met. Strange, really, how he provoked such a reaction in me. I truly wanted to throttle him."

Rather electric, to hear such truth spoken aloud.

Her heart beating faster, she ventured, "It's as though he has a force about him."

"Yes. Exactly." He said it so matter-of-factly.

She absorbed herself in passing scenery. "I thought it was me."

"Oh, he wanted you to believe so. Manipulative tyrant. And his wife!" Percy barked a cold laugh. "What a pathetic woman."

She stared at him. "There's nothing left of her."

He gave her a glance. "My precise assessment. Good thing you got out in time. She may as well have been a piece of wallpaper. Rather horrifying, how he took her over."

"Yes," Clare whispered.

His hands tightened fractionally on the wheel. After a moment, he said, "Can't imagine if that had happened to you."

"It did, for a time."

"Why do you always grab hold of that necklace?" he said sharply.

Her hand flew from her neck, but didn't know where else to go, and went to the locket again. Then she got angry, with herself or with him, and could think of nothing to say.

"That is to say . . . what does it mean to you?" His tone had softened. "Did it belong to your mother?"

"No." Then, "Well . . . sort of." She'd never told anyone this, not even the Shrew. "A few years ago, I went to see if my parents even existed. It was such an idyllic childhood. Oh, I was an only child and dearly wished for brothers and sisters, but nonetheless, we were quite happy, just me and Mum and Dad. When they died, I went to my uncle and aunt's the same day — never returned to my home. I wasn't allowed to retrieve any of my belongings. Not my clothes, or my books. My uncle had the home sealed off, and later he had an estate sale — sold everything. There was nothing left of my mum and dad. Not a dish or a vase. Not my mother's knitting, or her songbooks. Not my father's glasses, or his pipe. How I loved the smell of that pipe on his jacket. The jacket was gone. It was all gone."

She heard the squeak of leather as his

hands gripped the wheel. It was a reflex, like the fist on the envelope, like the teacup. She didn't think he knew he did it.

"Well, anyway, a few years ago, I found the house. We had lived in Manchester. It was very different from what I remembered. It wasn't kept up. It was all run-down — weeds, dirty windows — and I lost all courage to go up to the door. I merely stood on the street for quite some time. I was just leaving, when a middle-aged woman came out of the house next. She stared at me, as if she couldn't quite believe it, and said, 'You're not Clare, are you?' And I said, as if in a dream, 'Mrs. Cleary?' You'd have thought I was *her* child, come home at last. She cried and made such a wonderful fuss, told me about my parents, how much she loved them, how kind they were . . ." Clare sniffed, and swallowed very hard. "She said how hateful my uncle was, how she hated what happened to me — she was on holiday when he held the estate sale, and the only thing she could do for me was to try and buy back a set of dishes that had been sold to another woman in the village. But the woman wouldn't sell. Then she invited me in to tea, and told me there was one thing she could do. And she brought this out."

Clare pulled the locket up and showed

him. It was a small silver pendant shaped like a heart with intricate weavings, like silver ribbons, on the front. "My mother gave it to her as a keepsake when the woman's mother had passed. She said my mother's . . ." Clare paused, took a breath. "My mother's kindness meant the world to her, and she vowed that if I ever showed up, she would give it to me. When I left, I took a flower from Mrs. Cleary's garden. I dried it, and it's in here. This is a reminder of good and real people, that they existed, and that they still do. It is all the proof I have of a happy childhood."

"There's far more proof than that," Percy said, in what could be mistaken for a gentle tone. "There is you, Miss Childs. You are certainly not the child of your uncle and aunt. Never could you have come from them."

She felt light-headed, and teary, and would *not* cry yet again in front of this man she barely knew. She pinched her leg mercilessly to distract herself, and it didn't work.

It was the loveliest thing anyone had ever said to her.

Something like that *must* be inscribed on the back of the locket: *You are the child of Gordon and Ada.*

"Thank you, Mr. Percy," she whispered,

wiping her nose.

Presently, he said, "I want you to think back to when you came to the police station to murder me. I wondered what on earth I had done. Were you to prepare it again, that speech, what would it be?"

Buildings and people and automobiles flashed past, no trace of a sinister tinge. All was wholesome, and good, and dear . . . and vulnerable past imagining with the peril surrounding the BEF, and the oncoming calamity of Hitler.

But she saw in her mind a white fist on an envelope, and rounded on him.

"I don't know what spell Hitler cast that people should go along with him, and it terrifies me to death that this spell is nearing our island, but I'd say this: How can you possibly think you're alone? It's how you seemed when you'd left the café. Do you truly believe that England would put up with killing children? Or that the rest of the world would? In case it escaped your notice, it was *Germans* who got the information to the journalist. *Germans* who risked their lives to do it. That makes me quite sure that Nazism will be defeated in the end, for good people reside yet in a very dark place. Didn't you say that *I* did?" Her lips trembled. "That I am the child of Gordon and Ada? If Hitler makes it here, if he crushes our army and crosses the Channel, then let him find us holding high the picture of Erich von Wechsler as proof that *his own people* would not have his ways. So then, neither will we."

When the heat subsided, and her vision cleared, she smoothed her skirt and added, "I believe that version was a great deal longer than the other, but I don't care. And I don't care how it sounds." She lifted her chin and looked away.

"How do you imagine it sounds?" he asked.

"Frightfully melodramatic."

"Well, it does." Then, "Could you say it again?"

Clare smiled.

"Actually, do you think you could write it down for me? I'll slip it out when I'm feeling low. Take a little nip off it, like a flask. Perhaps visit a tattoo parlor, add it to my number five."

Clare laughed, and looked at him. If it wasn't exactly a smile that she saw on his face, it was an easing of lines.

14

It ain't our war.

Dead children are my war.

Murray's eyes flew open.

Conversations with the Fitz had tormented Murray throughout his sleep. No surprise he should find one when he woke.

If it's not funny, or pleasant, or happy, or fascinating — it has no part of your world.

You're just as blind as the people you draw those posters for.

Find that packet, Murray. You'll believe me.

"I ain't gonna give you that cigar, you keep that up."

He became aware of the gentle movement of a boat at anchor in placid water. He'd spent the happiest summer of his life on this boat, until that last day. He hadn't seen his father, or answered a letter, since. All because his father looked at a broad.

Murray liked to look at broads. But if you're in a restaurant in Barcelona, and your old man looks at the same senorita you're lookin' at with a look that in a younger guy woulda been no big deal but in an older guy was slimy . . . Nah, nothing had changed after all. He was the same man who left his ma for another skirt. She was a waitress, too. Ma didn't like waitresses. Or barmaids. Or cleaning ladies. Or hairdressers.

His old man got around.

He pushed up on an elbow and looked around his cabin. "Good to be back, Mags. Even if you are the original skirt."

This great old cabin. Same faint mildewy smell, same damp feel that would never go away, no matter where they sailed. He felt along the bottom edge of the bunk frame and found the hardened drip of shellac. He'd found it that summer, looking for a place to park his gum.

He eased back to look at the bottom of the top bunk. He'd had to clear away a lot of stuff last night, and stowed it up there. One of those things was a box, and in that box were surprises.

First was the little figurine of the dancing native girl. They were in some bazaar in Egypt or Morocco, and his father caught him admiring it. Her figure had made him think of Helen, the secretary who worked with his mother at Florsheim's. He'd blushed and put it back, afraid his father would think he was only a hormonal teen, but the old man picked it up and said, "A boat needs a talisman. I think a taliswoman would suit, don't you?"

Next was a sea sponge from the harbor at Paphos, Cyprus. Looked like one of those *National Geographic* pictures of coral, except it was bile yellow. Fascinating color, fascinating thing, and it came from the sea as is, nothing needed to add to its usefulness. "Nifty," Murray had said, and the old man bought it. It was the last thing Murray admired out loud to his old man.

There were a few navigation charts that brought back the old man's lessons. One chart was of the southern coast of Turkey. His father knew the waters well and couldn't wait to show Murray a special place — a channel opened into a secluded narrow lagoon flanked with high walls of rocky hillside. They anchored in the middle of the lagoon. Murray swam a mooring line out to a rock; then they dropped the dinghy to paddle for shore. They climbed for a spell, and Dad brought him to the ancient ruins of a tiny church. A cross was carved in the white stone above the entryway. You could look out a window to the lagoon below, where *Maggie Bright* sat, a beauty at anchor. Past her, through a crevasse, you could see the ocean. It became Murray's favorite place of the summer. They spent a whole week there, swimming, fishing.

Seemed as though the whole box was devoted to Murray.

He'd already taken out volume 2, number 11, and slipped it into a drawing pad to bring home to his mother. Crazy, finding her missing piece among his father's things.

He listened for Clare and Mrs. Shrewsbury, and smiled to think of the old lady because real fans made him smile, but all was quiet. Then he heard footsteps overhead, near the stern. They sounded heavier than what women would make, reminded him of the footsteps of his old man. The thought did not sadden him, which in itself was kinda sad.

He listened — definitely the footfalls of a man. Must be the fellow who owned the boatyard, the one Clare talked about. He got up quickly to use the . . . what did she call it?

"Loo," he said, chuckling. Crazy English. Where did they get *loo* out of *john*?

"Where should I park?"

"Pull round to the other side of that lorry.

Oh dear. I've forgotten the marmalade. Do you know," Clare suddenly mused, "this is the worst day of my life, all that I've learned, but now that I *know* the worst, now that I've had *time* with it, I feel better. I feel . . . pugnacious."

"Captivating word choice," William Percy commented.

"Agatha Christie just used it. All I want to do is grab a pistol and run for the front."

Percy nearly smiled, an action that with him was as good as. He put on the parking brake and switched off the engine.

"Was that amusing?" said Clare.

"The image, yes. You running with a pistol. Not *amusing,* but rather . . ." and curiously, he colored.

"Rather what?"

"I'm not going to say what." Then he said quickly, "Well, I was going to say *endearing* — which is the wrong word, of course — but you made me see grandmothers and aunties all ranged at the top of a fort, brandishing pistols. That's endearing." He thought for a moment. "Scary, too."

He got out of the car and came around to her door.

"An image of me with a pistol *immediately* calls to mind aged grandmothers and aunties," she said as he opened her door.

"Why wouldn't it?" Again, that easing of lines, that almost smile.

A clever retort was in the making when a shout cut it off.

"Oh, thank goodness you're here! Quickly — run for the police!"

Mrs. Shrew stood wild before them with a teakettle.

"If it hadn't been for that man to subdue him," the Shrew said, running behind them, "I don't know what we should have done."

Clare had a feeling she'd done all right with the kettle.

"I only hope the Shrew hasn't killed him so that you may," Clare said to Percy.

"I wish Butterfield hadn't taken Clemens off," he growled. "I *told* him not to."

They jogged down the wooden dock to Maggie's berth at the end. The murderer of Murray's own father was aboard the *Maggie Bright.*

"Is Murray all right?" Clare said over her shoulder.

"All is well," the Shrew puffed. "And his hands are fine."

Clare glanced behind, puzzled, and Mrs. Shrew said, "Famous violinists have their hands broken by thugs. His hands were the first I checked."

Percy threw up a cautionary hand when they slowed up and neared the boat. He put his other hand in his pocket, which Clare was sure concealed a gun.

"Stay here. He's a very dangerous —"

"I shouldn't wonder if my skull isn't fractured!" came a high-pitched voice from the boat. "Good Lord, that shrieking; I'll have nightmares the rest of my life. Am I bleeding?"

"Come now, guv, brace up — it's just a scratch." It was Captain John.

"I quite understand the threat of Fifth Columnists, with the lamentable influx of *refugees,* as they call them, but this is ridiculous. A German spy indeed."

Clare knew that voice. She stared at Percy. "Why — it's Mr. Hillary!"

It was indeed Mr. Wilfrid Hillary, family lawyer of the Childs clan.

He kept checking to see if the scratch had produced blood on the square of handkerchief he pressed against his forehead.

Maggie's crew ranged about on her deck. William Percy, in his yachtie apparel, sat on the aft sail locker. Murray, who had slept in his clothing, took up a sprawled post in the captain's chair at the helm, creased and rumpled from sleep and intensely interested in the ruckus. Mr. Hillary sat on a bench in the cockpit opposite Clare, with a formidable and arms-folded Captain John standing behind his right shoulder, flanked by Captain John's mirror image, Mrs. Shrew, at his left. She still held the kettle.

Clare's knees nearly touched Mr. Hillary's. Ordinarily, none of them would be in such close proximity to one another, but on a boat, one pretended more personal space existed than actually did.

"I'd tried to contact you via the telephone, only to discover you had none," said Mr. Hillary stiffly. "Twice I sent notification by post, but you hadn't answered my requests for an appointment."

No, she hadn't. The two envelopes from Messrs. Hillary and Sprague remained unopened on the captain's table.

"Your dear uncle —" here, Clare sent a swift glance at William Percy, gratified to receive one in return — "said you'd not been into the shop in months. There. Look. Blood."

He showed it to the closest person, Murray, who said, "Boy, I'll say. You want me to get a tourniquet?"

Mr. Hillary scowled. "This isn't the sort of thing to occupy a solicitor, you know —

making house calls." He glanced around distastefully. "Rather — house*boat* calls. It isn't done."

"Awfully appreciate you should take your time —" began Clare meekly.

"It's not as though I have several names on *my* door. Hillary and Sprague it may read but there is no Sprague about it, not for years. Threw me off for a London firm."

This Clare knew. "Yes, well, I'm awfully sorry —"

"No, I'm quite on my own except for a clerk in the village I occasionally hire when work is backlogged. My time is valuable and I am unused to *two* unanswered summons. Did I have an incorrect address?" His tone and a high eyebrow indicated he was sure he did not.

She couldn't say in front of Murray that the envelopes had struck a sick dread in Clare — anything legal did, for it came with a threat that this dream she'd been living was over, and Maggie would be seized because of more undiscovered debt, or unrevealed taxes, or any number of unimagined bureaucratic infractions. Or . . . that she actually belonged to someone else, someone the will had missed. Like Murray.

She remained silent, but before it grew awkward, William Percy said, "Mr. Hillary, please get to your point — I have very important business to attend to in the area, but wish to hear this business first."

He drew himself up. "Well, it's certainly none of yours."

"It's all right, Mr. Hillary," Clare assured.

"Miss Childs, this is a private matter. I couldn't even tell your dear uncle. I am quite uncomfortable disclosing —"

And Clare laughed.

Mr. Hillary's eyes inflated with shock.

"I'm sorry — it's just . . . Look, I've heard the most awful news today. Shocking and dreadful and . . . you will all know soon enough, though I suspect Captain John may know some of it already. The truth is, I don't feel that any matter is private anymore. Not now." She looked around at Maggie's crew, at this young man she barely knew, at the captain and the Shrew, at the man searching for blood on his handkerchief, at the hazel-eyed man on the aft locker with the photo of his sister in his wallet. She felt a rush of affection for these friends and strangers. She could lose them all. Nothing much mattered now, except to say no to a man who kills children.

"You can disclose anything you want in front of these." She raised her chin. "It's a day for the worst possible news, so do your worst, Mr. Hillary." And in her heart, she braced.

"Suit yourself, Miss Childs," said the lawyer, with the long-suffering air of one accustomed to the poor judgment of the young. "A few weeks ago, I was filing some papers I'd received from the lawyer of Arthur Vance. And something struck me, which I believed warranted further investigation on behalf of longtime clients. You see, Mr. Vance's lawyer had suggested that your father, Gordon Childs, was a boyhood friend of Arthur's. He said as much in his letter. But it isn't true."

Clare blinked. "Whatever do you mean?"

"Your father was born and raised in Manchester. But one of the papers, a deed of ownership transferal, stated that Arthur Vance was born in a little village called Ockham, Surrey, where he lived for many years."

"That is odd," said Clare slowly.

"Those places far apart?" Murray asked, looking from one to the other.

"About a country apart," Clare said.

"Miss Childs," said the lawyer patiently, "do you not remember? *You* were born in Surrey."

"Well, yes, I know that. I was adopted out when I was —" Clare broke off.

"You were born in Ockham."

After a moment, William Percy said sharply, "Are you all right?"

She was clutching the locket.

"Adoption records of course are sealed," Mr. Hillary continued, "but not the full disclosure of wills. For a shilling you can read one at the Sommers House in London. A few weeks ago, I went to London, paid the shilling, and read the will of Arthur Murray Vance. It turns out that he had left his houseboat to his firstborn. A daughter. Her name listed in the will is . . . Clare Ada Childs."

Clare remained very still, until at last, she found the eyes of Murray Vance; she likely had the same sort of look on her face as he.

"In the event of refusal, it was to be passed on to his second born, Murray Arthur Vance, of Bartlett, New York. For reasons unknown, Arthur had instructed his lawyer to say that the behest came from a boyhood friend of Gordon Childs. In any correspondence, you were never referred to as anything other than the daughter of his boyhood friend."

"My old man got around," Murray said softly to Clare, adding a quick artificial grin. "Prob'ly one of us in every port."

"*That* was unnecessary, young man." Mr. Hillary gave him a very stern look. "Perhaps it's how you talk in America. It isn't done here, and not to my client." He turned to Clare. "I gave it long thought, and decided you should know. *I* would have wanted to."

"Well. It's good to know this *now,* isn't it?" said the Shrew, hands on her hips. "I had you two married off, but this is even better — his *blood* runs in your veins. Right, then; would anyone like some tea? I'll just go make some. That and a few digestives seem just the thing." On the way to the companion hatch, she gave Clare's shoulder a quick squeeze, said quietly, "We'll sort it out later, my dear," and went below.

"You need not pay back the shilling," Mr. Hillary said magnanimously.

"How do you like being the daughter of a two-timin' snake?" Murray said.

"Now see here," Mr. Hillary began severely.

William Percy rose. "She's the daughter of a national hero."

Murray rose. "Must be you're talkin' about her adopted daddy. On behalf of my ma, ain't no one callin' my old man a hero in front of me." He looked him up and down with clear disdain. "Who are you again? Some kinda bobby?"

"Detective Inspector William Percy. Scotland Yard."

"Yeah? Why don't you go solve a crime?"

"Murray," Clare began. "He's here because —"

"What did you say I already knew?" asked Captain John, the anxious expression from this morning on his face. "Do you know anything about my Jamie?"

Clare hesitated, then said carefully, "It appears that the army is in desperate straits."

"*Who* is in desperate straits?" asked Mr. Hillary, twisting to have a look at everyone.

"The BEF," said Percy. "They are cut off and surrounded. The entire army."

"What?" cried Mr. Hillary, jumping to his feet. "Impossible! I haven't read this in the newspapers! I haven't heard it on the wireless!"

"Belgium is all but finished. They are expected to surrender anytime. For France, it could be a matter of days."

"But we are allies!" said Mr. Hillary. "France would never surrender!"

"No," said Percy grimly. "But they will fall."

"Great scott! What's to become of England? There's no one left! Mussolini is an onerous piece of tripe, and if Roosevelt is anything like his sorry ambassador, then —"

"Please," said Captain John, looking from

Clare to Percy. "Do you know anything of the Queen's 9th Lancers? Only, I haven't heard from Jamie in weeks."

"Nothing, I'm afraid," said Percy. "I do know they're converging on Dunkirk, and that a rescue operation *is* under way. My brother-in-law serves under Admiral Ramsay. Best stay close to the wireless. The king is sure to make an announcement soon." To Clare, he said, "I'm going to canvass the area and ask if anyone has seen Klein."

"Mr. Percy, I've thought of something — I do have an extra cabin. It's filled with junk, but I could clear it for you."

"Thanks, but I noticed the Anderson shelter at the boathouse. I'll stay there. Better vantage. He'd have to pass by me to get to — the *Maggie Bright.*"

"Wait. Who's Klein?" asked Murray.

"Oh, dear me," said Mr. Hillary, shoving his handkerchief in his pocket. "I must get home. I must see to my dog. I must cycle out my Anderson perishables. Must get the mail, and I have an order at the butcher's." He quickly made his way off the boat, and hurried down the dock.

"Mr. Hillary!" Clare called. "Thank you for coming!" He didn't answer.

"My good fellow," Percy said to Captain John, "would you mind terribly if, for a few

223

days, I posed about your boatyard as a hired hand? Perhaps as a fisherman?"

"Wait, Mr. Percy." Clare looked at his clothing. "I think a yacht owner would be far more plausible. You fit that bill much more believably. There is that lovely little *Argo* in dry dock, Captain John, the Chris Craft with the beautiful mahogany hull; perhaps Mr. Percy could pretend to work on it. Act as though he's readying it for the water."

"I haven't the faintest what you're talking about," said Captain John, bemused.

"Yeah — what's goin' on?" Murray asked.

"I'll leave you to Miss Childs for that," Percy said to Murray. He looked at Clare, and his eyes briefly held hers. Then he turned to Captain John. "Come, my good fellow, I will tell you what little I know. You'll likely read about the BEF before the day is out, but there is another matter, about a man named Klein."

When they stepped from the boarding plank to the dock, Clare heard Percy say cheerily, "You're an old navy sod, correct? Well, as far as the BEF is concerned, they've got the entire Royal Navy on the job, pulling in destroyers from everywhere. The navy to the rescue of the army — now that must be a very entertaining thought. . . ."

With one of Maggie's crew in the keeping of William Percy, whom she felt to be another, Clare called down the hatch, "Mrs. Shrew, can we take tea up here?" She couldn't go below. She had to be in the bow, near the foremast where she loved Maggie most. She had to be in the open air, facing south, where the hope of England lay on a foreign, embattled shore.

"Certainly," the Shrew called up. "How many? I heard some go off."

"Three. Counting you."

"Righty, then."

For the first time, brother and sister were alone.

"No wonder you're good-lookin'," Murray quipped.

"No wonder you talk so much." They regarded one another for a moment, and Clare blurted, "Maggie is just as much yours as she is mine."

"Nah — for once, my old man did the right thing."

"Oh, Murray — he's done so much more than that. I don't know where to start." She hesitated. "Please, I would like to . . . If it's not . . . Do you mind?" And she stepped closer. How very strange to see some of the same traits she saw in the mirror.

Hesitating, she touched his cheek, for the

set of the face was hers. The bridge of his nose, the shape of the nostrils. His eye color was a deeper brown, but the way his eyes turned downward slightly at the edges . . .

"The worst day of my life is turning out to be one of the best," she said.

A charming grin came, as if he'd held it back. "Ain't it a kick? Can't wait to tell the Fitz. Say — what did the bobby mean? Who's Klein?"

"Murray, I have to know — what was the photograph that changed your friend?"

"What?" he said, confused. "Oh — the senator. Boy, we must be related. You don't stay on track."

"I hope it changed him for the good." Her breath caught. "I saw a picture today. I have to know I'll come out all right."

Eyeing her, he put his hands in his pockets and jingled change. Then he looked up at the top of the mainmast. "Come on. Let's go forward. I like it best, there."

"Me too," she said, surprised.

They sat next to each other on the locker near the foremast, watching the east-flowing waters of the Thames.

This young man was her brother.

She couldn't absorb it. It was too enormous.

226

"About that picture," Murray said. "They said I should read the papers to get ideas for my work, and I did, and maybe political satire is where the dough is but I figured out it ain't me. So I do my own thing, but one guy got my attention when I was lookin' into politics — Senator George Norris, Nebraska. Old Georgie pie was all isolationism and noninterventionism up 'til Shanghai. Changed when he saw a picture of a baby."

Erich von Wechsler's face came laughing before her.

"The picture's called *Bloody Saturday.* You prob'ly seen it. A baby's sittin' all alone in bombed-out Shanghai, when the Japanese took the Chinese by surprise. It was all over in the papers and newsreels. He's just sitting there, cryin'. All by himself."

"I remember." No one could forget it.

"Norris changed after that."

"For the good, do you think?"

"Some said no, some said yes. But you know what I liked? He followed his conscience. Didn't care what any party said. I got two questions: *A,* what picture did you see today, and *B,* what about that Klein fella?" He jerked his thumb to where William Percy had gone. "Why's he got that bobby all Eliot Ness?"

227

"Who?"

"Ness? Guy who got Capone?"

"Oh. Capone the crime lord." Clare's stomach fluttered. "Capone's a fairy godmother compared to Waldemar Klein. Murray — did you know that your father had been working with Scotland Yard? That Maggie had been used to save lives? Did you know that they're killing defenseless children, the ones they say have no use in society? The picture is one of those children."

He watched a seagull alight on a dock piling. "I knew. The Fitz told me. Rocket Kid saved 'em."

"What do you mean?"

He gave a short chuckle. "People thought I stopped drawing. I got a whole stack of unpublished strips where Rocket Kid and Salamander save them kids, and Hitler and the Nazis get theirs, and I think it's some of my best work. But guess what? It's all fiction."

She shrugged. "You try to make things right, with your work. What's so bad about that?" She muttered darkly, " 'It's all fiction.' Nonsense! I see shades of my uncle in that."

Murray went still. "Say that again."

"I see shades of —"

"The other."

And she said it clearly and with all her heart to make the words sail home: "You try to make things right with your work."

Murray shot up as if propelled by what Clare now saw in his face, excitement made golden by the sun's waning rays. He paced a few steps and put his hands in his pockets, withdrew them and rubbed his fingers together, looked at them as if expecting to see something.

"I gotta draw."

"But — I have so much to tell you!"

"Tell me while I draw. I hear best that way." He ran for the hatch and swung below.

Murray sat in the curve of the bowsprit with a drawing pad propped on the rail. He'd shimmied easily into the spot as if long accustomed to doing so, and Clare could easily see him younger, and sunburned, and could imagine a presence in the stern watching the boy draw, a man who was her own father.

The only presence behind her was that of Mrs. Shrew, who sat on the locker near the skylight of Murray's cabin, holding a cup of tea. She was the one who watched Murray now.

"Murray," Clare began.

"Hang on, hang on." He finished some strokes, put in some shading, and pulled away from the drawing, tilting his head. A grin came. He stuck the pencil behind his ear, slid from the bowsprit to the deck and brought the drawing pad to Mrs. Shrew.

She studied it — and gasped. "*That's* how you intend to bring back Salamander?"

Murray stuck his hands in his waistband, grinning, while she carried on, flapping her hand and saying, "Oh, bravo!" Then he eased the pad from her grasp and climbed back into the bowsprit. He touched the pencil to his tongue, hesitated, then began to draw.

"Where *did* you come up with that?" said Mrs. Shrew, wiping tears.

"I think my editor's gonna love it."

"Perhaps Salamander is the one paddling the banana boat, and the ray gun is actually his paddle," the Shrew suggested. "What do you think? And then — no. No, don't listen to me. I will *not* interfere. Worldwide implications, right here on this deck. I shall get my knitting, and remain calm. Everyone — give him space."

"Murray, have you heard of a place called Grafeneck Castle?" Clare asked.

The pencil hesitated.

It resumed.

"You hear of Hadamar?" Murray asked, not looking up from his drawing pad. "Brandenburg?"

"What's this?" The Shrew looked from Murray to Clare. "What are they?"

"Killing places," said Clare faintly.

"Oh, not just any old killing places," Murray said, now making broader strokes. "They're killing kids. Deaf kids. Retarded kids. Blind kids. Kids born with bad spines. Sometimes before they kill them, they do research on 'em, see. Can't miss a chance for science." He pulled back from his drawing, and tilted his head. He turned the pad about to face Mrs. Shrew. "Whaddya think?"

Mrs. Shrew stared at him, frozen. She glanced at the drawing. "Brilliant. What do you mean, they're killing children? Who is?"

Murray resumed drawing. "Nazis."

"It's what the BV told me," said Clare quietly. "And later, Mr. Percy and Mr. Butterfield, from Scotland Yard."

Mrs. Shrew was speechless.

"Murray's father sailed *Maggie Bright* four times from Holland, saving five of those children. Five lives, saved. One day I will carve that number on Maggie's foremast as a record of her exploits." She took hold of the locket. "Murray — I have something awful to tell you. Your father was murdered by a man named Waldemar Klein."

The pencil stilled.

"My old man died of a heart attack."

"No." She let go the locket. "He refused to give him that packet of documents. He was . . . tortured for it."

"See, that's what I'm sayin', Clare. Rocket Kid can't make that right." He suddenly winged the drawing pad into the water, the pencil after it.

He slid to the deck and said brightly, "I'm starvin'. How 'bout I get cleaned up and take you girls out for dinner? You ain't got Prohibition here, do ya? We're still smartin' over that."

He made his way past, and went below.

The two women watched the drawing pad in the water. A gentle eddy caught it, turned it lazily about, and slowly bore it east.

"Tell me everything, my dear," said Mrs. Shrew quietly.

15

After a few days in the company of these men, Jamie had a fair idea of who ran the group, and it wasn't the ranking man by three weeks, Lance Corporal Grayling.

Their squad consisted of Grayling at the top, then Balantine as his right-hand man, then Baylor, Curtis, and Griggs, and now Jamie and Milton. If Grayling gave a direct order, he expected it to be obeyed, but he didn't give those often enough. Balantine, in Jamie's mind, had the sort of leadership qualities that made him the best soldier of the lot; but exactly because of this, he supported Grayling. Jamie discovered that Baylor, despite his lack of soldiering qualities, was the one he most liked to be around — in part, because of the way he looked out for the captain. Curtis was the sort of guy with the unfortunate personality of admiring whoever dominated, and the person who dominated this group wasn't Grayling; it was Griggs.

Because Griggs talked the most, because his annoying opinions were always assertive, because he was handsome and sometimes funny and carried himself with supreme confidence, because he was often right in his assessment of situations (maddeningly so), all seemed to defer to him whether they liked it or not. But Griggs was finally challenged when Jamie and the captain came along.

Baylor had brought out this observation to Jamie when, the previous night, they'd found shelter in a barn, and Griggs went on first watch.

"He doesn't like the captain because he's afraid he'll give us away," Baylor had said. "Of course, the captain says things he can't understand, and that provokes outrage because nobody can be smarter than Griggs. But he likes you even less, partly because you take care of the captain, partly because you don't give way to him. I must say, Elliott — it's good to have someone knock him off his perch a bit. Arrogant twit."

Today they moved through fields and meadows, taking as direct a route north as they could without taking the roads — yesterday they'd had a narrow miss when a Stuka appeared out of the bright blue, diving with a hellish onrush of shrieking whistles, to pull up and strafe the road at car height. Bullets sprayed the area, and one shot through Curtis's kit bag; it was as close an encounter with death as any of them had faced, and all agreed with Griggs that they should abandon the roads and strike cross-country for the sea. Slower, but safer.

"What in me is dark, illumine. What is low, raise and support."

"I think that's his favorite," Baylor now observed, walking behind the captain. "He says it a lot."

"That one, the most," Jamie agreed. But today he didn't like the way he'd said it. The captain's voice had lost a lot of its pep.

"And I will place within them as a guide my umpire conscience," the captain said thinly, "whom if they will hear, light after light well used they shall attain, and to the end persisting, safe arrive."

"He really *says* something, you know?" said Baylor. "I read the book because I had to, but now, I want to."

To the end persisting, safe arrive. Jamie saw in his mind an insistent Captain Jacobs in a moonlit patch. A captain who was stronger than this.

The squad of seven men marched sometimes through fields of knee-high corn or waist-high wheat, sometimes through woods and meadows, often through the backyards of abandoned homes, and once through a potato field, where they dug up new potatoes and ate them raw. Bray Dunes, and the sea where they were supposed to find it, was much farther away than they had originally thought; they were two days out from the town where Jamie and the captain hooked up with the five.

"From imposition of strict laws to free acceptance of large grace, from servile fear to filial, works of law to works of faith."

"Oh, just shut it, will you?" Griggs called from the back. "Annoying sod."

"Here it comes," Baylor muttered. Over his shoulder he said, "I don't know what your problem is. You can barely hear him from there."

"I think he's making it all up," Griggs announced. "He's probably an actor. This is his big chance to show off."

"Just let him talk," Baylor warned, for Jamie's ears only.

"It's brilliant, really. Make everyone think you've gone daft by quoting a bunch of fancy lines, and there's your ticket home." Curtis laughed.

"Why is he such an idiot?" Jamie said, not for Baylor's ears only.

"He's baiting you," Baylor said.

"Yes, but why?"

"Because he knows you hate it when he goes after the captain."

"Probably even faking that head wound," Griggs said.

Jamie gripped the stock of his Bren.

"Don't. You'll upset the captain," Baylor said. Jamie glanced at him.

Baylor pushed up his spectacles, and kept his tone low. "He gets agitated when Griggs agitates you. Always seems aware of the *climate*. Aren't you, Milton?" he said, a little louder, to the captain. "There's a good chap." To Jamie, "Remember when Grayling kept you from killing Griggs yesterday? You should have seen the captain. Whenever Griggs provokes you, I look to see how he reacts. I wonder if it means he's getting better." He reached to pat Milton's shoulder, and said louder, "I really think you are, mate. I should say, sir."

"He doesn't look it," Jamie said darkly. "He's whiter by the day. He's slower. And he's not eating much."

"Not that there's much to eat. I can sort of *feel* the captain's rank. Can't you? Wounded or not, deranged or not. Maybe it's because I admire his Milton, but he does seem to have an air of quiet authority. I would have liked to have known him sane."

Jamie did not respond. He was tense for whatever Griggs would say next. He always was, and hated it. Not for the first time he wondered if things weren't better when he and Milton were on their own.

They kept to the same formation as the day before. Balantine walked ahead with Grayling. The captain followed them, with Jamie and Baylor behind the captain, and Griggs and Curtis bringing up the rear. Jamie felt best right where he was, between Griggs and the captain.

"Yet once more he shall stand on even ground, against his mortal foe, by me upheld . . . while by thee raised, I ruin all my foes." He stumbled, nearly fell, and regained his footing.

"Oy, Grayling — old Captain Show-Off is slowing us down," Griggs called ahead.

Balantine, who rarely spoke when walking, said over his shoulder, "We're not leaving him behind, Griggs. You want to take off on your own, have at it."

"And good riddance," Baylor muttered.

The day was clear and warm. Lovely, really. The only thing they missed was a decent breakfast and boots that wouldn't blister. Jamie tried to think of sore feet and an empty stomach, instead of Griggs.

"That thou art happy, owe to God; that thou continuest such, owe to thyself, that is, to thy obedience: therein stand."

"Rather heartening, isn't it?" said Baylor.

"He's utterly bladdered," said Griggs.

"Good he made thee, but to persevere he left it in thy power — ordained thy will by nature free; not over-ruled by fate."

"The whole Victoria Cross thing is probably a myth. They just wanted a babbling lunatic off their hands."

Jamie turned and headed straight for Griggs.

"Grayling!" Baylor shouted.

Jamie shoved Griggs. "Mind who you're calling a lunatic! He outranks you."

Griggs shoved back. "I see no stripes."

"You and I are gonna have some words pretty soon."

"Why don't we have them now?" He unshouldered and dropped his kit bag. Griggs was half a head taller than Jamie, and seemed to inflate. "Little pansy."

A firm hand clamped on Jamie's shoulder. It wasn't Grayling, because Grayling showed up alongside with a bellowed though barely heard "Knock it off, you two!" Jamie heard instead firm and quiet words from the one who restrained him, words aimed not at himself but at Griggs:

"Thyself not free, but to thyself enthralled."

The captain's authority came unmistakably through.

"Oh, well done! You want me to explain that one to you, Griggsy?" said Baylor.

Griggs turned on Baylor. "Shut it!"

"Griggs, I'm warning you." Grayling put himself between Jamie and Griggs. "You keep up all this needling, and you're gone."

"What do you mean, gone?" Griggs demanded.

"You're out. You're not with us anymore. Is that clear enough? You will not endanger this group. This stupid bickering means less watching."

"Oh, really? Look who's endangering the group!" Griggs pointed at the captain. "Every night that loony bin is up and barking at the moon!"

Jamie reached around Grayling to shove him. "Mind who you're calling loony bin!"

Grayling rounded on Jamie. "And why do you let him provoke you? You should know better." He looked Griggs up and down. "You too."

"That's right," said Baylor, and spat.

Griggs sneered at him. "Since when have you got so bold?" He looked at Jamie. "Since your boyfriend came along?"

"Close your mouth and fall in line. Both of you." Grayling went back to his position.

Griggs snatched up his kit. "If any of us should go, it's not me," he muttered. "I was here first. It's not my fault I got separated from my men. Any one of them is better than this entire lot."

"What about me?" Curtis protested.

"Oh, shut it."

The squad of seven took up the march to the sea once more.

"You don't back down from Griggs," Baylor presently observed, after the sting of the encounter had died down. "You haven't from the first. It's put some sand back in the rest of us, but I warn you — because of it, he won't go after you. He'll go after the captain."

"Then that's his mistake."

After a moment, Baylor said, "I think Griggs is a good soldier. But he does have a hateful streak."

Jamie said suddenly, "Baylor, listen. If anything should happen to me —"

"Nothing will," Baylor cut in. After a moment, he said, "And if it does . . ." He looked at Milton. "I'll get him home."

16

"Hail, below!" came a call from above. "Are you decent, Mr. Vance?"

"Depends who you ask." Murray came to the companionway, wiping the last of the shaving cream from his neck with a towel. He looked up and got an unflattering angle of a beaming Mrs. Shrewsbury. "You ask Betty Reynolds, no, I ain't decent. But that was a long time ago."

"There's a lovely little place called Evelyn's, just up the road. Best sticky toffee pudding in all of England."

"I'm game. Let me get some dough. They take American cash? It's all I got."

"I doubt it. Perhaps we can pop into the bank in Teddington to exchange."

By the time they got to Evelyn's place, the sun was setting. It took much longer than expected to exchange Murray's money, as the bank was mistrustful of the brand-new bills. Apparently America's paper currency had gone through a redesign and did not match the pictures in the Teddington bank's currency book. They had to go all the way to London, where one of the banks had an up-to-date book.

"What do you call this stuff?" Murray asked, his mouth full.

"Sticky toffee pudding," said Clare.

"Ain't never had anything like it." He swallowed. "My mother would go nuts. She's got a sweet tooth to shame every kid who trick-or-treated. Sea foam's her favorite. They make the best on Long Island, Ruby's Confectionery."

"Sea foam?" asked Mrs. Shrew, perplexed.

"Brown crunchy stuff, covered with chocolate? Don't you have that here? Aw, I wish I had some with me, you'd —"

"Your father's last words were for you."

Murray poked the pudding with his fork, then put it down. "You can sure rain on a parade."

"It's a little hard for me to carry on as usual, knowing what's going on just over the Channel."

And indeed, the words of the men from Scotland Yard proved true: the early editions in the newsstands in London were now filled with ominous updates on the situation with the BEF.

Some of the papers, it was true, down-played the news with a lot of hearty bravado as they usually did. But in others, like the *News Chronicle,* one of the papers Mrs. Shrew had bought and read aloud in the cab on the way back to Bexley, the news was far bolder:

In his brief statement on the war situation yesterday the prime minister made it clear that the tide of German penetration into Belgium and northern France has not yet been stemmed.

And from the *Evening Standard:*

First let us have no ostrichism in our preparations against an invasion of this island. There are still some who scorn the idea. Can Hitler succeed where Napoleon failed? No, they say, the Channel is impregnable. We would do better to prepare for the worst.

"Your father did something brave, and it cost his life." Clare felt the heat rise. "But when I say, 'Your father's last words were for you,' you don't show the slightest inter-est to know what they were."

"You wanna know what it's like standin'

in a soup line with your mother?" Murray looked up at her. "And she's tryin' hard not to show she's cryin', wonderin' how she's gonna make rent, how she's gonna put clothes on your back? You wanna know how it feels when she acts like she's not hungry so *you* won't go without? And your old man's off sailin' on some boat with your mother's name on it and not sending anything to help, livin' free and easy and makin' misery wherever he goes? You think I *care* what his last words were?"

He fell to his pudding with a glower. He took the fork, and then put it down and shoved the plate away. He rubbed his forehead.

After a moment, he said, "What were they?"

"He said, 'Tell Murray I'm sorry it all went to bilge.' " Clare watched him worriedly.

"What kinda last words are those?" He looked up at Clare, confused. "Say it again."

" 'Tell Murray I'm sorry it all went to bilge.' " She winced. "Oh, I wish it were more than that, but I'm sure he said it *all* with that — I love you, I'm proud you were my son. Mr. Butterfield said your father's greatest regret was leaving you and your mother."

"I'll bet. Like he left you and a dozen other kids." He pulled over his plate, took his fork — and a very peculiar look came to his face.

"What is it, Murray?" asked the Shrew anxiously. "Do you need paper? A pencil? Everyone — hush."

"Bilge, eh?" he said. He looked at Clare and said, "Why didn't he give the packet to the bobbies?"

Clare shrugged. "He was waiting for the BV to come for it. Mr. Percy said he didn't trust Scotland Yard. It really seemed to bother Mr. Percy. I suppose he felt that after all the time they'd spent together —"

"But he trusted me," Murray said, gaze drifting.

"What do you mean?"

The gaze came back to Clare. "I know where the packet is."

"But I *looked* there," Clare complained, watching Murray.

"Nope," Murray grunted. "Not here, you didn't. You can't see this place; you can only feel for it."

Murray had removed the companionway ladder and pulled up the boards over the engine, opening up the lower deck in Clare's captain's room. He lay on his stomach along

246

the edge of the opening, reaching into the space as far as he could to an area on the other side of the engine.

"Cylinder head," saying what his hand felt. "Valve cover. Ah. Holding tank."

"What *is* it, exactly?" Clare asked, trying to see through crevices, but it was impossible, he blocked the whole space. Mrs. Shrew held a lantern in one hand and a torch in the other, aiming it fruitlessly at Murray's back.

"It's a fake compartment, made to look like a small holding tank. Bolted right to the engine mount, other side. It's even insulated. Dad had it put in when he started sailin' waters where there's pirates."

"Pirates? These days?" said the Shrew, delighted. "Excellent!"

"He stashed extra money there, in a waterproof pouch." He grunted, and pulled up his hand. The Shrew shined the torch on it; it was covered with oily gray-and-green goo.

"Disgusting," said Clare.

"That's bilge," said Murray. He sifted it between his fingers, then shook it away over the open space. "Water rolls around up there in a bad storm. Gets ugly. Lemme try again, I ain't done this before. My hand keeps slippin'."

He readjusted himself, and reached farther.

"You can see it if you got a couple of mirrors," he grunted. "Hang on — okay, cover's off." They heard a dull thump. "Yep — there's something inside. It's kinda big. Bigger than his money pouch. I don't know how I'm gonna . . ." He grimaced, strained, and then sat up, sliding something out of the compartment. Mrs. Shrew's torchlight fell upon a cellophane-wrapped bundle.

The three looked at one another.

"Open it," said Clare.

"My hands are dirty." He held it out to her. "You open it."

She reverently took the bundle with both hands.

Murray's father, and her own, had died to keep it safe.

"We must get it to William Percy immediately," she said softly.

"It's quite late," Mrs. Shrew said. "Don't you think tomorrow is a better idea?" She added a bit reluctantly, "I saw the light on over there, and I know Mr. Percy is talking with that man. I don't wish to interrupt. I am sure it's doing the captain good, the man talk. Always did my Cecil good. I'd run him down to the pub on a blue day."

"I won't let him spend another night

wondering where it is." She smoothed her hand over it. "All his hope is in this packet. Hope for America to wake up."

Then Clare stilled and looked up, listening.

"What was that?" Mrs. Shrew said sharply.

It came again, a sliding thump, not from above but from the side — sounded as though something was bumping up against Maggie's starboard bow.

"What on earth?" said the Shrew, steadying herself.

Clare shoved the packet into Murray's hands. "Hurry — put it back."

"Where's my teakettle," Mrs. Shrew murmured, turning into the galley.

Murray dropped to his stomach and went to work.

The next noise came from the stern, port side. Heart racing, Clare stared at the curved wall of her cabin. She could feel the vibration of whoever was there. What were they doing? She whirled — that thumping slide at the starboard bow again. Noises from opposite places at the same time.

There were at least two out there.

"Quickly, Murray."

The companion hatch ladder was lying on its side. She started for it. She had to secure the hatch, but couldn't reach it without —

She grabbed the captain's table to steady herself. "Did you feel that?" she whispered. "They've cut the anchor."

Murray's arm was deep in the compartment, his face red with effort. "There — it's back." He reached for a compartment board.

She turned to him. "Murray, whatever happens, they must not get that packet. Your father gave his life for it."

The *Maggie Bright* gave a terrific lurch, and Clare fell sideways into the engine's open compartment.

So Clare Childs was the daughter of Arthur Vance, one of the few men William Percy had truly admired. How interesting.

"Of course, it seemed vain to me at the time," Captain Elliott was saying. "I likely said as much. But now I'm glad. It really captured him."

William wished Clare had known Arthur. And he wished Arthur had known her.

"He shook the hand of King George, once, when he inspected the regiments. Wish my wife could've seen that. She was there, in spirit. Always with Jamie in spirit."

Arrogant and insufferable became eccentric and tolerable, the more you got to know him. You began to suspect that something else lay beneath all the smug trappings of a fashionable expat. Something did.

"Yes," William said, because something was expected of him. "Handsome lad."

Captain Elliott replaced the picture frame on the shelf. "There's the cot for you, Mr. Percy, over there. Mrs. Shrewsbury's very clever; she's got the place all kitted out. Right up to specs. Look there." He pointed to a line of gas masks, hanging on pegs. "And there's the list of who should be in here. Look at that neat handwriting. She's a retired schoolteacher. Of course, Minor Roberts came and crossed his name off. He doesn't like his name on anything. Lives in that old river tug, year-round. Dodgy old sod."

The way Clare came straight for him at the police station. The way she cried when looking at the picture of Erich.

Let him find us holding high the picture of Erich von Wechsler as proof that his own people *would not have his ways.* So emphatic. So uncomfortably demonstrative.

It had been so long since William felt any hope.

Without the army, Hitler would crush them. But to be crushed with hope was far different than to be crushed with despair.

251

Fred told him today that it would take a miracle to save the army, and William wasn't sure he believed in miracles; but for the first time in a long time he felt hope, and if it wasn't hope *exactly,* because he wasn't even sure what that felt like, then it was a lessening of despair; and that alone felt like a miracle.

Things felt lighter around her.

She said things and displayed things that William never could. Freely. Effortlessly. It was another thing about Arthur Vance that he had come to admire. Now that was something to think about: were character traits genetic?

"Who the devil's out at this time of night?" said Captain Elliott, and went to the door.

"What do you mean?"

"That's a boat engine," he said over his shoulder. "A big one."

After a heartbeat, William ran after him, cursing himself for a fool.

We have no allies.

We are alone.

The BEF is gone. Vanished, you see, by the man who cast the spell.

Then a grandmother ran with a pistol, and the pistol became a teakettle, and there was a smashed teacup and a white-bandaged hand and Clare put a kiss on the palm.

Someone was shaking her.

Clare tried to open her eyes. "Murray . . ."

As consciousness came, so did an awareness of pain. Something hurt. She wasn't sure what. "Murray?"

A wave of nausea, oh how she hated to throw up, if she could just get some ginger ale . . .

"Where are the papers, Miss Childs?"

A foreign accent.

Her eyelids fluttered, she tried hard to open them. "What papers?"

"Arthur Vance came aboard with them. I was watching when he did."

She rolled to the side and vomited. The action sent out shock waves of pain. She clutched her side. Surely a rib was broken.

She opened her eyes, fought to keep them open.

"We are on our way to a warehouse in London. You will save us the trouble of tearing apart this boat board by board if you simply produce the papers. It is a nice boat. A beautiful boat. I am sure it is worth a lot of money."

Waldemar Klein stood over her.

"I have no interest in you or your companions. Give us the papers, and we will

253

cut you loose."

She was lying on the couch that lined the port side of the living area. She tried to sit up, but nausea and pain kept her down.

"Where is Murray? Where's Mrs. Shrew?"

"I'm here, Clare," said Murray, somewhere behind Klein.

"You will not speak," said Klein over his shoulder. Clare looked to see Murray at the dinette, a man in dark clothing with a gun standing beside him.

"Are you all right?" Clare said. His mouth was bleeding. "Where's the Shrew?"

"They locked her up."

The man in dark clothing struck Murray, and Clare cried out.

"You will not speak," Klein said calmly. He turned to Clare. "The papers."

"I don't know what you're talking about."

He struck Clare.

Murray lunged from the table for Klein. The other man tackled Murray, scuffled with him, struck his head with his fist, and then yanked a dazed Murray to his feet and threw him back to the dinette. Klein pulled out a gun, and aimed it at Murray.

"No!" Clare screamed.

The gun came around and pointed at Clare's face.

"You do and I'll kill you!" Murray

shouted.

And Waldemar Klein smiled.

He turned to Murray. "Where are the papers?"

"What papers?" Murray said.

His eyes on Murray, Klein kept the gun pointed at Clare's head. Then he lowered it, aiming at her leg, and pulled the trigger.

"Murray . . ."

Banging, pounding, and somewhere Mrs. Shrew was screaming.

She reached for a place of fiery pain.

She opened her eyes. She was looking at the port bookshelves, above the couch. *Murder on the Orient Express. Jane Eyre.*

A clatter of boards — Murray had opened the engine compartment.

"Don't give it to him."

It's all the hope William Percy has.

"*A*, I got a sister, now." His voice was shaking. "*B*, I ain't gonna risk her for some papers."

But we have no allies.

We are alone.

"William Percy has a sister too," she heard herself say. "She has Down syndrome."

Those papers are meant to . . . make an impression . . . cause a fuss. . . . She couldn't recall what they were meant for, she was sinking fast, but knew they were very important.

"That is interesting, he has a sister like that," Waldemar Klein commented thoughtfully. "Too bad."

She roused a bit. "Too bad for you. Those papers will show the —"

"Those papers will one day show how to solve problems like the inspector's sister. For now, they are pearls cast before swine. The Führer will be misunderstood."

"We understand him at last," Clare murmured. She'd not last long, so she tried one last time, clear as she could: "Murray — your father died to keep them from him."

"*A,* he was your father, too." A dull thud as the lid came off the fake holding tank. "*B,* given the same choice, our old man woulda picked you."

17

Time passed, and things happened, though she wasn't sure what.

She heard voices, and they were close. She wanted to assure them all was fine, for these were *good* voices, and that with vision, courage, and singularity of purpose she'd rise from this bed in no time.

It was just that she couldn't *fully* wake up. She was in some kind of pressed-down, sluggish stupor. She couldn't even open her eyes.

"What're your intentions?" said one of the good voices. "Maybe I ain't sayin' it right. I ain't got practice bein' a brother. You got references? I gotta ask around. We ain't got an old man to do the vettin'. This is old-man territory. Maybe the Fitz can —"

"What the devil are you talking about?" said another good voice.

"You like her, bobby."

"Don't be ridiculous."

"Yeah? I saw how you was when you got there. How long you known each other?"

"We've just *met.*"

"Oh, don't gimme that, frosty pants."

"Look, I quite assure you —"

"Boy, I can't wait to get home. 'I quite assure you.' My friends don't talk like that. Father Fitz'll —"

"*Fadda* Fitz." A snort. *"My* friends don't talk like *that.*"

"You got friends? Ha! You make the *room* cold, bobby boy. I can draw, but that's some feat."

"That's quite enough," said Mrs. Shrew. "She may hear you. I think she's waking up."

"I must go," said William Percy quickly.

"No, no, please wait!" Mrs. Shrew called. "I'm sure she'd like to see you."

No, she wouldn't, Clare thought bleakly, and stopped trying to wake up.

She couldn't bear to look at him. The packet was gone.

The last thing she saw was Murray handing the packet to Waldemar Klein.

"There she is," someone sang.

Clare opened her eyes to a rather alarming close-up of Mrs. Shrew, sprouting bright blue-eyed sunshine. She withdrew, satisfied.

Clare sat up a little and looked about. Maybe she had dreamed that earlier conversation. Murray and William Percy were not in the room.

It was a private hospital room, clean, bright, orderly. Afternoon light came in at the window. There was a vase full of flowers on a narrow table at the foot of the bed.

"You'll never guess who those are from: a desk sergeant at a police station."

"How long have I been here?"

"This is day three. They've had you on entirely too much morphine. I shouldn't wonder it feels like a week. I told them to back down the grains by two or three and give you a chance to *feel* pain and wake up."

"Actually, I could use a few more grains." Curious word. That's what Agatha Christie called units of morphine. She didn't know the medical profession did. Never had a chance to find out. "What have I missed?"

"You had surgery to remove a bullet."

"I think I remember that."

"Good, because there is *so* much to tell you. All of London is in an uproar."

Clare stared. "Because *Maggie Bright* was —"

"Oh no, no, no." She reached for a newspaper and her reading glasses. "They've printed some of the king's speech. My dear, brace yourself: the king has called Britain to a *day of prayer.*"

She came fully awake. "He's done *what*?"

"It's true. For the BEF and our doomed nation. The balloon has gone up, my dear, and all is black as night." She pulled up the newspaper and looked through her glasses. "Listen to this, it's right from the king's speech: 'Let no one be mistaken: it is no mere territorial conquest that our enemies are seeking. It is the overthrow, complete and final, of this Empire and of everything for which it stands, and after that, the conquest of the world.' "

"He said that?" Clare breathed in awe.

"Oh, this is verbatim. I heard the speech, *as* he spoke it, *with* my own ears. The nurses have a wireless down the hall. It was quite a moment to share with my countrymen."

"I'll bet it was."

Mrs. Shrew laid down the paper, and lowered her glasses. "Whenever has a monarch called our people to *prayer*? To a *day* of prayer? Do you know what this means?"

"That all hope is lost for the BEF," said Clare, her head falling back on the pillow.

"Rubbish! Why do we assume that to *resort* to prayer is some kind of death knell? Is it not to prevent such a death knell? No,

I meant this: King George has *acknowledged God.*"

"Well . . . we *are* a Christian nation."

"If that were true, how many of us go to church? Isn't that what one does when one is a Christian? For the 'fellowship of the saints,' to learn how to love people, and how to stop being annoying, and live a good useful life and all that? But who actually goes to church these days? Monarchs and old ladies, to keep up a good show."

"*You* go to church."

"I'm an old lady."

"Keeping up a show, then?"

"No, I am not." She drew herself up. "I *believe.*"

"Ow." Clare adjusted her leg, wincing. But she'd have to assess injuries and shriek for more grains of morphine later — there was too much to find out. "When is this day of prayer?"

"Sunday, the twenty-sixth. I am *lightheaded.* Cecil must be dancing. I wonder if he'll see the prayers ascend. What a sight that would be, if they were actually visible. I'd planned to go to services at Westminster Abbey, as this occasion seems to demand, but upon further reflection I feel it quite appropriate to fall in with my usual gang at St. Mark's." A very small smile, and:

"Captain John wishes to go. For his son."

It was the first time — that Clare could recall — Mrs. Shrew had referred to him as something other than "that man."

"He told me something interesting. A man at the pub said he'd never go hat in hand to God that way. And Captain John said, 'For my son, I'll go. Hat in hand.' It was quite poignant."

"What day is it today?" Clare asked.

"Today is the twenty-fourth."

"Good. I should be up and around by the twenty-sixth. I shall join the masses."

"With a shot-up leg and a broken rib?" Mrs. Shrew raised a brow. "And after all the time I've tried to get you to go to St. Mark's . . ."

"Well, this is for England. And for the BEF."

Mrs. Shrew softened and patted Clare's hand. "Yes, it is. Good show, my dear."

"Now." Clare tried to control the stomach flutters and braced herself. "What's the other news?"

Mrs. Shrew snatched the newspaper and peered through her glasses without putting them on. "They're making plans to evacuate the children. Some have already arrived in London from Dover. And listen to the response from Mass-Observation regarding the king's speech: 'Just what was wanted,' said a man from Bristol. Others said, 'A grand effort . . . greatly appreciated.' " She snatched another newspaper. "This is from the *Daily Telegraph:* 'Now is the time for the British people to show the stuff of which they are made. . . .' Hm, hm . . . ah, here: 'Hitler's peace propaganda before the war was directly designed to spread terror. Duty calls us to close ranks at home against the slightest sign of national disunity.' " She thumped the paper. "Close ranks! That is proper journalism!"

"Mrs. Shrew. Not that news."

She lowered the paper, and looked at Clare.

"Not that I can bear to hear it."

"Bear to hear what?" said Mrs. Shrew, perplexed.

"That Klein got away with the documents. That all of William Percy's hope is gone."

"But my dear," Mrs. Shrew protested, "he *didn't* get away with the documents. Though he did get *away.* And that did provoke a cascade of despair in the young detective inspector. *Despair* puts it mildly — Mr. Percy wanted to *kill* that man. He would have preferred the loss of the documents over the loss of the criminal. He told me so. I've gotten to know him, you see. He's been

263

by to visit you every day."

Clare reached for Mrs. Shrew's hand and held it tightly. "The documents are safe?"

Mrs. Shrew smiled and squeezed Clare's hand. "They are safe."

The nurse gave Clare a dose of morphine, took her temperature and frowned at the result — a frown was automatic with this nurse — then plumped the pillows, and left.

At Clare's anxious request, Mrs. Shrew had gone home to the *Maggie Bright* to make sure she was truly secured in her berth at Elliott's Boatyard. But when Clare had suggested hiring a cleaning crew to clean up the vomit and blood, Mrs. Shrew got a high and formidable light in her eyes and said, "Rubbish. That man has already dug up the anchor, and has *splayed* the lines back together. Or whatever the word is. Maybe *spliced.* It's quite nautical, and it's an art form. Fascinating to watch. Anyway, the two of us plus Murray makes three to put things to rights. Vomit and blood, nonsense; I've cleaned up buckets of the stuff as a schoolteacher, and I've just the remedy to get the blood out of the couch cushions."

Clare was shot in the thigh, just above the knee. The surgeon had removed the bullet and asked Murray if he thought Clare would want it for a nice little souvenir since it was a German bullet. Murray punched him, was escorted from the hospital, and was asked not to return.

A light tap came at the door, and it came open a few inches.

Looking very uncomfortable, it was William Percy.

Clare sat up, surprised. "Why, Mr. Percy. Do come in."

"I've brought someone with me. I can never say no, the little vixen. I think Fred put her up to it." He looked down at a small someone behind the door. "Did Uncle Fred put you up to this?"

A little girl with blonde hair, blue almond-shaped eyes, a pink dress, and a white sweater peered around William Percy, clutching the hem of his suit coat.

"It's all right." He gave her a very gentle push. "Go on then. That's Miss Clare. She's got something for you, Miss Clare."

"You must be Cecy," Clare said warmly, holding out her hand.

"So you know my vixen?" Percy frowned. "I cannot trust Fred."

Cecy went shyly to the bed, sucking on two fingers. She held out something with her other hand, and Clare displayed her palm. Cecy dropped a sticky sweetie into it.

William waved to get Clare's attention. "You don't have to eat that," he mouthed, shaking his head, eyes wide. "Heaven knows where it's been."

Clare regarded Cecy, and popped the slightly furry sweet into her mouth. She concentrated, and then rolled her eyes. "Oh — absolutely delicious! How did you know peppermint's my favorite?" The little girl smiled around the fingers. "Thank you *ever* so much. I get *no* sweets in here. Isn't that tragic? I dearly love them." She followed Cecy's gaze, which had wandered to the vase of flowers. "Aren't they lovely? You can play with them. Mr. Percy, could you please take them down for her? Perhaps you can make a garden, Cecy."

"Are you sure?" Percy said doubtfully. "I guarantee, they won't look the same when she's done with them."

"Of course I'm sure."

He took the vase, glancing at the card. "Sergeant Blake?" He snorted. "Yes, you did seem to make an impression on him. Too bad he's old enough to be your father." To Cecy, he said, "As for you, my little pink poppet, why don't you sit here." She sat on the floor, and held her hands up for the vase. He set it in front of her. She looked

266

very small and sweet next to it, and Clare smiled.

"All right, Cecy-Peacey. Take them out one by one. Like this." She watched him solemnly. "Give it a go." She carefully selected a daisy, and laid it on the ground. She looked to him for approval. "Oh, well done. Try again." She did so. "You've mastered it. Go on, then. Make us a lovely garden." He rose, and watched her for a moment.

"Please sit down, Mr. Percy," Clare said.

He took Mrs. Shrew's chair near Clare, and pulled it out a little from the bed. He settled in and watched Cecy. He looked uncomfortable. He brushed at a surely non-existent spot on his trousers, and just when it seemed neither of them could find something to say, commented, "You *can* call me William."

"All right then. William. I'm warning you: I'm on morphine."

"Excellent. I'll extract your worst secret and blackmail you later."

Clare laughed.

"Of course, I'll wait until you're better. Wouldn't be sporting."

She laughed again, a little too hard. The morphine *was* quite pleasant. It not only took the pain away, it made Clare feel rather carefree.

She sobered; it also made her feel not quite in control.

"I'd rather have the tiniest edge of pain," she said distinctly. "It grounds me. I do not wish to abdicate control."

"Of course you don't. Especially you."

She narrowed her eyes. "I'm not sure if that's an insult."

"On the contrary," William said, not taking his eyes from Cecy.

Clare turned away.

"What's the matter?" he asked, his tone still gentle.

"I wish you weren't being nice to me."

"Whatever do you mean?"

"It makes me feel dreadful."

"I don't understand."

"I don't either." She laid an arm across her face.

Good heavens, what troubled her? This pain in her chest, and the sort of cry that rose within — it was the same as when her parents died, when she had cried herself deaf. Oh, please, *not* in front of this man. . . .

And then she realized it was because of this man that she wanted to cry. The instant Clare saw Cecy, this sweet little girl put a face on Erich von Wechsler.

"I'm on morphine. All must be excused,

even this, when I say that I —" a little gasping sob for which she hated herself — "I'm so very sorry Klein got away."

Clare heard a little sound at the side of the bed. She pulled away her arm. Cecy stood beside her, offering a daisy.

Clare gave a small involuntary cry, and sat up, wiping tears. "Oh, you darling thing!" She took the flower. "Thank you, Cecy." She smelled it, pretended it smelled heavenly. "You've made me feel ever so much better."

Cecy seemed pleased, and then shyly displayed her dress. "I like pink."

"So do I."

"This is pink."

Clare dashed at a tear. "So it is. Lovely sweater, too — a little kitty cat on it." She touched the appliqué.

Cecy cupped her hands around her mouth. "Kitty cat says *meow.*"

"So it does."

She went back to her garden. She squatted over it, surveying, then sat on the floor and began arranging.

Clare twirled the daisy by the stem. "I'd feel eviscerated, too."

"I really can't trust Butterfield," William said coldly.

"By the way, I need to thank you." Clare

snatched a tissue from the bedside table and pressed it to her nose. "Mrs. Shrew said you saved my life."

"*That* is an exaggeration," he snapped.

"Not according to the Shrew. You stopped the bleeding. You took me to the hospital. She didn't even know which one, you were gone so fast."

Eyes on Cecy, he adjusted himself in the chair and said angrily, "Well, you wouldn't have been hurt in the first place had it entered my thick skull that Klein could come by water. Such an *obvious* error."

"I didn't think of it either."

"You weren't supposed to; it's not your job."

"Not my job to think?"

"You know what I mean." Less heated, and back to his discomfort, he said, "It's why I'm here. I wanted to apologize."

"For what?"

"For . . . you know." He impatiently crossed his legs. Not for a moment did he take his eyes from Cecy. "Putting you in danger like that." As if the next bit would cost him the most, he said stiffly, "It was unprofessional in the extreme."

She stared at him. "You saved the documents, you saved my boat, and you saved me. That is hardly unprofessional."

270

He steadfastly watched Cecy.

"Oh, William, don't be ridiculous. Klein had a river tug, a crack team of bad men, and a warehouse in London ready to tear Maggie apart. Bad men *will* occasionally outthink us. My uncle did it all the time. And just look at Hitler." She was starting to feel better. Chiding him seemed to do the trick. "Now. Mrs. Shrew was locked up and only heard scuffles and grunts. I don't like that word, *grunts,* but it's what she used. By the time she got out, you were gone with me, and Klein and the rest had vanished. She later tracked you down for details but said you were evasive."

"What's there to say?" said William, clipped and cold. "There was a fight; I grabbed the packet; he got away. Why do women always need the nth degree of detail?"

Cecy got up and went to William and climbed into his lap. She settled in as if she was accustomed to doing so, and he wrapped his arms about her and held her close. He rested his chin on her head.

"Cecy-Peacey is tired," he said, rocking with her gently. His voice had gone low and rich. "Aren't you?"

"No."

He pulled back to look at her. "You're

quite sure about that?"

"Where's Mummy?"

"Right. Time to get little vixen home. Up we go. Say bye-bye to Miss Clare."

She slid from his lap and went to Clare. She patted her arm.

Clare smiled. "Thank you for the sweetie, sweetie."

He nodded at Clare for good-bye, and said to Cecy, "Come along, then." He shepherded her to the door.

"There's to be a prayer service at Westminster Abbey," she suddenly said.

"So I've heard." He paused at the door, and said wryly, "Rather unsettling, isn't it?"

"Well, that's what *I* thought. Mrs. Shrew seems to think it a positive thing. Would you take me?"

Now serious, he said, "Clare, don't be foolish. It's too soon. You need to heal."

"I can't think of a better place." Then, "I *must* go. For Captain Elliott's son. For the BEF." The little girl in the pink dress plucked petals one by one from a daisy. "For Erich von Wechsler." She lifted her chin. "If you don't come to get me, I shall go alone and will likely fall."

For the first time since she'd met the man, William Percy smiled. It was quite charming, and produced an odd little *lift* in her stomach.

"Well, we can't have that," he said. "Where shall I pick you up? Here?"

Goodness, that smile. It was gone but she felt it. Or maybe it was the morphine.

"Rubbish. I'll be home before the sun sets."

"That's the morphine talking."

"Perhaps. I feel bold."

"Fancy a dash to the front with a pistol?"

"I'm glad I *wasn't* drugged when I said that," she said haughtily. "It came from my heart."

"Bye-bye, Miss Clare," said Cecy.

Clare melted, and blew her a kiss. "Bye-bye, darling. Visit me again, will you? I'll take you for a ride on my boat."

"See you Sunday." William nodded, and they left.

Clare lay back on the pillows and stared at the ceiling.

A strong, cold man tenderly holding a little child.

Is there anything more fiercely attractive?

18

"I'm very happy not to be the one who makes the decisions, but I'd at *least* like to know what is going on. Surely there is some sort of trap waiting for the Jerries — we'll fool them somehow, we'll pull something off. The leaders have *something* up their sleeves."

The seven men trudged along in usual formation, Balantine and Grayling out front, Milton in the middle, Jamie and Baylor next, with Curtis and Griggs bringing up the rear. They moved through a long, grassy field under a fine, unseasonably sunny sky. At least, it was unseasonable for May in England; maybe here in Belgium, or France, or wherever they were, it was just right. A lively breeze shook the leaves in the trees, birds dipped and soared. Jamie shook his head. Hard to believe men were killing each other under a sky like that.

"Haven't we *historically* allowed advances

such as these, only to stick 'em in the ribs as they passed by?" said Baylor.

"This is a defeat," Griggs announced. "Pure and simple. Whole army is retreating. There is nothing up their sleeves, Baylor, except hopefully a plan to get us home."

"Well, you don't have to say *defeat* so well enunciated," Baylor said over his shoulder. He moodily readjusted his pack. "You hope it's all worth it. You hope someone's not mucking things up. Do you know that the German Army has not reached the English Channel — by land, at any rate — until now? Not once in the Great War, twenty years ago, did they get this far. Does that alarm anyone else?"

Talk fell once more to the retreat, and nothing new was said.

"All I know is a *red* Very light followed by a *green* Very light is supposed to signify withdrawal."

"Yes, but they change it up to cause confusion."

"We're the confused ones."

" 'Defenders ordered to disengage and head for Dunkirk.' That's the last I heard."

"Where *is* everyone else?"

"We could be outflanked even now, heading straight into a German ambush."

"There is no one else. They made it home

and they're laughing their guts out at the sods left behind. Your girlfriend left you for a victor."

Nothing new, except what Milton could add: "To mischief swift. Earth felt the wound."

"All right, then, Milty? Do you know, he seems a little better today," said Baylor, pleased. "Don't know how that can be, all this walking. All this not eating and not drinking. I feel like an empty cartridge."

Talk fell once more to food and drink.

"Where's our tea? The British Army marches on tea."

"Or hard liquor."

"All I want is a boiled egg. And salt."

"A nice, lovely plate of chips and fried fish."

"And salt."

"I'd eat bully beef and be grateful."

"My mother's Christmas pudding. I'm desperate enough for my aunt Isabel's Christmas pudding."

"When's the last time he had water?" Baylor asked of Milton. He took off his helmet and wiped sweat from behind both ears. A red impression circled his forehead. He took off his glasses and wiped the sides of his nose. He tucked up the helmet straps and put it back on, then refit the glasses.

"That would be the last time any of us had water," said Jamie. "And I can't remember."

"At least things aren't so bad now, taking the back route," said Balantine over his shoulder. "We have no refugees to deal with."

"I believe that was my idea," said Griggs.

"No, but we do have farmers who either want to kill us or refuse us food or water," said Baylor. "Still can't believe the bloke who wouldn't let us drink from his well. What was his problem? What would that bloody cost him?"

"No clue," said Jamie. "But then I'm still not sure if we're in Belgium or France."

Suddenly Balantine halted and held up his fist. The squad stopped, and eased to a knee. He watched and listened, a little longer than usual.

Things *were* awfully quiet, and Balantine seemed on edge. Presently, he gave the okay and they resumed the march.

"What I want to know is who is holding the perimeters," said Baylor. "By some luck of the draw, some random turn of fate's wheel, here we are because *we* were not on the outskirts when the balloon went up. They are buggered, and we are not."

"I'd rather have someone else buggered

than me," said Griggs.

"What will happen to them?" Baylor wondered. "Will they be taken prisoner? Killed?" He added darkly, "Both?"

"I can understand a fighting withdrawal better than this," Jamie muttered.

"*They* are the ones fighting. Giving us a chance to get to the sea. But what will happen to them?"

"They're doing their duty," Grayling said over his shoulder.

"How many of us will get to Dunkirk by their duty? Who will be left behind?"

"Shut it, Baylor," said Griggs. "You think too much."

"I'm with Griggs on that," said Grayling. "Our orders are Dunkirk. That's it. Stop thinking." He added dryly, "You're a soldier, you're not supposed to think."

"There's a very dark truth in that," said Balantine cheerfully.

"It just unnerves me, no communication." Baylor pushed up his glasses. "We are cut off. How do we know where things stand?"

"Baylor, *shut up,*" said Balantine, now walking backward. "It doesn't do any of us —"

A dull pocking of bullets, and Grayling fell.

A heartbeat of shock, then all was confusion and shouting and trampling.

"Take cover!" Balantine roared, grabbing Grayling by the collar.

Jamie hauled Milton down beside him, looking wildly about. Cover? What cover?

"Where are they shooting from?" shouted Griggs.

"Get down! Take cover!"

"Can anyone see? Where are they shooting from?"

"Seest thou what rage transports our adversary . . ."

"Where's the shooter?" Griggs bellowed.

"Baylor, get over here," Balantine shouted. Hand on his helmet, Baylor ran at a crouch to where Balantine had dragged Grayling, a place with not much cover at all, just a few low bushes. He unshouldered his kit and knelt over Grayling.

"Over there!" Jamie shouted to Griggs, and pointed to the east side of the field at a collection of white beech trees. Behind one huddled a gray-helmeted form. Milton tried to stand up and see. Jamie hauled him back down.

Griggs dropped low and took aim. But his rifle jammed, and cursing, he brought it to his knee, frantically slamming the bolt with the heel of his hand.

"Griggs!" Jamie tossed over his Bren.

Griggs threw aside his rifle, grabbed the Bren, flicked off the safety, set it to multiple bursts, took aim, and fired on the copse of trees.

Jamie saw movement and shouted, "Over there, left!"

Griggs trained the Bren left and gave a burst.

What had they walked into? A recon squad or a whole regiment?

Another muffled pocking of bullets.

"We've got to get out of the open!" said Griggs. He looked about, then pointed west to a slope across the clearing, maybe fifty yards away. "Other side of that hill! Curtis, when I start shooting, get them over there and then turn and cover me. Move!"

"He's not going anywhere," said Baylor of Grayling, sitting back. "He's shot in the chest."

Balantine tore off his helmet. "Grayling!"

"Griggs, get them out," Grayling said thickly, waving him off.

"We're not leaving you!" Balantine shouted.

Grayling felt for his .38 sidearm, and before anyone could move, put it under his chin and pulled the trigger.

After several heartbeats of shock, Griggs snatched Balantine's helmet out of his hands and shoved it on his head. He pushed him into Baylor, and then went to a knee with the Bren.

"Curtis, get them moving! Now, now!" He hauled the Bren to his eye and fired. "Move!"

"Come on!" shouted Curtis.

Jamie grabbed Milton, and ran.

"Mercy first and last shall brightest shine," said the captain softly.

No one told him to shut up. They knew he spoke of Grayling.

They knew that these strange Milton words were just for him, and with them, the captain told them what sort of soldier was he.

They had taken cover behind the hill, and when no one pursued, pushed on northwest mile after mile until twilight. On the outskirts of a deserted town, they fell in for the night in a long concrete greenhouse, with a slanted ceiling open to the sky. The moon, a few days past full, shone brightly.

The men had fallen in exhausted, some sitting against the concrete wall, some against the dry trough running down the center of the greenhouse. Only the captain now stood, gazing at the moon.

"With good still overcoming evil, accomplishing great things . . ."

Balantine dragged off his helmet.

It was Grayling's benediction, spoken in moonlight over a grave they never had a chance to dig.

"For so I formed them free, and free they must remain. God toward thee hath done his part." All watched one hand come slightly from his side, saw his fingers stretch and reach out a few inches toward them, as if to bless, as if to commission. "Do thine. And to the end persisting, safe arrive." The hand held, then relaxed at his side.

"He wants us to get to Dunkirk," Baylor said softly.

"Yes, I think we've worked that out," Griggs said, in a mild return to sourness. He began to take apart the Bren.

"He knows Grayling bought us time," Jamie said to Balantine. "He could easily have said 'Grayling toward thee hath done his part.' "

Grayling and Balantine had been in the same unit for eighteen months, before the war began.

"He would've died of that chest wound in an hour," Baylor said to Balantine. "He did a brave thing, mate. I'll never forget it."

Balantine put his helmet on, and pulled it low over his face. He wrapped his arms about himself, and slid a little lower on the wall.

"Tomorrow we strike north and don't stop until we hit the sea," said Griggs, cleaning the Bren by moonlight. He'd offered it back to Jamie earlier, but Jamie told him to keep it since he was a better shot. It was Jamie's way of saying, Well done, and I'm glad you're a better soldier than you are a mate. "Elliott, take first watch. Curtis, you're next. I'll take last."

Exhausted, hungry, thirsty to the point of torment, Jamie made himself get up. He followed the captain's gaze to the moon.

Month after month of others doing the thinking for you, others telling you where to go, what to do, and suddenly you're cut away and cut off, floating free with no direction, no orders, nothing but confusion. Where was everyone? What was the overall situation? Did anyone at home know what sort of straits the BEF was in?

"We've got to make it home," Jamie suddenly said, looking at the men. "Who will defend them?"

"Oh, we'll make it," said Griggs. "I'm too angry not to. Now get your arse out on watch. The rest of you, get some sleep. That includes you, Captain . . . whoever you are."

"Jacobs," Jamie said, watching him watch

the moon. "He told me the other night."

"He did?" said Baylor, sitting up, looking from Milton to Jamie. "What else did he say?"

"That was it. One word." He touched Milton's arm. "Come on, Captain Jacobs. Get some rest."

He checked the captain's bandage but found he didn't need to change it; the wound was giving off far less fluid and actually looked a bit better. He took him to a corner and got him settled in, then went outside to look for a likely spot to keep watch.

He checked his wristwatch for when to rouse Curtis, and then settled snug into the split of a tree to gaze for moving shadows in this foreign, moonwashed landscape.

Did those at home know that Belgium was caving in? Did they know that France was being overrun? Did they know the army was running for its life?

The Empire responds to the King's call. And at Westminster Abbey, heart of the Empire, the statesmen, the soldiers, the ambassadors, and hundreds of ordinary men and women join the mighty congregation. Her Majesty Queen Wilhelmina of the Netherlands arrives a few moments before Their Majesties.

No one here today could foresee the grave news that has come from Belgium. All the more, it is well for us to show the world that we still believe in divine guidance. In the laws of Christianity, may we find inspiration and faith from this solemn day.

— PATHÉ NEWSREEL

There was a short service of Intercession and Prayer in Westminster Abbey on May 26. The English are loath to expose their feelings, but in my stall in the choir I could feel the pent-up, passionate emotion, and also the fear of the congregation, not of death or wounds or material loss, but of defeat and the final ruin of Britain.

— WINSTON CHURCHILL, The Second World War, Volume II: Their Finest Hour

Nothing but a miracle can
save the BEF now.
— DIARY ENTRY OF GENERAL ALAN BROOKE,
May 23, 1940

We shall have lost practically all our
trained soldiers by the next few days —
unless a miracle appears to help us.
— DIARY ENTRY OF GENERAL
SIR EDMUND IRONSIDE, *May 25, 1940*

19

Clare wasn't home before the sun set. In fact, to her seething chagrin she had to send word to William Percy to meet her at the hospital early Sunday morning, not at the boatyard.

"You look very white," he said with no other greeting than that, when he came in and found her sitting ready on the edge of the bed. He took off his hat, and shut the door rather firmly to show he was perturbed. "What are they thinking to let you go? You looked better a few days ago."

"It's just nerves. I'm keyed up." She frowned. "This is a day of historic importance — why aren't *you* keyed up? It's a day we officially acknowledge that *all is not good*. And I don't care if it's bad form to say that out loud."

"Clare, you don't look well. You can pray right here. I'll get you some beads. Or whatever they use."

"That's Catholic. My family is Protestant. Anyway, I have to go. I *know* it. I *feel* it. I want to be with people at a time like this."

After a moment, he admitted, "I do too."

"Do you believe in God?"

"I don't know, really. I believe in people."

"That's why I want to be there." She found she had taken hold of the locket, and let go before William called attention to this fact.

But there was something else. There was some other reason she wanted to go, but it felt elusive and, just when she thought she'd caught hold of it, ephemeral; she saw in her mind an image of Captain John with his hat in his hand, but it vanished before she made sense of it.

"The Shrew and Captain John are going to St. Mark's together." She smiled impishly. "An interesting first date, don't you think? Look — she was a dear, and brought me some proper clothing." She smoothed her favorite pale-blue skirt.

"So they *are* letting you leave?" he said doubtfully.

She was glad Mrs. Shrew had also brought some makeup, as well as the smart hat he had wanted to pinch for his sister when he knocked her to the pavement.

"Of course. They just took my temperature

and I've passed muster. I also told them Scotland Yard would escort me, which of course impressed them. If I do well this morning, they say I should be able to go home this evening." She added wryly, "You must have made your mark on the nursing staff — when I said who would be escorting me, Detective Inspector William Percy, they went all fluttery. You're quite well known here. How is that, in a hospital? You've taken multiple wounds, then, for king and country?"

"Must be the papers."

"What papers?"

He looked at his watch. "Clare, we really have no time for chitchat; the service starts at ten. How's your leg?"

She looked down. "They've bound it tightly, as I asked. Sutures are a bit sore, and I can't put much weight on it, but those crutches will suit fine. The nurse just brought them. Could you hand them to me, please?"

"Are you on morphine?" he asked lightly, walking over to the crutches.

"Certainly not!" she declared. "I will *not* attend church on morphine. I'm sure I'll want it by the spoonful for lunch, but I intend to do my beseeching with a clear head. My prayers will be more potent that way."

He chuckled. "Good girl. Well, I've heard there's a queue all the way to the Houses of Parliament. Perhaps they'll take pity on a cripple." He gave her the crutches. "Thanks for getting shot, might land us a decent seat."

"All the way to Parliament?" she said, rising from the bed, fitting the crutches under her arms — and hiding not only a rush of faintness, but a wince. Oh dear. She didn't worry too much about the leg, but could already feel a nasty pull on her left side. The doctors suspected not one but two broken ribs. She had a fleeting second thought about the morphine, and banished it for heresy. Some things ought not be done in a church. She'd pass under that arch and every saint in heaven would fall upon her for an addict. She'd just have to bear it, and felt sure the saints would cheer her determination for clearheaded beseechment.

William said, "I've heard Queen Wilhelmina from the Netherlands will be there, besides Churchill, the entire cabinet, the Admiralty, and of course, the king and queen. Movie stars, too. Most people are likely going just to see all the celebrities."

"At least they're going," said Clare fervently, a sudden pang on her heart. She couldn't bear the thought of Captain John losing his son. He was a boy she'd never met, but he mattered to her because Captain John did. He was the one person to put a face on the entire army for her. "The BEF will need all the prayers they can get. Even from not-quite believers, such as you and I."

He held the door wide for her, and put on his gray felt fedora. "Did your parents go to church?"

And there it came again, the image of Captain John and a hat.

"Clare?"

Captain John vanished.

She realized he was looking at her hand, which clasped the locket.

"Are you all right?" he said sharply. "You're sure you're up for this?"

"Yes, of course." She smiled and let go the locket. "With all my heart."

After days of unseasonable sunshine, the morning was overcast and with just enough snap in the air for Clare to be grateful for the long spring coat Mrs. Shrew had brought.

The queue was long indeed, winding

around the corner and down the road from Westminster Abbey, long past where Clare could see. They waited in line for a very long time before pity *was* taken on Clare by a strap-helmeted policeman who must have recognized William Percy, since he deferred to *him* far more than he conferred pity on Clare — to the point of fawning obsequiousness — and the two were picked up by car from their spot at least a quarter of a mile out, and then escorted to a place just yards from the front of the line, where they waited through the receiving of dignitaries to enter themselves.

"I'll bet everyone wishes they'd been shot," William said, noting the rather peevish looks they received upon assuming their new place in line.

"I've never been more grateful." Some seemed to wonder if they were dignitaries themselves, until they saw Clare's crutches and the wonder turned sour. She felt mildly indignant, and then mildly guilty, but this privileged place did indeed afford a dazzling chance for glimpses of *leaders* and *statesmen* and *royalty*, people she might never see again, all gathered in this one austere and beautiful and historic place . . . all for the purpose of *prayer*. Prayer! These *notables*, who very soon would figuratively (perhaps literally, and certainly publicly) bend the knee before God! No wonder, Mrs. Shrew's astonishment. From the moment Clare and William had joined the queue, she'd felt . . .

"I feel an overwhelming sense of *portent.*" She gazed enraptured at the beautiful, massive building.

"They probably wonder if you're faking it."

"The portent or the injury?"

His lips twitched in that rare smile. "The injury, my dear."

"Oh, I'll happily show off my sutures. The broken rib may be awkward. I may get arrested for exposure."

"Broken rib?" Any suggestion of a smile vanished.

"Or two. From the engine."

"Why didn't I know of this?"

"Don't ever fall on an engine. It's very uncomfortable. Stop looking at me like that. There's nothing they can do. It's not like they can cast it." She clutched his arm. "Look, is that — ?"

Winston Churchill strode past, a leather satchel in one hand and a walking stick in the other.

"How do you think he's suiting?" she asked thoughtfully, watching him go.

"Bit early to tell. Myself, I think he came in the nick of time. I find it interesting that he assumed power on May 10, the very day that Hitler began his western strike. Look what's happened in only two weeks: the swiftest overthrow of Holland imaginable, and now, Belgium and France." He glanced at Westminster Abbey, and muttered, "And you wonder why we're praying . . ."

"Who's that?" Clare pointed at a slightly thick woman who cut a very impressive figure, clad in a long, dark, fur-trimmed cape, wearing a dark, respectable hat, greeted by a frocked bishop holding a program who received her quite respectfully, and ushered her in.

"I think it's —"

"It's Queen Wilhelmina, from Holland," a young woman behind them quickly supplied. "She's here to pray for her country. Isn't that marvelous?" She gazed about, wide-eyed. "Isn't this terribly exciting? All these great people?"

"I can't *believe* it," Clare agreed firmly. "Did you see Churchill?"

"Yes! And look — doesn't that look like Vera Lynn? I *think* it's her."

"Really? Where?" She looked to where the young woman pointed, and agreed that it might be her.

Clare was glad to have someone with whom to share these bits — William seemed positively bored. If not *bored,* then deliberately unimpressed, and it peeved Clare.

As if he overheard her thoughts, he muttered, "Honestly. They're just people, Clare."

"They're *great* people. Churchill is a *leader,* and the leaders have a *great deal of pressure* on themselves."

"They have a job to do, and they'd bloody well do it."

"Well said, guv," mumbled the man standing next to the woman.

"They were elected to do it," William said, as if that settled any issue of greatness.

"Or *born* to do it," said Clare. "In which case, they don't have any choice in the matter."

"True. Either way, they have their duties and we have ours."

"Look — the king and queen!"

Murmurs swept down the queue. Fervent monarchists applauded.

"Oh, I'm so glad Edward abdicated!" said the young woman, a hand pressed to her heart. "Isn't King George handsome? Doesn't the queen suit?"

Their majesties came striding by, looking

quite heroically like anyone else in line. People they passed took off their hats to them. Hats . . .

"Oh, well done! The king's wearing his officer's uniform," the woman said, as if they couldn't see.

Clare put a hand to her cheek. "Look at the queen, how lovely — Mrs. Shrew would *love* that dress, so beautifully feminine. Nothing androgynous about it. Oh, look at those sleeves, look at that hat. It's quite inspiring."

"Inspiring?" William demanded.

"Yes, isn't it just?" said the woman behind them.

"Very much so." Clare turned to her. "She's lovely, and put-together, and —"

"Well, just look how she walks," the woman said.

"Exactly! As if —"

"As if, sod Hitler, I'll carry on if bombs are dropping and I've got a Luger up my nose!"

"Precisely!" Clare beamed at her.

The young woman smiled, and squeezed Clare's arm. "I wish we could sit together. I'm Blanche."

"Clare."

"Never in all my days . . ."

"Mine, either."

"It's all so terribly exciting."

"Horrible, and awful, and monstrous, and perilous enough to provoke something as incredibly momentous as *this* — this calling together of an entire *nation* to prayer, all to bow the knee — but *yes,* exciting. *Very* much so."

"Exactly." Blanche nodded firmly.

"We're *together.*"

"That's *exactly* it."

William made a very small and long-suffering noise. Blanche's husband made something of the same.

"What happened to your leg?" Blanche asked.

"I was shot." It was the first time she said it, and it was most satisfying.

"You never were!"

"By a German spy." She must learn how to say it without that twitch of a smile.

She must work at being offhanded.

Blanche gasped. She clutched Clare's arm. "You're not the one on the Thames? In the boat?"

Clare's composure faltered. She looked at William. "Is it news, then?"

"Is it news?" Blanche squeaked. She pounded her husband on the arm. "It's all over the newsstands! How your houseboat was hijacked by a group of Fifth Columnist

spies planning to bomb Parliament and —"
She gasped, a long and severe intake of
breath. "Oh — my — goodness." She stared
at William, eyes ready to tip out of their
sockets. Her cheek moved in a tiny rhythmic
spasm just below her left eye. It seemed to
affect her mouth, which trembled just a bit.
"You're not William Percy."

He gave a small and instantly disappear-
ing smile.

Strangled and hoarse, pounding her
husband's arm with every word, she said,
"He's — William — Percy! Hero — of —
the Thames/Parliament caper!"

For the first time, her husband showed
interest. He looked William up and down.
"Oh. Well done, guv."

"Can I have your autograph?" said an
eager listening teenager.

"This is the man who foiled the bombing
of Parliament!" Blanche glanced about
wildly for those who had ears to hear.

Just then, a young uniformed man came
to escort them to the door. Clare gave
Blanche an uncertain good-bye wave. She
did not wave back. She just watched them
leave, mouth open, eyes round.

"Hero of the Thames/Parliament caper."
Clare advanced carefully with the crutches.
It was getting a little harder to maneuver

the things.

"I told you, I have a friend at the *Daily Mirror.* I helped him write it. It's my penance."

"Seems Mrs. Shrew didn't tell me *all* the news." Clare glanced at him as they followed slowly behind the young man, who paused occasionally to make sure they came. She set her teeth. Every landing of the crutches spiked pain in her left side. "What do you mean, penance?"

"There's nothing more humiliating than being a hero, is there?"

"Yes, but penance for what?"

"Well, with the gunshots, the incident had caused quite an uproar. We had to scramble to make up a story. I'd never let Klein have the satisfaction of public truth, that he got away, and that Scotland Yard had failed. That *I* had failed." He smiled coldly.

Clare paused, studying him.

"This way, miss," said the solicitous young man over his shoulder.

"Someday the truth will be known about him," William said grimly, mostly to himself.

"So you're not done with him."

He looked at her in a flash of surprised disgust. But she was getting to know him, and knew the disgust was not in the least bit for her. "When was I ever done with him? I'll be done when I can write his obituary."

Perhaps it was quite wrong, the uprush of primitive pride.

Was this a proper thing to feel — pride at the thought of this man killing another? And just as she was about to walk into a cathedral?

She saw the laughing face of Erich von Wechsler, and a little girl in a pink dress, first plucking petals from a daisy, and then safe in the arms of a brother who would never let anything hurt her. She thought of the words of Mr. Butterfield, William Percy's "magnificent obsession."

Maybe it wasn't proper. But primitive pride was the truth of what she felt, and if she'd not had crutches to manage, she'd slip her hand into his.

They sat at the end of a row. The service began, and Clare wanted to hold every second close, she wanted to breathe it in and make it part of her cellular makeup forever, but the hats distracted her; all she wanted since the moment she came into this magnificent place was to observe pure portent, but instead, encountered a botheration of *hats*.

Hats, everywhere hats, doffed, slipped off,

held at sides, tucked under an arm, laid in a lap.

"It's so catastrophic you can't even think of it," Clare whispered to William over the roaring of the hats. "Look at all of this beauty. The lovely people. This cathedral. It could be taken from us."

Confound the hats.

What were they trying to say?

"Is that the way people get through crises like these?" she said. It was very warm in here. She unbuttoned her jacket. "They do their best not to think of it? They just keep moving forward, like the queen? I've never had a *real* crisis."

He turned a look upon her. He whispered, "You lost your parents when you were eleven."

"That wasn't a crisis. It was the end of the world." She gazed at the soaring ceiling. "I keep thinking of my father. And curiously, Arthur Vance. I would like to have known him. We must go for tea and you must tell me everything you know about him, to the nth degree, short of me hiring a hypnotist for the last scrap. Oh dear." She glanced about the massive cathedral. "That was a joke. Hypnotist."

An elderly lady in front of them turned and glared. She put a finger to her lips. Even

William gave a little sideways remonstrative glance of his own.

"Oh. Right. Sorry," Clare whispered, and put a finger to her own lips to show she got the message. She leaned to William and whispered as quietly as she could, "You really can't think of it. That they are coming. The Nazis. They will profane this place, like Klein profaned Maggie. I don't mean *this* place, exactly. I mean England. I think that's the secret of sticking to your duty — you *can't* think of it. You've got to look straight ahead." She gave a firm Mrs. Shrew nod. "You've got to be unemotional. Plenty of time for emotion later. What is called for now is singularity of purpose. This is . . . what did you say, earlier? The end of everything lovely and good. Someone said it."

Several people turned to look at her.

"Clare . . . ?" His look was not one of remonstration but of something else.

"Oh. Right. Sorry."

He took her hand and she smiled, and then realized he was taking her pulse.

Hats covered in gold braid and shiny golden emblems. Fedoras. Bowlers.

Policemen helmets.

And then things grew still.

Why do you take off your hat before church, Daddy?

Far off, in a dream, someone pontifical led the gathered supplicants in prayer for the safety of the British Expeditionary Force, for the empire, for guidance, for wisdom . . .

Because it's a sign of respect for God, my little Clare Bear.

The vicar's voice faded, and she looked around in a spell of silence, at monuments, at plaques, at stained glass . . . at pomp, at circumstance, at people, and at men with hats in their laps.

She rarely saw Captain John without his hat on.

For my son, I'll go. Hat in hand.

"Your pulse is racing."

She clutched William's arm. "There *is* a God. William." She stared at him. "We have an ally."

He grabbed his hat, secured it on his head. "I'm taking you back."

"But this is historic."

"You are historically white, my dear."

He picked her up, and headed for the entrance. A few ushers hurried to open the door.

"But I've had an epiphany." Pain to which she paid not much attention made itself

303

known, pressing against her ribs, or her ribs pressed against it. "Gracious, what an appropriate place for an epiphany, where they've buried Dickens."

"Call a cab," William ordered an attendant outside. "Immediately."

"It's because of the hats, the epiphany."

A cab pulled up. The cab driver leapt out and opened the door. William settled her carefully in, the cab driver assisting. Some thoughtful soul came running up with Clare's crutches. "How very kind!" Clare exclaimed. William snatched them, tossed them in the cab, and got in. He told the cab driver the name of the hospital.

"Did you say thank you? You didn't say thank you." She watched the man watch them as they pulled away. She looked at the soaring abbey. "William, this is important: We have an ally." Then she said, rather stupidly, "I'm sorry I'm white."

"You're not white anymore."

He felt her forehead, and his face went cold. "You're burning up. You have a fever."

"Yes. Since yesterday. It was just a *little* fever, but I was afraid they wouldn't let me go, so every time they came to take my temperature I sucked on ice. There. It *should* be confessed. I've been to church." Then she insisted, "But the *hats* aren't because of a fever. My epiphany isn't. You believe me, don't you?"

William told the cab driver he changed his mind, just find the closest hospital.

"You take off your hat for many reasons. To say hello, to say good-bye. To show respect for authority. Do you know what this means? If these men and women, just as sane as you or I, are taking their hats off before they go into church then there really may be someone they are taking their hats off . . . *to.*"

She looked out the window.

"My parents went to church. Not to keep up a good show, but because they believed. My mother sang, and my father took off his hat."

She felt lighter than she'd felt in ten thousand years.

"It's a pity to have an epiphany and a fever at the same time. No one will believe you. Think of Joan of Arc. I feel such empathizing kinship. She *was* sick, wasn't she? Maybe she wasn't. I can't remember. My point is, we have an ally. We thought we stood alone, but we don't. I want you to believe it, but I'm not finished believing it myself. I must *finish* believing it before I make you. Otherwise I'm a hypocrite."

Then, at a spasm of pain on the left side,

"Oh, drat. I *am* fond of morphine. It's all I want right now. You won't let me become an addict, will you?"

William leaned forward and said to the cab driver, "Can we step it up, please? I did say *hospital,* didn't I?" He dropped back. "Of all the cab drivers in London, I get the most incompetent —"

She laid a hand on his arm. "Don't be unkind."

He covered her hand with his.

"Oh, William. We are not alone."

She rested against him, and all faded to lovely hues of rose, and orange, and little-girl pink.

Clare's raised knees moved from side to side under the sheets. Her arms were one moment behind her head, the next at her side. The glimpse lasted only a moment. The nurse closed the door.

Mrs. Iris Shrewsbury, that competent woman William Percy was beginning to like, sat next to him in the hallway. Murray Vance sat in a slouch a few chairs down, bouncing a handball off the wall when the nurses weren't watching. They waited for the doctors, who were in with Clare now.

"All I can think of is Gibbs Dentrifice," said a dazed Mrs. Shrewsbury. "It was the last thing I read in the newspaper before we got your message. 'Your teeth are ivory castles. Protect them with Gibbs Dentrifice.' It's become a horrible singsong. She's a very —" and the capable woman caught herself, lifted her chin, and finished coldly, "She's a first-rate girl."

"When does the padre get out?" said Murray. He bounced the handball.

"Butterfield is sorting the paperwork," William said. "He'll take him to the boat-yard once papers are signed. Put that away, this isn't a schoolyard. You're only here because of me, you know."

"Yeah. The hero of the Thames." Murray caught the ball, was about to toss it again, then pocketed it. He folded his arms. His knee bounced up and down.

"Would you like to draw?" asked Mrs. Shrewsbury. She pulled a bulky satchel to her lap and opened it. "We are in the process of getting our muse back, Mr. Percy. Even in crisis, I came prepared. I've got a drawing pad, number 4 Kimberly pencils, a pencil knife, chewing gum . . . Would anyone like some digestives?" She stared into the satchel. "Why did I bring the teakettle?"

"I can't draw." Murray leaned forward on his knees. The knee resumed bouncing. "*A,* it's like my ma's in there, you know? I don't know her much, but she's family. Half family, but family, you know? *B,* Rocket Kid's gone AWOL."

"You'd better lay out some crumbs for him," said Mrs. Shrewsbury. "I do notice that you've only drawn Salamander since you've been here."

He pulled out the handball and examined it. Put it back in his pocket. "Where's the docs?"

"Give them time," William said. He took out a pack of cigarettes. Luckies. They were supposed to curb his anger. He crushed the pack in his fist, and returned it to his pocket. He realized his knee had started to bounce up and down, and discreetly laid his hand on it. He glared at Murray. "Will you stop fidgeting?"

The door to Clare's room opened, and William shot up.

One of the doctors came out. His face was too grave.

The doctor left them and went to prepare for surgery.

"Mr. Percy?" said a nurse at Clare's door. "She's asking for you."

"See? What'd I tell you?" said Murray quietly, all fidget gone out. "Asks for you,

308

and I'm her brother — how'd ya like them apples?" He had an arm about the capable and weeping Mrs. Shrewsbury.

William stood looking at the door to the room. All had gone tinny and hollow and distant, and the nurse spoke again. William took his hat.

"Say, bobby." Murray looked up. "You tell her her brother says hi."

She was no longer agitated. She was serene. Her face was lovely in fever, cheeks rosy, eyes bright if red, and the fear that the doctors had raised, as if flushing out a great swell of black carrion, came home to roost in his gut. Infection, infection . . .

William took the chair next to the bed. "Are you going to talk to me about epiphanies?"

"I'm going to talk to you about Murray and Arthur Vance."

"Then you'd better stick to your point," he said lightly. "They've given you something to make you sleep."

"I've not gotten used to the idea of being a sister. It's too wonderful. I can't let it close yet. I was deeply happy once, when I was eleven. I fear happiness."

He crossed his legs. He picked up a book on the bedside table, looked it over. "It's something I've been recently aware of myself." It was a Bible. He turned it over in his hands, put it back on the table.

"It would mean everything to me if you kept an eye on Murray."

He recrossed his legs. He checked the Bible again, it had a leaflet in it. A weekly radio program with a few circled time slots. A few emphatic notes were in the margin, surely Clare's. It seemed he'd known her far too long to not know her handwriting.

"When Waldemar Klein was in my boat, *intimately* there, in a place evil should not have gone, I could only think of Arthur Vance. I can't help but call him Arthur, I'm not used to the idea of . . ." She trailed off. After a moment, she narrowed her eyes. "Where was I?"

"Arthur Vance."

"Stupid spleen," she said crossly. "Did I ever dream at tea and toast for breakfast, that later in the day I'd combine those two words? Or 'internal bleeding'? Such unfortunate pairings."

"It isn't the internal bleeding they're worried most about." He folded his arms. He flicked at a spot on his trousers. He suddenly found it harder to breathe.

"Yes, yes, either the infection will do me in or the operation to clean it up. Well at least they'll give it a try. Right? I do feel a bit stupid. Apparently one is supposed to let the doctors know about things, and not be so . . ."

Abruptly he rose and went to the window.

"I'm so sorry, William," she whispered.

He felt in his pocket for the package of crushed Luckies.

He'd lost Waldemar Klein. But he'd rather lose Klein a thousand times over than . . .

He realized she was talking.

". . . that Maggie must go. The Small Vessels Pool came, and we had a chat. They've just left. Did you see them?" She paused. "No — no, that was weeks ago. I *am* damaging my credibility. But I know for certain that Maggie must go."

The nurse warned that she was confused. It was a symptom of internal bleeding. That and faintness — *why* hadn't he seen it? She had wavered when she stood to take the crutches, and he put it off to —

"He stood over me with the gun, and I wondered if this was what Arthur Vance knew — such dipping, plunging fear. And then suddenly . . . it's gone. Perhaps he felt the same, that moment to look Waldemar Klein in the eyes, that moment to see the one behind him, the one who comes for us, the one this is all about. I saw his master, his shatterer, the one who would kill

311

Cecy . . ."

A chill prickled the back of his neck. He stopped breathing.

". . . and I knew a surety I'd never known. I knew I'd choose good if it meant my life. I wish everyone had that dreadful chance. I'd not let him have those papers, and did not know until I saw his face. Everyone should have a chance to look evil straight on. Yet we put off the one thing that could change the world. Change ourselves." She paused. "Have you heard of Popsicles?"

And just like that, the spellbinding tone became that of a fevered young woman once more. William felt released, and took a long discreet breath.

"Such a whimsical little word. *Popsicles*. Murray spoke of them. I'm sure he meant ice lollies. Where was I? Oh yes. Do you know —" her tone went musing — "belief does something marvelous to courage. Courage is something to be *drummed up* without it, but if you have belief, *it* does the drumming. Am I making sense? I hope you don't think it's the fever talking."

He turned to her. "Oh, it's Clare talking. Every word."

And she smiled, most brilliantly.

"You literally knocked me off my feet. I wonder how many can say that." She touched the chair. "Come. They'll run off with me soon."

He came slowly back to the bed. He picked a daisy out of the vase along the way. He sat in the chair, and twirled the daisy by the stem, watching the petals go round. "If you see . . . anything at all . . . what could you possibly see in me?"

"It's hard to put into words, and you'll only get a big head. I shouldn't wonder if the nurses have already given you one. William, he has taken them hostage, and now he comes for us. We mustn't give in."

"Have you gone spellbinding again?"

"I can't tell you the personal relief. I feared I would scramble about and find something to make them go away. When you've suffered a great deal, you can't bear to suffer again. I feared . . ." Tears rolled down, and William took her hand. "I feared that those papers would become my personal appeasement, that I'd offer them up like one of England's territories. You see, I stood to lose everything once more. Maggie, my people, everything." She closed her eyes. "But I passed the test, and it's good to get down to the bottom of myself, and oh goodness, it's taking effect. Like morphine, except drowsier. I hope I am not an addict;

I *like* the effect. Very peaceful. Where was I?"

"Personal appeasement."

"Right." She slowly opened her eyes. "I passed when I looked him straight on and realized he'd never stop coming. He doesn't want territories. He wants it all. I knew then the bottom of myself, that something there would never stop opposing him. It is strong, and secure, and good." Tears rolled down, and she gripped his hand. "I knew what Arthur did. No wonder he went out ruefully serene. I must tell Mr. Butterfield the secret: We have an ally. The shatterer will not prevail. Maggie goes forth to meet him." Her fevered gaze wandered the ceiling. "Man the ramparts. Watch the road. Gird your loins, and collect your strength." Her eyes closed, and this time she seemed to wilt, as if the medication had taken full effect.

William rose from the chair. He started for a nurse, but she had come for him. "I think she's —"

"Mr. Percy, we need to prepare her for the operation. You can wait with the others. We will keep you informed."

"I have to tell you something important," Clare said weakly, eyes still closed. "Can't think what it is. . . ."

"You already did. It's all right, we'll talk when they've fixed you up." His breath caught. "You owe Cecy a ride on your boat. Don't disappoint her."

"He sees the prayers. It's the only thing he's afraid of."

William fingered the edge of her coverlet. "Who?" he said, playing along as with someone senile, even as it pierced his heart.

"The shatterer. He sees a great wall between us and him. Hopes it's made of glass."

"Glass *can* shatter." His fingers moved from the coverlet to touch the back of her hand. "Make it a great wall of iron, Clare, and keep us safe."

"He'll have a surprise . . ." And she was asleep.

"Mr. Percy." The nurse held the door open for him, and that was it, no more time.

He went to the door, took his hat from the peg, and went to put it on. Then he paused, staring at the gray felt hat in his hand.

"Just —" He held up a finger to the nurse, striding to the bedside table. He picked up the Bible and opened it to where the leaflet was. Nahum 2:1 was underlined: *The shatterer has come up against you. Man the ramparts; watch the road; gird your loins; col-*

lect all your strength.

He closed the book and set it on the table. He picked up the fallen daisy, laid it by her side, and left the room.

Across the English Channel, in an uncovered greenhouse, a bandaged man stood watching the moon.

Another came alongside.

"All right, Captain?" He looked down at a man sleeping against a stone trough, and nudged him awake with his boot. "Curtis. You're up."

"Such a foe is rising, who intends to erect his throne equal to ours throughout the spacious North," the captain said to Jamie, as if he were filling him in, giving him the lay. There was something about him this evening. He was watchful. Alert.

"He at it again?" Curtis said hoarsely. He scrubbed his face with both hands, and shook himself.

"You're on watch, Curtis."

"Yeah, I'm going." He yawned. "See anything?"

"No," Jamie said, watching the captain. "All's quiet."

The captain watched the moon and the stars. Something about the watching was quite lucid tonight, and tense, as if he expected nothing good.

"Let us advise, and to this hazard draw with speed what force is left, and all employ in our defense, lest unawares we lose this our high place, our sanctuary, our hill."

"Milty, let's get some shut-eye."

"What enemy, late fallen himself from Heaven, is plotting now the fall of others." His eyes narrowed, traveling the sky, and his fingers turned the wedding ring.

"I can't sleep unless you do."

He lingered a moment more, and followed Jamie.

"Sad task and hard, for how shall I relate to human sense the invisible exploits of warring spirits?"

The British Expeditionary Force today is almost surrounded. That is the very grave position caused by the surrender of the Belgian Army.

— Daily Mail

Nothing is gained by blinking facts or mincing words. The British Expeditionary Force and the French divisions with it are beset on three sides and from the air. All are in danger of being cut off from Dunkirk.

— Daily Telegraph

We must keep all our anger for our one enemy, Hitler.

— Daily Express

And oddly enough, I notice that since things got really bad, everyone I meet is less dismayed. . . . Even at this present moment I don't feel nearly so bad as I should have done if anyone had prophesied it to me eighteen months ago.

— C. S. LEWIS TO OWEN BARFIELD, *Oxford*

I hope the BEF is cut to pieces sooner
than capitulate.
— DIARY ENTRY OF GEORGE ORWELL

From Ramsgate the first convoy of "little
ships" sailed at 22.00 on May 29. By the
next day they were streaming across the
Channel in seemingly unending lines.
— Dover Castle: A Frontline Fortress
and Its Wartime Tunnels

20

"Every man for himself," Baylor mused, as they moved along. "Doesn't make much sense. We're sticking together. I'm sure everyone is, wherever they are. So how can it possibly be every man for himself?"

Baylor did a favor for everyone in the group. He kept talking. It gave them a focal point. It kept them from Grayling.

"It's every man for himself *together,*" said Jamie.

"Well, that makes sense then," said Baylor, and even Griggs chuckled.

Baylor looked at the sky, and pushed up his glasses. "You get the feeling if we just get to England, it's all over. We're safe, everyone's safe. We'll go back to living our lives just as they were before this bloody war started."

"It won't be over. We won't be safe."

"Yes, I *know*. You don't have to take everything so literally, Griggs."

"Why is life given, to be thus wrested from us?"

"Poetry," Griggs complained. He let the Bren slide from one shoulder and slung it to the other. "Why couldn't *Call of the Wild* be the last book he read? Now there's a book. Read it in school."

"Probably the last time you touched one," said Baylor.

"Milton has a point, don't you think?" Balantine said over his shoulder. He walked in front, where he usually did, without Grayling on his right. It put their minds on Milton's words, and no one answered.

Would the group dwindle yet again before they reached home? Jamie stiff-armed the thought. Every man for himself was an order, and if it was a desperate order, the last one they would hear, it was a directive and the directive somehow gave comfort: Get to Dunkirk, get home.

Do not think of Grayling, and Lieutenant Dunn, and Kearnsey, and Drake. Get to Dunkirk. Get home.

"They God's image did not reverence in themselves. What thou livest, live well."

"We are a world apart, aren't we, Captain?" said Baylor in admiring wonder to Milton. "I wish you'd come deliver a lecture at university. Just as you are."

"Ratty head wound and all," said Jamie.

"Yes, he can prattle on to all your incredibly smart friends and you can all have a jolly celebration of your incredible wits while the rest of us fight Hitler," Griggs said.

"Be not diffident of wisdom, she deserts thee not, if thou dismiss her not." Milton not only half looked over his shoulder to address Griggs, he had a small smile on his face.

Baylor caught it, and stared at Jamie, incredulous. "Did you see that?"

Jamie grinned. "I did."

"He actually smiled! I think he's starting to know what's going on."

Jamie thought of last night, and the uncanny way Milton had studied the sky. Did he know what was going on?

"Well done, Milty," said Baylor. "Keep at it. I should say, Captain Jacobs. Right? Jacobs?" He said the word a little louder as if hoping to jog something. Then, "What's wrong, Milty?"

For the captain had stopped, staring. They looked to where he did.

A black expanse covered the distant northwest sky, as if a great patch of thundercloud had broken from a stormscape to hover in one place.

"What in the world is that?" said Baylor.

"It's no thundercloud," said Jamie.

"It's smoke," said Griggs. "Oil smoke. I know there's a refinery on the coast."

Balantine held up his hand. "Shh, listen — do you hear it?" He turned to look at them.

Faint but unmistakable came the sound of distant gunfire.

"Don't tell me that's Dunkirk," Baylor groaned.

They listened hard, and at one particular sound all exchanged glances.

"That's not just gunfire," said Balantine. "The Germans are bombing. Come on, lads. Let's go."

Gripping guns, reshouldering their packs, picking up the pace they headed for the oil-black expanse.

"What are we walking into?" Baylor wondered.

"I guess we'll find out," said Jamie, swallowing down a bulge of fear.

He watched Milton as they went. The captain kept his eyes on the blackened sky, fingers twisting the ring.

Not long now, mate. We'll keep those bombs off. We'll get you home to her.

It was late afternoon when they approached Dunkirk from the south, walking fanned out, guns at the ready and Milton in the middle, the only one without a gun.

They had left the fields and took to a road for faster going. The closer they got to the city, the more the road began to fill with refugees. Days ago the British Army had moved with a flow of Belgian and French refugees heading west; they now threaded into the town against an unabated stream of civilians heading — on this particular road — south.

As the men approached the city, signs of war met every glance.

"I wonder what it's like on the beaches," Griggs said grimly, staring at a kitchen with no walls as they passed. Crumbled masonry half covered a stove. A woman picking through the debris with a full apron straightened, nearly fell, regained her footing, and noticed them. She was covered with plaster dust.

The German bombs had created massive havoc. They passed too many dead civilians to count — men, women, and children. It looked as though they were not given the chance to flee. On the outskirts they saw the still-smoking rubble of homes, barns, livestock, and as they came into the city proper, saw caved-in apartment buildings, churches, shops, restaurants. Barking dogs were everywhere.

"Halt! Who goes there?" someone shouted.

Balantine's hands came up. "British!"

"Say something else!"

"I'm starving and my feet are killing me!"

"I've got blisters on my blisters," Baylor added.

"Have you got any water?" Jamie asked.

The speaker emerged from around the corner of a half-bombed brick building. A few bricks tumbled down as he came out. "All right, all right — go on, then. Straight ahead to the beaches. They'll put you in groups of fifty."

"How bad is it?" The men gathered around him.

"How bad is what? Which part?" He took off his helmet and wiped his face, put the helmet back on. Looked as though he hadn't slept in days. "They're bombing the beaches to bloody pieces while the navy tries to take us off. They're bombing the navy, too, entire route to Dover, far as we can see." He pulled off his helmet again, squinted inside, shook it, replaced it. "As for our brothers who haven't arrived yet, there's one ever-shrinking corridor, and you were on it. This is it, lads — the end of the line. We're bloody surrounded. So I'd say it's bad everywhere. Last bus filled with civilian refugees just left. You should've seen the push to get on it, it was absolutely mobbed. I've no idea where the driver thinks he's headed. Any way he goes, he'll run into Germans."

"How close are they?"

"Close enough that the Jerries aren't bombing inland anymore — might hit their own men. They're mostly bombing the beaches. Communication's been cut off, and a patrol's been sent west to judge how far they've come, but they haven't returned. They're on all sides, east, south, and west." He pointed grimly at the sky. "And up there."

The six looked at one another. "We could've come right through 'em," said Baylor.

"Might have done. Many have. And wait till you see the queues on the beach, it'll fair take your breath away. But there's order for all that, even in the bombing. Captain Tennant of the navy's in charge, and thank God for him — it's chaos now, but you should've been here a few days ago."

"What day *is* it?" said Baylor.

"No idea."

"What about the town?" asked Griggs, looking around. "Are we supposed to defend it?"

The soldier shook his head. "That's all sorted. Just get to the beaches, find a place to fall out in the dunes, and they'll assign you into groups to approach the mole. Ships are coming alongside the mole to take the men off, but the going is precious slow for the amount of men on the beaches. It's just a waiting game now. Wait, and dodge."

"Dodge . . . ," said Baylor, not liking the sound of it.

He shrugged. "Bullets and bombs."

"Any food around?" asked Balantine. "Haven't eaten for days; we're done in."

"You and everyone else. There's only what you can scrounge, and the town's pretty much picked over. Supply lines can't get to us. Wait." He looked left, and whistled. "Murphy! Bring some of those pilchards. He found a cache of pilchards this morning in the basement of a grocer. Don't know how everyone else missed it. He's got an uncanny knack for finding things."

A private came at a trot, carrying a lumpy cloth sack.

He nodded at them and said cheerily, "Hullo, boys! Welcome to Dunkirk. Glad you made it. We've only some nasty pilchards in tomato sauce as part of your welcoming ceremony, but . . ."

"Grateful for anything you've got," said

Balantine.

The private handed out a flat tin to every man, then dug in the sack and produced a larger tin. "Plums. It's auntie food, but it's food. Share it out." He tossed it to Curtis.

"Enjoy yourselves!" He left at a trot.

"Cheers, mate! Thanks, mate!" the squad called.

"All right, get going," said the first soldier, motioning on with his head. "And be prepared for dodging — today's bombing started early this afternoon and hasn't stopped. They usually let off a bit at dusk, but they make up for it in the morning. Good luck."

The soldier started back from where he came, but Griggs called out, "What kind of bombs?" It was a question that would never have occurred to Jamie.

"Well, there, we're in a bit of luck as far as the beaches go — penetration bombs. There's no survival with scatter bombs, but many of the p-bombs don't explode 'til they're deep in the sand. They haven't figured that out yet. We'll take what we can get, right, lads? Still — look sharp. They take us out with direct hits, and you'll get thrown if —" He looked past them and brought up his gun. "Halt! Who goes there?"

"Friends! British!"

"Say some more!"

"Come on," Balantine said to the five. "Let's find a spot to fall out and eat, then head for the beaches. Whatever we do, we stay together."

"Every man for himself together," said Baylor, and all fell in behind Balantine.

They passed the remains of a bombed transport, and then a caved-in café with a café table on the path that was completely untouched, checkered tablecloth and white cups and a white porcelain pot still on it. It was coated with dust.

"Look at that," said Baylor. "Only wants a little French waiter next to it."

Everywhere, the crumbly dust of bombed and smoldering buildings, and everywhere, glass crunching under their boots.

Dust hung like fog, and permeated the city. Orange bursts of fire flashed in the haze, and sounds and smells and vibrations increased as they moved ahead. They could smell cordite, and salt, and fish from the sea, and they could now see the flash of explosions ahead, though they couldn't tell if the explosions were on land or sea. Planes overhead wheeled and dove, strafing and releasing oblong bombs; the last bomb from a peeling-off bomber fell very close, not a hundred yards away on the other side of a brick wall — it buckled the wall, and the concussive wave sent them stumbling. They heard a groan of steel and then a terrific crash, and all about them rained fine debris.

"Oh, this is fun," said Baylor, coughing.

"My mother told me to run from things like this," said Jamie.

"From this specifically?"

"Yes." He coughed and wiped his eyes. "Took me aside one day and said, 'Jamie, me lad, if ever Dunkirk is bombed and you're heading straight for it, divert.' "

"Smart woman, your mum," said Balantine, trying to breathe through his sleeve. "Come on, boys, keep moving."

"I thought we were going to eat," said Curtis. "I could chew right through the tin."

"There's a spot just ahead, over there. Stop!" Balantine yelled.

Milton halted, and Jamie ran into him.

They came upon . . . at first, Jamie wasn't sure.

Helmets and guns and mangled chrome in a storefront doorway; bodies and parts of bodies, blood and viscera, bricks, and empty boots, and dust-coated rucksacks, all tumbled together in a still, gruesome mishmash, the sight itself a ghastly storefront display. Blood ran from beneath the mess, different flows joining into one, running down the street until it slowed, congealing with the dust.

Griggs went to his haunches beside a body, touching skin. "Not long ago."

"Lads must've taken shelter here," said Balantine, taking off his helmet.

"God, have mercy," Baylor murmured. "How many are there?"

"Can't tell," said Griggs.

"Oh, this is nothing," a soldier told them, passing by with several others. Some had bulging sacks over their shoulders. One carried, of all things, a gramophone. "Wait till you get to the beaches."

One corpse stared from half-lidded blue eyes, his mouth askew from a shard of chrome through his cheek. The sight transfixed Jamie.

"Milton?" said Baylor. "What's he doing?"

"He's gone crackers," said an awestruck Curtis.

"He's already crackers," said Griggs, rising.

"Not like this," said Curtis, horrified.

It was hard to say, exactly, what Milton was doing.

Trying to match body parts to corpses was a good guess.

He worked feverishly in the mangled pile before Jamie could pull himself from a momentarily appalled state.

"Milton! What are you doing? Stop that!" He put a hand on his arm, but Milton threw it off and continued his frenzied activity. "Captain Jacobs!"

It had no effect. Milton turned over a body and tried to match a severed arm to it. Jamie grabbed hold of his shoulder, and once again Milton threw him off.

"Don't you see?" said Baylor in horrified awe. "He's trying to save his unit. He's trying to . . . put them back together. In his mind."

Milton gazed about for body parts, picking them up, testing them out, discarding and trying again. If he hadn't already unraveled, he did so now, and it shocked Jamie to inaction. Just when they thought he was getting better, just when he gave his name . . .

"My God, what do we do?" Baylor put his hands on his head. "How would the psychiatrists deal with this? Anything we do could have dire repercussions!"

"Oh, sod this." Griggs stepped over the mouth-skewed corpse and picked his way through to Milton. He grabbed a handful of Milton's jacket, twisting it into his grip, then dragged him backward, bumping over debris and the corpse out into the street, well clear of the macabre mess, where he threw him off with more force than needed.

Baylor followed, saying, "Freud would say he's undergoing —"

"Shut it, Baylor!" Jamie went to Milton and warily went to a knee, waiting first to see if he would pull away at the hand on his shoulder, then checking under his bandage when he didn't. "Hope you haven't buggered those stitches."

"Who — me or him?" said Griggs, lighting up a cigarette.

"Both of you!" Jamie shouted.

Milton sat, breathing hard. He made no move to get back to the bombed men, but that face — maybe Jamie expected what he saw in the moonlit bedroom, just haggard misery. This was something else. Milton's face was utterly blank.

Jamie tilted his head up. He pushed up the eyelids to look into his eyes. Patted his cheeks. "Come on, what's the matter with you? Wake up." It was like Milton wasn't even there.

He never thought he'd want to see that misery again. This blankness was far worse. He let him go, and looked to the sea. Wait till they got to the beaches, the man said? How bad was it? What would Milton do then?

"Will you stop making this so hard?"

Jamie all but shouted. "What am I supposed to do, blindfold you on that beach?" After a moment, with less heat, "Come on. Up we go." Baylor went to the other side and helped get him up.

"Did you notice, the whole time he was about that horrible business he didn't quote any Milton?" Baylor said an hour later, pushing up his glasses. "Hasn't since. I don't know if that's good or bad."

"I just want to get him home. I want to be done with him." *He'll be hers, then.*

They'd found a spot to fall out and eat pilchards and plums before they got to the beach, a relatively rubble-free bus stop at a street corner, and Balantine even found a tin of Carnation milk that must have fallen from the sack of someone on a foraging spree. They shared it around.

"This tastes absolutely smashing," said Baylor with his mouth full, passing the tin. "And I hate milk and fish."

"Then you haven't had pilchards the way my mother makes 'em," said Balantine, wiping his mouth. "She serves them in a mash, spread on toast. Salt, pepper, herbs. Brilliant."

"Sounds disgusting," said Griggs, who couldn't bear to go without being contrary for long.

Tired as they were, no one could sit, except for Milton and for Jamie who sat beside him, making him eat. The men watched soldiers and civilians hurrying about in different directions, and listened for the Stukas.

"Make an awful noise when they dive," Balantine commented, gazing under his hand toward the beach.

"I believe he's suffered a setback," said Baylor, watching Milton. "He was doing much better earlier."

"Baylor, would you just — ?" The fact that Jamie refrained from finishing the sentence was apology enough for his earlier eruption. He was used to telling Griggs to shut up, but not Baylor.

"Sorry."

Jamie tossed aside Milton's empty tin, and got up to stand beside Baylor.

"I'm worried about the beaches," he said, low enough so the others couldn't hear. "We're heading into nothing good, and I don't know what will happen to him. I don't know how he'll react. I wish we could . . . drug him or something. Have you got anything like that?"

"No. But don't worry, I'll help you with

him. There's something about him, isn't there?"

Sometimes he wished Baylor didn't say things so openly. But he was glad someone else felt it. "Yeah," he said.

"I want to read *Paradise Lost* again, with completely new eyes. It says something about epic poetry, don't you think? It takes things out of our hearts."

"Baylor, if my mates thought I might agree with you, they'd beat me up."

"I'd hold you down," Griggs said, passing by and flipping up the back of Baylor's helmet.

"Griggs, you are a twice-uncircumcised Philistine," Baylor observed, righting his helmet and his glasses, "yet, you do have your qualities."

"Twice? How is that possible?" said Jamie.

"I wanted emphasis."

"Come on, let's go," said Balantine. "We're almost there, I can see the Channel through those buildings. Fall in." He waited until they were in usual formation, started walking, then stopped and turned. He briefly looked each in the eye. "Whatever happens, we stick together, right?"

"Yeah, you said that once," Griggs complained. "Never met such a group of women."

"I'm glad you're the prettiest," said Jamie. "Lots of men on that beach. *We* won't get bothered."

"Oh shut it, Elliott. It's the captain who's the prettiest but I don't think they'll fancy a lunatic."

Another time, not long ago, Jamie would've had a go at him. This time he only said, "Well, then you're twice safe."

Even Curtis laughed.

And Milton, first time talking since the bombed-out storefront, said softly, "What in me is dark, illumine. What is low —"

"Raise and support," the others chorused. A delighted Baylor added, "Well done, Milty! You're back!"

21

William Percy pulled into Elliott's Boatyard and parked on the other side of the lorry. He turned off the engine and rested his wrists on the steering wheel. He couldn't see *Maggie Bright* from here; she was at her berth at the end of the dock, obstructed from view by the boathouse.

He had no logical reason to be here, yet he couldn't stay away.

The operation, day before last, had gone well. Quite well, in fact. *It was boring,* one of the surgeons had told them in an effort to ease their minds. *Just how we like it.*

The infection surrounding the spleen had been cleared out, and part of the spleen was removed — they were assured that Clare would get along fine with a partial spleen. Then the surgeon said, with the first hint of gravity, that now all they had to do was wait for several days to make sure no vestige of infection had entered her bloodstream. She was allowed no visitors during that time.

He got out of the car and pocketed his keys, shutting the car door. He jingled the keys in his pocket, looking around. He heard singing, wasn't sure where it came from.

What could he say to explain his presence? He'd known her less than a week.

He had the keys out of his pocket and the car door opened, when something about the boatyard made him look again. Where was John Elliott's fishing trawler? And the ratty house tug they had commandeered from the old recluse to follow after *Maggie Bright*? What about the Chris Craft vessel with the mahogany hull, laid up in dry dock?

Mrs. Shrewsbury came singing around the corner of the boathouse, wearing a dress and a hat, carrying gloves and a purse. She stopped short when she saw him and waved enthusiastically.

William cursed under his breath and produced a wave.

"Hello, Detective Inspector!" she sang as she approached. "I was just on my way to St. Mark's to pray for Clare, and the BEF, and Captain John, and Minor Roberts. Would you care to join me?"

Minor Roberts — the recluse who owned

the ratty house tug. Handy in a pinch, that man.

"Actually, is Murray about?" he asked, the first thing that came to mind to get out of it. He shut the car door.

"Yes, he's on the *Maggie Bright,* in the bow. *Drawing,*" she added significantly, leaning in with a raised brow. "I couldn't resist a *very* clandestine peek, and there he was for the first time in five months: Rocket Kid." She withdrew, beaming, as if William should know what she was talking about and rejoice.

"Oh. Yes. He's an illustrator or something. Well, I best get along then. Got a bit of news for him about Father Fitzpatrick."

"He's to be released?"

"This afternoon."

"Wonderful!"

"Butterfield will pick him up from the American embassy and bring him by. They are making arrangements to get him home to the States."

"Arrangements for the States. Think of it: ordinary travel plans. Isn't it lovely that we are all carrying on just as if the barbarian were *not* at the gates? I must pick up a cake for the dear Burglar Vicar, and just think of that: an ordinary cake. Of course, I'm sure I have a far better recipe, but that awful galley stove does not deliver consistent heat. Not for a cake. It shall be a Dundee cake, then. Oh, you must come for the cake, Mr. Percy! Mr. Butterfield, too. We'll have a regular party." She put a hand to her cheek. "*Such* a pity that Clare cannot be here. And that man. She's the heart of the boat, and I do believe Maggie misses her. Well, there's nothing for it. Stiff upper lip." She gave a firm nod. "Off I go. Infection doesn't stand a chance, all the prayers that have gone up in this land. Heaven is stormed, Mr. Percy, and our prayers for Clare ride some very formidable coattails. I wish I could actually *see* it, the whole cosmic scope, as my Cecil does. Right, then. I will see you soon, Inspector." She started off.

"Mrs. Shrewsbury — what did you mean, to pray for Captain John and Minor Roberts?"

She stopped short, surprised. "Haven't you heard? They've gone."

"Gone where?"

"Why, Mr. Tough from the Teddington boatyard came by the other day — the day our Clare was in surgery. They're collecting boats. Bringing them down to South End. He had a weather eye upon Maggie and other worthies."

"For what?"

"Well, no one knows *exactly,* though they can't think we are complete idiots, can they? All the things we're hearing from Dover and Ramsgate? Surely . . ." She softened, gazing toward the boatyard, likely at the place where Captain John's trawler had been. "Surely, for an heroic venture. 'Awake, awake, English nobility . . .' " Then she smiled at him. "Shakespeare. Henry VI. What must be borne shall be borne, and we shall fight on. Yes, Inspector?"

"Yes, Mrs. Shrewsbury."

"Good day, then."

He touched his hat. "Good day."

She started off.

"Mrs. Shrewsbury!"

She turned, and he never felt more foolish in his life because it was one thing to bandy words with a fevered woman, quite another with a lucid woman off for church and Dundee cake.

"How do you suppose prayer works?"

Mrs. Shrewsbury tilted her head, very interested. "What a wonderful question. I'm not sure how it works. I can say what I believe it *does.* I believe prayer kicks things out of the way. I believe it does so to make room for a better outcome. I believe prayer illuminates our paths so we can see more clearly, choose our way more wisely."

"Clare spoke of a shatterer, that it has come against us." Good Lord, what was he trying to say? He gripped the car keys short of puncturing skin.

"Did she?" She came a few steps back, her expression thoughtful. He didn't like that thoughtfulness. She shouldn't take him seriously. "Well, why do you think the king has called for prayer?"

"I say shatterer, and you seem to know what I'm talking about."

"We all go to war, Mr. Percy. You shall go to war, and so shall I." Then the stark-blue eyes crinkled into a smile. "And I shall doubtless come again rejoicing, bringing my Dundee cake with me. Good day to you, sir."

"Good day."

He watched her leave.

She had a bit of Clare in her. Something spellbinding.

He was here because she was right. Clare was the heart of the boat, and that is where he wanted to keep vigil. And if he wasn't sure he believed as she, that prayer could actually *do* something, he was glad Mrs. Shrewsbury was praying.

Murray was in the bow, but he wasn't drawing. He sat on a coil of rope, a drawing pad and pencils at his feet. He watched the river.

"Three boats missing," said William. "It's a small boatyard. You feel it."

Murray looked over, but didn't answer.

William sat on a sail locker. "May I have a look?" he asked of the open drawing pad.

Murray shrugged. He pushed the pad over with his toe.

William did not know art, but these drawings were good. Very good, in fact. He flipped through a few pages.

"So this is the famous Rocket Kid."

Murray didn't answer.

He read the captions and studied the drawings. He chuckled. "Good to see justice *some*where. If Hitler saw these, you'd be enemy number one on the Nazi hit list." He looked closer at one particular drawing. "I don't think they'd fancy . . . whatever it is this fellow is doing to Hitler."

"Zappin' his guts out with a ray gun," Murray murmured.

"And all of this is . . . ?"

Murray looked. "His guts flyin' out. Kids like guts. Editors don't. Sam will ax the guts, but before he does, I want the colorist to see it. He'll love it. We think alike. Then afterward, we'll have ourselves a requiem for the axed guts."

"A requiem?"

"A wake to say good-bye to the good stuff."

"Who's this little fellow? He has some . . . *guts* on him."

"Salamander."

He handed back the drawing pad. He found a pack of uncrushed cigarettes in his pocket and offered one to Murray. Murray cupped his hand around William's lighter, and withdrew. He lit one for himself and they smoked in silence, watching the waters of the Thames.

William closed his eyes. He could actually feel her here. This boat was so her, everything about it, the paper Chinese lanterns, the decorated *Bed and Breakfast* sign, all so light and free-spirited, so aching to spread canvas to the wind, and yet held at anchor for a time. The first woman to single-handedly circumnavigate the world, she'd said at the restaurant; so declarative and projecting — to think he once thought it perversely naive and boasting. It was utterly sincere.

"Why are you here, bobby?"

"Because she's here." His eyes flew open. There was no recovering from that one, so he said quickly, "I'm here because the B— because Father Fitzpatrick is released. He's at the embassy for travel arrangements. My associate is picking him up and will bring him by." He added, "I saw Mrs. Shrewsbury. She's getting a cake for him."

Murray half smiled.

"Butterfield is arranging for dual passage. You can accompany him, if you like."

For the first time, Murray looked directly at him. "What if I don't like?"

William eyed him and drew on his cigarette.

"What if I wanna stay and fight Nazis?"

An eyebrow rose. He pressed out his cigarette on the bottom of his shoe, and tossed it overboard. "The other day Mrs. Shrewsbury told me you're an isolationist. You're in some group."

"That was before Waldemar Klein shot Clare."

A scalding red flash to his gut.

A boat motored by. William mustered a smile and a nod, the skipper nodded back.

"Klein killed my father?"

Another scalding flash. "Yes."

"You know what their mistake was, bobby? They went after kids. They do that . . ." Murray shook his head. "Ain't no politics no more."

"That's what your father believed."

"Look there." He turned and pointed with his cigarette to the base of the foremast.

"That's to honor Mags and my old man. Clare said she wanted a record of her exploits." The number 5 stood out, carved neatly into the wood. "Our press always showed up Hitler as a joke, you know?" He flicked the cigarette overboard. "Just an empty-headed, jumped-up sad sack with these big old delusions, and we all figured it was just a matter of time before he got his butt kicked back to where it belonged."

"That didn't happen."

"Now it will." He hesitated, then said, "You think Clare'll make it?"

"I know Mrs. Shrewsbury's praying." He was glad he came, just for that. She was so sure of herself. She believed prayer worked, she wasn't the sort to go off and do it if she didn't believe it would help, and something about that was old-fashioned, and stout, and . . . needed.

You shall go to war, and so shall I.

"Hope she's handy that way, like with the kettle." Murray chuckled. "You shoulda seen what she did to one of Klein's men."

"If you stay, what will you do?"

Murray shrugged. "I dunno. I wanna fight. Maybe join one of them foreign legion things. I can't wait around for America to go to war."

"You might wait a long time for that."

"I don't know. Roosevelt said something that stuck with me. Remember when Warsaw was bombed? And all them innocent people died? Frankie made a speech. He said even a neutral can't be asked to close his mind or conscience. And he left it hanging, what a person should do with that. Left it to *you* to follow *your* conscience. Wasn't sure I liked that. It was too broad, you know? Anyway, it gives me hope that America will get involved." He looked at the drawing pad at his feet. "And if I can't join up someplace, there's something I *can* do. And make people laugh at him to boot."

"Excuse me — is the owner of this vessel about?"

They looked to see a thirtysomething uniformed seaman standing at the end of the dock. He carried a clipboard.

They rose, and went to the port rail.

"That would be my sister, and no, she ain't," Murray said.

The man consulted the clipboard. "*Maggie Bright* has been registered with the Small Vessels Pool for privately owned craft. Actually, she's one of the few craft that *was,* only about forty, when the call went out." He looked up. "I'm Lieutenant Wares, Royal Navy. We're looking for any vessel with a shallow draft."

"How shallow?" said Murray.

"Ideally, three feet. Capable of inshore ferrying work."

"Her draft is closer to five."

"At this point, I don't care."

"What's this about?"

"Saving the British Army." He tucked the clipboard under his arm. "With no guarantee she'll make it back. Germans are already shelling the direct route between Dover and Dunkirk. We now have to take a long detour to get there — makes an eighty-seven-mile trip out of what should be thirty-nine. We're now rounding at the Kwinte Buoy."

Heroic venture, Mrs. Shrewsbury had said. William looked to where Captain John's trawler had been.

"What do you mean, saving the British Army?" Murray asked.

"They're trapped on Dunkirk beach. Entire army. Including a lot of French soldiers, I've heard."

"What's Maggie got to do with that?"

"The destroyers cannot get in close enough to load from the beaches, even at high tide. It's too shallow, a mile out. Motors get clogged with sand, propellers fouled by debris. We're working only from a flimsy mole in the Dunkirk harbor, nothing more than a breakwater, really, not built to take the weight of queuing men. So, there's a call out for all the small craft that can be mustered. We were here the other day, but no one else was." He nodded at the boat. "Mr. Elliott wouldn't let us take it without permission. Of course, we're a bit past that at this point. Things are quite desperate. Looking at conscription."

"Not this one, you ain't."

"You mean to say they're taking yachts like these?" said William. It was hard to believe. "This can only hold maybe — forty, fifty men, tops?"

"A vessel this size, they're packing in twice that, I've heard; and they'll take anything that floats. Fishing trawlers. River tugs. Lifeboats. They're all going over. Even holiday ferries, like the *Brighton Queen* and *Gracie Fields.* London fireboats, cockleboats — you name it. Hundreds have gone over already, but they need more. Lots more." Some emotion passed over the man's face, a momentary interruption of naval competence. "We've already lost some, either by direct bombing or by mines in the water." He looked at *Maggie Bright.* "She has a wooden hull; at least she won't attract any magnetic mines."

"Like I said — she ain't goin' anywhere,

pal. Not without my sister's say. And she ain't sayin'. She's in the hospital."

He looked at the clipboard. "I have here a Clare Childs who registered the *Maggie Bright* two weeks ago. I'm assuming she's the owner?"

"You're saying that's some kind of permission?" Murray nodded at the clipboard.

Bluff called, he said with a trace of stiff reluctance, "Not exactly . . ."

Murray paced in a very small area, hands in his waistband, staring hard at the naval officer. "*A,* Clare ain't here to say it's okay. *B,* this boat is her *home.* It's all she's got."

There came again a mild break with naval composure. "Look, I've been dealing with this all day," he said testily. "You'd think people would actually jump at the chance to save human beings. They have *no* idea how bad things are." He pointed the clipboard south. "Don't you understand? If the army goes, so goes the country! Doesn't anyone understand that?"

"You're having trouble collecting boats, then?" said William.

The officer looked blankly at the clipboard, and sighed, dropping it by his side. He wearily rubbed his forehead. "Don't get me wrong. Most are quite willing, and people like that brighten my day.

They even want to go themselves. But some fuss about compensation, some fuss about their boats being crewed by the navy —"

"Oh, she for *sure* wouldn't be crewed by anyone but me," Murray said, jerking his thumb at his chest. "I know her. I know that motor. I know how she runs, I know how she *thinks.*" He looked south. "But I only know the Med. I don't know the Channel. Not them waters."

"I do."

Murray looked at William. "Yeah? So?"

"I can go with you."

"She ain't goin' anywhere without —"

"I have no time to run to a hospital for permission," said the officer. "There isn't time for protocol, there's only time for action. Those men are *dying.* I've seen some of the destroyers come into Ramsgate — those soldiers have been through hell. Look, just — both of you talk it out. Arrive at some conclusion, will you?" He looked at Murray. "If you're her brother, *you* decide, but be warned: I'm a hairsbreadth from conscription, and I can do it." Less severely, he said, "I'll be back later, but if I'm not, if you should choose immediately to do the *right* thing, then strip her down of anything that can make room for a man, and get her down to the Tower pier. Boats are rendezvousing there, and then it's on to Sheerness, where they'll be taken over by tug to save fuel for the ferrying work. They're mostly crewed by the navy, but . . . look —" he paused to scratch his head — "we *are* low on men. They're reporting in spurts from all over the country, but . . . if you know the engine, you'd be a —"

"Thornycroft. Six-cylinder. Starts up with gas, switches to paraffin, and I know how to keep her from starting fire when she does."

The officer looked at Murray appraisingly. "They will need a man aboard each vessel strictly to keep the engine running. If you're game, report to the Port of London Authority, down by the Tower."

"They take Americans?"

"They'll take anyone and are grateful. Talk to Lieutenant Sanderson, tell him Lieutenant Wares said you'll crew this one for the engine — that is, if you decide to go." He made a mark on the clipboard. "Right. Onward. Good day, gentlemen."

He started to leave, then snapped his fingers and said, "Bandages. If you decide to go, take everything out but what can be made into bandages. Towels, tea towels, curtains, sheets — whatever you've got. Ample dressings are needed, but ambulances in Dover and Ramsgate are running low. Good day." He turned to go.

William called out, "Good luck, then."

The officer paused, and said, "We need all we can. The truth is, we need a miracle." They watched him go.

"Easy for him to say, do the right thing. Ain't *his* boat. Ain't *his* home. It's all she's got." Murray paced. "*A,* she's gonna circumnavigate the globe someday, bobby, single-handed. She's got vision and purpose and other stuff and I for one believe she's gonna do it. *B,* I don't know what I'm gonna do if she — Because *C,* I just met her. And *D,* this ain't fair! What kinda decision *is* this?"

He ran for the bowsprit. He shimmied out and sat at its peak, hooking his feet around the lower brace. By the set of his face he looked like a thunderous male version of a clipper ship's figurehead.

William felt for the packet of cigarettes, and crushed it in his fist. Then he cursed — fat lot of good *that* just did.

He went to the bow.

"I wanna get Clare outta here, I wanna take her to the States. I want her to know my ma." The young man stared at some distant spot. "My ma could be her ma, you know? She ain't got one. I wish Ma was here. I wish the Fitz was here. Came down in cement for me. I could kill him for makin' me that kid's godfather, but it was the proudest day of my life, you know? These are the ones who help me figure things out." He shook his head, staring at the distant spot. " 'Cause I ain't got the heart to take this boat from her."

William folded his arms and leaned on the rail. "Look. Mrs. Shrewsbury will be back soon. And Father Fitzpatrick *will* be here, along with my associate, Frederick Butterfield — what do you say we have a council of war on Clare's behalf? We'll talk it through and give it our best to sort out what Clare would want."

"You know what she'd want."

"Perhaps. But it's not my decision."

"No! It's mine." Murray scrubbed his hair with both hands, and then looked with sudden hope at William. "Say — any chance one of them nurses could sneak us in?"

"Not likely. And you heard the man — there's no time. We'll wait for the others, we'll put our heads together, and we'll do our best. All right?"

"Yeah." This small plan for action seemed to calm him. "Yeah, okay, bobby."

And then a thought came creeping. William slowly turned, staring to where the naval officer had left.

"Whatsa matter?"

"I do know what she wants," he breathed. "Small Vessels Pool."

"Say what?"

Clare was in her morphine fit. Or spellbinding fit. "I know what she wants." It was what *he* wanted, before he exploded to bits, before he tore things apart from this helplessness.

"What're you talkin' about?"

He looked at Murray. "Before she went into surgery she said something about Maggie meeting them. Or him. I thought she was talking nonsense. But she specifically mentioned the Small Vessels Pool. And she said this: Maggie must go."

Murray unhooked his legs from the bottom brace. "Maggie must go?"

"I'm sure of it."

"Cut it out, you're giving me goosebumps all over. Look at that." He scratched his arms. He slid to the deck. "How could she know to say something like that?"

William paced the bow. "I don't know, she was in a state. She was in a *strange* state. Something about a shatterer. I thought she was delusional. She'd gone spellbinding."

"Spellbinding?"

"Spellbinding, prophesying . . . You had to be there. But it didn't feel like a delusion, and she didn't say it once, the part about Maggie — she said it twice."

He gripped the rail. Then he turned, looked at the carved *5,* looked up the foremast to the flag fluttering in the wind, a Union Jack.

Clare, would you lose it all? Would you lose your home? Would you lose your dream?

Maggie must go.

It wasn't spooky or metaphysical or prophesying or anything like that. It was simply what she said, and that was good enough for him.

"We have her answer." He looked at Murray. "I want you to believe me."

He jerked a shoulder. "Why wouldn't I?"

"Because I want to sail this boat. Now."

"Why, bobby?"

"Because it's all I can do!" He stepped back from the rail.

He couldn't save Erich von Wechsler. And Klein got away. But he could sail.

It cleared away the last bit of uncertainty.

"She'd haul things out of this boat in an instant. She'd tear it apart to make room, she'd crew it herself, she'd do anything she could. And she'll tear *us* apart if we don't help her. I can't do anything. But I can sail for her."

357

A spasm of emotion crossed Murray's face. He went and picked up his drawing pad, flipped through it, laid it down. He shoved his hands in his pockets. After a moment, he said thickly, "You shoulda seen her with Klein."

And then, a change came to his face. Tension flowed out. He looked at William. "That's how *I* know what she wants. She was gonna die for that packet."

Murray looked at the number *5* on the foremast. He looked at William. "Let's get out of here."

When Mrs. Shrewsbury came humming around the corner of the boathouse with a freshly baked Dundee cake, *Maggie Bright* was not there. But piled high at the end of the dock was all manner of things. The dinette table. Fishing equipment. Stacks of books. Clare's pots of herbs and flowers, the red and yellow Chinese paper lanterns, the little grill, the deck chairs, the foldout table that went with the deck chairs, and boxes and boxes of Clare's things from Murray's cabin and the back cabin.

She certainly hoped to find things from her own cabin in that pile, and she hoped they didn't wreck that priceless treasure trove of a newspaper collection, *Rocket Kid*

358

and Salamander. She'd collect *that* from the pile straightaway, and store it in the Anderson shelter. *Someone* had to look out for things.

"What am I going to do with you?" she asked the cake. "They've gone to war."

Later, when Frederick Butterfield arrived at the deserted Elliott's Boatyard with Father David Fitzpatrick, he found a Dundee cake sitting on a note in the middle of the walkway to the dock, directed to, of all people, himself.

Dear Detective Inspector Butterfield,
We've gone to war. The others, to France; myself, to Dover or to Ramsgate, where I am sure to be of good use to receive our boys home. Do check in on Clare — she will be lonely without us. And I am sure she would very much like to see the dear Burglar Vicar.

Do enjoy the cake.

Regards,
Mrs. Iris Shrewsbury
P.S. Do you know? I feel as though I were born for such a time as this. Of course, I feel as though I were born for many things. It is wonderful to be 67, retired, and of good use.

P.P.S. Apologize to the BV for me. My actions with a teakettle are entirely reflexive.

May 30–31, 1940

"Well, how many small boats do you want? A hundred?"

To [Captain Eric] Bush it didn't seem then that any man as yet appreciated the full gravity of the situation. His voice tight with emotion, he answered: "Look, sir, not a hundred boats — every boat that can be found in the country should be sent if we're to even stand a chance."

— RICHARD COLLIER,
The Sands of Dunkirk

The rich and the famous, the poor and the unknown, as motley a bunch as ever set sail made up this mercy fleet.

— RICHARD COLLIER,
The Sands of Dunkirk

Let's hold our nerve, and see how many troops we can get away.

— WINSTON CHURCHILL

Lieutenant Ian Cox, First Lieutenant of the destroyer *Malcolm,* could hardly believe his eyes. There, coming over the horizon toward him, was a mass of dots that filled the sea. The *Malcolm* was bringing her third load of troops back to Dover. The dots were all heading the other way — toward Dunkirk. . . .

As he watched, the dots materialized into vessels . . . they were little ships of every conceivable type — fishing smacks . . . drifters . . . excursion boats . . . glittering white yachts . . . mud-spattered hoppers . . . Thames sailing barges . . . dredges, trawlers, and rust-streaked scows. . . .

Cox felt a sudden surge of pride. Being here was no longer just a duty; it was an honor and a privilege. Turning to a somewhat startled chief boatswain's mate standing beside him, he burst into the Saint Crispin's Day passage from Shakespeare's *Henry V:*

And Gentlemen in England, now abed
Shall think themselves accurs'd they
    were not here.

— WALTER LORD,
The Miracle of Dunkirk

22

The squad of six men crested the rise of a dune and beheld the beach for the first time.

The nightmare scene before them was so vast and dark and flashing and thunderous, so unbelievably frightening, that at first no one could say a word.

Like prehistoric terrors of the air, wheeling Stukas and Heinkels harried their prey on the beaches and the harbor, flying overhead in groups of two and three, diving, strafing, bombing. They had just caught a glimpse of the man-clad pier in the harbor on their left when diving planes drew their attention to a ship that had slipped from the mole. They watched the destroyer take pounding after pounding of bombs and bullets until finally the deck exploded in flame. They heard men scream as they leapt, flaming, into the water; and suddenly the ship blew up, obscuring the entire harbor with first a blinding yellow flash and then a geysered veil of water and concrete, flying steel, flaming rubble.

The six men who'd crested the dune cried out in horror and rage, and realized that others did too, a great roar of wrath from massive black patches on the beaches.

The massive black patches ranging over the sands first brought to mind a continent of seaweed, until it materialized as thousands and thousands of men stretched out before them in milling dark groups, in great snaking queues. They saw these patches en masse first, and then as their minds adjusted they saw smaller patches, and smaller yet, down to individual spots scattered and walking about, some joining a group or leaving one. Finally, they saw patches not moving at all, at least not of their own accord; these lay scattered upon the beach, or rolled stiff and oil-slicked in a blood-frothed surf, or were stretcher-borne to an aid station or a place where they piled the dead.

"You had the feeling that if you just got to Dunkirk, it's all over," said Baylor, his voice small. "Everyone's safe."

"That was England, remember?"

"What's this?"

"Not England."

Blazing wrecks dotted the harbor amid a

forest of masts where boats had sunk. Straight down at the beach itself, they watched a blue-painted fishing trawler fifty yards out from the shoreline try to navigate wreckage with one man hanging off the bow, watching intently and calling back orders to the skipper.

"Look there!" They looked to where Griggs pointed.

Boom, boom, boom. A destroyer lying a mile off, its Bofors guns angled high as they could manage, blazed away at a dive-bomber and clipped its wing. Trailing smoke, the bomber banked from the dive and looked as though it might pull out when it suddenly veered, caught a wingtip on the waves — then cartwheeled on the surface of the sea, and exploded.

A roar went up from the seaweed continent, and the men on the dune pounded each other on the back.

"Cheers for the Royal Navy!"

"Did you see that, Milty? Did you see it?"

"What fine shooting, what an impossible angle!"

"Lads, will you look at that!" Balantine yelled with a grin. He pointed at the blue-painted trawler. It had tied up to what looked like . . . "They've made a pier out of lorries!"

"Ran 'em out on low tide the other day," said a soldier close by, a flush of lingering joy on his face from witnessing the plane wreck. "Brilliant, hey? Made it easier for smaller craft like that to get in. Loading goes faster. There's some British ingenuity, hey?"

"How long have you been here?" Jamie asked him.

"Two days."

"Two days?" said Jamie. He stared down to the harbor. "That's how long the queues are taking?"

"Some have been here longer than me. They can only load by that eastern mole and by the lorry jetties they've thrown together, two or three of 'em so far. I heard there's another up by Bray Dunes. You better get your men into a group. They take us off in order, best as they can. Until then, you can amuse yourself by staying alive. But look over there — see? We're starting to see smaller craft like that come straight in to the beaches. Lifeboats, day sailers, you name it. They're taking us off by tens and twenties and fifties out to the destroyers. You know what they do then? They come straight back for more. While hell rains down. Never seen anything like it. They're civilians." He shook his head. "Brave, brave lads."

"I'll say," said another next to him.

"Some of 'em ain't lads," another ginger-haired soldier added. "I seen old 'uns out there, old enough to be me grandpap."

"Why are there bodies in the water?" Jamie asked.

"Well, you saw that ship blow up. Some are killed by the bombs, and some just can't swim."

Jamie looked around, and said, "Where do we go to get into groups?"

"Incoming! Incoming!"

"Take cover!"

A droning field of planes appeared from the east in three columns, some in formation over the waters, some over the beaches, some over land. Jamie watched, mesmerized, as a single plane dropped . . . four, five . . . ten, eleven . . . fifteen bombs.

Milton dragged Jamie down to the sand and threw himself on top of him.

Wet sand filled Jamie's mouth, and he kicked and struggled and finally shoved Milton off. Coughing, spitting, he righted his helmet and wiped his mouth only to be pushed down again, his face shoved once more into skin-scouring sand. He couldn't breathe, and frantically threw Milton off.

He spit sand, scrubbed his mouth, and roared at Milton, "Mind those stitches! I

367

can't have you comin' apart!"

"He's already done that, hasn't he?"

"Shut up, Griggs!" shouted Jamie, Baylor, and Balantine.

Each man emerged from wherever he'd dove into the sand on the dune, took stock of himself, brushed off sand and righted kits and helmets, and then took stock of each other.

"Everyone all right then?" said Balantine. He looked down to the beach. "We need to find out where we're supposed to be. That's one bloody massive queue."

"Go see that man with the megaphone," said their earlier informant, brushing off sand and pointing west. "There — that's Captain Tennant, actually. He's in charge."

The man with the megaphone, dressed in naval blues and wearing a helmet with some sort of sticker on the front, moved along with another man trotting behind, calling out, "Maintain order! Stay in your groups! Queue in an orderly fashion!" His naval blues stood out in fresh, welcomed contrast to filthy army greens and browns.

"Nice to see someone clean," said Griggs.

"Griggs, keep everyone together," said Balantine. "I'll see where we're supposed to go." Hand on his helmet, he went off at a trot, glancing at the eastern sky.

■ ■ ■ ■

Jamie and Baylor sat watching the beaches. Curtis dropped where he stood and fell asleep in an instant. Milton sat gazing at the sky, and Balantine had not yet returned. Griggs sat apart, cleaning his gun and glaring at the east as if daring a bomber to come — as if a Bren could take down a bomber.

"You ever see so many people in one place?" Jamie said.

"I went to the Olympic Games in '36 with my cousin. That was a lot." But Baylor sounded as though it didn't quite compare to what lay before their eyes.

The entire beach, once a place for holidaymakers, was a shambles of debris. In the dunes, you couldn't take a step without landing on something bomb-strewn; a bit of a brightly colored beach umbrella, a piece of what looked like a café table thrown hundreds of yards from the line of bombed shops fronting the beach, broken army equipment, and broken men.

They lay everywhere, and not just soldiers; they saw dead civilians, same as inland, the old and the young, men and women. Some of the French townspeople, weeping, collected their dead on stretchers and bore them away.

"Bullets are the worst," said their informant, whose name was Peter. "You can avoid the bombs, but when they come in strafing, that's another thing. Seems they always come out of nowhere. That one's buggered," he said with a nod, and they followed his line of sight. At first Jamie thought he referred to Milton, and felt a flash of offense; but past Milton, down in the surf of the beach, soldiers began to roll out of a stalled-out motorboat, and wade back to shore.

"Poor sods. You wait all that time. Bit anticlimactic. Especially if you get bombed on the way to a destroyer. I'll come back just for that. You see that happen, and all you see is bloody murder. Killing men who can't shoot back. It's just wrong. I don't care if it's war. It's wrong. I'll be back for that." Peter nodded. "I'll be back for a lifeboat I saw. Crewed by two kids, all shoutin' and friendly and helpin' the lads. One of 'em jumps in the water to help push a bloke up — gets strafed to pieces, cut right in half. Then a bomber comes, finishes off the boat. Blew it to kindling." He pulled out a pack of cigarettes. "Couldn't see the name of the boat, so I named it in my head. The *Endeavor*. I'll be back for that. I hope I get the chance to kill 'em just as defense-less."

"I'll kill them now," said Griggs with a shrug.

"You have ammo for that?" Peter asked of the Bren.

"One magazine left."

"Heavy things, they are," Peter said vaguely, lighting his cigarette. Jamie noticed then how bleary-red his eyes were. There probably wasn't much sleeping on the dunes. "They're being slaughtered for us, you know. Right in front of our eyes." He watched the surf. "They're civilians. It's just wrong. We're supposed to do the saving. But we have to watch it every day, and not a bloody thing we can do. They keep coming, more and more of them. We have to watch when they're blown to bits."

"Just shut it, why don't you?" said Griggs.

Peter blinked, looked at him in surprise.

"Don't mind him. He's just ornery," Baylor told him. "Since birth."

Griggs pulled up his gun and aimed for Baylor. Jamie felt a rush of weakness, and then Griggs swung the gun to the sky and let loose a continuing burst on a passing plane. The plane strafed their area, stitching a sand-pocked line right beside Griggs as men dove frantically for cover. Griggs continued shooting at it long after it passed, the only one standing when it came and when it left.

"Belay that!" someone shouted at Griggs. "Oy! Get your man under control!"

"It does no good, you moron!" A soldier sat up, brushing himself off. "You think we haven't tried it? Save it for the German infantry, they'll be here soon enough!" He looked around. "Everyone all right? Peter — you all right?"

But Griggs, to the astonishment of all, took the Bren by the end of the barrel and slammed it repeatedly on the packed sand. The magazine snapped off, the stock cracked and broke apart.

"Griggs!" Jamie bellowed.

"It jammed," said Griggs.

"Oh, that's smart!" an onlooker jeered. "That's tellin' 'em!"

"He's gone mad!" said Curtis, wildly looking about. "Where's Balantine?"

Effort noises erupted from the red-faced Griggs with each blow of the Bren upon the ground.

Milton rose and went to Griggs, hands raised. "My name is Captain Jacobs," he said. "My name is Captain Jacobs."

Griggs stopped, breathing hard, staring at the captain. He wiped spittle from his

372

mouth, looked at Jamie, back at the captain. And the captain looked back at him, straight at him, brown eyes earnest beneath the dirty white bandage.

"My name is Captain Jacobs." He lowered his hands.

Griggs looked at the ruined Bren in his hands, threw it aside. "All this time, you can't come up with anything more interesting —"

"That's all you need to know, Griggs," said Baylor, but the men turned at the sound of his voice.

He lay on the ground, gazing proudly at Milton, blood running between the fingers clutching his side.

"Do you know, the word *exodus* is actually Greek," Baylor said weakly. "It means a departure. You'd think it would be a Hebrew word. It should be, shouldn't it? I wonder what the Hebrew is for *exodus.*"

Milton sat beside Baylor, watching the medic work.

Baylor looked up at him. "You'd probably know the Hebrew. Locked up in that head of yours." He winced, and looked down. "I'm not dying, man. Let's keep it that way. It passed right through."

"Passed right through, and took a chunk

of you with it," said the medic.

"Baylor?" Balantine appeared, carrying a box. He set it down. "What happened?"

"Ah. There you are. I thought Griggs was going to take me out, but at least it was an enemy bullet. There's an understatement — feels like an orange went through me."

Balantine took off his helmet and went to a knee beside him.

"Where have you been?" Baylor asked crossly. His face was very white. "We were worried. You'll never guess: Milton said something new. Go on, Milton, say it."

"I got lost coming back," said Balantine. "Then someone pulled up with a load of bully beef." He looked at the medic. "How is it?"

"Come on, Milton, say it. He said a full sentence. Come on, old boy. Ouch."

"Bully beef?" the medic said, pressing a thick pad against the wound. "Where did they get that? Haven't eaten in two days."

Eyes on Baylor, Balantine felt in the box for a tin and held it out to him. The medic took it with bloodied fingers, and dropped it down the front of his shirt.

"How is it?" Balantine asked.

"It did miss the vitalities, but he's lost an impressive amount of blood. He'll be all right — under normal circumstances, that is." The medic threw a dark look at Griggs. "King Brutus here won't let me take him to the aid station."

Griggs shrugged, and said to Balantine, "You said to keep us together."

The medic gave Milton a nod. "Come on, chap, let's sit him up. I need to wrap the bandage. Sorry, mate, this is gonna hurt and I'm out of morphine." He and Milton gently pulled Baylor to a sitting position. Baylor groaned. "Easy there. Right, hold him steady." Milton kept his arms about Baylor's shoulders while the medic finished wrapping the bandage. He tied it off firmly, checked its sturdiness, and ignored Baylor's protest that it was too tight. They eased him down. The medic sat back on his heels and took up a handful of sand. He rubbed it vigorously between his hands to get rid of the blood.

"Did you see that, Balantine?" Baylor, taking shallow breaths, nodded at Milton. "He did as asked. Well done, Milty. Elliott, he's coming around."

"My name is Captain Jacobs," the captain offered. When the men chuckled at Balantine's amazement, the medic glanced at them all, puzzled. He shook his head, and got to his feet. He said to Balantine, "Look, if you're in charge, you should know they're not taking any wounded, not on stretchers." He nodded at the loading ship in the harbor. "Stretchers take up too much room. Best get him to the aid station. There's a temporary one set up over at the church, St. Eloi. Middle of town, south of the quay."

"He stays with us," said Griggs.

"We won't leave him for the Germans," said Jamie. His attention kept going back to Milton. He was his best yet. The expressions, the little things, like waving off a fly or rubbing sand from his eye; there was a new ease about him, and except for the new sentence from which he did not deviate, he looked and acted like any other bloke around.

"Suit yourself," said the medic. "But if you keep him here, he'll have a long wait, no water, no food, and he needs both. He'd at least have that at the aid station. Thanks, by the way," he said to Balantine, and tapped the tin through his shirt. "Well, carry on, lads. Off to save mankind." He came to attention, snapped a comical salute, and clicked his heels. "Wish me luck." He picked up his medic bag and left.

" 'He stays with us,' " Baylor said. "I will treasure that speech. Griggs, it appears *you* are the pansy for at last, we know you are in love with me."

Laughter from most, but not from Griggs. "I should have shot you."

Baylor chuckled, and then winced. "Oh . . . oh . . ."

"My name is Captain Jacobs."

"You couldn't manage a little more Milton, could you?" Baylor asked. "For old time's sake?" He closed his eyes. "I'm tired."

"Don't go to sleep just yet," said Balantine, patting his shoulder and rising. "We've got to join a group west of here for our spot in the queue. They'll call us down to embark when our number's up. They say things are speeding up, with the smaller craft. They're now loading from the beaches as well."

"We've seen it."

"Surf's kicking up," said Curtis, looking down to the water. "Unless it changes, won't be loading there for long."

"Yes, and that's why I was thinking of the word *exodus.* We could use a parting of the Red Sea, couldn't we? We could use a miracle." Baylor's eyes were still closed. "Pharaoh's army, bearing down upon the entire nation of Israel. Milton? How about you play the part of Moses, Balantine can be Aaron, and maybe Griggs could be God. Acts like him, at times."

Balantine motioned with his head to Jamie, and they stepped a few paces away.

"How is he, really?" he asked quietly.

"You heard the medic. He's lost a lot of blood."

"How do you think he'll do? Do you think he can — ?"

Griggs joined them at that moment, and Balantine looked less ready to talk. It was a little odd, really; technically, Griggs was in charge by order of enlistment. But it came clear to all of them where Griggs's skill lay, and it had to do with leading men in combat, but not in other ways. He seemed to look to Balantine for those other ways much as Jamie did.

"Do you think he'll manage?" said Balantine.

"He's a pansy, but he'll manage," said Griggs.

"I heard that," Baylor said.

Jamie said, "I think he'll be all right. We'll help."

"Yes, but you heard what he said." Balantine rubbed the back of his head, thinking hard. "They won't be able to lay him out. If they see that he's wounded —"

"We'll prop him between us." Griggs said over his shoulder, "You *can* suck it up for a *small* amount of time, can't you, Baylor?"

"Now that I know you care, I've got something to live for."

Even Griggs cracked a smile. But Balantine looked out at the sea.

His shoulders came down. He looked at the other two. "Look, it'll be a hard crossing. If he's already lost a lot of blood, how will he stand it? What's better: risk it and lose him, or —"

Jamie grabbed his arm and pulled him a few steps farther away, Griggs following. "Do you really want to leave him for the Germans?" Jamie tried hard to keep his tone low. "How do we know how our men will be treated? Will there be a prisoner exchange? We don't know. We have no idea! Balantine, listen: when I first met you, you said you'd never leave a man behind."

"That was before this!" Balantine hissed. "If it comes to wondering if he'll even *survive* that passage, there's a choice to be made!"

"We've lost Grayling," said Griggs. "No more."

That came closest to deciding it.

After a long moment, Balantine nodded.

He called Curtis over. "You and Griggs scrounge up some water, as much as you can. I don't care what you have to do, just get it. We'll stay put 'til you get back, and then we'll head for our group. See if you can find something to lay Baylor on to get him down there. Mind our position as you go; I got lost coming back." He looked about, and pointed inland. "Look — we're straight out from . . . whatever that is. That bombed redbrick place with the yellow canopy."

Curtis and Griggs collected canteens, and started off.

" 'We're gonna hang out the washing on the Siegfried Line . . .' " a few men sang nearby with gusto, one raising a bottle to the sky.

"Bring us back some of what they've got," Jamie called after Curtis and Griggs, and Curtis called back, "We'll do our best!"

"Too late, mate!" one of the singers roared. "This is French champagne! We got it all, and we ain't sharin'!"

"Oy!" one of his compatriots remonstrated. "That ain't fittin'. Where's the manners yer muvver raised you wif? We share with the wounded."

"We do?" said the first, perplexed.

"Oh, aye! It's fittin'! It's noble! You, there — rouse up a bottle and share wif the man what's spilled his blood for England." He held up his bottle to Baylor. "To the man!" Then he resumed leading the men in song: " 'We're gonna hang out the washing on the —' " he cupped a hand to his ear, while the others roared, " 'Sieg-fried Line!' " One came unsteadily over with a bottle of champagne and handed it to Milton, sitting next to Baylor. "Cheers, mate!" he said to Baylor, raising his own bottle, and then he staggered back to his group.

Balantine and Jamie went back to Baylor.

"From imposition of strict laws to free acceptance of large grace," Milton was telling Baylor. "From servile fear to filial, works of law to works of faith."

"Is that how you like your bedtime stories, Baylor?" Jamie asked, settling down beside him. He took the bottle from the captain. "Here's your warm milk."

"Those thousand decencies that daily flow, words and actions," Milton said. He gazed at the sky. "Love leads up to heaven — is both way and guide."

"You hear that?" Baylor opened his eyes. "He almost sounds happy." He looked up at Milton. "Do you know, Captain? I wish I had served under you."

It was a shame that he closed his eyes before he saw the look on Milton's face. Jamie couldn't wait to tell Baylor later. *You should have seen it, Baylor. He looked like you were one of his men.*

Milton laid his hand on Baylor's arm. "Be strong, live happy, and love. Thou to mankind be good and friendly still, and oft return."

"Will do," Baylor murmured. "Wish I had paper to write this down."

Jamie worked the cork off the champagne with his teeth, and watched a ribbon of mist curl from the bottle. He went to take a drink, and then handed it to Milton. "You first, Captain Jacobs. Cheers."

Milton took the bottle, turned it in his hands, seemed to read the label, and then looked to the sea. He watched the waters and then the sky, and absently handed the bottle back without taking a drink.

Jamie received it with a sigh, glanced at Balantine, who was looking at him. He gave a little shrug and took a sip — and then made a face. "Oh, that's nasty! How can anyone drink that?" He wiped his mouth and handed it to Balantine. "What I wouldn't do for a good stout from Evelyn's. I'd eat her soggy chips, too."

He suddenly felt a dizzy wash of fatigue, and wondered when he'd lain down last. He stretched out on the ground for the first time in what seemed like days, and groaned for the pleasure. Felt like he was melting into the sand.

"I could sleep for a week."

He had no sooner covered his face with

his helmet, than a drone of the next bank of planes came, and with it men shouting, "Incoming! Incoming!"

23

Murray and William milled about the lobby of the Port Authority building near the Tower with dozens of other volunteers. Most had come when they heard from those with family and friends in the Royal Navy that volunteer crews were needed; others learned from coworkers or neighbors whose crafts had been requisitioned.

"Clare'll be mad she missed this," Murray said.

William sipped his coffee. He wished he had time to change his clothing. He still wore his suit for the office, and his shoes could not be more unsuitable. He looked around, peeved to see men outfitted exactly the way he wanted to be: deck shoes with sailcloth trousers and warm jerseys beneath rain slickers. One chap wore the gear of the Royal London Yacht Club, topped by a yachting hat with the club's insignia; contentedly smoking a pipe, he looked as though he were ready for a pleasure cruise.

He kept an eye out for John Elliott and Minor Roberts but didn't see them in this crowd. They'd likely already gone over. He wished them well and hoped Mrs. Shrewsbury did them justice with her prayers.

Men from every walk of life crowded the lobby, waiting for assignments and doing the same as he, sipping coffee or tea and looking about. He recognized some from the Royal Yacht Club, and nodded to an old instructor from the first yacht he'd crewed when he was in his teens. He smiled a little, recalling that first lesson in how to tie a bowline. Something about a rabbit chasing round a tree, jumping into the hole . . .

"Glad I'm not the only one dressed for Whitehall." A man who looked like he had stepped off Savile Row stood next to William, sipping coffee from the same sort of paper cup. "I didn't dare run home. Terrified I'd miss out."

"Oh, I don't know." William sized up a few men nearby. "I think we could take those two — I fancy that one's shoes."

"I like the other's slicker. Shall we give it a go?"

"Hmm. Perhaps not. That one's got more muscle in a single nostril than I do in both biceps."

They shared a chuckle, and the other said, "I'm Peter Goodson. Someone told me you're William Percy. Hero of the —"

"Complete bollocks. Every word. I should know, I wrote it." William put out his hand. "Very long story."

Amused, the man shook his hand. "Sounds like an interesting one."

"Not half as interesting as this." They looked around at the milling volunteers. "So what do you do for a living?"

"Typographical designer. My friend over there is an advertising exec with Montblanc. He's my weekend sailing mate — my wife gets seasick just walking on a dock." He gestured with the paper cup. "He's talking with a car salesman, and that other bloke is a garbage collector. All walks, eh?"

"All walks."

"It's rather heartening, you know, this pulling together. Glad for a chance to do our bit. I get tired of inked fingers as my red badge of courage." He raised a brow, and took a sip. "I do hear things are interesting over there."

"I hear they're bombing the route to Dunkirk. And that some boats are blown up from beneath. That is interesting."

"Do you know anything else?"

"Nothing more than that. It's all a bit

386

vague and terrifying."

He nodded. "No one seems to know much. Well, we're in for a bit of an adventure, then. Can't remember the last time I dodged a bomb with a yacht."

William smiled. "Nor I."

"Good luck, then."

"The same." They shook hands, and William watched the man walk back to his friend.

"You see Cap'n John and the creepy recluse guy?" asked Murray.

"No."

"Hey — how far is that hospital? We got time to drop in on Clare?"

"Not likely. I don't want to risk it. Look — there's the fellow who told us to wait."

Lieutenant Sanderson, the man they'd met an hour ago, appeared at the door to an office. "Percy and Vance?" he called.

William raised his hand. "Here." They made their way over to him.

"Right. I've sorted your paperwork and got you assigned. I'll need signatures." He handed them each a clipboard and a pen. "Per Lieutenant Wares, you'll be crewing the *Maggie Bright*. She's been taken down to Sheerness, where they'll assign her a naval rating who will outfit her for the journey. She'll go over tonight around 2200 hours. Pulled by tug to save fuel."

"What's this?" Murray asked of the paper.

"This is the T.124, because we are desperately fond of paperwork and even more fond of giving it names. Makes you a volunteer for one month in the service of His Majesty's Royal Navy — welcome aboard, Yank." He gave Murray a wink and a grin. "You're the second American I've signed. The other's an accountant. Well done — glad *some* of you won't listen to your ambassador." He pointed across the room. "You see the man over there with the ridiculous hat? He'll get you down to Sheerness with the others. Your ride leaves in about an hour. Right? Thank you, gentlemen." He shook their hands. "God bless, keep safe, and come home." He consulted his list. "Randall? Goodson?"

They didn't leave in an hour; they left in two. And by the time they finally made it to Sheerness and were reunited with the *Maggie Bright,* they hardly recognized her.

They were dropped off at a quay with several other men, where a great tug stood off in the harbor. Several automobiles positioned at various angles along the quay and headlands trained their headlights on the docks to illumine the bustling work; many vessels were tied to the dock, and naval men moved swiftly at their work, loading vessels with stores, painting fixtures, checking lines and engines, sometimes talking with boat owners or crewmen.

They found the *Maggie Bright* only because an officer led them to her, not because they recognized her.

"Oh no," Murray groaned. "What've they done to you, Mags?"

A young naval rating, who couldn't be more than twenty years old, looked up when they came aboard and gave a nod.

"Welcome aboard, shipmates. Smudge is the name. What do we call you?"

"Smudge, what've you done to my girl?" Murray jumped down from the boarding plank to Maggie's deck.

"I'm William Percy. This is Murray Vance," William said, grabbing hold of a line as he stepped down to the deck. He shook Smudge's hand, then took off his suit coat and tossed it on a bench. He rolled up his sleeves and looked around.

Oh, Clare. No, it won't do for you to see this.

All of Maggie's beautiful brass fittings had been painted black, including the lovely brass bell. The salon windows and portholes had been taped over with brown paper. Any area of steel or chrome — grommets, railings, rings — had been darkened with paint. And unfortunately, some of that paint had ended up on the deck and the wood trim. Worst of all, her beautiful white transom with *Maggie Bright* spelled out in such artistic lettering had disappeared beneath a still-shining sheath of black.

"Anything that catches light has to be doused," said Smudge. "Otherwise, we're nothing but a bright shining target for the night bombers. They drop magnetic mines along the routes at night, and see what other havoc they can manage when they do."

"Looks like she's goin' as the grim reaper for Halloween," Murray muttered. "What kinda name is Smudge?"

"Smith, in some parts."

"Smudge. Like ink. I like it. What's this?" Murray asked, nodding at a barrel in the stern.

"That's oil."

"For what?"

"Dousing phosphorescence. A clever lad aboard a destroyer came up with it, a bloke who serves with my best mate." He pointed to other barrels and boxes. "There's petrol, paraffin, and rope. We've got rations below for three days. Here — you'll wear these once we're under way." He gave them each a tin navy hat.

Murray held it out from him. "I ain't wearin' that. I'll look stupid."

"Um . . . yes, you *will* wear that. Those are orders." A challenging flicker came to the young man's eyes; he looked ready to put down any rebellion, and seemed to welcome the chance.

"Oh, for heaven's sakes, Murray," said William in a bored tone. "You've officially signed on with the RN, remember? I assume a signature in the States means the same in England? Rather oathlike?" To Smudge, he said, "Have you been there yet?"

Smudge finished staring down Murray, and turned to William. "No. But my mate has. He says it's worse than we can possibly imagine."

"I can imagine a lot," said Murray unhappily, idly swinging the tin hat by the strap.

William looked around. "What's to be done?"

"You can go below and tear up anything you can for bandages — apparently some of the fellows are in quite a state. My mate said he's seen it all. Other than that, all is ready. We're just waiting for the others." He looked about. "There wasn't much to do, readying this one, she's in very good shape. Her engine hasn't been run much. Cleaned out some sludge and now she's tip-top. You should see some of the other craft. They're desperate enough to take anything." He consulted his watch under the light of a dock lamp. "Shouldn't be long now. We'll tie on to that Leviathan out there, along with three or four other vessels, and then we'll rendezvous at Ramsgate to join up with an armed convoy."

"Armed convoy," William murmured, shaking his head.

"Hopefully we'll get our orders at Ramsgate, as far as what we're supposed to be doing on the beaches. And then —" he looked at them, excitement and apprehension and old-fashioned naval superiority on his face — "well, then we're off for Dunkirk."

Ten minutes out of Ramsgate and William put his suit coat back on. Half an hour, and he huddled behind Smudge in the cockpit, wrapped in a stiff piece of deck carpet. Why didn't they think to save some of Murray's clothing when they emptied her?

Maggie Bright followed behind a great powerful tug to which three others had tied on: a Thames fireboat which had never been to sea, another yacht similar in size to Maggie, and a beamy coastal fishing boat made for the mud flats, which had also never been to open sea. They traveled in the company of six other boats not pulled by tugs, though shepherded by an armed tug on one side, and an armed vessel on the other, one that William didn't recognize — someone called it a Dutch 'scoot.' Silly word.

Everyone should have a chance to look evil straight on.

Conversation with Clare went round and round in William's head, snatches from when they sat together at Westminster Abbey, the cab ride to the hospital, the day he met her when they sat at the restaurant and he had no clue that the girl he'd knocked over in the street would come to be . . . the sort whose words he would replay.

She took the things he felt and packaged them into sentences and spoke them aloud. She spoke them bitterly, or with joy, or with the sort of *feeling* that made William want to look away in distaste, only to listen keenly for what might come next.

Let him find us holding high the picture of Erich von Wechsler as proof that his own people *would not have his ways.*

It was the reason he carried Erich's picture next to Cecy's. Clare put it into words. When she had done so, it solidified what was already there into iron. Her spokenness made stronger his unspokenness.

"I'm sick," Murray said from where he'd wedged himself in the companionway. "She's gonna need a squad of carpenters when we're back. Thank God Clare can't see this."

William, too, had a hard time not wincing every time one of the accompanying boats missed one of Maggie's rubber fenders and thumped her hull.

From various delays, the little convoy didn't leave Ramsgate for the Kwinte Buoy until nearly 1 a.m. They were told of three different routes mapped out by the Admiralty to Dunkirk, and theirs was called route Y. It was the longest route, stretching northeast until it doubled back toward Dunkirk at the Kwinte Buoy — but, as the skipper of their towing tug had informed them when they first set out, it was so far the safest route; easier to navigate and, so far, unseeded with magnetic mines.

But traveling in convoy meant they traveled at the top speed of the slowest boat, and a tug pulling four boats was steady but not fast; they'd heard it took a destroyer and a hospital ship six hours to complete route Y, but they were coming up on four, and had not yet rounded the buoy. William had no idea how long it would take to reach Dunkirk after that — they didn't say.

"Channel's uncommon calm," Smudge said for the third time. It was his turn at the helm. He and William took turns by the hour. "Haven't seen it like this, this time of year. Look at that — a gray carpet." He nodded to the other boats. "Some of these skippers have never been out of sight of land. They don't know how unusual this calm is. I *am* a bit worried about the Kwinte Buoy light — I've been up there on night patrols, it almost blinds you when you're upon it. Anything could be hiding up there, you'd never see it."

Smudge didn't stop babbling. It interrupted his conversations with Clare. Then again — the droning was a nice backdrop to the picnic in his mind. He and Clare sat on a picnic cloth in the park, talking, sharing a lunch, she was laughing at something amusing he'd said . . .

"Another thing that worries me: if Dunkirk is the last Allied-held port on the continent, then straight out from the buoy to the land is enemy-held territory. Enemy-held! I wonder if they've occupied it yet. You know — with artillery and whatnot. If so, will they shell us from the land?"

You knock someone over on the street, you end up with: *William, we have an ally. And William, we are not alone.*

Maggie Bright followed obediently behind the tug on her tether, and other than the occasional nudge and spray from another boat, the passage was indeed remarkably smooth for waters known to be choppy. William kept his eyes on the tug ahead. He was assigned the task to watch for the tug's signal if they were about to be cut loose — the tug's skipper said if the enemy zeroed them, he'd cut them free as fast as possible to break up a large target. Smudge had to be ready to start the engine if that happened, and Murray had to be ready to watch over its transfer from petrol-start to paraffin-run. He stood on the top rung of the companionway ladder, resting on folded arms on the hatch, watching the sky.

Murray straightened, gazing ahead into the darkness. "Bobby, listen — you hear that?"

"Why do you call him Bobby, if his name is William?"

" 'Cause he's a bobby. Somethin's coming. Somethin' big. Straight ahead, port side. Listen to that churning."

"What is it?" William asked, sitting up. A sudden thought came. "Are we armed?" he said to Smudge. "Do we have any guns?"

A more ridiculous question was never asked. A gun from a yacht against a German battleship or U-boat.

Hand on the helm, Smudge rose, peering ahead to port. "No guns."

William put off the piece of carpet and went forward. He grasped the port rail, midships, and leaned an ear into the darkness.

"Them Germans got those U-boats out there?" Murray said, coming to his side.

"Shh."

William finally heard what Murray did, and suddenly the gray carpet of the English Channel darkened as a huge form loomed left. Passing very close against starlight and a crescent moon was a massive shadow.

After an unnerving moment . . .

"Well done, mates!" someone called down, and then comments rained down from everywhere.

"Good luck!"

"Cheers for the mosquito armada!"

"Well done!"

"Thank you, men! Thank you!"

"God bless you! God keep you safe!"

Churning phosphorescence outlined the ship. The massive size could merit that of a destroyer. Smudge called out between cupped hands as she passed, "Douse it with oil!"

"Oy! Keep it down!" someone from the tug called back.

"God keep *you* safe," Smudge murmured, as they watched the great live humming shadow ease away into the night.

The passing encounter, so brief, left William with an odd sense of loneliness. The shadow had teemed with life — he had sensed a great company of souls.

He'd taken no real thought of where he was bound or what awaited.

You shall go to war, and so shall I, said Mrs. Shrewsbury.

He looked southwest. What was out there, at Dunkirk? When first they left England, they'd seen a distant red glow and could hear faint explosions. They were too far away to see or hear it now, but would soon round Kwinte Buoy. What then?

Perhaps the others felt something of the same.

Smudge: "I wonder what it's like, over there."

Murray: "Don't know. But I think we're in for it."

"Good and hearty," said Smudge, settling back into the captain's chair.

"Well, then, bobby," said Murray, turning to William. "In case we get bombed I got somethin' to say. You know that packet? *A,* it proves something bad got inside us. But *B,* there's something else in us, too, that can beat the crap out of the bad. It's in Clare, and Mrs. Shrew, and most of all, the Fitz. But it's in you too, bobs. You came crashin' down that hatch for Clare, and that's good enough for me. That's all I gotta say." He banged the heel of his hand on the hatch, as if to settle it. "Anyone want somethin' hot to drink? Might be the last for a while."

"Tea, please. Sugar and milk," said Smudge.

"Milk inside tea. Ain't never gonna get used to that. Bobby?"

"The same."

"Figures. Comin' up." He disappeared below, talking to himself. "Wonder what my editor would think of a Brit guy. Salamander finds him swimmin' in a tank of milky tea. Cute little strap under his chin. Ha! Bobby the Bobby . . ."

"He's an odd one," commented Smudge. "What does he do for a living?"

"He's an illustrator. Draws for the funny papers." William pushed away from the rail and came back to the cockpit. He settled in and pulled over the carpet, then resumed watch of the tug. "He's rather good at it, actually. *Rocket Kid.* There's a longer title. I don't read the funnies, but I've seen his work."

"Not *Rocket Kid and Salamander*?"

"Yes, that's it."

"You're not serious."

William glanced at him. "I am. His sister owns this ketch."

Smudge made strange little stuttering noises. "And he's below. Making my tea. I am trying very hard to act normal." Then, "Well, in my defense, the name didn't *register*! How could it, how could I think he was *the* Murray Vance? He's supposed to be dead! Drowned off Sicily or Minorca or something. There was never a newspaper account, but that was the rumor. I can't believe it. What am I going to do? *The* Murray Vance!"

William thought idly, Thus will I ever be known as the brother-in-law of *the* Murray Vance.

The shock of the thought roused sense.

You've known her *one week,* he told himself severely. Be reasonable, man. Pull yourself together. No more picnic conversations.

"There was one comic strip where Rocket Kid and Salamander invaded a tribe of pygmy cannibals who'd taken the president of the United States and four other world leaders hostage while on safari . . . but the *president* wasn't the focus, you see; it was

400

his attaché. . . ."

Off Smudge went, while William thought of his frightening subconscious. What things went on in the deep? He was deeper than he thought if something down there had the presumption to cast up very presumptuous thoughts. He snorted. He despised the fashionable celebration of *depth*. His job called for clarity in the shallows: snap decisions, intuition on the fly, no mention of shatterers. Wasn't that depth in its own right?

"— changed my life. On a personal level, you know? He's the reason I finished school, and there he is below. Making tea." He laughed nervously. "Won't know how to act when he comes above."

"I'm sure you'll manage," William snapped. "Shall we turn our minds to other things, such as actually steering clear of that cockleboat?"

"Oh. Right." He adjusted to port. "I named my dog Rocket Kid. Got him a little companion dog just to name him Salamander. I'm very nervous."

And Clare said softly in William's head, *Don't be unkind, William.*

After a moment, he offered the anxious Smudge: "Cheer up, man — he's as down-to-earth as they come. He's actually worse than down-to-earth. What *I* wonder is, how did Murray Vance manage to keep you in school?"

Off Smudge went on a happy monologue.

The little convoy would soon be upon the Kwinte Buoy, there to swing west for the beaches of Dunkirk. The first suggestion of dawn came in the east, and on the convoy sailed.

24

Jamie woke with a shout.

"Wonderful. Now it's not old loony bin; it's his master."

Night had fallen upon the beaches at Dunkirk.

"You should've seen yourself," said Griggs. "Jerking around like a frying fish."

"Just when I start to think you're all right, I remember you're not." Jamie sat up and looked around. They had fallen out with a group of about fifty men, and they were still in the dunes, a few hundred yards up from the surf. "What time is it?"

"We're maybe an hour or so from dawn," said Balantine, the red glow of a cigarette to show where he sat. "Bombing should start anytime. Griggs, you ought to try and get some sleep yourself."

"I don't need sleep," said Griggs. "No more than loony bin. Besides, who can sleep in this? Only Elliott and Curtis. Oh, and

Baylor, 'cause he's half-dead anyway."

"That isn't very nice."

"How about you, Balantine? Have you slept?" Jamie asked.

"Some."

"He doesn't trust me," Griggs said.

"Funny — I actually do."

Milton sat beside Baylor, studying the sky, twisting his wedding ring. Baylor was sleeping. "How is he?" Jamie asked.

"I don't know." The red glow intensified for a moment. "He's quiet. Has been for hours. Captain Jacobs checks him now and again. I don't dare check the bandage. He needs stitches, lots. Likely a lot of other repair work. Can't get home soon enough."

Jamie chuckled. He rubbed sand from the back of his neck. "Last time I had someone do some stitching for me, it was at gunpoint. Seems like forever ago."

"I heard of a French doctor and his wife who work the beaches, sunup to sundown. Maybe we can find them, come daylight."

"In hundreds of thousands of men," Griggs said. "Good luck."

"We can try. What else have we got to do?"

"Sure, you can try — and if you do, there'll be a bloody queue."

Jamie got up, brushed off sand, and rubbed away the grainy crust from the edges of his mouth. He stood and stretched, taking in the sight and sound of the ocean. He couldn't see much, just a white line of washing surf at the beach. He took a drink from his canteen — cold tea that Curtis and Griggs had managed to beg off an aid worker in town — and went over to drop down beside Milton.

"What do you say, Milty? How went the night?" He gave him a nudge. "How about you and Balantine fix us breakfast? I'll take hot tea, eggs, bacon, sausages, and a plate of toast high as my armpit. Jam, butter . . ."

Milton's bandage gave off a white-lavender glow in the darkness. He continued to gaze at the sky and move his wedding ring. He had the vague, lost look again. Maybe it was simply fatigue, but with head wounds, who knew? Jamie found himself thinking to God, What in him is dark, illumine; what is low, raise and support.

Jamie gave him another nudge. "You'll be all right, Milty. Not long now. When the sun comes up, you'll see England from here. You can point out where your wife is."

He looked about. To the west, a refinery still burned on the outskirts of Dunkirk, still casting up oily black billows and an occasional furnace blast of fire. The razed town itself smoldered in hazy pockets of red and orange, the sporadic sound of a tumbling wall or a muffled explosion coming from everywhere. The sound of the sea was comforting, but not the pitiful sounds of the wounded. Medics and naval personnel moved about. Down at the harbor, large ships still loaded at the flimsy eastern breakwater, and very small ones loaded at the beaches, from lorry jetties or the sand itself.

"They're really making a difference, those little ships," Balantine commented. "I counted a hundred and twenty-seven men taken off in the last hour from several different small craft. That's only what I could make out — maybe lots more than that. They all come back for more."

"A hundred and twenty-seven in an hour. Not much," said Griggs. "We need another pier like that." He nodded at the harbor.

"Ask the hundred and twenty-seven if it's not much," said Balantine.

"Where are Baylor's glasses?" Jamie asked, when his eyes had finally accustomed to the dimness. "He didn't lose them in the shooting, did he? Haven't seen them since."

"Might have done." Balantine continued to watch the beach. "Strange thing to be waiting for rescue."

Jamie scanned the shores, and at first, a

thing perplexed him: in the dark seaweed continent of men came the glow of thousands of orderly pinpricks of orange, like stationary fireflies. It took Jamie a moment to realize those pinpricks were cigarettes.

A muffled boom drew his attention to the far eastern perimeter.

"How close are they?" he asked.

"Closer," said Balantine. "I talked to a naval lieutenant a while ago. Up till now their shells have fallen short. Not anymore. On the far east end of the beach, we saw a shell land on one of the little ships. At first we thought it escaped any major damage, and all of a sudden it burst into flames. It had just loaded." The cigarette glow deepened. No one spoke for a moment.

"They've been shelling at night?"

"Some."

"We really are cut off," Jamie said, hardly believing the words.

"Good and true."

"We still don't know how big their army is," Jamie said.

"I think we have an idea," said Balantine, "if they could rout numbers like this. I'm still trying to work out how it happened so fast."

"I'm still trying to work out how we'll face

those at home," said Jamie.

It was a stinging admission.

Griggs laughed. "You think we'll make it home?" He jerked his thumb to the perimeter. "Can't you hear that? It's coming from the west now. We're surrounded. We barely have ammunition to hold them back, and even what we do have, how long will it last? Panzers should be here anytime, and if they don't get us, then ho lads, just wait 'til dawn — bombers back in force."

"Well, we mustn't panic," said Balantine.

"I'm not *panicking,*" Griggs snapped. "I hate the bloody uselessness. I hate being *rescued.* If I die in battle, so be it. But let it be battle — not this. Not chased, and surrounded, and so bloody *helpless* and *useless.*"

Tactfully, no one brought up the gun Griggs himself had made useless.

"Try to think of it this way, Griggs: we're not being rescued — we're just all in it together. Civilians and military." Balantine's tone took on a heartening cadence. "They're getting us home so we can fight again. That's it; that's all. We're in it together."

If it didn't make Griggs feel better, it helped Jamie.

Then Jamie suddenly sat up straight, staring down to the beaches in the predawn dimness. He got to his feet.

"What is it?" asked Balantine. He put out the cigarette in the sand, and joined Jamie.

It couldn't be. It was dark, very hard to see — it was impossible.

Yet . . .

"I swear I'm seeing things. Only — look, do you see that boat straight out from here? To the left of — whatever it is, with the ladder sticking out. See the man on its deck?"

"No."

"There."

Balantine looked down the length of his arm.

"That's Minor Roberts."

"Who?"

Jamie lowered his arm, a grin rising, a flush of delight. "It's Minor Roberts! I'd know him anywhere! I'd know that old tub of his blind! He's lived in it all my life, at my dad's boatyard. Took me down to Evelyn's for a beer before I shipped out. Good old Minor!" He shook his head, incredulous. "What's he doing here? That lunky old river barge, it's never *been* to the —"

And the next thought took his breath.

"Elliott?"

If Minor Roberts was here, it meant his dad was too.

"Elliott, what's the matter?"

He turned to Balantine. He could hardly get the words out, they came so thick.

"The shelled boat you saw — was it a fishing trawler, was her name *Lizzie Rose*?" When Balantine shrugged and shook his head helplessly, he stared down to the beaches. "He would've come with Minor. My dad's here, in this. What am I gonna do?"

"Easy, Elliott," said Balantine. "It'll be all right."

"It won't be all right!" Jamie bellowed.

He realized that up until now all had been well with him, all the rotten things they'd come through, the death they'd seen, losing his mates, losing others on the way — all had been well because what mattered most was safe at home in England. Before his eyes, he'd lose everything.

Fear, panic, madness swirled. Jamie stumbled a few steps forward.

Was he gone already, while Jamie slept? Did he die right there, within shouting distance?

The captain was at his side, words at his ear. "God towards thee hath done his part — do thine." Of course he came for you, Jamie. It's what fathers do. Let him do his part — do yours.

He clutched his head. "I can't lose him!"

410

"The mind is its own place, and in itself can make a heaven of hell, a hell of heaven." Think clearly. Don't panic. And come — sit with me. We'll watch for him, and if we see him, why, we'll run on down and shout, "Well done."

Jamie pressed his face in the crook of his arm until hard breathing subsided.

After a moment, he nodded. The two sat on the crest of the dune.

Griggs watched Elliott and the captain. He watched Balantine standing like a sentry behind them. He unscrewed his canteen and took a sip.

25

May 31, 1940. Or is it June 1.
From: A Barn in Dover
To: The London Hospital
Whitechapel Road
Whitechapel
Room number unknown. Please deliver
to: Clare Childs, she who recently
underwent a partial spleen-ectomy.

My Dear Clare,
There is much to tell and little time to
tell it for the need is ghastly great; and
for the first time I curse the fact that I
am 67. My body, I have discovered in
this test of tests, is inhabited by a spirit
who thinks it is 27. I am weary, and appalled by this treasonous fact. I feel the
day in my spine.

I shall explain.

I arrived at the Dover train station not
by rail, as the entire railway system has

been commandeered. Our men are being received in Ramsgate and Dover, where they are revitalized by extremely necessary stopgap measures, and then shuttled off to all parts of England. They arrive at the harbor shipload by shipload, boat by boat, in every condition you can think, bodies as well as boats. One ship literally sank in the harbor as men disembarked. What heights of exaltation to watch men dive into the water to save others! I wept aloud. We all did.

Some ships come in blackened and burning. Some, without a scratch. Every time one comes, anyone present rejoices aloud, as angels do when a sinner comes home. I am part of something never before seen in England, perhaps never to be seen again, acutely aware of the historicity, and it is marvelous to behold. We are free with expression and feelings. We weep, we rejoice, we encourage, we pray, and we do so freely, and there is a wide-open place for it.

At present I am in a barn, tucked in a corner and guilty for taking time to write this, but my feet must rest if I am to soldier on. A farmer has put up wooden planks for tables, and we endlessly make sandwiches from endless loaves of bread made by housewives and ladies' societies and schools and churches. We cut cheese and ham, we spread butter. The food comes from everywhere. A timid young lady with a child on her hip came bearing a basket of boiled eggs. For all of the acts of generosity I have seen, this one touched me most. She set it down, and left, and I watched her go, a sweet patriot of England, a deed unthanked and unsung and unseen but by me, who shall remember it always. Of all that my Cecil has seen, looking down, at this I am sure he wept. Indeed I whispered, "Did you see what I know has moved heaven?"

Oh, what a state the boys are in — one so dazed, I put a roll in his hand and he did not know what to do with it — and oh, what pulling together on their behalf. What love from strangers for strangers, but we find after all that we are family. (Do not mind the spots on this page; they shall be dried and wrinkled by the time you read this. Forgive bits of illegibility.) Our poor boys are famished and dehydrated. Some are wounded, previously or during what must have been a frightful passage home. They have not slept since only God knows when, and some fall asleep drinking tea. They bear the mark of one who has passed through a night of terrors, grateful it is over though not quite believing it.

Did you hear the news of the *Grafton* and the *Wakeful*? They were two of our destroyers, en route to Dover from Dunkirk, and they were lost, lost, only two days ago. (Or was it three? I am bemused.) 700 souls. 700, my dear! It is believed the ships were torpedoed by U-boats, a bit unclear at present. 700 souls, and I hope to God one of them is not Private Jamie Elliott, son of that man.

I find that I want a teakettle at times. It is a weakness, I fear, this desire to seize a kettle and shriek.

A situational snapshot: When a boat comes in, we greet it. We escort men to a stopgap place — a cinema, a church, a factory — and feed them whatever we have on hand: sausage rolls, meat pies, biscuits, cakes, bread, boiled eggs, along with great quantities of tea, coffee, milk, hot cocoa. Then the lads "fall out" as they are, often asleep with food in hand, and we women push them bodily into lines, and remove their battered equipment, hats, and boots, and socks. Their feet are in a pitiable state, and the socks are soaked with blood; we take the socks outside to wash them, and bring them back to lay over their boots to dry.

Some women weep when we wash the socks, and I let them weep for me; some of us are fated to show a strong face, and thus inspire others to constancy and courage. Dear Lord, how hard it is at times, when I scrub the blood from my nail beds.

But you mustn't think all is sodden and weepy! Dear me, it is not the case. There is great laughter, and good chaos, and all manner of joking, with a blanket of jubilant relief upon all, and sometimes unexpected delight. Just hear what happened this morning: I led a stupefied group of five or six to a spot in the barn, filled their hands with food and their heads with soothing declarations of comfort, and I was about to run off for the next lot, when one of them said, quite surprised:

"It's not the Shrew, is it?"

I discovered beneath the grime and the stubble, "Danny Morgan!" I thoroughly sized him up and said, "Well, you've gone and made something of yourself.

There's a pleasant surprise. Your parents must be shocked."

Said he with a bonny grin: "It's the Shrew, all right. Lads! My teacher from West Kirby!"

Oh, it was grand.

How good it is to be here.

There is a banner hanging in the barn. I've seen many like it in town, and I am told they line the rails so the boys can see them on their way home. There are many versions, and this one says: WELL DONE, BEF! Well, I happened to overhear one of them as he stood staring at the banner. Said he, quite loudly, and with angry surprise: "Well done? What have we bloody done?"

It provoked me to quick thought.

You see, I saw it all in a moment, the curious reason why some looked so deeply dejected and even fearful as they came upon land, as if waiting for the back hand of a looming nasty old nanny.

I immediately went to this fellow's side. Said I: "Well, you have bloody well come home, and you will bloody well go back, so that banner is bloody good enough for me and for everyone else. We are bloody glad you are home, and if our gladness erupts in ways that you think are bloody inappropriate, then you must bear with us for a time as bloody old well-meaning fools." Now note: you are well accustomed to the fact that in my day-to-day discourse, I refrain from common language. I felt compelled to its use so that this young man, by the juxtaposition of vulgar commonality and my serene aged countenance, would be startled into a better state of mind. It was a tactical move, and worked splendidly. The lad smiled most brilliantly, threw an arm around me, and said, "Thank you, mum." I said, "Welcome home, boy. I'm glad you're here." (Drat the spots. Forgive them.)

A destroyer is in. I am wanted. Must go.

Bemused with fatigue and having the time of my life, yours affectionately,

The Shrew

P.S. I do hope all is well. Please mend quickly.

P.P.S. There you are in all your ordinary living, and you are called upon to do something marvelous.

P.P.P.S. Do I not see answered prayers before my eyes, in every sense that prayers can be answered? To a great degree, we are the answer, in hurried organization, in every sandwich made, every cup of tea thrust into a weary hand — so pray, my dear, pray. Pray for our sustaining, pray for theirs. Pray to kick things out of the way and get this army home, for it works; before my eyes it works. Don't mind the spots. Must go. Loads love. Shrew.

Clare folded the letter.
Acutely aware of the historicity. Marvelous to behold.
Well.
I'm not beholding historicity. I'm not in a barn; I'm not welcoming them home. I'm not called upon to do something marvelous. I'm not even boiling eggs. Here I rot, "like a dead daisy!"

She snatched a pillow and hurled it at the vase of wilting daisies. It sailed off the table and crashed to the floor. She pulled another pillow over her face, and burst into tears. I'm not taking care of the Shrew! I'm not convincing a soldier of his worth! Worst of all, I am *not* sailing Maggie to fetch them! She *rots* at her berth, same as I!

"I can't even get *up* to clean a mess I've made," she wailed, and sobbed like a child.

She heard the sound of broken glass scraped together.

"It's all right, I've got it," came a pleasant voice.

She froze.

She pulled aside the pillow and didn't see anyone. Tried to sit up, couldn't. She hadn't had a look under the bandages yet, but good heavens, the incision on her stomach felt a foot wide.

"Hello?"

"Good to see you again, Miss Childs. I hear you're doing much better." Father Fitzpatrick rose from the end of the bed and waved a fistful of wilted daisies. "They make a nice little broom." He looked about and spotted a trash bin.

While he finished cleaning up the mess, she hastily cleaned herself up, snatching tissues, wiping her face, blowing her nose.

"It's good to see you as well, Father Fitzpatrick," she said civilly. It was anything but. Did he see her throw the pillow and burst into tears? "I'm sorry I can't sit up yet."

"I can't imagine you could," said the American vicar, returning the trash bin and pulling up a chair. "Had my appendix out years ago, couldn't move for days. Then again, clergy and doctors make the worst patients." He nodded to the table at the foot of the bed. "I've brought you some cake. What's left of it, anyway. It's very good. I also brought something you might like to take a look at, before I bring it back to the States. Mr. Butterfield thought you would."

He produced a gray-green folder and handed it to her.

She started to open it but got a funny feeling. She gave him a swift glance. "This isn't . . . ?"

"It is. Cleaned up a bit. Still smells moldy."

Her heart picked up pace, and tears began before she even saw the papers for which Arthur Vance died.

Every item was a photograph of an original. She saw copies of ledgers with columns of names and dates and diagnoses and treatments. She tried to act as though she read every word, but the tears blurred them. She saw again Waldemar Klein, and Grafeneck Castle, and Erich von Wechsler. She saw pictures of children and adults with deformities — physical deformities or, by the looks on their faces, mental.

The last picture was a thin, naked child about nine or ten years old. The backdrop was very dark to show his malady clearer. His hips were out of alignment, his right leg hung curved and shortened and shrunken, but that wasn't the most pitiable; on his white and thin and lucid face was terror and confusion as he either stared at some spot he had been commanded to look, or at a spot that caused terror and confusion.

"I wanted you to see the reason Arthur Vance died."

It was the worst picture she'd seen in her life. Worse than the crying baby in Shanghai.

"Sometimes we need to see why we fight," said the Burglar Vicar gently. "We need to see what God sees. Then we can understand a little better his wrath, and his justice, and his love."

He slipped the photograph from her hand, put it in the folder, slipped the folder from her. She pulled the pillow over her face and wept.

She'd not forget that image, not for the rest of her life.

She cried herself deaf for the child, and for Arthur Vance; for Murray, whose Rocket Kid did not save this child, and for William, because she finally understood how it felt to be eviscerated.

She wept that she could not go and die for this boy. That sprightly Maggie, anchored at dock, missed her chance to continue Arthur Vance's heroic exploits.

"I'm utterly useless!" she screamed into the pillow, and finally came to her defeated senses. A good cry, and she did *not* feel better.

She blotted her face with the pillow, and pushed it away. She wiped damp hair from her face. Her ears were plugged, her face felt puffy.

"You are hardly useless," said the Burglar Vicar.

"Oh really? I can't even sit up." Lovely — her voice had gone nasal and pinched.

"You can pray."

"Pray!" she said in disgust. "I can't think of anything that feels less like pulling a doomed soldier aboard *Maggie Bright.*" She glared at the ceiling, a blank white landscape with which she'd grown far too acquainted. Blank as her life.

After a few seething moments, she realized the priest sat quietly. She slid him a look.

"Your king called your nation to a day of prayer. At the police station, the desk sergeant came to my cell, and I had the privilege of leading a collection of prison guards and inmates in prayer, anyone who wanted to, and most did. I sat feeling pretty useless for weeks. The inmates feel useless, and so do the guards. Yet we prayed."

"How do you know it does any good?"

423

Clare said.

"It's better than moping, which does no good at all."

Surprised, she said nothing for a moment. She wasn't moping. Was she?

"Well . . . *that* was a bit abrupt." And refreshing. He was as forthright as the Shrew.

She supposed it *would* be better to pray than to mope. The Shrew said prayer held them to their tasks. She said she saw before her eyes that it worked.

"How do I pray?" She tried to sit up, but bother the sutures, couldn't. "I don't have practice."

"Why don't you start with the Lord's Prayer?" He took the Bible from her bedside table and opened it on his lap. He paged through it, found what he was looking for, and marked the place with the radio program. He closed the book and replaced it. "Read it over, pray it a few times. Then go off on your own. And get specific. I think God likes it when we're specific."

Clare felt a little better. It was *something* to go on. Felt good to do *something*. Better than nothing at all.

"Right, then. What sort of prayer shoots straight to the top of the pile?"

He chuckled. "No idea. If you find out,

let me know. But I'm not sure that our prayers jockey for position. In fact, I wouldn't be surprised if some prayers help others make it to the top. Maybe some prayers give others a leg up." He shrugged. "I don't know how it works. I only know we're supposed to do it."

Just sitting with this man made her feel better. She knew Maggie liked him. She looked at him anew.

He was a medium-size man with a thinnish build, thinning hair. But there wasn't anything medium or thin about him. Instead there was something clear-eyed and purposeful that provoked a galvanizing surge.

Which brought her full circle to uselessness.

"All I want to do is leap from this bed and run for Maggie." Her lips trembled. "We'd fly across that Channel and scoop up as many brave soldiers as we could, then fly for England like Pegasus. But she's as useless as I am." Clare added blackly, "Yes, yes — I can *pray.*"

The Burglar Vicar tilted his head. An uncertain look came to his face. "But . . . Miss Childs, you know that Maggie has gone over, don't you? Oh. No. I suppose not. Are you all right?" He poured a glass of water and handed it to her. "Mr. Butterfield found his partner's car at the boatyard. Then we found a great pile of Maggie's things on the dock, but no Maggie. No Murray, either." His face softened. "He's gone over with Mr. Percy. Captain Elliott has gone, too."

She sat up, not minding the pain. "Truly?" she breathed. Her eyes smarted, and her nose ran fresh. "Well, if they've gone . . . then some of me went, too. Oh — thank you." She seized his sleeve. "Thank you! You have no idea."

She sank back, but what played across the blank white landscape was not a heroic Maggie bashing the waves, but a shatterer who snapped the picture of a terrified child, who now fell upon England's army, who now fell upon men she knew and loved. Fear rolled over her in weakening waves, and tears spilled.

Father Fitzpatrick leaned forward and took her hand. "Let's pray, Miss Childs. It is not the least you and I can do. It's the best."

26

Third-watch sailing became sunrise sailing, and the skies promised a clear day — perfect for bombing boats, William noted grimly. But so far, the skies were empty of malicious intent, though as they traveled west, closer to Dunkirk, the ominous sounds of malicious intent began to grow. He hadn't slept all night, just on-and-off dozing, but those distant, muffled sounds felt like the jolt of a hundred cups of coffee.

The convoy had rounded the Kwinte Buoy an hour before without incident, no lurking U-boats or German battleships ready to blow them to the afterlife. They moved steady on course with the tug in the center of the configuration; the tethered Thames fireboat lay on Maggie's starboard stern, the other two tethered vessels on her port; the fishing trawler ahead lay off her port bow, and the other yacht moved farther out on her port beam.

The entire convoy had fallen into a good rhythm of careful navigation so that the tethered boats rarely touched, and the untethered boats minded manners. The armed Dutch scoot sailed a hundred yards out on Maggie's starboard beam, while the armed tug lay ahead off her port bow. The untethered six cruised in or about their flanked presence, and all felt tight and trim.

All felt tight and trim when William was at the helm, that is; it became quite evident — at least to William's eye, and no sailor can help sizing up seamanship — that Smudge, Royal Navy or not, had not spent much time on the water. His movements were not fluid. They were correct, but as stiff and careful as if he had just finished a sailing course and was minding his p's and q's for the examination. He knew what he was doing, and one day promised to be a good sailor, but for now clearly lacked practice. William wondered how he'd do in Dunkirk.

"We're coming up on the Zuydcoote Pass," Smudge announced, after a glance at a chart.

"Whatever that is," said Murray, standing near the top of the companionway ladder, leaning on the hatch. He stood with his feet apart, easily wedging himself stationary. His movements about Maggie were unconscious. He knew his way around a sailboat.

"Look, there's a buoy," said Smudge, an edge of excitement in his voice. "I'm sure it marks the pass. Won't be long now."

"*Boy?* You sure it ain't a girl? Where do you get that? You Brits need a lesson in how to pronounce things."

"Well, I don't think *mother* is pronounced 'mutta,' " said William pointedly.

"Lemme ask you this: *queen* is pronounced 'queen,' right?"

"Correct."

"And *quilt* is 'quilt'?"

"Brilliant."

"Then how come you call a *quay* a 'key'? Huh? Key? Where do you get that? There ain't an *e* in it."

"That's La Panne, I think," Smudge said, watching the shoreline on the left. Land was now only a few miles off. "Just west of that is Bray Dunes, and then it's Dunkirk."

"Yes, we can see that, thanks," said William, eyeing the western end of their sight line. "I don't know what other harbor would be burning."

"We're maybe an hour out." Smudge lifted up in his seat, looking around. "Wind's backing. My mate said they're loading from the beaches but I shouldn't wonder if today that won't be a bit tricky." He pointed. "Look at that line of surf."

"At least the skies are clear for now," William said.

Smudge squinted where he had pointed. "What's all that in the water? Near the shoreline?"

"Bombing debris, perhaps, washed over from Dunkirk. Or maybe they've bombed right here." He rose and took a pair of binoculars from a small shelf near the helm. He trained them on the surf, adjusted the surf into focus, and then answered carefully, "Yes . . . bombing debris." He lowered the binoculars. It wouldn't do to describe it more than that. He looked toward Dunkirk.

It came upon him, then, the enormous here and now. An enemy had taken the continent and crouched at the door of England. All the land his eyes fell upon — Flanders, France — last week it was friendly. Every tree, every housetop, anyplace you put down your foot. Now it was enemy held, every inch of coastland as far as he could see, save that shrunken patch far west and under siege. He shook his head. It was something out of a dusty history book. It belonged to an age when Shakespeare was new and people said, "My liege."

Twenty-four hours ago he was on the way to the office, giving no thought to piled sandbags and gas-mask posters. He thought instead what rubbish it was that sugar was now taxed, that wartime rationing should apply to *him,* and that his cleaning lady wanted him to buy his own Hoover so she wouldn't have to lug hers. He had arrived at the office in his usual state of ill temper, made worse with worry for Clare.

Twenty-three hours ago, for the first time in his life, he left the office without telling anyone where he was bound, without knowing it himself until he showed up at Elliott's Boatyard. His car keys were still in his pocket, and no one at the office knew where he was.

They'd never imagine what came to his eyes through those lenses on shore — dead men, and women, and children. Wandering dogs and horses. The smoking wreckage of bombed buildings, bombed businesses, bombed homes — bombed lives. He was here to see it because Clare had gone spellbinding with *Maggie must go,* and so Maggie did, and William too. He was skimming along the coast of enemy-held France, realizing for the first time that they truly *had* an enemy, feeling its presence all around, land, air, and sea. They came in

431

numbers no one really knew, but enough that they should rout not a company, not a battalion, and not even two — but the entire bloody army. To this shatterer of lives, *Maggie Bright* now went.

The incongruity of her name and of other boat names he knew — *Lizzie Rose, Gracie Fields* . . . the absurdity of tiny civilian ships marching forth to battle . . . He had a flash of a pink-bedecked Cecy holding a popgun to Waldemar Klein.

"Do you suppose I could get an autograph, Mr. Vance?"

"Smudge pie, lemme ask you this: Ain't I your age?"

"I'm twenty-one."

"Yeah? I'm twenty-three. *A,* you don't owe me a *mister* 'cause the last time *I* called anyone *mister* and meant it, it was the president. *B,* he likes *Rocket Kid* and he had me over for these little spongy cakes with pink curlicue icing in crinkly paper cups, which I pocketed for my ma. Tried to do it on the sly, but old Frankie saw. And guess what? He slipped me some more when no one was looking. Swell guy. Slipped me an ashtray, too — a White House ashtray. Now that's a souvenir. He gets a *mister* for it. But am I a president, Smudge pie? Did I give you an ashtray?"

He seemed ready to say more, but paused, listened, and swiveled to look at the southeastern sky. He shaded his eyes from the rising sun. "Bad news, fellas. Look who's had their morning coffee."

William raised the binoculars. Dozens of aircraft darkened the horizon, coming straight for them like a parading flight of mechanized birds. He wasn't sure if it was the sight or the rising sound of them that inspired the most fear.

He adjusted the focus. "Well, good morning, Herr Hitler. How *do* you do? Looks like he wants to shake hands, and that makes me a bit uneasy."

Murray chuckled.

"Here's the problem with our destroyers," said Smudge, looking about for one. "Look at that — we've got a rotten degree of elevation with our guns for fighting the dive-bombers. I know they're trying to jury-rig for better firepower, but what good —"

"Let's get ready to start the engine," William said, eyes sharp on the stern of the tug. He shoved the binoculars back on the shelf, and glanced at the engine switch on the helm console. "Murray, get below and pull up the boards over the engine compartment. We'll start it from below. Can't have any stalls."

433

"Aye-aye, bobs." Murray swung below.

"Be ready to grab hold of something in case we have to dodge," William called down. He looked again at the tug, and shouted down, "That would be *now*! Start the engine!"

Against the mounting sound of the planes, men on the tug sawed frantically at the tethered lines. William pulled Smudge out of the captain's seat and took the helm, shouting, "Get forward and call it out!" He had to know which boat they cut loose first, so he could try to avoid collision. Smudge instantly ran forward.

He set the pieces in his mind: the other yacht, far to port on the far side of the fishing trawler; the fishing trawler, immediately on Maggie's port side; the Thames fireboat on her starboard. Which will they cut first?

"Don't cut us all at once!" he growled at the sawing men.

The bomber planes came roaring, and William looked up in time to see them directly overhead — then rectangular objects began to fall, and the sight was irresistibly horrific. Down they came, and compared to the roar of the planes they were eerily quiet in their descent, all the more terrifying for that.

Maggie's tether line snapped and, for a

second, floated high and white-snaked in the air, and then it plummeted, and all forward motion was arrested. *Maggie Bright* rose and fell on a backwash swell at the same moment her engine sputtered to life — and then everything happened at once.

"Trawler!" Smudge shouted back. "Hard to starboard!"

Maggie took a crashing glance off the trawler's starboard stern, throwing Smudge to the deck, William against a cockpit bench. He lunged forward and grabbed the helm in time to see the Dutch scoot off Maggie's starboard bow explode in a shower-burst of wood and water and crewmen. Maggie's windows shattered and she rolled on the percussion swell — debris rained down, a chunk of something shearing down the side of William's neck. Another explosion sent him sprawling once more, a wave came drenching down, whelming all.

He rose coughing, soaked, threw off splintered boards, and fought his way back to the helm, almost there, just an arm's reach — but the other yacht cut free from the tug slammed Maggie's port stern and sent him down once more, barking his chin, biting his tongue. He lunged with a growl for the helm, seized the stick, powered her up, and Maggie leapt forward.

435

"Smudge!" William shouted. He spat blood. But Smudge did not appear. "Murray, get up here!"

"We're on paraffin!" Murray surged up the companionway. "Holy smokes, who got hit?"

William pointed forward. "Pull in that tether line before it fouls the engine! Then see to Smudge!" Murray raced forward, grabbing rail as he went, and William called, "It's the Dutch boat — she's gone."

He tried to look for survivors, but the convoy was in chaos and he had all he could do to steer clear of boats and wreckage. Too much wreckage. Surely others had been hit. A swift glance about — the cockleboat from the mud flats was gone. The Thames fireboat.

She had to get clear, her props would foul, she'd be dead in the water — he peeled away toward the shoreline, veering round a lifeboat-size chunk of flotsam.

The side of William's neck burned, from the back of his ear to his shoulder. He clapped a hand to it and looked to see blood on his palm.

Movement caught his eye, and he watched the squadron of mechanized birds fly west. They'd only dropped a few bombs, on a whim it seemed, unable to resist such easy targets. The real target lay ahead, precisely where they were going. But what destruction they'd left behind, on a passing whim.

Movement drew his glance to the bow. Murray was helping Smudge up. He put an arm around him, helped him move aft.

"Smudgy's conked." He eased the dazed young man to the bench behind the captain's chair. "Easy does it, Smudge pie. You got some shiner comin' on. Good thing for the stupid hat. Might've caved your noggin."

"Who's hit?" said Smudge, looking about.

"Several," said William thickly. His tongue began to swell. He spat blood and wiped his chin. "We're leaving the convoy, making straight for Dunkirk."

Smudge shook his head at William. "Don't know how you got out of that. Well done." The side of his face looked nauseatingly spongy. His eye had already swollen half-shut.

"Pure luck."

"I don't think so." He watched the mechanized birds diminish on their death flight to Dunkirk. "We're in for it, lads."

"I got a Jewish buddy," Murray said. He began to clear the wreckage, tossing splintered pieces overboard. "He draws too. I ain't got the heart to tell him his work stinks, but he's studyin' to be a rabbi so maybe he'll do better at that. Anyway, he's always quotin' a thing called the Talmud, and one day he says this: You save one life, it's like you saved the whole world." He examined a piece of floppy rubber, realized it was a deflated fender, winged it over the side. "We pack old Mags with a bunch of guys, get their fannies home . . . just think how many worlds we save. *That's* what we're in for, Smudge pie. Savin' a buncha little worlds."

"I hope my world is saved, too," Smudge murmured. "I've got a girl."

"Me too," said Murray. "My ma. Ain't no one to take care of her but me."

"There's Clare," said William. "And Father Fitzpatrick."

"Clare, you think? She'd do that?"

"Well, you are family."

Murray looked ahead. Breeze ruffled his black hair.

Smudge rose, looking aft, and said in awe, "Will you look at that?"

They turned and saw three boats trailing behind. Now a fourth joined, and then the armed tug — five.

Murray grabbed the binoculars. "Six! Seven . . . eight. Our pulling tug's coming. She made it, she's bringin' up the rear —

nine!" He let out a wild whoop. "They got some of us, but not all! There's spit in your eye, Adolf!"

Murray waved widely at the boats following behind, and received many waves in return. One boat sounded its horn, and others echoed. One rang a bell.

The three men looked at each other, laughing.

Murray shoved the binoculars back in place and ran for the bow. He climbed into the bowsprit and anchored his feet, then stood tall, shouting and waving fisted arms.

William and Smudge laughed, and then William couldn't resist, he veered the helm in a quick move to port, quartering the waves to send a drenching spray over Murray. The crazy young man only whooped all the more.

Let him whoop, William thought. He can do it for me. I do *not* whoop.

But I am beginning not to mind those who do.

Maggie Bright bashed on, chasing lethal birds and leading the way to Dunkirk.

27

"Freely we serve because we freely love."

Jamie watched the shoreline, head in his hands.

Milton sat beside him, the others ranged about behind. It was a few hours past dawn, and all dawn did was illuminate everything they didn't want to see. Jamie had always associated dawn with hope, but the light showed only hopelessness. It showed thousands of men who were nothing but fish in a barrel. It showed the heartbreaking efforts of rescuers with such little return on their costly investment.

For some reason the bombers were late this morning, but not the strafers. They came and went in endless lethal rhythm, spitting off mad, gleeful bursts to end lives with no cost at all to themselves. What a contrast: great effort from the rescuers to save few lives; little effort from the enemy to end many.

He hadn't seen the *Lizzie Rose.* He had no idea if this was good or bad.

"It didn't hurt at first, the new window to my soul," said Baylor, who had woken at dawn, cheery and with better coloring in his face. He'd spoken of nothing but his wound since waking. "It was the shock, I suppose. I was blown right off my feet. All I perceived was *great pressure,* and then all went numb. It's not numb now. I can't move an inch without pain. I do hope it leaves a decent scar. Did anyone see? Something permanent must show for this misery."

"You won't have to worry about that," said Balantine.

"Curtis, what's that goo in your hair?" said Griggs, who couldn't manage to say anything without sounding disgusted, insulted, or revolted.

"French pomade. It does stink," Curtis admitted. "Smelled better in the bottle. At least this perfume is nice. Got it for my girl."

"Yes? And where did you get that?" Balantine's tone had an edge.

"Same shop I got a nice boules set for my parents," said Griggs, and his tone had a nasty smile. "Spoils of war, Balantine."

"Except that the French are not our enemy," Balantine snapped.

"They're foreign," Griggs said. "Same dif-

441

ference."

"It's theft."

"Germans are gonna come take it," said Curtis. "Why not us?"

"At last, some logic." Griggs shook his canteen. "Anyone have any water left?"

"I think Milton's got some," Curtis said.

From the corner of his eye Jamie saw Griggs reach for Milton's canteen. "Leave it," Jamie growled, and snatched the canteen. He shoved it into Milton's hands.

"If he's not drinking it, someone else might," Griggs complained, though he withdrew.

What difference did it make if Jamie watched for the *Lizzie Rose*? He couldn't save his father no matter what he did. He'd blow up before his eyes, like another civilian boat had done since he and Milton sat watch. Two men sat the oars in a rowboat that had launched from a beamy craft standing out a hundred yards. They came on like heroes for the lorry jetty, and then a plane came strafing, and all went to chaos as men dove or tumbled from the jetty. When the plane pulled off, the rowboat and the two men were gone, shot to mush and kindling.

His dad would go up in a fireworks display featuring the *Lizzie Rose*. Or he'd continue to load and run them out, over and over like the others, and have a heart attack because he was old.

He was sick to death of watching innocent people die with nothing he could do about it. A sweat broke on his neck.

"A scar would've been nicer on my arm. It's hard to display an abdomen scar."

"I can't stand it — go soak your head in the surf," Griggs said to Curtis.

"The palpable obscure," Milton was saying.

"I'm going to look for food and water," Jamie said, getting quickly to his feet. Griggs tossed over his canteen, Curtis doing the same. He took Milton's and slung it over his shoulder, then Baylor's and Balantine's.

"Curtis, you go with him," said Balantine.

"I'm going alone!" He was sick to death of them all.

"Mind our position," Balantine called after. When Jamie didn't respond, he called, "Elliott?"

Jamie just kept walking.

Were Lieutenant Dunn and Kearnsey and Drake somewhere down in that seaweed continent? Or did they get it in a ditch like those little girls, or on a transport stuffed with men heading home at last, only to go up in a geyser of oil and debris not a hundred yards out of port?

He passed a soldier sitting on a wooden crate, peeling bloody socks from his feet. He passed an old Frenchman with a mole-dotted and age-spotted face slumped over a cabinet, blue eyes shocked, lower half of his body nonexistent.

Soldiers and civilians roamed the ruined town of Dunkirk, singly or in groups, scavenging for food or water, poking about in piles, pocketing things. Some men likely wandered about as he, thinking to escape carnage on the beaches only to find it here. He passed a collection of soldiers who prayed in a group, led by a short man in a black frock coat with a red sash draped about his shoulders. Jamie hesitated, watching them. The sight made him feel a very small bit better, and he moved on.

"Keep calm, and stay under cover as much as possible," a naval officer was telling a group of terrified French civilians huddled in the entrance of a church. Jamie wondered if they understood a word. The man had gold stripes, brass buttons, and authority. Maybe that was all they needed for now.

"Not an unbroken pane of glass anywhere," said someone at his side. "Can you believe all this?"

It was the man he'd seen on the beach

yesterday, the naval officer in charge. Couldn't remember his name. He wore a hat with *SNO* taped to the front — *Senior Naval Officer,* Jamie supposed. He walked briskly, and Jamie picked up pace to keep stride.

"No, sir," Jamie said. "Never seen such destruction."

"None of us have."

"Do you think there's enough time to get everyone away? Lot of men on that beach." Jamie raised his head at the sound of faint rumbling, like distant thunder. Was it artillery? Was it bombs? Panzers?

"How close are they, sir?"

"Very close now." The officer smiled wryly. "I'd say this is all getting a bit personal, wouldn't you?"

"How long have you been here, sir?"

"Came over on the twenty-seventh. No idea what day it is now."

"Nor I."

"What about you, then, soldier? When did you get here?" He nodded at Jamie's canteens. "Arrive with your unit?"

"Came in yesterday. I'm on a run for food and water."

"Well, there's no food to be had unless you can glean some from the pickings, but you can try for water around the corner, up to the left on Rue Jean Bart. There's a wonderful old Frenchman sharing out water from an in-sink well in his kitchen. You can't miss the queue. But don't get locked into conversation with him; you'll be there all day."

"I don't know French."

"He knows English — or thinks he does. Well, this is my stop — carry on, soldier. Next time I see you, let it be Dover." He gave a little salute, along with a smile and nod, and turned off the path to an apartment building, where an iron rail led down several steps to a door. A few naval personnel came trotting up the steps. Must be headquarters for the evacuation.

"Good luck, sir," Jamie called, again feeling a small bit better.

Perhaps he'd just needed to leave the beach for a time. Thoughts about his father didn't press so hard, and it was nice not to see men under fire.

He took a few wrong turns, but at last tracked down Rue Jean Bart and the house of the Frenchman with the inside well. The queue went all the way down the street and attracted those who came on the double to see what was worth queuing for. By the time it was Jamie's turn to fill the canteens, at least an hour had passed.

An elderly little man received his guests at the pump at his kitchen sink, gesturing widely every time the next man appeared in line, displaying in one elegant and graceful motion the sink, the pump, and his willingness to share. Contrary to what the naval officer had told him, the little Frenchman didn't say a word. Perhaps he was talked out.

Jamie filled the canteens, nodded to the man with a "Thank you, sir. Cheers," and slipped through the press of men back outdoors.

He was trying to arrange the canteens around his neck and over his shoulders, when someone called out, "Elliott?"

A soldier trotted over from across the street, tilting his head as he came near, as if not quite sure . . . then stopped in his tracks.

"It *is* you! I don't believe it!" The man grabbed his shoulders and shook him silly, jostling canteens. "Where have you been? Drake! Get over here! You won't believe it!"

Jamie stared, but couldn't get words out, couldn't make true what was too good to be. He finally whispered, "Kearnsey."

Drake came walking up, shaking his head, a huge smile on his good-natured face. "I *don't* believe it! We were just talking about you!" He threw his arms around Jamie for a

447

fierce moment, and then stood him back to look him up and down. "Where have you been, old man?"

And just like that all fell away, everything squalid and wrong.

Jamie could breathe again, first time in forever. "I was commandeered. Making my way here ever since, and looking for you sods along the way."

"Dunn sent Avery after you, but HQ was overrun," said Kearnsey, pushing up his helmet. "We figured you'd bought it right there or got swept along with their retreat."

"I was ordered to escort a wounded captain to Dunkirk. We threw in with another lot. Where's Lieutenant Dunn?"

"Saving our spot in the queue. A medic is working on him. He's had a bullet in his foot for three days, didn't even know. Isn't that just Dunn? He was limping and brushed it off as sore feet, till Foster asked what was leaking from his boot. Come on, man, he'll be over the moon to see you! Blamed himself for days when we lost you."

He fell into step with them, felt like he was floating.

"I can't *believe* it!" Kearnsey laughed joyously, and pounded Jamie on the back. "Thought we'd lost you for true."

"Dunn was a wreck," Drake put in.

"He wasn't a *wreck,* and he'd punch you for saying that, but he *was* angry."

"He's always angry," Jamie said, grinning. "How is everyone? How's Avery and Foster?"

Kearnsey and Drake exchanged swift looks. Then Kearnsey said, subdued, "Avery's gone. We woke up one day to a German patrol. They didn't know we were there, and we might've got away, but a squad of Belgian soldiers came tramping through. All of a sudden there was a firefight, and . . . we were caught in the middle. Lost Cates and Scotty in that one, too. That was a bad day, our worst. It was the day after we lost you." He brightened a little. "But everyone else is intact, more or less. Except for Dunn's foot, and Foster caught a bullet in the shoulder but it's not too bad, and then of course —" He looked over slyly at Drake.

"Oh, shut it!" Drake said. Then, grudgingly, "Got a nasty case of . . ."

Kearnsey put a finger to his ear. "Yes? Didn't quite catch that."

"Diarrhea." He glared at Kearnsey. "It isn't funny. You should have it, you wouldn't be laughing. It's bloody inconvenient, especially at night."

"How long have you been here?" Jamie asked.

"Four endless days, and we are starving to *death*. I am not joking. I'm just short of eating boot leather."

"And we're sick and tired of being bombed," said Kearnsey. "Can't believe we're almost *used* to it. Do you know, I can actually sleep through it? Here, here's a present: a tin of asparagus. An old grandmother just gave us a sack load. From what we could make out, she was looking for soldiers who were *worthy* of it."

"Convinced her we were angels."

"How in the world did you manage that?" said Jamie, grinning. He pocketed the tin.

"No idea," said Drake, and they laughed. "We ate two tins each and drank every drop of the tin water — and we're not telling the others."

"How long have you been here?" said Kearnsey.

"Got in yesterday."

"Well, you're in luck. Our number's almost up. We'll be out of here today, maybe early this afternoon."

"What do you mean?"

"We're almost to the front of the line, man!" Drake whacked him on the back. "It's bangers and mash by sundown!"

"You'll join us, of course," Kearnsey added.

"Or steak and kidney pie . . . pork pie . . ."

"My mother's apple and blackberry crumble . . ."

"You're killing me. Stop it. I'm burping asparagus juice."

"If I join you, isn't that queue jumping?" Jamie said slowly.

"No, they want to keep units together if they can, keep things easier to sort back in Dover. Lieutenant Dunn will tell them you're with us." Drake gave him a little push. "Anything could happen now, and I just wouldn't care. I owe God something, as I made a few entreaties on your behalf. I can't remember what."

"Your life in his service, I think," said Kearnsey.

"I'm sure it was much more reasonable than that. A box of Weetabix. A parakeet."

"A parakeet?" Kearnsey hooted. "Did you hear that, Elliott? You're worth a parakeet."

"I'll slaughter it in thanksgiving on some great altar, like a bullock or a ram."

"You couldn't slaughter a thing."

"You're right. I'll pluck a feather and call it good. You're awfully quiet, Elliott, when I've gone and made sacrifice on your behalf."

Drake and Kearnsey, his two best mates in the world.

His steps slowed.

"What's the matter?"

Jamie wished Balantine didn't worry so much, didn't try so hard to keep them all together. He wished Baylor hadn't vowed to look after Milton. He wished Griggs hadn't gone after Milton and dragged him from that pile of bombed men. And he wished Milton . . .

"I've got to get back."

"What do you mean?"

"I've got to get back to the captain."

"You were supposed to get him to Dunkirk, right?" Drake shrugged. "Job well done. You're with us again, mate."

"I was supposed to get him home."

There was no explaining it, so he didn't try.

"Say hello to Dunn and the rest." He thrust out his hand, shook each of theirs heartily. "Best of luck. I'll see you in Dover."

"Elliott, wait!"

"What's the matter with you? This is us!"

"Come back!"

"Elliott! Good fellow! Wherever have you been?" Baylor called when he neared.

"We were afraid they'd move our group

and you wouldn't find us," said a very annoyed Balantine.

Baylor lifted high a bottle. "We have passed a mildly alcoholic afternoon with this excellent chap who has shared round his case of — what do you call it?" he asked the man sitting next to him. Milton sat on Baylor's other side. He seemed relieved at Jamie's return, if the only thing to show it was fleeting eye contact.

"Cointreau," said the bleary-eyed man.

"Cointreau! I recommend it highly. I am back to a state of pleasant numbness."

"I'll bet you are." Jamie tossed Griggs a canteen.

"What happened to you?" said Griggs. He opened the canteen and drank it half down. He wiped his mouth.

"Got lost. I did find some asparagus." He tossed him a tin.

"I hate asparagus." Griggs flipped it to Curtis. "How could you possibly get lost? The sea is *north.* You just sort of face north and walk until your feet are wet."

Jamie handed out the other canteens and went to drop beside Balantine.

After Balantine had taken a drink, he asked quietly, "Feeling better?"

"I am, actually."

"Good."

"Did you see the *Lizzie Rose?*"

"No. Griggs watched with me, but we can't really make out names from here. A lot of the names are blacked over. I wonder why. Anything much to see in town?"

"Nothing much. Place is bombed to bits. I did have a chat with — the fellow we saw yesterday. The naval man in charge. Good bloke."

"Tennant. He gets around. I saw him not ten minutes ago. Seems a good leader."

Jamie smiled a little. He wondered if Balantine knew that he himself was a good leader.

The two took up the only thing there was to do: watching. They watched the slow-moving lines of men, they watched the small boats on the beaches, they watched men wade out from lines and clamber aboard whatever awaited, one by one.

They watched a sea littered with flaming flotsam and jetsam, patches of burning oil, and the bobbing, oil-slicked faces of men trying to swim back to shore or back to a boat.

"What's that?" Curtis suddenly sat up, gazing wildly about. He looked up and groaned. "Oh no. Not again."

"I wondered where they were," said Balantine stoically. "They're late this morning."

They watched the eastern sky fill with a grid of dark, droning dots growing ever larger.

"This time I am *not* dodging," Baylor declared. "I shall fend them off with my bottle." He waved it in the air. "They will respect my — what is it again?"

"Cointreau."

"You're such a good chap."

"Baylor, you're not in any position to dodge," said Griggs crossly. All understood. It meant they had to shield him. Not one of them would leave him exposed.

"Gather round, men!" said Baylor, raising high the bottle. "I will keep you safe! Me and my Cointreau."

Milton patted Baylor's arm. "What in me is dark, illumine. What is low —"

"Raise and support," the men chorused with the captain.

After a surprised moment, Milton's lips twitched into a faint smile. The men glanced at one another, grinning.

Then planes came on and bombs began to fall.

"Keep us safe, Baylor," said Balantine, as he rose to stand over him. One by one, the others followed suit.

28

The *Maggie Bright* closed in on a scene straight from an alien nightmare.

A black ball of smoke hung over Dunkirk. Flaming wrecks of every size dotted the far harbor, and a first glance at their own immediate approach afforded an ominous sight, dark obstructions everywhere in the water; but nothing could compare to the sight of the beaches themselves.

"What is that?" Murray said slowly, gripping a mast stay.

"Men."

They covered miles of sand like great oil spills; they wound like wide, curved asphalt roads from where they stood in the water, up through the beaches and up into the dunes, into the city, past what they could see.

"So this is what an army looks like," Murray said faintly.

"And a lot them got off already."

William slowed the *Maggie Bright* to a crawl to try and take stock.

"But — where do we go for orders?" asked a stunned Smudge, looking about under his hand.

"You're tryin' to find who's in charge of this mess?" said Murray. "Good luck, pal. I think we're on our own."

"Look there — what is that?" Smudge pointed. "That line, with all those . . . things in the water. What are the men standing on?"

"Lorries," William said, hardly believing it. He rose, one hand on the helm. "Transports. Must've driven them out at low tide. Brilliant!" At least *one* worry dropped off. "Look at some of those wrecks further in. Maggie would've grounded same as them. Well, that's a relief. I wasn't aching to get into that harbor. We'll load from the lorries, then, and head out for one of those ships." He grabbed the binoculars to look north and see what ships were standing out — they had to be a mile off. "I see a destroyer, and another — some sort of other battleship, a bit smaller. Hang on — can't be." He brought the focus tighter, hardly believing what he saw. "It's the *Medway Queen*!"

"The what?" Murray asked.

"Why, a paddle steamer! A holiday craft! I've seen her on the Thames. Can't believe she's here." He suddenly thought of Clare, and aged aunties and grandmothers running for the front with pistols — it was that bizarre, this decorative bit of England that should belong to a civilized world, here in a warring one. It was a sharply poignant mix he felt, seeing the *Medway Queen:* pride, and fear, and hope.

Murray shook his fist at the appearance of the next set of bombers. "Give us a break, will you?"

"That's quite a traffic jam of boats at the jetty," said Smudge. "Can we get some on faster than that?"

William looked through the lenses, mentally mapping a way through wreckage to the lorries, sickened at the thought of wreckage *not* seen. Soldiers were lined up in the water, high as their armpits, holding their weapons above their heads. He watched a lifeboat, surely from the Ramsgate station, run straight up to the sand: a man leapt out and waved men down. A young naval rating hurried over to supervise the embarkation.

William picked out other naval personnel; they walked the beaches, patrolling, calling out instructions, keeping order, most with revolvers in hand. No one broke order that he could see, but the revolvers said they had or might. He briefly trained on the mass of soldiers — helmeted Tommies, smoking, talking. Waiting.

"Getting closer," Murray warned, eyes on the sky.

"How's she running?" asked William. He lowered the binoculars.

"She ain't gonna quit. We just gotta keep her fueled and clear of junk."

They watched the lifeboat load.

"Well, what do you think?" said Smudge, anxious to get moving. "Can't we try and follow suit? We'd get them on faster than that queue of boats."

William wanted nothing more than instant action, but caution had to be the watchword if they were to keep it up. He carefully considered, and shook his head. "Her draft is too deep. It's either the end of that lorry jetty, and even then we've got to look sharp, or else we make for the harbor."

"Getting closer . . ."

"Look at that!" Smudge shouted. "It's the RAF!"

Two English Spitfires came roaring, chasing down four German planes. Machine gun fire erupted from the navy ships at the same time the Spitfires opened up. One of the four exploded, and another suddenly belched black smoke and peeled off, a Spitfire hot on its tail. A great roar of cheers went up from the beach.

But immediately came the whistling dives of planes attacking destroyers, and bombs began to fall from planes now overhead — a spume of surf erupted near the lorry jetty, men dove or were blown into the water . . .

"Bobby!"

William looked where Murray pointed, north, toward the standing-off ships, and wasn't sure what he saw.

"That big boat got hit! There's a bunch of men in the water!"

"Smudge, run forward and call it back. Murray, get the ladder net ready."

William powered up Maggie, and surged ahead for the flaming wreck.

Maggie Bright delivered her first load of nineteen men to a destroyer, none taken from the jetty or the beach, all survivors of the sinking river barge that had just loaded and was heading out to sea. It wasn't long before Maggie's decks were slippery with oil and congealed blood.

It took ten minutes to pull the men aboard, twenty minutes to make it out to the destroyer, dodging obstructions on the way — other boats, floating debris, bodies. It took ten minutes to help the nineteen off Maggie and onto the rope nets and ladders hanging from the destroyer's side. Some were so exhausted they could barely hold on to the nets and had to be half carried up by the destroyer's deckhands or Maggie's.

Forty minutes, one load of nineteen, and the three men were already exhausted.

"My arms are noodles," Murray said. He sat beside Smudge on the bench behind the helm.

"No wonder they load from the lorry jetty," said Smudge. "They can jump aboard."

"Didn't figure on 'em bein' starved," said Murray. "Wish we had food for 'em. I pull in a guy charred and half-drowned, first thing he says, 'You got anything to eat?' "

"That's not our focus," said William. "We catch the fish, others will clean them."

"Yes, and now we haven't any food for ourselves," Smudge accused Murray. "You gave away all our rations."

"No more 'Mr. Vance'? Attaboy. All I gotta do is make you mad, and you'll treat me regular."

"Well done, Maggie." William patted the helm console. "How's the petrol and paraffin?"

"I better go see," Murray said. " 'Cept I can't move."

"Well, you'd better call up some reserves. It's going to be a very long day. Smudge, why don't you clear the decks. Won't do for new guests to see it. Should be a bucket in one of the lockers."

William suddenly thought of Mrs. Shrewsbury.

"We're being prayed for, you know," he announced, feeling only a trace foolish. "We'd better act like it." It seemed the responsible thing to do.

Smudge said, puzzled, "How do you *act* like you're being prayed for?"

"By producing things prayer should produce, I suppose."

"Like what?" Murray asked.

"Stamina," William enunciated. "Get moving."

"Then am *I* makin' it happen, or is it the prayers?"

"Both."

"Ha! Sounds like somethin' the Fitz would say. How's your head, Smudge pie?"

The two rose and started toward their tasks.

"It'll mend. Say, Mr. — Murray. What were you thinking to kill off Salamander? My mates and I see a possibility for bringing him back. I could tell you our ideas."

"Well, I got a secret. Swear you won't tell, but — he ain't dead."

"He ain't? He isn't? Fantastic!"

They moved off, talking, and William finally allowed the sensation within to well up and tip the banks — an exhilaration he had never known, and it had to do with nineteen worlds plucked from the sea.

Nineteen little worlds.

The number *5* was carved on the foremast. Now *19* would be added, and if things went right, if they kept dodging bombs above and wreckage below, then more numbers after that, more little worlds, more of Maggie's exploits. Just wait until Clare saw it.

Don't forget her, Mrs. Shrewsbury.

William put Maggie in gear, powered her up, and swung back toward the hellish fray, praying that Mrs. Shrewsbury was praying.

29

Balantine emptied the last drops of his canteen into his mouth and screwed the cap back on. "Look how often they're running groups down to the beach, not just the harbor. It really is going faster. We may be off by tomorrow. I thought we'd be here for a week."

"We'd never last that long," said Griggs, a bit muffled, from beneath his helmet. He lay stretched out with his hands behind his head.

"The little boats are really making a difference," said Balantine.

"Yes, you've said that before," said Griggs. "About fifty times."

"Do you sail?" Jamie asked Balantine.

"No." He studied the small craft on the waters. "I've just never seen anything like this."

"It is inspiring," said Baylor sweetly, and then his tone went acid. "That is, it *would*

464

be, if anyone would lift me up to *see*."

"No," they all said, and Balantine added patiently, for the fiftieth time, "You've got to save it for the journey home."

Twilight was not far off. It would be the second night the men passed on the beaches. The Cointreau and its bearer had long gone, leaving Baylor out of sorts.

"Well, I can *prepare* for it, can't I, with a nice bit of exercise to get me up and looking around? Can't see a bloody thing except your arses or faces when planes fly over — so I can't even see planes! My one bit of entertainment, gone."

"Yes, you're missing a lot," Griggs said into his helmet.

"I wish you all would leave me alone!" Baylor's tone went forlorn. "Don't you understand? If any one of you is hit because of me . . ."

"Bit of luck about them bombs, eh?" said Balantine. "Just like the bloke said. Unless they hit you direct, they don't do to us what they do to . . ." He nodded to the sea.

"Does anyone have a toothpick?" said Curtis.

"What is there to pick?"

"I want to be ready. I have a gap between two molars."

Idle chatter helped drown the cries of the

dying and the wounded, some of those very close by; it helped distract from hunger and thirst. It helped turn a blind eye to sights that would ordinarily send them running to help or running for help; instead, great hulking ships exploded into concussive infernos they could feel, and men bobbed in the water, choking on oil and petrol if they were alive to choke at all, and here they sat chatting idly, clinging to any bit of sanity they could with talk of the cinema, and home cooking, and girls, and toothpicks.

"Curtis, why do you bite your nails?" Baylor said, back to his peevish tone. Curtis shrugged, and continued nibbling his pinky nail. "I can understand tobacco, or too many profiteroles. And for the first time in my life I understand alcohol. But what sort of actual pleasure could you possibly derive from biting your nails?"

Curtis shrugged and nibbled.

"I want my Cointreau," Baylor said plaintively.

"I wish you had it," said Griggs. "I like you better drunk."

"If ever I have a postwar party, you are not invited, Griggs," said Baylor. "I shall invite Elliott, and Balantine, and Captain Jacobs, and even Curtis, but your invitation will *not* arrive."

466

"Thank God for small favors."

"What do you mean, 'even' Curtis?" asked Curtis.

"I *genuinely* dislike you, Griggs. I've been taught I can never say *hate,* I can never *hate* another human being, but oh, the day I discovered I could *dislike* them."

"Let's keep it civil, shall we?" said Balantine, and employed his usual trick of distraction. "Elliott, what will you do after the war?"

"Open a pub."

"Will you serve Cointreau?" asked Baylor hopefully.

"If it's good. It's got to be good, not like that other French swill. I'll serve Jenner's, Bass —"

"My mum says they're taxing beer," Curtis said indignantly.

"— and Guinness. I'll have a state-of-the-art wireless where —"

"You and I will look at each other across the room, and we'll lift our mugs. I think you quote Milton because your heart is broken, mate, not your head."

It took a moment to realize it was Milton.

A riot of goosebumps rose on Jamie's arms and raced into his neck.

Griggs lifted his helmet to squint at Milton. "Was that you, loony bin?"

"It was," said Baylor in hushed amazement. "I was looking right at him."

"It's what I said to him," Jamie said slowly, sitting up. "I was telling him about my pub. . . ."

Captain Jacobs took no notice. He watched the sea, idly twisting his wedding ring.

"I told him the little girls we saw would be avenged. I said we'd be back in force, and Hitler would get his. I said we'd lift our mugs to each other . . ."

The five men watched Milton closely, but he performed no more verbal acrobatics. He twisted the wedding ring and watched the sea, his expression the same as ever, one that managed to be watchful and pensive and vacant at the same time.

Griggs lowered his helmet, and Curtis went back to his nail.

Maybe the others could go back to business as usual, but not Jamie.

You're in there. You're not a Milton box; you're a man. You're my friend.

"We *will* lift our mugs to each other," said Baylor, the only other still eyeing Milton.

We *will* get you out of here, Captain Jacobs. We'll see you right.

The Stukas and the Heinkels came, and with them their bombs, and all got up as a matter of course to stand shelter over Baylor, while Baylor cursed them away.

"Elliott! How can he possibly sleep in this? Elliott — wake up."

He'd dreamed of his old dog Toby, who wore Milton's bandage and seemed ready to say something wise.

Balantine stood over him. "They're moving us down to the beach." He nudged Jamie with his boot. "Upsadaisy."

Jamie sat up and looked about. Everything was dove gray. The air was damp and chilly. "What time is it?" he asked hoarsely.

"Dunno," said Curtis. "It's early."

"The night's gone?"

"Wish I could sleep like you," said Balantine. "That's one way out of this nightmare."

"Not if you dream that your old dead dog is about to speak Milton and mean it." He looked down at the harbor. "We're loading, then?" The other men in their loose group of fifty were gathering up their gear.

"Don't get your hopes up." Balantine shouldered his knapsack. "We're not moving to the harbor itself, but we are moving closer."

"Milton?" Jamie said, looking about.

"Over here," called Baylor. "Look, I'm vertical. Griggs and Milton have actually al-

469

lowed me to *stand.*"

Milton said, "To the end persisting —"

"Safe arrive." They looked in surprise at Curtis, who looked surprised himself.

"Oh dear," Baylor said, his face gone pale. "I rather liked being horizontal. . . ."

"Oh, be a soldier," said Griggs. "We can't let anyone see you're stretcher material, you moron." His shoulder was under one of Baylor's arms, Milton under the other with his arm securely about Baylor's waist.

Balantine watched Baylor closely. "All right? Easy does it, lads. Take it slow."

Jamie rubbed his face awake, got to his feet, and grabbed his knapsack. He grabbed Milton's, too, and fell in.

As they came down from the dunes, it felt as though they'd fallen into their old retreat formation, Balantine out front and watching, the rest following behind. The only difference was that Griggs walked with Baylor and Milton, and Jamie walked with Curtis.

"Step carefully here, there's a drop-off." Balantine looked over his shoulder. "How's he doing?"

"Griggs, you can let me walk," Baylor complained. "I'm not even walking. You just wanted to be close to me."

"You're right. Easier to vomit on you."

Jamie chuckled. Baylor was caught,

somehow fittingly, between the man he liked least and the man he liked best — between Griggs, the born soldier who would've fit well with his old unit, and Milton, the locked-up and poetical and strange. One strong man and one wounded man, supporting another.

The three moved carefully along. Milton had to be on automatic pilot, drawing upon reserves made of stuff Jamie couldn't imagine. Stuff he hoped was in him, too.

"I would like to have served under you, Captain Jacobs," Jamie suddenly said aloud.

Milton's head lifted a little. He'd heard, he understood, and Jamie just didn't care when Griggs said, "I *am* going to vomit."

It was far better up on the dunes. Here, the six were not the onlookers but part of the great seaweed continent, wide open to the skies.

Here on the flat beaches, there was no cover. Here the bombs fell heaviest, closer to the ships where the bombers concentrated their payloads. Here there was no burrowing in the sand — and since the sand was harder packed, the bombs created far more havoc.

They had just found a place to fall out, had just tossed down knapsacks and got

Baylor settled in, when a naval rating came up to their group of fifty.

"Any 2nd Grenadiers?" he called. "Is there someone here from the 2nd Grenadiers artillery?"

"Over here!" Balantine raised his hand.

Strange, to remember everyone came from different units.

"Come with me. Any more of you?"

"Six of us!" said Balantine. The man waited until Griggs and Milton got Baylor back up, then beckoned them to follow. They headed for the eastern mole in the harbor.

Balantine turned and mouthed, "You're all from the 2nd Grenadiers. Got it?"

The eastern breakwater of Dunkirk harbor was not built to hold thousands of men. It was flimsy and in some parts bombed, yet things were found to plug bombed holes, with duckboard laid over that, and so by some miracle in the incessant pounding it had taken over the past few days, it held.

The six followed the naval rating past hundreds of men, maybe a thousand, until they were on the quay itself, until they were on the flimsy breakwater where the wind came stronger and the waves tossed up water, until they stood next to a destroyer with rope ladders down the side and seamen up at top, calling down encouragement to men crawling up. The six glanced at each other, not understanding their luck, until a middle-aged man rushed forward.

"Balantine!" The man thrust out his hand. "Donnelly thought he saw you!"

"Captain Wellard!" Balantine's face livened with joy, and he shook his hand heartily. "Good to see you, sir!"

Again, strange to feel this small separation from Balantine, to see him know someone that Jamie didn't.

"The same, the same! Come, half our unit is aboard and below. Follow me."

"Get moving, men!" An embarkation officer waved them on. "All the way to the end if you're for the end. Let's not bottleneck!"

"That's us, we're the ship at the end of the mole."

They hurried along, passing two vessels tied up on the left, loading with men. Captain Wellard glanced back at the men following Balantine. His delight came down a bit. "Where's Grayling? Where's Portman?"

"Gone, sir."

Any remaining delight disappeared, and his face took on a look Jamie was beginning to associate with Dunkirk. "Very sorry to hear it. The others?"

"Don't know, sir. We were separated when the line broke through. *These* are my men, sir." Balantine glanced back, taking them all in.

"Move it along!" a naval man called.

"She's about to cast off," said Wellard. "We must hurry."

They passed six smaller craft docked and loading on the left, two rows of three abreast. Men clambered over the first two as a bridge to get to the last. How did they manage to navigate past those harbor wrecks? Some wrecks were partially submerged with bow or stern stuck in the air, some visible just feet below the surface. Jamie stared at the six boats as he passed. They must have very shallow drafts and skippers of incredible skill and luck. *Lizzie Rose* was not among them.

"Come on, men, move it!"

"Incoming!" someone cried.

"I hate that word," Griggs said, refitting himself under Baylor's arm. He said to Milton, "Look, you're slowing us down! I've got him. Elliott, see to him."

They hurried along the mole for the end destroyer, but the beckoning men on the ship's deck suddenly disappeared as they dove for cover.

"Incoming!"

"Come on, men!" Balantine bellowed.

A high, whistling whine, a deadened second, and then a blinding flash, a concussive implosion . . .

Jamie fumbled for clarity, tried to get up, tried to get up . . .

. . . and a concert of destruction fell upon the breakwater.

A blinding deluge of shrapnel and water and foaming debris. You clear yourself, coughing, only to see lancing streaks and wheeling planes, only to see falling rectangles meet pier, ships, men, and sea, and the concert of destruction starts over again.

You clear yourself, coughing, get yourself up.

Jamie, back on his feet, reaching for Milton next to him. Griggs stumbling forward with Baylor, Balantine shoving Curtis forward, shouting them all on.

A rectangle fell, met the destroyer at the end of the mole. A great explosion, and then a groaning shriek of steel — the pier shuddered and buckled where the ship ground against it, crushing men caught on the rope ladder between.

The rush for the ship ceased. Jamie stood horrified, but not Griggs.

Griggs swung Baylor to the left, pushed

him down into the first boat in a line of three tied to the pier. He reached for Milton next, pushed him down next to Baylor and turned for Balantine and Curtis, shouting them over. Balantine pulled a staring Curtis from the sight of the destroyer, which now listed heavily starboard and, engines roaring, metal shrieking, stern deck flaming, began to pull away from the mole.

Balantine shoved Curtis toward Griggs, then reached into a pile of men for Captain Wellard. Jamie came to help, and between them they dragged the dazed and bleeding man toward the boat where Griggs shoved off other men trying to board, some into the water, some into the next boat over.

A plane came strafing low, buzzing the curve of the breakwater.

Balantine collapsed with his captain, buckling Jamie's knees, taking Jamie down.

A cry from Milton, and he climbed over men in the boat, past Griggs, who tried and failed to catch him back, past frantic men surging forward to come aboard. Griggs vanished, shouting, beneath them.

The Junkers 88 peeled off from the breakwater, soared in a roaring climb and came about in a smooth banking turn.

Balantine, get up, get up. Jamie shook him.

The Junkers 88 angled in and lined up

low for another breakwater pass.

"Balantine!"

But Balantine was dead, beside his dead captain.

Milton came for Jamie, pulled him away from Balantine. He shouted something, but Jamie couldn't hear over the roar of the oncoming Junkers. Milton righted Jamie's helmet, seized his arm, and turned for the boat.

The plane roared strafing past, bullets rattling through the man-clad pier.

Milton went down, Jamie beside his captain.

Griggs fought through the frenzied press, shouting back for Curtis to mind Baylor. He used oncoming men to pull himself onto the pier, pulling some into the water, shoving others aside to get to where Elliott and Milton had gone down.

Balantine was gone; he'd seen that from the boat, gave him no more than a swift glance.

For a heartbeat Griggs stood over Milton and Elliott, then quickly knelt to check. Milton was gone. He checked Elliott, whose helmet bore a new bullet crease — Elliott's eyes fluttered, and Griggs hauled him up.

30

"What ship is this?" said a man close by. "I want to know the name of the ship that will carry me home."

"You're on the HMS *Wolsey,* mate," said a cheerful seaman. "She's an old girl and she's taken a beatin'. Might have to sit the next dance out, but she's done us proud."

Hundreds of soldiers covered every inch of the *Wolsey*'s deck. They sat on railings and ammunition lockers, they packed in tight, right up to the swivel line of the gun turrets. Many slept on each other, while others watched the skies for enemy action. Some kept to themselves, some swapped stories of perilous escapes.

They were two hours out from Dunkirk, no one in pursuit. Nothing exploding. All quiet.

Baylor was wedged between Griggs and Jamie. Curtis sat nearby.

They were no longer six. They were four.

None had spoken since coming aboard, since the little ship that Griggs had commandeered had ferried them out to a river barge, which then took them to the *Wolsey,* standing off a mile out. Griggs kept them together when a medic wanted to take Baylor below. Griggs made sure they all got a share of the tea that came around in helmets. Griggs repacked Baylor's dressing.

"It's all wrong," Baylor said, voice soft, face stricken.

"I just wanted to get him home," Jamie whispered.

He nearly did. Duty so nearly accomplished. He failed, and he'd never know anything more about this man. Never know the unit he came from, never have a sound conversation, never raise mugs in the pub. Captain Jacobs died in the Milton box.

"He wanted you to get home, and he did it," said Griggs. "You were his mission, Elliott. Don't take it from him."

Jamie pulled his helmet low.

God towards thee hath done his part — do thine.

Jamie's part was to get home. Why wasn't it Milton's part to live?

Why Milton, and why Balantine? Why not men who meant nothing to him? Why not Curtis, who seemed to fill a blank spot, as if

479

he were just along for the ride? He glared at Curtis, but Curtis was silently crying, tears running down his face as he gazed south to Dunkirk.

"Balantine led from the front." Baylor's face was white and empty. "Somehow, Milton led from the back. The two who kept us together are gone."

"I have something for you," Jamie heard himself say.

He dug into the captain's rucksack and came up with *Paradise Lost.*

It was the one thing in the world he wanted for his own, and he knew with all his heart Milton would've wanted it for him, and for a moment he gripped it hard. Then he handed it to Baylor, who took the book, turned it over in his hands, and looked off to sea, bleak as Curtis. At the moment it didn't mean anything more than anything else.

It wasn't any different from what Jamie felt. But he knew what the captain would do if he were here. He'd speak Milton.

What in us is dark, illumine. There's a lot of dark.

"Baylor. I'm going to open a pub when this war is over." He bit his lip, waited it out. "A man can come in who's down on his luck, get a meal for free."

And the vision came before him, illumined, illumined . . . illumined by the soft yellow glow of the great fireplace, details like Jamie had never seen.

"There's a great fireplace, with a mantel made of an old barn beam. A beautiful wireless, top of the line, is at the end of the counter. On the wireless is King George, and I can hear him. He's telling how a mighty force came back with Lord Gort, whipped Hitler and all his men. I see you across the room, Baylor, whole and strong. I see Griggs and Curtis, and we're lifting our mugs. For Milton, for Balantine, and for Grayling. For two little girls I saw in a ditch. For all the men Milton lost. And for his wife, who lost him."

He could see it in the golden glow of the fireplace and knew it was a true vision because the glow touched his heart and the pain lessened.

Baylor looked at the book. Turned it over in his hands.

"You should call it Milton's Men," Griggs said.

Jamie liked the sound of it. Then he looked at each one of them earnestly. "You have to be there. It's not some dream. It's real. You have to be there, every one, or I'll find you and kick your arses."

481

"I'll be there," said Curtis, wiping beneath his nose.

"Me, too," said Baylor, gazing at the book.

"Then we have to promise to stay alive," said Jamie. "We'll be in Dover soon. We'll get split up. We may not see each other for the whole of the war. I live in Bexley-on-the-Thames, up from Teddington Locks. That's where Milton's Men will be. Find me at Elliott's Boatyard, if the pub's not built yet. Now look me in the eye and give me a promise to come."

"I promise," Baylor said.

"Promise," Curtis whispered.

Griggs was silent.

"Griggs," Jamie prompted.

"I'll not make a promise I can't keep," said Griggs. He looked Jamie straight on. "But if I'm alive . . . I'll be there."

Jamie put his head back and closed his eyes, and when he awoke, he was in Dover.

31

Nineteen.

Nineteen little worlds saved.

Then ninety, and did William ever imagine to see the ketch take on so many? There on out he stopped trying for a precise count. It was impossible.

Then twenty — bombs came heavy on that one, they had to leave fast.

Eighty.

Ninety.

Twenty — another survivor pickup not five minutes back from the destroyer, when one of the Dutch scoots sank.

A day passed. Two days. On went *Maggie Bright* and her crew without pause.

Bombs fell, planes came strafing, magnetic mines blew holes in steel hulls, and all throughout this hell called war, the English Channel remained uncommonly calm. Little ships motored about less hampered by its usual chop, saving time, using less fuel. Maybe William did believe in God. He certainly believed in Mrs. Shrewsbury.

Ninety.

Seventy.

Seventy.

William carved the number of each ferried load on a piece of console trim. Clare wouldn't mind, not this record of Maggie's exploits.

They took on fuel and rations and water. At each load delivered, William wanted to crawl up the nets with the soldiers, he wanted to be done, he wanted out. He could summon neither hatred nor hope to keep going. He felt nothing at all. He simply wanted it to end and would not mind if a bomb answered all.

Did he ever imagine that one day, he would grow adept at timing the fall of an object the size of a suitcase, at knowing exactly when to lay her over hard to port or starboard, depending on the waves and the feel of the wind?

Forty.

Fifty.

He had nothing left, and he knew it, yet he sat in the chair and motored round wrecks, said "Oops" if he glanced off another boat, or if another glanced off them. The crew of three could no longer speak, not to one another, not to oncoming or off-going men. Their eyes were red and grainy, their feet swollen; their bruises and small abrasions, numerous. Sea salt crusted their skin and stiffened their hair.

Smudge and Murray had the worst of it, hauling men in, pushing men up, jumping in the water if one fell. They loaded only from the lorry jetties now, to conserve strength in order to keep going at all. When they left a destroyer after delivering a load of men, Smudge and Murray lay down wherever they stood, in whatever the soldiers had left behind — oil, blood, vomit. They were asleep in seconds.

William helped when he dared leave the helm, usually when tied to a destroyer. But back and forth along the routes or at the lorry jetties or the pier in the harbor, he had all he could do to make sure Maggie didn't run aground or hit other craft. He had a fending pole at his side, had to use it ceaselessly.

Clare, how are you healing? Hmm? All the infection go bye-bye?

Mrs. Shrewsbury, pray.

I cannot lose her, you see, she who will circumnavigate the world. She who holds high a picture.

By the by, I have nothing left. Pray.

485

You have your job, I have mine. Did I say that, or did you?

Eighty.

Ninety.

One hundred twenty. A bit tender on that one.

Ninety.

He watched his hands make the knife carve this last number onto the console. He watched his hands withdraw the knife, fold the knife, slip the knife into his pocket, because doing things like watching one's hands kept one's mind in step with one's body, and this was important when one was losing one's mind. Yet he'd barely had time to be satisfied with the accomplishment of pocketing one's knife when shouts came from above, shouts from the men on the destroyer they had tied to, they were shouting down something dire, dear me, something important, he was to *do* something, they were frantic, they were waving him forward — he watched his hand move to power her up, but Maggie crashed into the destroyer.

He picked himself up, and there was no getting out of this, no shrewd maneuver, no time to be indignant at the poor seamanship of whoever bashed into her. Her crushed stern took on water in seconds, and there it loomed, a great powerful barge bearing down on the little ketch, crushing it like dry crackers, soldiers tumbling from the barge, some into the drink, some onto Maggie, some thrown straight to the climbing net on the side of the destroyer — at that he could only think, How clever, how very efficient.

Get Murray, get Smudge, get out.

But curse the inconvenient sense of duty, he first helped those thrown onto Maggie because she wasn't going down yet, as the barge pinned her against the destroyer, and he prayed the pilot wouldn't do something as foolish as back away *now.* Let's work together, man; this is going to be tricky.

He looked for Smudge and Murray as he helped men gain the net, but didn't see them. Where could they be? I could use some help.

"Orderly, now," he called hoarsely to men scrambling down to Maggie from the barge. He grabbed one, he steadied another, he dragged one up from the water and pushed him to the net. The barge ground against Maggie, kept her neatly propped as a bridge, and he looked to catch eyes with the pilot, but saw no pilot in the cockpit for there *was* no cockpit, and that's when he realized the barge had been bombed.

The barge listed to port, and her grip on Maggie slipped. Maggie's crushed stern slid several feet, and water began to pour in.

Then Maggie fell away beneath him, and William scrambled and leapt and caught the bottom of the net, climbed a few footholds, and frantically searched the area for Murray and Smudge.

"Murray!"

"Bobby! Bobby, up here!"

In the crowd of soldiers leaning over the rail, William finally picked out the anxious faces of Murray and Smudge. He'd sort out later how they'd managed that feat. He sagged against the net in relief.

"Come on, bobby, climb!"

"You can do it!"

"Oh, shut up," William muttered. Why couldn't they sail back to England this way? He was secure enough. He looked up. It was a long way up.

He saw a few soldiers swing legs over the rail, ready to sprint down for him like a couple of agile little monkeys just brimming with vigor.

"I'm coming!" he growled, waving them off.

Cursing the world and all that was in it, he began his ascent of the destroyer but, oh, oh, how tired he was.

One handhold, one foothold, up we go.
One handhold, one foothold, up we go . . .

Murray and William sat on a . . . Actually,
William didn't know what they sat on,
something uncomfortable and covered with
a tarp. Smudge lay asleep at their feet, a
neat bandage about his head.

It was a time for philosophical reflection,
a moment Butterfield would have adored.

"Well, *that* woke me up," said William
hoarsely.

"Me too," Murray whispered. His voice
was gone.

"I hate to discover that I have reserves."

"Me too."

"I mean very *deep* reserves. I can be
pushed far more than I ever imagined. It's
disturbing."

"Yeah."

"Let's not tell anyone. A thing like that
can't get out."

"I'm just tryin' to care that we lost *Mags.*
I don't."

"Neither do I."

"Is that bad, bobby?"

A deckhand came by and put cups of hot
cocoa in their hands. He knuckled his
forehead, grinning a gap-toothed grin, and
backed away.

"Thank you. There's a good chap. It's *likely* bad. Right now I suspect that I have poor judgment. I care only that I lost a piece of trim. I'd carved the number of each rescue on it. I wanted to show Clare."

"How many did we save?"

"Oh, lots. Lots of little worlds."

"That's great. But right now . . . I don't care. Is that bad?"

"Oh, that *is* bad. That's definitely bad. But you *can* care later."

"I can?"

"I give you permission to care later," William said grandly.

"Gee. Thanks, bobs."

"A nice little sleep for a night or two, you can wake up and care, care, care."

After a moment, Murray said, "Care about what?"

"I haven't the faintest."

A few soldiers came by and said some nonspecific things, whacked William on the back and spilled his cocoa, moved on. He glared at the spot on his trousers, but then saw, amazed, many spots.

"I'm still trying to work out how you got to the deck so fast," said William.

"They came down and got us. Wasn't fast."

"Yes it *was* fast," William said peevishly.

"The barge hit, I looked, you were gone."

Murray stared at him. His eyes were inflamed, caked at the corners and rimmed with salt. His face was swollen and streaked with blood, grease, and grime.

"Good heavens," said William, dismayed. "I hope I don't look like you."

"Wasn't fast, bobby. Smudge got conked again. Had all I could do to keep him from goin' in. Took 'em half an hour to get us up here."

"Nonsense."

A middle-aged uniformed officer came up, a younger uniformed man at his side. Though William was past bleary, he saw brass and bars and tried to sit up straight and make himself a bit respectable. He discreetly crossed his legs to hide the cocoa stain.

"I've seen many things this past week." The older officer took off his hat. "Nothing like that." He put out his hand.

William shook it. Poor man. He looked very tired.

"I'm putting you in for an order of chivalry," he said.

"Don't be ridiculous," William snapped. "Help a man off a barge, they want to award you for it. It's spectacle gone to seed. Next they'll award you for getting up in the morning."

"Bobby," Murray whispered. "You was at it for an hour."

William stared.

Murray jerked a thumb at the officer. "*This* guy knows his stuff — kept nosin' this mammoth into Maggie and the barge so you could get 'em off. You was some team. Attaboy, Sailor Bob." He nodded at the officer, then looked at the younger man. "Junior Bob — put him up for the same award."

Junior Bob smiled brilliantly and gave a nod. "It will be a pleasure."

Bits came prickling back, just bits . . .

William stared at the middle-aged officer. Wonderingly, he said, "You kept us together." He shook his head. "That is seamanship. What is your name?"

"Phil."

"Well done, Phil." He would stand and salute, in the flush of admiration for this skilled and very tired man, but he couldn't move.

"Mr. Vance . . . would you sign this, please?" The younger officer unfolded a piece of paper.

"Sure, Junior Bob."

Junior Bob handed Murray a pen. He made an X on the paper.

"It's all I can do," he whispered.

"I quite understand."

"What is that?" William asked. Junior Bob held it up for him to see.

"It's you, bobby. And the guys you saved. And the last of Maggie. All they had was a grease pen and the back of a chart."

William studied the drawing. "Why did you do it?"

"It hollered to be drawn."

Junior Bob folded the drawing and said some nonspecific things — many men did, they kept coming by, kept coming by, kept shaking hands with the officer and William, and William tried hard to control the trembling in his body and wished they'd all go away. Their congratulations taxed and vexed; he found it more exhausting than sailing.

They finally left, and it was time for philosophical reflection once more. He thought of Mrs. Shrewsbury. He saw her on her knees, hands clasped, a Dundee cake nearby.

"Thank you, Mrs. Shrew," he whispered. To Murray he said, "Is your face numb?"

But Murray was sleeping, and William took his cocoa before it spilled. He patted Smudge, sleeping at their feet, and took a sip from his cup.

■ ■ ■ ■

"Which hospital, mate?" the cab driver said.

"Can't remember," William said hoarsely. "Are we in London? Are we here?"

"We are."

"Good."

The *Maggie Bright* was gone. How could he tell her?

"I need a name, mate."

"Hospital," William said, irritated. He closed his eyes and stood in a clearing with ever-diminishing perimeters as unconsciousness came crouching in assertive gray billows. But not yet, not yet.

"Look at you. Can't imagine what it's like over there. Poor sod."

The pity angered, just what he needed, and his eyes flew open. "I have to get to her before it . . . I can't think of the word. Caves."

"But I need a name, mate."

One William battled the gray with a sword, while the William in the clearing said, "Whitehall."

"Whitechapel?"

"Whitechapel! That's it. London Hospital."

"We're in business, mate." He wheeled the

car into traffic.

"Don't let me fall asleep." Curse the trembling! He stared at his hand. He couldn't stop it.

"When's the last you slept?"

"Don't know."

What soon would be Clare's loss made heavy his heart and beckoned the gray all the more. His tricks to stay awake were failing. He smacked his face, he put his head out the window, sang a song as loudly as he could. He stomped his feet up and down, or thought he did, but found they did not move.

"Were you in one of the little boats we're hearing about?"

"Her name was *Maggie Bright.* She went down." Such a deep, hoarse, tired voice. William would pity it, were it not his own.

"Bad luck."

"Yes." He looked through the window. "Bad luck."

Trees passed by, people, sandbags, buildings.

"What was it like over there? What did you do?"

A white glow came to William's heart, phosphorescence in a dark sea. "Well, there's a bright spot. We did something wonderful. I just can't remember what it was."

The cab driver pulled up to the London Hospital, and helped William out of the car. He held on to William and walked him into the building. When the receptionist gave them directions for Clare's room and rose to watch them go, the cab driver helped William find the room. He was about to leave when William cried, "Wait!" and, stupefied, patted his trouser pockets.

"No charge, mate." The cab driver smiled, winked, and walked away whistling.

William opened the door and staggered into the room. Clare was in bed, bright as a button, and on seeing him, sat up.

He held on to the doorknob. His hand twitched convulsively, moving it back and forth.

"You're all right, then," he said hoarsely.

"I am."

"No infection."

"None."

He let go the doorknob, made it to the bed, lay down beside her. He pulled her close, as great gray billows crashed upon the clearing, and passed from consciousness.

He reeked of petrol and oil and fish and

sweat. He was blackened and blood-smeared, scruff-faced and swollen-eyed, his hair stiff and spiky with sweat and salt. His detective inspector clothing, the office shirt and trousers, would have to be thrown away.

Clare looked about the room, taking note of little things — the leftover cake, the sunlight at the window. His right arm lay heavy across her. She took his hand and inspected his palm. It was blistered and grime-creased. There was the cut from the teacup at the restaurant, dirty and inflamed.

She kissed the cut and snuggled in beside him. She loved the weight of that arm.

32

A day had passed and William Percy had not yet woken, and his appearance had not changed. He still slept in Clare's bed, with Clare beside him. It was a snug fit, but they managed.

Clare was pleased to see that any hint of impropriety that this might cause was completely ignored by all, hospital staff and visitors alike. The Hero of the Thames was now one of the many heroes of Dunkirk, and far more visitors came to peek in on William than they did Clare. William's mother and father came with little Cecy, who brought another furry peppermint for Clare and flowers for her brother. Frederick Butterfield made an appearance, and the desk sergeant from the Westminster precinct.

Father Fitzpatrick came for a brief farewell visit and did something lovely before he left: he *blessed* them. She'd never been part of a blessing before. He stood at the door and raised his hand to them, and said something about the Lord blessing them, keeping them, causing his face to shine upon them. It was lovely, and glowing, and then he left.

Mrs. Shrewsbury arrived with a bag of things she'd collected for Clare from the Maggie Has Gone to War pile.

"How's Murray?" Clare asked as she came in.

"Still sleeping," Mrs. Shrew whispered. "He's on a cot in the Anderson hut, snoring to shame a jackhammer. How's our sailor?" She drew up a chair. "Gracious. I smelled him the moment I walked into the room. Very different from the soldiers."

"We've tried to freshen him but gave up," Clare whispered. "I can't bear to wake him."

"He'll have a good long wee when he does. How do *you* feel, my dear?"

"A kitten could beat me up. But I am happy." She reached for Mrs. Shrew's hand. "Dear me, I am so happy."

"Even with the loss of *Maggie Bright* . . ." Mrs. Shrew reached for a tissue from the bedside table and pressed it to her eyes. "I feel so terribly bad. I know how much she meant to you."

"She went down for a child whose name I'll never know. On the contrary, Mrs.

499

Shrew, I do not feel sad. Perhaps that will come later when I stand beside Maggie's empty berth. For now, all I feel is joy."

She took a tissue from Mrs. Shrew, and they wept, and blotted, and composed.

"I have William, who will never be more handsome to me than he is right now — I clipped a piece of his shirt to remember this beautiful filth forever. I have you. I have Murray, who happens to be my brother. I have Captain John, who has his son back. I have the knowledge that my birth father was a good man, and I have a new friend in an American Burglar Vicar. It's as if *Maggie Bright* brought our hands together to touch, and now she's slipped off, but look what she's left behind. I'm the richest woman in the world. Oh! And I've been blessed!"

"You've been what?" said the Shrew, startled, mid-blow on the tissue.

"The Burglar Vicar did it before he left. You would have loved it. He is somewhere between Catholic and Protestant, so it was nice middle ground, and he raised his hand right there at the door and said the loveliest words I've ever heard. Something about blessing, and keeping, and shining."

William suddenly sat up. He looked about, confused. He seemed ready to say something, then fell back to the bed,

500

instantly asleep. His slightly altered position revealed a cut on the back of his neck. Clare touched it.

"The wee will have to wait," Mrs. Shrew said regretfully.

"Oh, goodness . . ."

The Shrew sighed. "My dear . . . I can't help but think of the jar with your coins. I found it in the Maggie Has Gone to War pile. I confess I wept." She sniffed. "Your dream to circumnavigate the world sank in the English Channel."

"But I've already done so! I've come full circle. I'm back to real people once more, and I've been *blessed.*" She lightly brushed crusted salt from William's eyebrow, and smiled when the eyebrow twitched. "I have a new dream, you see. This man and I shall round Cape Horn together one day. Lashed to the foremast for fun."

33

On June 2, just before midnight, Captain Bill Tennant of His Majesty's Royal Navy signaled Dover Command: "BEF evacuated." Then he boarded the Motorized Torpedo Boat-102 and headed home, under enemy fire, for England.

In the nine-day siege of Dunkirk, Churchill and the Admiralty hoped to save 30,000 to 45,000 men through the efforts of the Royal Navy, the Royal Air Force, and any available civilians.

They saved 340,000.

At 10:20 a.m. on June 4, a swastika was hoisted on the eastern mole of the harbor.

Dunkirk had fallen.

War would change him, and so it did.

His boy was older, wiser, and heartbroken. He never said a word to tell it, but John Elliott knew. He'd been there, twentysome years ago.

They sat on the old whitewashed bench in front of the bait shop, watching the boats go by on the Thames.

"Dad. I met a man."

He got no further than that, and John Elliott put an arm around his son.

"It's all right, lad. We'll get through it together. So we will." He took out a cloth and blew mightily.

Jamie chuckled at that old, familiar sound, and wiped his face.

He looked about the boatyard. He looked where Minor's old tug used to be, and he looked at the *Lizzie Rose*. She came into Ramsgate with never a scratch. Dad had taken off four loads of men.

This dear, familiar place. He'd not see it again for a long while. He had to meet in twenty-four hours for reassignment. They were sending them off to camps all over England to prepare for invasion. He wondered where Griggs and Curtis would go. Baylor was in the hospital at Dover. They'd send him when he was ready.

"I'll miss old Minor," said Jamie.

"I will, too. Dodgy old sod."

"What happened?"

"Took off three loads before a torpedo sank a paddle steamer, and Minor was too close." He blew his nose again. "You never know about a man."

"No. You don't. Dad, when I come back I want to open a pub. I want to call it Milton's Men."

Jamie told Captain John all he saw in his mind, and when he was done, the worried old man was at peace. His boy was going to be fine.

It was a lovely day, and Mrs. Shrewsbury wanted to be alone, and she wanted to be alone at Maggie's empty berth.

She slipped off her shoes and sat on the edge of the dock. She tried to put her toes in the water but they did not reach. She squinted at the sky.

"What did you see from your glorious vantage when we prayed?" she asked Cecil. "When the shatterer went forth, and prevailed not?"

Did you see the prayers kick things out of the way?

Did you see them make the English Channel smooth?

Did you see them hold men to heartbreaking tasks, which is love disguised as duty?

Only love can bring men home looking as they did. Though of course, men would have none of *that* — calling it love.

Did you see the prayers seep down and

make them strong, hold them together, help them do things they thought they never could?

Cecil had a front-row seat to all the marvelous things.

She took a newspaper article from her sweater pocket and unfolded it. "Listen to this. It's Churchill, the new prime minister. Yes, the same Churchill. Winston. It's from his Parliament address, a few days ago." She scanned the article for the bits Cecil would find most interesting. "Yes, here. This is what I heard on the BBC. Wasn't Churchill himself, but the fellow did him credit. Listen: 'Even though large tracts of Europe and many old and famous States have fallen or may fall into the grip of the Gestapo and all the odious apparatus of Nazi rule, we shall not flag or falter. We shall go on to the end.'"

Her throat tightened. She blinked quickly.

" 'We shall fight in France, we shall fight on the seas and the oceans, we shall fight with growing confidence and growing strength in the air, we shall defend our island —' "

Pause.

" 'We shall defend our island whatever the cost may be. We shall fight on the beaches, we shall fight on the landing grounds, we shall fight in the fields and in the streets; we shall —' "

Pause. Rapid blinking. She rested the paper in her lap.

She thought of her student, Danny Morgan, already back to the fight. She thought of Jamie Elliott, son of that man, off to some camp in the north. She thought of Clare's detective inspector, who went down to enlist with the Royal Navy the day after he woke up. Murray Vance had enlisted, too.

She cleared her throat and resumed.

" 'We shall never surrender. And if, which I do not for a moment believe —' nor I, Cecil — 'this island or a large part of it were subjugated and starving, then our Empire beyond the seas, armed and guarded by the British Fleet, would carry on the struggle, until, in God's good time, the New World, with all its power and might, steps forth to the rescue and the liberation of the old.' "

She gave a hard glance toward America. "Did you hear that? Wake up, thou that sleepest."

Wake and pray. Wake and fight.

The paper rested in her lap until she noticed, folded it, and slipped it into her pocket.

"There's more, Cecil, but I'll finish with this: Winston called the Dunkirk operation 'a miracle of deliverance.' He also warned us, because of so many lunatic gadflies going about like drunk orangutans, that we must *not* regard this rescue as some sort of victory, as wars are *not* won by evacuations. Some think it's done. They think they can go back to normal. There is no going back. It isn't done. It's only begun. Dear me — I do wonder what you see, from your glorious vantage."

Then she jabbed her finger to the south, and said severely, "You! You shatterer. You shall *not* prevail!" And she slowly smiled a smile, which she knew to the shatterer was a chilling smile indeed. "Not when people pray."

She rose and took up her shoes, gave a last long look at the end of a lovely day, and strolled barefoot back to the Anderson shelter.

You are sixty-seven, retired, and with a great deal to do, for the war is not yet won.

It has only begun.

A NOTE FROM THE AUTHOR

In the midst of our defeat, glory came to the island people, united and unconquerable; and the tale of the Dunkirk beaches will shine in whatever records are preserved of our affairs.

WINSTON CHURCHILL

The evacuation of Dunkirk shines as the greatest military rescue in history. Approximately 340,000 men were saved from certain death or imprisonment by the Herculean efforts of many.

Yet what of those left behind?

Many British and Allied soldiers paid a heavy price to buy time for others to make it home. They defended the retreat by protecting the ever-shrinking corridor to Dunkirk, often fighting down to the last man and bullet until they were killed or taken captive. Thousands of these defenders died. Forty thousand spent five years in captivity.

Forty thousand.

One of these men was John Borland.

John Borland was a Cameron Highlander serving with the 51st Highland Division. He never reached Dunkirk but was forced to hold the line further west. . . . As he was marched away to five years of captivity, Mr. Borland spotted a scrap of paper blowing across his path. He has it still. "It was a biblical text, with the words 'Don't give up' scrawled in pencil, probably by the man who'd dropped it. Those words stayed with me through my time in the POW camps." [Borland was asked,] had he ever given up? The answer was unequivocal: "Never."

ROBERT HALL, BBC News UK,
May 28, 2010

Let this shine, too.

Authors of historical fiction often face conundrums in deciding what words to use for sensitive topics or conditions. I faced such a dilemma in identifying the disability of the young German boy, Erich von Wechsler. I chose to use the contemporary name for his condition, Down syndrome, although at the time he would have been described as a mongoloid. I wanted to make sure readers understood, and I did not want to risk giving offense over what has become, in our society, an offensive term. This condition was specific to the T-4 program; I wanted you to be as astonished as I was when you learned children like him were being experimented on and euthanized.

I have also played with the time line in giving Clare a Revised Standard Version of the Bible, although this version was not published until 1946. Its specific wording of Nahum 2:1 fit perfectly into the image I wanted to develop. I hope careful readers will forgive my artistic license.

Many books are available on the story of Dunkirk. Some of my own favorites include Richard Collier's classic, *The Sands of Dunkirk,* and *The Miracle of Dunkirk* by Walter Lord. For an in-depth study of the withdrawal of the BEF, check out *Dunkirk: Retreat to Victory* by Major General Julian Thompson.

ACKNOWLEDGMENTS

Writers are haunted by the thought that they may forget to thank someone who has contributed to a book in some powerhouse way — and even small ways are powerhouse. I hope I have forgotten no one. If I have, dinner is on me, next time I see you. (Wait, that sounds fun; maybe I should forget someone on purpose.)

I am indebted to the following folk for the gracious and multitudinous ways they contributed to this book. They did things like: loaned a pile of WWII newspapers, gave a tour of the *MTB-102,* gave tours of privately owned craft registered with the Association of Dunkirk Little Ships, loaned a cottage in which to hole up and write, read the manuscript, steered me in good directions, and answered endless questions. They are: Neil Barber, Alan and Margaret Childs, Susan and Nigel Cole, Terry Crowdy, Alison Hodgson, Melissa Huisman, Alan Jackson, Debbie King, Don Pearson, Trevor and Alison Phillips, Aaron Smith, Elena Studebaker, and Robert John Tough.

Thanks also to Kathy Helmers and Meredith Smith at Creative Trust, dear friends and Core Competencies. Thanks to the talented team at Tyndale, with whom it was an honor once more to create something good. And thanks to my husband, Jack, an implacable encourager and the only man on earth capable of putting up with me. I don't know how you do it. I'm glad you do.

Finally, I wish to thank my best-friend-cum-research-assistant, Tami Huitsing, who ran off with me to England and France and did the following: took a million photographs, offered invaluable suggestions, tramped all over kingdom come with never a complaint, prevented me from killing a taxi driver, sampled endless tastes of sticky toffee pudding once I'd discovered it, and endured my often-graceless ADD-on-steroids personality for the entire trip with magnificent aplomb. Many best friends have done nobly. You leave them in your sparkling dust.

DISCUSSION QUESTIONS

1. How much did you know about the "Miracle of Dunkirk" before reading this book? Did the book pique your interest to learn more about this historic event or other aspects of World War II?

2. When Murray finds Father Fitz in jail, he is quite angry with him for leaving his wife and newborn child. "If you won't take care of them, savin' the world don't matter. It's lost already if a man can't take care of his own." Do you agree with Murray's statement, that taking care of our own families is our most important priority? Does knowing what Father Fitz's mission was — trying to stop Hitler's atrocities — affect your answer? If so, how do we determine which causes are important enough to risk neglecting or endangering our loved ones?

3. Calling the nation to a day of prayer — even in the officially Christian nation of Britain — strikes some of the characters as unusual. Do you think political leaders have the right or obligation to ask their citizens to pray? Has this changed in the last century?

4. William Percy asks Mrs. Shrewsbury how prayer works, and her answer is, "I'm not sure how it works. I can say what I believe it *does.* I believe prayer kicks things out of the way. I believe it does so to make room for a better outcome. I believe prayer illuminates our paths so we can see more clearly, choose our way more wisely." What do you think of her answer? How would you answer William's question?

5. William isn't sure he believes in God, but he believes in Mrs. Shrewsbury and the power of her prayers. When have other people held you up in prayer, even if you weren't sure you believed in praying for yourself? How has that impacted your life?

6. Clare receives the unexpected news that the man who bequeathed *Maggie Bright* to her was her birth father, and that Murray is her half brother. What did you think of

her reaction to this news? Have you ever learned something that changed your perception of yourself? How do you think this revelation plays into the story? How important is it?

7. Jamie Elliott is given a mission that seems impossible — getting a critically wounded man, who is essentially unable to communicate, to safety. And he is faithful to the mission, even when he is told that wounded men are to be left to fend for themselves. How would you have responded to such an assignment? Do you think Jamie's choices and actions are realistic? What do they say about the kind of person Jamie is?

8. What did you think of Captain Jacobs, "Milton"? Did you find him amusing? Annoying? Did you feel sorry for him or for those tasked with caring for him? Have you ever had to care for someone with a physical or mental disability? What are some of the challenges and rewards of such a role?

9. In the final rescue before *Maggie Bright* sinks, William loses track of time and is shocked when the others tell him he spent

an hour working to save people. Have you ever been in a crisis situation where time seems to slow down? Why do you think that happens? How is it that people can find hidden reserves of strength to do what should be physically impossible?

10. The end of this book is just the beginning of the story of World War II. How do you think each of the main characters will spend the duration of the war? What will happen to Clare and William? Murray and Father Fitz? Mrs. Shrewsbury? Will Jamie ever open his pub? Will his former comrades meet there? If you were to imagine a sequel to this story, what would be its focus?

ABOUT THE AUTHOR

Tracy Groot is the author of *The Brother's Keeper; Stones of My Accusers; Madman,* a Christy Award–winning novel that received a starred *Publishers Weekly* review; *Flame of Resistance,* also a Christy Award winner; and most recently *The Sentinels of Andersonville.*

She loves books, movies, knitting, travel, exceptional coffee, dark-chocolate sea foam, and licorice allsorts. She lives with her husband, Jack, in a Michigan home where stacks of books must be navigated to get anywhere, and if she yet lives at the reading of these words, she is likely at work on her next historical novel.

For more information about
Tracy and her books,
visit www.tracygroot.com.